By the same author

The Viceroy's Captain
The General's Envoy
The Colonel's Renegade

The Brigadier's Outcast

ANTHONY CONWAY

The Brigadier's Outcast

Hodder & Stoughton

First published in Great Britain in 2003 by Hodder and Stoughton
A division of Hodder Headline

1 3 5 7 9 10 8 6 4 2

A CIP catalogue record for this title is available from the British Library

ISBN 0 340 82210 4

Typeset in Plantin Light by Phoenix Typesetting, Burley-in-Wharfedale,
West Yorkshire

Printed and bound in Great Britain by
Clays Ltd, St Ives plc

Hodder and Stoughton
A division of Hodder Headline
338 Euston Road
London NW1 3BH

Prologue

There was a purity in the heavens altogether absent on earth, the airman reflected as he surveyed the billowing sea of clouds several hundred feet beneath him. Indeed, with thick layers of cumulus blanketing the ground from horizon to horizon he felt he could imagine himself to be a visiting creature from another world. His environment had become a magical place, comfortably divorced from the filth and carnage he knew to exist many thousands of feet below. Gone was the network of trench systems and the blood-soaked mud between them. Gone were the tumbled ruins of the numerous shattered villages. Gone, even, were the pathetic little vapour trails of the squabbling fighter aircraft, twizzling around like bothersome gnats, their frail wings held together by wire and glue.

The heavens were pure but bitterly cold. He shrugged down into his fur-lined leather flying overalls, attempting to shrink himself like a mouse in a nest. Inside he felt his body shivering, the layers of clothing failing to fight back the penetrating iciness. Purity came at a heavy price.

'Gustav! Where are you?'

The airman glanced round, opened his mouth to respond but remained silent. Dieter would find him soon enough. Dieter and his dull banter, his heavy bonhomie, his forced cheeriness. Of course, Gustav understood that most of it was disguise. A barely adequate cover for the terror that all of them felt.

He looked up into the voluminous interior of the Zeppelin. A gust of wind rising through the open hatchway beneath him swept upwards into the dark void, rippling the sides of the nearest gas cell, the vast hydrogen-filled bag billowing at its moorings. Flanking it, a further seventeen were strung inside the Zeppelin's giant cylindrical hull. Together they held over a million cubic metres of gas. Hydrogen. Lighter than air but highly flammable. Like all of his fellow crewmen, Gustav viewed the gas with mixed emotions. It held them aloft, while at the same time enveloping them in the most deadly of cocoons. It could ignite at the slightest spark transforming, in an instant, their temporary home into a plummeting inferno.

He shuddered again, this time not from the cold.

'There you are, my friend.' Dieter had found him, approaching silently along the gangway in his soft-soled boots, the undersides covered in thick layers of cotton to prevent sparks and all the dangers associated with them. 'Has the order come yet?'

Gustav shook his head. Dieter let out a heavy sigh and lowered himself down beside his comrade, similarly dangling his legs out through the hatchway and into the cold night air. A short drop below them, the wicker of the small observation basket creaked as it swung on its supporting ropes.

'Can't be long now,' he observed nervously.

Once again Gustav shook his head. Then, feeling suddenly mean-spirited, he looked at the young man beside him and said, 'No. Not long now.'

Dieter chuckled, slapping himself warm. 'You know, before we left Nordholz I had a letter from Friedl. She is pregnant again.'

Gustav was about to offer his congratulations but stopped himself. The tortured expression hacking its way brutally through the brave smile on Dieter's face betrayed the man's agony. What must it be like to have left his wife looking after two young children and expecting a third, while he, Dieter, was gingerly suspended thousands of feet above the North Sea in a flying incendiary device on its way to bomb England, where anti-aircraft guns and fighter aircraft undoubtedly lay in wait?

Instead, Gustav reached into the satchel slung across his shoulder and took out his thermos of coffee. He unscrewed the lid, carefully measured out a cupful and offered it to Dieter. 'Let us toast the coming infant,' he said kindly.

Dieter smiled, gratefully accepting the cup. Gustav could see the struggle on the man's face as he sipped, courage and self-control vying with an almost overpowering well of emotion.

They sat without speaking, sharing the rapidly cooling drink to the accompanying drone of the four powerful Maybach engines, each one in its own gondola slung beneath the five-hundred-and-fifty-foot-long Zeppelin, driving it forward at a cruising speed of forty miles per hour through the icy upper air.

There was the sound of voices briskly approaching.

'Here they come,' Gustav said grimly, retrieving the empty cup from Dieter, shaking out the last few drops and then screwing it back onto the thermos. 'Time to go.'

The ship's captain and two of his officers worked along the narrow gangway towards the open hatch. Gustav and Dieter stood up as they approached, slapping their legs to encourage the circulation.

Captain Baron Ulrich von Staaden surveyed the two airmen with only mild interest and then peered over the edge into the abyss outside the hull. Far below they could see the upper surface of the clouds writhing slowly, massaged by strong winds.

'All set?' he asked, his eyes briefly leaving the patterns of cloud.

Gustav and Dieter nodded.

'Into the basket, then. Once again we will disturb the sleep of our English friends.'

The two men saluted and then crouched down to help each other out of the Zeppelin and into the small wicker observation basket precariously suspended underneath. It was a job that Gustav loathed, however much he understood its necessity. Since the advent of the so-called height-climbers, the high altitude Zeppelins, the need for accurate navigation and target information had become paramount. Bombing raids with the early generation Zeppelins, flying at around three thousand feet, had proved disastrous once the initial shock effect had worn off. The British had swiftly learned to employ anti-aircraft defences as well as aircraft using incendiary ammunition and the Zeppelins, opposed by such fast and agile opponents, had fallen out of the sky one after another.

The answer had been the height-climbers. Flying at anything up to twenty thousand feet, they were impervious to the British fighters who reached their own ceiling at about thirteen thousand feet. But increased height meant decreased bombing accuracy, and the problem was exacerbated by cloud cover. The solution was to lower a small observation basket down through the clouds. Suspended on two slender ropes in the vastness of space, observers could relay target information back to the Zeppelin far overhead, giving instructions for the release of the payload of bombs.

Gustav lowered himself into the basket, feeling the wicker creak under his weight. Once safely beside him, Dieter tested the mouthpiece of the communication tube that would link them to the Zeppelin's control gondola. Receiving a muffled reply, he gave the thumbs-up.

With a final check that they were securely aboard, the Captain gave the signal for the basket to be lowered. There was a sickening series of shudders and jolts, and the basket dropped away from the Zeppelin at an alarming rate, the ropes speedily unfurling. Off to one side, the nearest of the Maybach engines roared, its seventeen-foot propellers of laminated West African mahogany and American walnut powering the floating colossus through the night skies.

Gustav looked up, and his last view of the Zeppelin was of the Captain's interested face staring into his own. There was a detachment about the man's expression that Gustav found disquieting. It reminded him of a boy observing a specimen in a jam jar, considering his options. The odds were even, Gustav imagined, as to whether the boy would decide to set the specimen free or pull its legs off.

A sudden jarring of the unfurling ropes tore Gustav's eyes away and when he looked back, the basket's descent having steadied, the Captain had disappeared and the hatch was closed. The noise of the Zeppelin's engines began to fade, gradually being replaced with the sighing of the wind through the basket's ropes.

The cloud rose up to meet them and for a moment, as they brushed the surface, it was like standing on a vast undulating plain. It appeared so solid that Gustav imagined he could step out of the basket and stroll calmly away from the whole damnable business, hands in pockets and whistling a tune. The next moment however, the plain dissolved. Mist closed about him, removing the vista and ending the illusion. Giant swirls spun around the descending basket like ghostly spectres, encircling the ropes and humming eerily in the communication tube. Gustav glanced at Dieter. He was clinging to the sides, eyes wide with poorly-concealed fright. Gustav had left his stomach behind when the basket had first fallen away from the Zeppelin, and only now, as the rate of descent began to slow, did it return. With it came a rush of nausea. His head spun, partly from the turbulence and partly from the sudden change in altitude.

'Are we there yet?' Dieter asked.

A jolt on the cables answered the question for both of them. The savagery of the halt made the two men stare at the ropes, expecting one or both of them to snap with the sudden force.

Gustav snatched at the communication tube and blew into the mouthpiece before speaking. 'We're still in cloud.'

In response, the basket began to descend again, more slowly this time. All of a sudden the enveloping mist vanished and Gustav and Dieter found themselves suspended beneath the clouds. Far below, they could make out the pathetic twinkle of lights.

'Where are we?'

Gustav struggled to make out a coastline, searching for the mouth of the Thames, the shining pathway that would lead them all the way to the very heart of London and their target for the night. The City. Instead he looked down upon farmland. A larger cluster of lights denoted a town but he had no idea which one.

Exasperated, he shook his head as if that alone might clear the confusion that reigned. Dieter leaned over the edge, unfolding his map case in an attempt to match it to the sparse information glimpsed beneath them.

'Kent,' he said thoughtfully, losing a modicum of his fear to a technical interest in the problem at hand.

He pointed to the cluster of lights. 'That's Ashford.' He studied his map eagerly. 'If we go to the west of it we can follow the Vale of Kent. It points straight at London. Look.' He offered his map for Gustav's inspection.

Gustav did not bother. 'From this height and in this visibility the Vale of Kent will be invisible. We have to head due north until we cut the line of the Thames and then turn west.'

Dieter shrugged, folding his map case again. 'How could we have been so far out?'

'It's the same with all the height-climbers. The winds of the upper air are unpredictable. It's a foreign realm altogether. They can blow you miles off course and you'd never know it. The other month when you were on leave we bombed France instead of England. How's that for an error?' He jerked a thumb at the ground. 'This, tonight, is accurate. Believe me. This is pure marksmanship.'

He spoke into the communication tube, issuing instructions. This done, he took out his thermos and poured some coffee, positioning the steaming mug on the narrow wicker seat. A further rummage in his satchel produced a salami and a chunk of hard black rye bread. He pulled out a lock knife, opened it and began to saw at the two items. When he had cobbled together two indifferent sandwiches, he passed one to Dieter and took a bite of the other.

He peered over the edge of the basket, chewing, and spat out a sliver of salami skin. As far as he could tell they had not changed course. He paused, looked up towards the Zeppelin but could see nothing but the base of the clouds close overhead.

'What the hell are they up to?'

'Probably having supper like us,' Dieter said with a smirk.

Gustav put his sandwich down and checked the compass. The bearing was exactly the same as before. He reached for the communication tube and hailed the control gondola.

'The change of bearing,' he shouted into the mouthpiece. 'What's the problem?'

He listened for the reply from the officer of the watch.

'What does he say?' Dieter asked.

'Ssh!'

Gustav strained to hear, his expression becoming pained. 'What do you mean, the Baron disagrees?'

Again he listened hard, struggling to make out the words being projected down the tube from the Zeppelin thousands of feet above.

As understanding dawned, he started to protest but quickly gave up. The control gondola had cut him off.

'Well?' Dieter pressed, catching Gustav's suddenly altered mood.

'Of all the stubborn bloody nonsense!' Gustav picked up the remains of his sandwich and hurled it out into the darkness. 'The Captain says I'm wrong.'

Dieter stared, puzzled. 'But we're the observers. He can't even see the ground.'

'The arrogant fool's used radio bearings. A German destroyer and a frigate in the North Sea. They've convinced him he's on course, and naturally he believes them and not us. Their bearings support his own navigation. What's more, he's descending to three thousand feet.'

'What the devil for?' Dieter asked, amazed.

'Accuracy. He wants the six hundred pounders to hit their marks in the City tonight.'

Dieter thought for a moment. He did not have to voice his fears aloud. They had struck Gustav as well. He leaned over the edge of the basket and began to scour the night sky for the British fighters. Radio bearings were a mixed blessing. They assisted navigation but, if intercepted, they acted as a beacon for the enemy fighter aircraft, drawing them to the target, the vulnerable Zeppelin.

The ropes supporting the basket shuddered as the Zeppelin began to wind it back in. However, as the Zeppelin itself was now descending, the overall effect was that the basket appeared to hang uncertainly at the same height.

Just then there was a break in the cloud. Looking up, Gustav stared in wonder at the spectacle of the giant Zeppelin looming out of the towering banks of cloud. Some miles away they could make out the *Rheingold*, similarly descending.

'This is madness,' he said. 'Absolute madness. The *Fafner* and the *Rheingold* have been built to outreach the fighters and yet the Baron's bringing them down within their range. And all because he refuses to have it said that he, Captain Baron von Staaden, missed his targets. He'd rather risk the lives of all his crew.'

'Well at least when he gets down here he'll see for himself that he's off course,' Dieter remarked.

'For all the good it'll do him,' Gustav replied, his voice suddenly ice cold. 'Look! Fighters!'

Dieter could just make out the sinister shapes of the British fighters, still some distance away but closing fast, rising up from the dark ground like spirits disturbed from the grave.

Gustav snatched up the communication tube and yelled a warning into it. Listening for a reply, he heard instead the alarm the news created amongst the crewmen in the control gondola. Cutting through the noise came the Captain's stern command, barking for silence. Then the tube went dead. Gustav stared at it a moment, then checked to see whether it was blocked. He tried to hail the ship again but there was no reply.

'What the devil's he up to?' he said, peering up through the intermittent cloud at the vast belly of the Zeppelin. 'Why doesn't he climb?'

'He'll pull us up, won't he?' Dieter asked nervously.

'God knows.'

The *Rheingold* was starting to veer away, heading back towards the coast. In stark contrast, the *Fafner* continued doggedly on course.

Suddenly the night sky lit up. Gustav and Dieter shielded their eyes and stared in horror towards the *Rheingold* as it burst into flames. Within seconds it had become a vast blazing torch. Silhouetted against the glare they could just make out one tiny black shape. A single fighter banking away from the stricken Zeppelin, its work done. It had turned in the direction of the *Fafner*.

Gustav screamed into the communication tube once more in a last effort to get through to the control gondola.

'Climb! Climb!'

At last they felt a rush of air and were able to make out the beginnings of an ascent, but it was painfully slow.

'We're not going to make it,' Dieter said quietly.

Gustav stared up at the Zeppelin and saw the bomb doors open. 'They're going to jettison the bombs. Good. That'll lighten the load so we can gain height more quickly.'

'But it won't be in time!' Dieter muttered, terror breaking into his voice.

'Quiet!' Gustav hissed, his eyes searching for the fighter which had disappeared behind a cloud bank.

A rain of bombs cascaded past them. Gustav glanced down at the earth and amidst the dark expanse of farmland, could just make out a single tiny light glimmering weakly, a lone farmstead in the middle of rolling fields. He watched as the dark shapes of the bombs disappeared from view, heading towards the ground. Several seconds later, bright orange flames burst like flowers down in the darkness, their accompanying thuds reaching the two occupants of the basket some moments afterwards. As Gustav watched, he saw the largest of the bursts erupt exactly on top of the frail glimmer, expunging it completely in its own brighter light.

Beside him Dieter whistled softly. 'What did they do to deserve that?'

Gustav was silent, turning his thoughts deliberately away from the death of innocents. After all, they were in enough trouble themselves. Any moment now they might be joining the dead farmer.

Their heads were snapped upwards by the sound of machine-gun fire from the Zeppelin. From the gun nests in the gondolas and on the top of the Zeppelin's fat body, machine-guns began to spit fire.

'Where is it?' Dieter said. 'Can you see it?'

In answer, a British fighter shot out of the clouds barely fifty yards away and screamed past the basket, its wing-tips narrowly missing the supporting ropes. Gustav and Dieter ducked instinctively, regardless of the fact that the wicker would shield them from absolutely nothing that the fighter could throw at them.

'Do you think he saw us?'

Gustav shook his head. 'I doubt it. The pilot's attention would have been on the *Fafner*.'

Sure enough, the fighter rose straight towards the other Zeppelin, approaching from directly beneath it in an attempt to find a way in under its machine-gun cover. Gustav and Dieter watched in horror as the fighter began to fire, a stream of scarlet incendiary rounds hosing up towards the massive gas bag. The pilot's aim was disrupted as one of the German guns found him and fired burst after burst in the direction of the attacking aircraft.

But the damage had been done. While most of the incendiary rounds had missed the Zeppelin, the final rounds of the burst arched towards the tail of the giant beast, catching the very tip of the rudders. To Gustav's horror, he saw a glow remain clinging to the rudder after the last of the rounds had died away, the fighter banking sharply and dropping back towards the earth to watch the result of its attack from a safer distance.

The glow spread and then, a moment later, a gust of wind caught at it and Gustav and Dieter saw the tell-tale flicker of a tiny flame, still some distance away from the nearest of the gas cells, but edging closer by the second.

Gustav snatched up the communication tube again and yelled into it. 'Fire on the tail. The rudders are alight!'

A violent change in the Zeppelin's direction told him that the occupants of the control gondola already knew. Like a dog chasing its tail, the Zeppelin began to circle, trying to get the wind itself to extinguish the growing blaze.

Gustav knew that the crew aboard the Zeppelin now had only the slightest chance of survival. To keep the weight down, no parachutes were carried. The only hope would be if the machine were to dive towards the ground and reach the safety of the earth before the fire could spread as far as the nearest of the gas cells. Once it reached that, the hydrogen would explode, igniting its giant neighbours, and the entire vessel would be consumed in a tumultuous conflagration within the space of seconds.

It was as if the captain had read his thoughts. The nose of the *Fafner* went down and she went into a steep dive. From behind her, a thin trail of fire leapt up, growing ever more out of control. In the observation basket, Gustav and Dieter clung to the sides as it was thrown this way and that by the turbulence of the rapid descent.

'We'll be smashed to pieces,' Dieter sobbed, the realization of his desperate plight striking home with full force.

Gustav knew he was right. The captain's main concern now was the fate of the *Fafner* itself and its crew. He had probably even forgotten about the two men in the basket. They had become an irrelevance now. Even if the captain was able to set the Zeppelin on the ground before she blew up, the basket, suspended far below, would be dashed to pieces several seconds before the beast touched down.

The next moment the two men felt the shock waves of an explosion. They looked up and saw the entire tail section of the Zeppelin consumed by flames.

'Oh my God,' Gustav murmured. 'The gas cells.'

Instinctively Dieter crossed himself. His face was illuminated by the light of the explosion and as they both watched they saw further detonations work their way along the entire vessel. As the blaze reached the midsection where the observation basket's supporting cables were attached, there was a gut-wrenching lurch and then the two men were falling, their ropes severed by the flames.

The basket dropped like a stone, the men, clinging to the sides, staring at each other in horrified wonderment, each witnessing the other's rush towards obliteration and seeing his own terror mirrored in his comrade's face. As the basket gathered speed it became increasingly unstable and the next second it flipped over, tossing Dieter aside. His piercing screams disappeared rapidly into the night and at the periphery of his vision Gustav caught the sight of flailing arms and legs tumbling out of control towards the earth.

Instinctively he clung to the basket, his mind shying away from the hopelessness of his situation. The wicker was going to be smashed to pieces and himself along with it. He prayed for a parachute, for wings, for a guardian angel to pluck him out of harm's way. But his solitary plummet earthwards continued, cartwheeling now, spinning like a top.

His head felt as if it was bursting. Rational thought became scrambled, fragmenting into shards like a plate glass window smashed with a hammer.

A momentary surprise registered that there were no profundities. No great insights into life and death. Instead there was only trivia. A snatch of a popular song, an item from a menu at the restaurant in Nordholz where he had eaten the previous day. And anger. Anger with himself and with everything, for suddenly rushing him like this. He had always supposed there would be time. Like a bumble bee that meticulously washes itself and folds its wings before settling, bowing its head, and resigning itself to the greatest of all mysteries.

For Gustav there was only the violently spinning basket, the confusion, and an overpowering sense of injustice. It wasn't fair. It simply wasn't fair.

I

He had chosen to walk, preferring the early morning exercise to a ride on a crowded, smoky bus. It was late summer. So late that the city reminded John Caspasian of an apple one cannot quite decide whether to eat or discard. Certainly past its best. Autumn was about to bring a momentary golden respite before the long dismal slide into the decay of winter. Ever shorter days, with dark falling in the rain-glistening streets, fog rolling in off the Thames, further corrupted with the smoke from forest upon forest of chimneys and the fumes from the cars.

The number of cars shocked him. It had increased dramatically since the end of the war eleven years ago. They were changing the very nature of the place, taking command, seizing the heights, as it were. From this new vantage point, they would soon dominate the landscape and people would be obliged to dodge and weave between them, apologetic secondary beings in their own city.

Caspasian was strolling down the Mall, not in any particular hurry despite the urgency of the summons that had called him to a meeting at the Air Ministry in Whitehall. Tall and lean, he moved with the self-contained ease of an athlete; an athlete in the classical sense whose limbs and build reflect the philosophy of the competent all-rounder. But if physically he was Renaissance man, in spirit he was something far less definable. Beneath tousled fair hair, his sharp blue eyes gave the impression that he was used to staring into great distances, like a sea captain surveying a horizon or an explorer scanning a desert's furthest and most inhospitable reach. one could imagine that neither spectacle would overly concern him.

He inspected the sky from beneath the brim of a tired brown felt hat and detected rain. But the air was brisk and a blustery wind was busily taunting the trees in the adjacent park so he reckoned it would be a light shower at worst. Refreshing even.

Entering Trafalgar Square he paused for a moment to survey the rush and bustle before him. The scale of the place was so much smaller than Lutyens' Delhi with its grand avenues and boulevards. The light was meaner too, carefully rationed in grey parcels. It was little wonder, Caspasian thought, that everyone looked so miserable and preoccupied.

He sighed heavily and turned towards Whitehall. Two passing gentlemen of military bearing eyed him scathingly, caustic eyes rolling over his stone-coloured suit, starkly in contrast to the dark greys of their own and everyone else's. Caspasian ignored them but was perturbed to find that their contempt had stung. He had imagined he had left such vulnerability behind. Apparently not.

As he continued on his way, his back a little straighter, his gait more measured, he was unable completely to fight off a feeling of shabbiness. It had crept over him together with their scrutiny, but while the latter had passed on to some other target, the former remained. With it came a whole uninvited and unwelcome host of accompanying sentiments, but, chief amongst them, a resolution. A decision that he had been combating ever since setting foot in the country some two weeks previously. Something he now knew he had to do. Come what may.

But first there was the meeting to attend. Now he had made up his mind regarding the other matter, he resented the intrusion of everything else that was keeping him from his goal. It was bothersome. He checked his wristwatch, flicking back the cuff of his jacket irritably and quickening his pace towards his destination, which was now in sight on the other side of the broad avenue of Whitehall.

The Air Ministry stood a little back from the main thorough-fare, sitting at an odd angle between the road and the Thames, lying fat and bloated on the far side of the building. Caspasian made his way to the main entrance and jogged up the pale stone steps and strode between the towering columns. The reception area was the sort that might herald admittance to a provincial library or impoverished gentleman's club. Bare tiles covered the floor and together with the whitewashed walls created an air of pecuniary embarrassment that was not wholly out of place in the context of the Air Ministry.

'Can I help you, sir?'

Caspasian cut short his survey of his surroundings and returned the cold stare of the guard seated behind a high wooden counter to one side of the lobby.

'I'm here to see Air Commodore Mannion. The name's Caspasian.'

The guard consulted a ledger concealed behind the counter. 'You have an appointment, I assume?'

'I do.' Caspasian smiled but as the guard was not looking he returned to his study of his surroundings. No sooner had he done so than his attention was snapped back to the counter.

'Ha! Found you.' The guard winced rather than smiled. 'Captain Caspasian, is it?'

'That's the one.'

'Do you have some form of identification, sir?'

Caspasian produced his papers for the guard's lengthy inspection. At last they were handed back.

'Straight up the stairs to your right. Third floor. Turn right, along to the end of the corridor. Left, through the passageway and report to room three-six-three, all right?' He noted Caspasian's blank expression. 'Would you like me to write that down?'

'No, I think I'll manage.'

Caspasian removed his hat and set off for his destination, taking his time although he had barely five minutes before the scheduled start of the meeting.

The staircase was functional, lacking any sort of unnecessary adornment, and when he arrived at the third floor, pleased to note that he was not even slightly out of breath, the corridor that stretched before him was flanked with unimpressive offices visible through their glass-panelled doors, all of which appeared to be shut. As he progressed towards the end, the occupants looked up one by one, their faces busied with scowls. Caspasian had worked in a headquarters himself and had detested the experience. The staff officers resembled laboratory mice futilely spinning their treadmills. He could sympathise with them in spite of their ill-humour.

A young officer was fretting outside room 363 and the moment he caught sight of Caspasian turning the far corner, rushed upon him. 'Captain Caspasian?'

'The very same,' Caspasian answered, bemused.

'Honestly, this really is too bad.' He furrowed his brow at his watch, staring closely at the hands.

'Am I late?'

'No, but . . .'

'Well then, what's the matter?'

A voice barked out from the interior of the room. 'Is he here?'

The officer scuttled back towards the open door of his room, half-dragging Caspasian behind him lest he change his mind and abscond. 'Right here, sir!'

Room 363 proved to be merely an anteroom to a much more spacious office beyond it. A narrow desk, an uncomfortable-looking chair and a vast filing cabinet were the only furnishings of the anteroom where the staff officer, the Air Commodore's aide-de-camp, was enduring his two-year posting. On the far side of the room, another door opened into an altogether different world. The Air Commodore's office was bright and spacious, with a wall full of windows opening towards the river. Elsewhere pictures depicted either the present inhabitant's various stern predecessors or an assortment of fighter aircraft in heroically dramatic settings.

An immense leather-top desk cut across one corner of the room, the chair behind it empty, and to Caspasian's right, an inspiringly-stocked glass-fronted drinks cabinet towered over a sofa and four armchairs, all the same colour as the sunshine that blazed in the aircraft pictures.

Puzzled, Caspasian looked around for the Air Commodore. A door beyond the nest of arm chairs gave him the clue.

'Here he is, sir,' the ADC said proudly as if brandishing a prize trout.

The Air Commodore poked his head round the door. 'Splendid. And bang on time too.'

He came into the room and walked straight up to Caspasian, hand outstretched. 'Knowing the army, I bet you've been waiting round the corner for the last ten minutes waiting for the second hand to hit the mark.'

Caspasian did not like to disabuse the apparently pleasant individual before him by saying he could not have cared less. He smiled indulgently. 'I am unmasked.'

The Air Commodore grinned and shook Caspasian's hand enthusiastically. 'Delighted you could make it, and so sorry to have to call you in from your leave.'

He was a good head shorter than Caspasian and was inexplicably tanned. The baldness of his head was offset by a pair of ferocious eyebrows, each one rising to a sharp point not dissimilar to the RAF wings he wore on his chest. Small but sparklingly blue eyes gleamed playfully in the shadows and a single tooth pushed forward from the upper row, projecting

between his lips like the tip of a cat's tongue. He looked like the
sort of man who would be incapable of artifice. Everything in
the shop was displayed in the window.

'Do you know Brigadier Percival?'

As far as Caspasian was concerned, the Air Commodore
might as well have shoved him clean through the drinks cabinet.
Feeling himself stiffen like a cat that rounds a corner to find itself
nose to nose with a bull mastiff, he turned to face the lanky figure
of Brigadier James Percival standing coolly in the same doorway
from which Air Commodore Mannion had just entered.

The Brigadier advanced on him, eyes as cold and unwel-
coming as flint. From the facial expression struggling to escape
from the Brigadier's iron control, Caspasian suspected that the
meeting was as much a surprise to the Brigadier as it was to him.
Also as unwanted.

To Caspasian's surprise, the Brigadier held out his hand.
'Yes, I know Caspasian,' he said to his host as his eyes bored a
warning into Caspasian's soul. 'Don't I, John? What was it, four
years ago?'

After a moment's hesitation Caspasian accepted the
Brigadier's handshake, finding the flesh as cold as a corpse. He
released it the second it was no longer impolite to do so.

If the Air Commodore had noticed anything of the animosity
between the two men he gave no sign of it. 'Excellent. That'll
help us to dispense with the formalities. Get straight down to
business and all that.'

Caspasian thought this was a good idea. Anything to get it
finished and get out of the room.

'And what exactly is the business, sir?' he asked, never taking
his eyes from Percival's. The Brigadier was hardly likely to
assault Caspasian but given their past dealings, it would not
have surprised Caspasian in the slightest had he done so. The
expedition of 1925 into the North-West Frontier Province of
India in pursuit of the fabled diamond, the Eye of the Storm,

had hardly ended in a manner conducive to the furtherance of Caspasian's career prospects.

'Let's have a seat first,' the Air Commodore said breezily. He ushered his guests into the armchairs, Caspasian settling himself uneasily as far away from the Brigadier as the seating arrangements allowed.

'A little refreshment perhaps?' the Air Commodore said to his ADC. Caspasian began to wonder whether the supposed suntan was more the result of such refreshments than exposure to the elements.

'I had no idea you meant Captain Caspasian, Jules, when you said you had found the man we needed for this little job,' the Brigadier said, leaning back, legs crossed, one arm draped casually over the back of his chair. He smiled icily at Caspasian. 'I didn't realise the two of you knew each other.'

'Nor do we,' Mannion replied. He leaned forward. 'What'll it be?'

'Gin and tonic,' the Brigadier answered.

'And you?' Mannion said, addressing Caspasian.

'Scotch, please. Ice, no water.'

Mannion turned to the ADC to check he had noted their preferences and then winked. 'The usual for me, Charlie.' Settling back in his chair he grinned, enjoying himself hugely. 'Caspasian was recommended by a chap in personnel. Sent his file over. One glance at that and I knew we'd found our man.'

The Brigadier acknowledged with a slight incline of the head. 'I'd have liked to have been involved, but no matter.'

A shadow of doubt crossed the Air Commodore's face. 'I'm sorry James. I hope I haven't . . .'

The Brigadier cut him short. 'Not a problem, I assure you. Why don't we get down to business?'

'Quite so, quite so.' Mannion's eyes fussed at his ADC until the drinks were proffered on a small silver tray whose inscription was partially obscured by the glasses. Caspasian could just see that it had been presented to Mannion by someone on completion of a previous staff appointment. But he was primarily aware of his old adversary's eyes upon him. The shock of their sudden meeting was only just beginning to diminish, replaced by an alarm call in his head telling him that he had entered upon treacherous ground.

'The maps please, Charlie.'

At the Air Commodore's request, the ADC disappeared into his office, returning a moment later with a rolled map which he unfurled on a low table placed before the chairs. Securing the corners of the map with an assortment of improvised weights, he paused for a moment to see if he was required further, and at the absence of any sign from the Air Commodore that he was to stay, withdrew from their company, closing the door to his office without a sound.

Caspasian stared at the map, puzzled. Far from being the sort of map he had expected, detailing an area of operations or the like, it was a map of the entire world, oceans and all. He looked up to find the two senior officers observing his reaction with amusement, one kinder than the other.

'Bet you're wondering what all this is about, eh?' Mannion said.

Caspasian returned the smile and shrugged, understanding that no answer was required. For now he was the plaything of a couple of one-star officers. He just hoped the reason was worth calling him in from his leave.

'The Imperial Intelligence Service has received a coded message from their man in Georgetown, Guiana,' Mannion began. 'Concerning the disappearance of the *D100*.'

'The Zeppelin?'

'Airship, if you don't mind, Captain,' the Air Commodore corrected him with a pained expression. 'Dirigible, if you must. Count von Zeppelin might have given his name to the German products, but not to ours. After all, who won the war?'

Caspasian smiled, duly chastened. He had always called them Zeppelins ever since sitting as a five-year-old beside his grand-father in Yokohama in the summer of 1900, hearing the old man read aloud from the newspaper about the Count's first tentative flight over Lake Constance. During the war the Count's inven-tion had been employed for aerial bombardment, mostly of targets in England. But now, by 1929, Zeppelins were being developed for peaceful purposes once again, for the transport of passengers, mail and cargo around the world, with Germany leading the field and a select few other nations following.

The Air Commodore studied Caspasian. 'What do you know of the *D100*?'

Caspasian swirled the ice in his drink, enjoying the sound of it on the cut glass, particularly as he could tell that it irritated Brigadier Percival. 'Lost with all hands over the Caribbean two years ago. Late summer, nineteen twenty-seven. Elements of wreckage washed up along the Venezuelan coast, some of it as far as the Antilles.'

Caspasian was surprised that the Air Commodore should test him. The incident had been the major news item for days. The deliberations and eventual findings of the inquiry had been the main topic of conversation in messes the length and breadth of the Empire and the front page item in every newspaper. It was hardly the sort of clandestine subject matter with which the Imperial Intelligence Service normally concerned itself.

'The inquiry deduced from the burn marks found on some of it that there had been a fire,' Caspasian continued, 'resulting in a catastrophic explosion of the hydrogen gas cells.' He regarded the two officers. 'Have I passed?'

Air Commodore Mannion laughed. Brigadier Percival found something on the arm of his chair to concern him. As no one answered him directly, Caspasian continued. 'You mentioned a coded message from your man in Georgetown?'

'Yes,' the Air Commodore said thoughtfully. 'To be more

precise, we received part of a coded message. The transmission was cut short in midstream.'

Caspasian was becoming interested. 'Nothing unusual in that. Comms fail. Happens all the time.'

'Yes, Caspasian,' Brigadier Percival cut in rudely. 'But eventually they're re-established. This transmission was not. What is more, our agent was found several days later with his throat cut from ear to ear, his body floating in a river. Occupational hazard, you might suggest?'

His sarcasm alarmed the Air Commodore whose glance rebounded between his two guests, coming to rest on the Brigadier, who concluded, 'He was a damned fine man too. One of my best.'

'But you did receive at least part of the message?' Caspasian prompted, fighting the urge to rise from his chair and propel the Brigadier through the opposite window.

'Yes,' the Air Commodore admitted. 'Hence this meeting. You see, the message said the *D100* had been sighted.'''

'Sighted?' Caspasian stared. He searched for the appropriate words, failing to suppress a smile of incredulity. 'Where? When?'

'Well, actually our agent mentioned two sightings. One was over a place called Sansaka up the Karanato river. The other was just east of the Windward Islands.'

The Air Commodore leaned over the map and indicated the area with an unhelpful sweep of the hand.

'That's a lot of sea,' Caspasian observed. 'I don't suppose you can narrow it down a bit?'

'Unfortunately not. That was the point at which the message was terminated, just when he started with the coordinates.'

'Anything further about the sighting over . . . what was it . . . Sansaka?' Caspasian said, searching for the place on the map.

Brigadier Percival reached beneath the world map and pulled out another map, this one showing the Caribbean and the northern coastline of the Latin American continent in greater detail. Gruffly he thrust a finger on the spot.

Caspasian flicked a glance at the Brigadier to find Percival's eyes boring coldly into him, the hatred barely concealed. 'Direction of travel? Altitude? Anything like that?' Caspasian asked hopefully.

'Afraid not, old man,' the Air Commodore answered with a weary sigh, sinking back in his chair and contemplating his drink, which had turned out to be an enormous cognac. 'Just the bare bones I've given you.'

Caspasian considered for a moment. 'But what credence can you give to the report? I mean, bearing in mind the results of the inquiry, the wreckage and all of that?'

'The credence associated with one of my top agents, Caspasian,' the Brigadier said sharply.

Caspasian was about to ask what a top agent was doing posted to a dead-end place like Georgetown, but thought it better not to. Instead he responded, 'A top agent who was reporting what he had heard or what he had seen with his own eyes?'

'What are you implying?' the Brigadier snapped.

'Nothing. It's just that sailors have been reporting monsters since men first went to sea, and jungle tribesmen are hardly more reliable witnesses, are they?'

The Air Commodore gauged his two guests for a moment and then retrieved the map of the world, placing it on top once again. 'Let me explain what's at stake here, Caspasian.' He paused, considering his words carefully. 'In the last war the Hun caught us on the hop. When they first sent over the Zeppelins we had nothing with which to counter them. Nothing at all. At first. It was unnerving to say the least. In one leap they had outmatched our technology with something we simply didn't have. As you know, gradually we turned it around, although even then we never managed to counter the height-climbers. Not so long as they stayed above the ceiling of our fighters.'

He looked at the map. 'The world is changing faster now than at any time since mankind emerged from the cave. In the air the Germans are leading the way once again. This time their airships have an apparently peaceful purpose. But in some ways that's an even bigger threat. The British Empire is totally reliant on sea power. The Fleet keeps the sea lanes open, trade flowing, the economy functioning. If the Germans develop a fleet of new, much more capable Zeppelins, they are once again going to steal a march on our technology. Their *Graf Zeppelin* can outdistance and outclimb any plane we've got. It can carry many times the payload in passengers and cargo. They are establishing new trade routes that make the old ones redundant. Trade routes of the air.'

'Which is why Britain, America and others are developing airships of their own, surely?' Caspasian said. 'In order to compete commercially.'

'Exactly. Until the *D100* disaster.'

'There are those in the government who are all for cancelling the entire airship programme,' the Brigadier added. 'It would be a commercial disaster if that were to be allowed to happen. A military disaster, too. Airships are invaluable, especially in the maritime role. Now they want to cancel the programme and give the air to the Germans.' He sneered. 'All because of one slip-up.'

Caspasian stared at him. 'Slip-up? Over thirty people were incinerated!'

The Brigadier glared at him. 'Nonsense. If my man was correct, nothing of the sort happened.'

'Do you really believe, Brigadier, that the *D100*'s just swanning around over the Caribbean? Surely the fire theory is the most logical explanation?' Caspasian held up his hands, searching. 'I mean . . . who's flying the thing? Is this the new *Marie Celeste*?'

'Don't be facetious, man,' the Brigadier snapped.

The Air Commodore stepped in quickly. 'Look at the map, Caspasian. Given time and resources, we can establish a link from England to Delhi, taking in Cairo and Karachi en route.'

He swept his hand majestically across the world map. 'We can have another route down to the capitals of South America, another linking the great cities of Europe, and yet another across the Atlantic to the States. This is the future. We cannot allow one loss to hold back progress. How many died in ships exploring the globe, for God's sake? How many died crossing continents, deserts and mountain ranges?'

'But according to the Brigadier there was no loss.'

The Air Commodore looked at him earnestly. 'That is what we have got to establish. If something else happened, if the airship was, for whatever reason, shanghaied, then we have to know who did it, how and why. That's where you come in.'

Caspasian took a stiff drink of his scotch, starting to feel uneasy. 'Go on.'

'The *D200* has finally got its certificate of airworthiness. It is now ready for its maiden voyage and it's taken every effort of this department to ensure that the flight goes ahead. It will be following the same route as the *D100*. You're going to be on board.'

Caspasian smiled. 'Me? In one of those flying crematoriums?'

'Yes, you Caspasian,' Brigadier Percival said, smiling with the first genuine pleasure of the meeting.

'But there's a garrison in Georgetown . . .'

'Which will render you every assistance you require,' the Air Commodore interrupted.

Caspasian shook his head. 'I might be being stupid, but I don't understand. Why not send a frigate to the Windward Islands to have a look around? There's probably one on station thereabouts anyway.'

The two senior officers swapped glances. The Brigadier shrugged. 'Tell him,' he said.

Caspasian looked from one to the other. 'Tell me what?'

The Air Commodore sighed. 'It's not just a matter of looking around. For a start there has to be a degree of confidentiality about the business. We don't want to start a panic or create a field day for the press. Our investigations have to be conducted discreetly.'

'You mean you don't want to be made to look complete idiots when it all turns out to be a wild goose chase, and that the *D100* did simply blow up?' Caspasian said.

'There's an element of truth in that, though I wouldn't have put it in quite the same way myself had I been in your position, Captain,' the Air Commodore replied tartly.

There was a moment's silence. Caspasian waited, wondering, observing the two men, and then said, 'There's something more, isn't there?'

The Air Commodore shifted in his seat. 'It's possible there might be a threat to the *D200*.'

'What sort of threat?'

'Can't say.'

'Don't know or won't tell me, sir?' Caspasian asked candidly.

'Look, Caspasian,' Brigadier Percival said brusquely, clearly becoming tired with the Air Commodore's gently coercive approach to the conversation. 'The *D100* either blew up or was shanghaied. If it blew up, there's a good chance it was sabotage. Possibly the Germans trying to knock out a rival. If it happened to the *D100* it can just as easily happen to the *D200*. That's why we need a man on the airship when she flies from Cardington in three days' time.'

Caspasian grinned. 'You mean you want me on board when it blows up instead of one of your own men from the Imperial Intelligence Service?' He put his glass down on the table. 'Brigadier, I'm flattered. But forgive me if I decline the poisoned chalice.'

The Air Commodore chuckled. 'Nonsense. It's because

we'll have someone like you on board that the *D200*'s not going to come to any harm.' He frowned. 'You were supposed to have been made aware of the mission before you left Cairo I signalled your Commanding Officer, Colonel Humphreys, who . . .'

'Was all too keen to volunteer my services,' Caspasian sighed. 'Yes, I know sir. His briefing was . . . well, brief.' Caspasian stared at the two of them, now thoroughly bemused. 'Sir, I'm as willing as the next man to accept a challenge, but I have no knowledge of anything you've spoken of. Zeppelins, airships, dirigibles, whatever. I'm an infantry officer. I'm not even a spy. Surely the Imperial Intelligence Service and the Air Ministry between them can come up with someone better qualified?'

'Certainly less insubordinate,' the Brigadier snorted.

'James! That's hardly helpful.' The Air Commodore sighed. 'We need someone with your . . . eclectic experience, Caspasian, if I can put it like that. And frankly, no, we can't come up with anyone better . . . who's available,' he added with an air of mystery. Caspasian suspected it was simply because they had not looked hard enough. They had gone for the first name pulled out of the hat by some minor clerk in personnel. The name of the first officer to fit the general criteria. And someone not too valuable in the likely event of loss. He could imagine his CO back in Cairo laughing all the way to the Mess, boasting to the adjutant how he had rid himself and the regiment of the troublesome Caspasian.

Mannion indicated the smaller of the two maps. 'Look at this,' he said, fingering the large green expanse south of Georgetown depicting the interior of Guiana. 'The Karanato rises deep in the jungles that roll all the way back to the Amazon. Tributaries flow north into the Orinoco and south into the Amazon itself. Sansaka is here,' he said, pointing. 'Surrounded by virgin jungle, much of it mountainous. You're going to have to find out who reported seeing the *D100* and make contact with them.'

'And the Windward Islands?' Caspasian asked, incredulous. 'Once I've combed the jungle presumably you want me to paddle downriver and swim out to the Antilles or thereabouts, treading water until I run into a mermaid who's . . .'

'Caspasian! That's enough.' Brigadier Percival got to his feet and stood over Caspasian threateningly. 'The *D200* flies in three days' time and you're going to be on it. You will be contacted from time to time to receive whatever other leads we've been able to find in the meantime.'

'So I'm going by myself? You're not coming too?'

'I am not,' the Brigadier answered, blushing almost imperceptibly.

Well that's one relief, Caspasian thought. 'And when I'm on board . . . ?'

'You watch the other passengers. Get to know them. If there's a saboteur on board you're to identify him and take the appropriate action.'

'Which is?'

'I hardly have to tell you that, of all people, Caspasian,' the Brigadier said with a grim smile.

'I see. And when the airship reaches Georgetown?'

'You will alight and continue your search from there. If a saboteur is going to strike it will be over the ocean. The waves leave precious little by way of evidence.'

'So does the Amazon jungle,' Caspasian added.

'Be that as it may,' the Air Commodore said, 'it is our estimation that if the *D200* has not been sabotaged by the time it makes landfall at Guyana, the greater threat will have passed. You are therefore to continue your investigations on land. The commander of the garrison will be informed, and instructed to render whatever assistance you deem necessary. Within reason. As I said before, our investigation must be . . .'

'Discreet,' Caspasian concluded for him. Hence the choice of himself as expendable lackey, he reflected bitterly.

'One thing, sir,' he ventured delicately. 'Are you requesting that I volunteer for this task? I mean, is there any choice involved?'

Brigadier Percival smiled, again with genuine pleasure. 'What do you think, Caspasian? I would have thought you'd been in the Army long enough to know.'

The Air Commodore coughed loudly and continued at speed. 'I don't doubt you have numerous questions, which is why Brigadier Percival is going to see you off at Cardington. He will brief you more fully there. You are to rendezvous at the Carlton Hotel in Bedford the day after tomorrow when you will receive a full passenger manifest and other briefing notes.'

He consulted his watch. 'And now I'm afraid you will have to excuse us. Brigadier Percival and I have to be across the road for a meeting in Charles Street before a briefing at Number Ten.' He looked up and smiled. 'Charlie will show you out.'

His head spinning, Caspasian stood and shook hands with Air Commodore Mannion, noticing that Brigadier Percival had conveniently placed himself well out of reach beside the furthest of the windows from where he gave a brief nod of his close-cropped head.

Some minutes later Caspasian stepped out into an un-expected shaft of sunlight at the north entrance. He turned right for the Embankment but stopped two paces later. He had almost forgotten his earlier resolve. As he stood there immobile in the sunlight firing from between the scudding clouds, he considered carefully what he was about to do.

He turned suddenly on his heel and headed in the opposite direction. For Horse Guards, the parks, Knightsbridge, and finally Kensington. As he walked, feeling the yards roll beneath his feet, Caspasian felt the slightest twitch in his stomach. Butterflies. It was a long time since he had felt those. Nothing so determinate as fear to which he was well accustomed. Somehow he associated butterflies more with the adolescent state. Childhood even. All of which, in his current circumstance, was highly appropriate. He had someone to meet. Or if not meet, then see.

2

He found the house without any real difficulty. Although he did not have an exact address and had never been there before, the approximate directions were remembered from conversations of many years ago when they had stuck in his young mind. Indeed, they had been unwittingly branded there. Along with them had been a description of the home that he had never visited, and now, all of a sudden, Caspasian found himself standing within sight of it.

He had positioned himself where he could observe the house without being conspicuous. A small, well-tended garden stocked with mature trees lay across the road from the front entrance and Caspasian located a bench and sat to contemplate his find. A thin screen of foliage complicated his view but he was content to remain obscured behind it. He stretched one arm along the back of the bench and crossed his long legs. His uppermost foot tapped the air with interest rather than irritation. He was evaluating the prospect before him, measuring it against the inner image that had haunted him since early childhood. Not surprisingly, the house differed considerably from his boyish vision, but only in the mass of trivia. Colours, dimensions, adornments. In the essentials of general aspect and design it matched admirably his mother's account, even though she herself had only observed it as an outsider, as he did today. An outcast.

Eventually, when he judged it safe, Caspasian delved more deeply into his contemplation to see how he felt about it all.

Instead of a direct answer he received an image, of himself as a young boy in his room in Yokohama. The image recorded a real moment in his life, one that he remembered well. It had been following a conversation with his mother in which she had, again, talked to her son of the house now standing across from the adult Caspasian. Their chat concluded, the boy had withdrawn to his room, easily masking his confusion with a cheeriness that came naturally to him in those days. He had stood for some time thereafter, staring out of the window at the trees spanning the hillside behind the house, the wooded slopes stretching down towards the sea, yet not really seeing the view before him, his focus elsewhere. He could no longer recall what had occupied his thoughts for such a long time but this was nevertheless the image that now assailed Caspasian as he sat on the bench. A young boy staring out of a window.

It was strange to be here at last, in front of the house plucked straight out of his imagination. It was like finding oneself suddenly confronted with an unknown place previously only seen in the muddled tableau of a dream. There was a similar sense of shock, a feeling that something was at the same time amiss and yet somehow quite fitting. An uncomfortable juxta-position of emotions usually experienced only in isolation from one another. Oddly, Caspasian found their sudden and un-expected close proximity exciting. It heralded a state in which anything was possible. To be here in Kensington like this, to have brought about this confrontation of dream with reality, made him feel like an enchanter and a mover between two worlds. Anything was not merely possible, but probable. He could effect material change through an exercise of will.

He recalled some lines from Goethe. *Faust*, he thought. 'Whatever you dream you can do, attempt it. For boldness has power and magic in it.' Caspasian's maternal grandfather had maintained something similar. 'In dreaming,' the old man used to say, 'one injects an almost unbelievable force into the universe. We set out our steps and we walk in them.' He might have been quoting from another but Caspasian thought not. He smiled, recollecting his grandfather's voice. And was it true? Was there any connection between the inner and outer worlds? Sitting there, Caspasian almost felt himself starting to believe that there just might be.

The illusion lasted until the moment the front door opened and, with a chill feeling of dread, Caspasian saw a figure dimly appearing from the dark interior of the house. Dreams might indeed shape the world. But then so did nightmares. Instinctively Caspasian checked his cover. A lively breeze was agitating the undergrowth around him and the leafy trees were noisy with it. The pavements were less than alive with passers-by, but there were just enough to make his own presence unremarkable should he be detected. Nevertheless he fingered the brim of his hat, unobtrusively lowering it over his blue eyes. The urge to rise and walk quickly away from the place was almost overpowering and he was humbled to discover that contrary to his outrageous confidence of only moments earlier, the most that his willpower was capable of achieving was to resist the desire for flight and remain seated on the bench.

Voices accompanied the spectacle unfolding before him. Not just one, but four figures came out of the house, all of them engaged in animated conversation. Three of them were girls, one of whom Caspasian estimated to be about twelve years of age. He judged one of her two companions to be in her late teens and the other in her mid-twenties. Despite their disparate ages, the similarities between them and their manner with each other were sufficient to identify them as sisters. But Caspasian's attention was focused on the fourth member of the group, a man. He was tall and slim, and an unruly shock of grey hair protruded from beneath the brim of a dark hat. He was enjoying the gently chiding attentions of the girls and appeared to be every inch a proud and contented father. His upright bearing was compressed into the most reluctant of stoops, his sixty or so years showing their effect. The impression was of a longbow whose natural inclination for straightness had been drawn into the slightest of crescents by the tensions of the string.

Caspasian was suddenly aware that in observing the man he himself had stopped breathing. Irritably he pulled the air into his lungs, propelling it out again in an effort to regain his composure, even though no one but himself had noticed its momentary absence. From his position of concealment he scrutinised every visible detail of the elderly man with increasing resentment. He found that he was looking less for information than for faults. Yet it was scrutiny nonetheless, and of an intense kind.

With some alarm he noticed that the group was headed in his direction and as they set about crossing the street the voices clarified. Caspasian could make out the young girl's the most clearly as she was dancing around and loudly playing the fool. The eldest girl was holding the lead of a bored-looking spaniel who seemed to be anticipating the exercise without any great enthusiasm. The middle sister was studying her own boots, possibly new, viewing them this way and that as she walked, almost tripping over the curb stone as a result. The man strode in the middle of the girls, a smile lighting his face as he listened to the youngest girl's rambling tale.

To Caspasian's relief the group angled away from his bench when midway across the street. Of all of them, only the spaniel glanced briefly in Caspasian's direction, though noticing more the trees and bushes, no doubt, than the grave spectator partially concealed behind them.

Caspasian waited until they had passed him and moved on some distance before rising from the bench, checking that he remained unobserved, and then following them. Tailing the group was a simple enough matter so he was surprised to find himself unreasonably anxious. To counter it he fell back, allowing the group to gain ground. He took his time, holding back until they rounded a corner and were out of sight, but before moving towards the same junction, he crossed the street so as to approach the corner from the other side of the road and thereby avoid any chance of a confrontation should they have retraced their steps for any reason and be walking back towards him at that very moment.

Once at the corner he saw with relief that they had continued on their way. He thought he could guess where they were heading and several minutes later his hunch was proved correct when they turned into the south-western entrance to Kensington Gardens. Unlike the relatively deserted street in front of the house, here the number of walkers enabled Caspasian to move with a greater sense of ease. He watched the group make their way gently into the park, climbing the steady rise towards Kensington Palace. The spaniel was released from his lead but far from bounding away with exuberance, promptly sat down until urged to continue by the youngest of the girls who nudged his rump with the toe of her boot.

The two older girls linked arms with their father, one on either side of him, while the twelve-year-old skipped ahead, the dog finally managing an interest in the exercise and ambling after her at something approximating a run. The three adults made a relaxed group and though viewing them from the rear, Caspasian could imagine the contented smiles on their faces. He sunk his hands in his pockets and selected a brace of pram-pushing nannies to hide behind as he started up the incline. True to his expectations, his targets beyond them veered towards the Round Pond where they halted to contemplate the ducks.

A small boy in a sailor suit crouched beside a model yacht, organising the sails before launching it with such a mighty shove that it was almost sent straight to the bottom. The spaniel took too close an interest in a mallard that scudded away across the

surface of the pond, eventually tiring of the effort and subsiding
with outraged squawks on the far side.

The nannies chatted their way across to a bench where they
settled themselves, wholly ignoring their charges, both of whom
were crying. Denied his cover, Caspasian chose another bench
further along, half of which was occupied by an elderly man
reading a newspaper. Sitting down beside him, Caspasian
nodded in his direction as the man lowered his paper with an
angry display and glowered at him.

'Nice afternoon,' Caspasian said, tipping his hat.

The man snorted, shook his paper as if freeing it of considerable layers of dust, and returned to his study of some article
or other.

When he looked back at the group Caspasian's heart stopped.
From the opposite side of the broad pond, all four of them were
staring straight at him and the eldest of the girls was pointing,
her forefinger directed exactly at Caspasian himself. He froze,
wondering whether to get up and go to them, or turn and walk
away. A meeting was wholly out of the question. It was a nonsense even to consider such a thing. So retreat then.

With as much dignity as he could muster, Caspasian rose
from the bench and turned to leave, tumbling straight into a
woman who had been approaching the pond from behind him,
the woman at whom the group were now vigorously waving. As
he mumbled apologies Caspasian was aware of the spaniel
barking in the distance, suddenly invested with life as it came
running round the edge of the pond to greet the newcomer with
a special fondness. Fortunately for Caspasian the collision had
caused the woman to drop an umbrella she had been carrying
and in the lucky confusion as he bent to retrieve it for her, the
dog arrived on the scene and launched itself at the new arrival,
enabling Casaspian to keep his face averted and slip away with
a polite and embarrassed tip of the hat.

Amidst the greetings overheard as he walked away he caught

the word 'Mama'. It fired into him, striking bone. He shuddered and coughed into his hand. Once at the tree-lined path he wheeled towards the Bayswater Road but despite his brisk step and the urgency of his departure he was unable to resist a backward glance. The woman had recovered and had been reunited with her daughters and husband, all of whom were attempting to converse at once. All except the eldest of the girls who this time really was staring straight at Caspasian. Having no part in the exchange going on around her, her eyes were levelled at Caspasian and he was still just close enough to detect her questioning frown and to recognize an expression not dissimilar to his own.

He regarded for the last time the mother of the girls, his heart fending off a rain of blows from a myriad unexpected directions. He was angry with himself. Livid. For having made the visit in the first place and, now, for allowing himself to be so affected by the outcome. He was a grown man, for God's sake. What the hell had he expected? Of course there had been a chance that such feelings would result from a confrontation like this. And there they all were before him, the happy shadow family that had so often haunted Caspasian's blacker reveries. A husband, now grown old, and his forgiving wife who had decided all those years before to overlook his dalliance in Japan with a girl of exotic European descent. A girl who had been wholly unaware of the wife's existence when she encountered the man now standing beside the water's edge. Sir David Edward. Caspasian's father.

The train headed north out of London, threading with a mercifully increasing speed through the grim flat bleakness of the suburbs and on into the equally unexciting countryside that stretched interminably for mile upon mile between the capital city and Bedford.

Brigadier James Percival yawned viciously at it, wishing it

would go away. He was a son of the Empire. The home mother-
land that had spawned it was, to his mind, like some dastardly
old hag that has unaccountably given birth to a radiant princess.
For Percival, that princess was India, the British colonies of the
east, the possessions straddling the African continent, the glittering islands in the Caribbean. How the devil they had ever
grown out of something as common as this was completely
beyond him. In certain parts of the country he was aware that
tidy little corners of old England resided behind drystone walls
and rose-covered trellises, but that was just it. They were tidy
and little. Percival believed himself to be a man of open spaces,
unkempt ruggedness. He even admired a degree of chaos, so
long as he himself might regard it from an elevated position that
placed him safely beyond its reach. As such, India superbly
suited his tastes, for there chaos, filth and ruggedness were the
order of the day, and his own position as an officer of the Indian
Army and, above that, of the Imperial Intelligence Service, did
indeed remove him to a position where he could observe with
detachment the squalid doings of the natives.

Oddly, it was a taste that both linked him to John Caspasian
and at the same time separated him from the man. For while
Caspasian was similarly a son of the Empire, unlike Percival he
was not averse to entering the chaos and dwelling there. Indeed,
Percival even suspected that the fellow thrived upon it. For
Caspasian, the desert, mountain and jungle were not abstract
concepts. They were his habitat and he was completely at home
in them. He was capable of submersing himself in the chaos that
Percival enjoyed only from a distance, and surviving there.
Flourishing even. Percival was sufficiently self-aware to admit
to a grudging admiration for the chap.

That aside, he detested him. To his mind Caspasian was
unable to sacrifice his principles to the wider good of the
Empire. Honesty got in the way. His view of the great imperial
direction of march was obscured by a vaporous blanket of

honour, a quality that was all very well in theory but impractical if one attempted to apply it to real situations. It was best confined to the lowliest of the officer ranks, and even then it should really be left at the gates of Sandhurst on commissioning.

He leaned back and pushed out his legs to their full length, inspecting the distant toecaps of his Highland brogues, the sternly polished black leather peppered with a symmetrical pattern of holes as if a woodworm had been at work, its industry driven by a fanatical sense of proportion.

'Tickets, please.'

Brigadier Percival slipped off a pair of black leather gloves and reached inside his jacket pocket to retrieve his wallet. Finding the ticket he presented it to the inspector who clipped one corner and returned it to him.

In India he would have been shown considerably more deference and Percival resented its complete absence in the surly man who now turned his back on the Brigadier and shrugged back into the shaking corridor. Mind you, in India he would hardly have been travelling in the compartment in quite such comfortable isolation. It would have been packed to the gunwales with humanity in a broad variety of guises, most of them either absurd or objectionable. Faces would peer down from the train's roof, grinning inanely at the Brigadier within, and boys clad in rags would proffer trays at the windows bearing cups of thick milky sweet tea, bananas, peanuts in shells and slices of watermelon to the unwary traveller. Westerners who accepted such wares usually spent the rest of the trip hanging out of the same window, retching into the wind. God help anyone further down the train who happened to look out. Percival smiled maliciously at the memory of one hapless missionary, new to the subcontinent, who had stuck head and shoulders out of the window to be met full in the face by such a greeting from further up the speeding train. To say the least it had put an end to his obnoxious proselytizing.

Bedford was grey with drizzle when the Brigadier alighted on the platform. He was travelling light so waved away the porter who came scurrying towards the single valise which contained his belongings for the overnight stay. All being well he would be back in the capital the following day and Caspasian would be soaring like a bird fastened to a ton of explosives.

A taxi transferred him swiftly to the front entrance of the impressive Carlton Hotel which stood on the north-eastern outskirts of the town. This time, to avoid the stigma of miser, he allowed a porter to carry his valise up to his room while he himself registered at the reception desk. Smiles proliferated, the receptionist's as insincere as his own, and he made his way up the stairs as indicated and found his room to be moderately sized, modestly furnished and overlooking the backyard which was garrisoned with dustbins and a ferocious-looking but slumbering dog on a chain. Percival twitched the net curtain aside to run a gloved finger over the sill. It came away clean.

With plenty of time before dinner and his prearranged rendezvous with Caspasian in the lounge bar, he stripped off his jacket and shoes, loosened his collar and tie, punched the pillows on his bed into a haphazard stack, and lay back with the contents of his briefcase to review the fat manila folder. It was fastened with scarlet ribbon which Percival's fingers untied with a single deft tug. Page by page he leafed through it, studying only cursorily the passport-sized photograph pinned to every top right-hand corner. He only paused and looked more closely at one of them, raising a recently trimmed eyebrow interestedly at the woman depicted. Frozen in time, she maintained her brilliant smile into the unseen camera lens, presenting the world with the image that the public on both sides of the Atlantic had come to love of Miss Emma Lavelle, star of a score of moving pictures.

Completing his survey, he dropped the folder onto his lap and stared into the milky folds of the net curtains, thinking. He remained in this position as the hands on the mantelpiece clock wound their way inexorably to seven-thirty when, with a sigh denoting anything but boredom, he swung his legs off the bed and stood to prepare himself for dinner.

The bar was tended by a neatly attired member of staff who was busy serving a small group of hotel residents perched in a row on stools too spindly to permit even the mildest slouch. Without warning, Caspasian was at the Brigadier's side.

'Ah, so you made it,' the Brigadier said peremptorily. Caspasian smiled and Percival could not help thinking that the man looked distracted. 'What's your poison?' he asked.

'Poison?' Caspasian said with a start.

'Drink, man, drink.'

'Oh. Scotch.'

'Soda?' the Brigadier said as he moved to the bar.

'Ice, please.'

When Caspasian's drink was in one hand and a gin and tonic in the other, Percival motioned towards a table in a secluded corner well away from the increasing volume of the chatter bordering the bar. They sat down, Caspasian accepting his whisky with thanks.

The Brigadier regarded him resolutely for a moment and then raised his glass. 'New beginnings,' he said.

Caspasian returned his toast suspiciously. 'New beginnings, sir.'

They drank, each holding the other's eye over the top of his glass like poker players anticipating a drawn gun.

When the glasses had been set down and the two men were satisfied with their mutual sizing-up, Brigadier Percival began his verbal brief, keeping his voice low and checking, every so often, that they remained isolated and out of earshot from their fellow drinkers.

Caspasian listened closely, refraining from making notes but committing to memory names and other details as he judged fit.

When the Brigadier reached Miss Lavelle, Caspasian stared in disbelief.

'What's the matter?' the Brigadier asked, sensing a protest.

'Surely if there's a danger of sabotage it would be wise to keep high-profile passengers off the flight?'

The Brigadier smiled icily. 'And how do you propose we do that?'

'There must be ways,' Caspasian said, hunting for them in his swirling scotch.

'These bookings were made long ago. You don't just wake up in the morning and decide you want to go on an airship. Miss Lavelle's presence on the flight is part of a publicity campaign by her studio. Apparently they feel her career needs a lift.'

'Well it'll certainly get that,' Caspasian could not resist saying.

'Ha jolly ha,' the Brigadier replied laconically.

'I suppose you're going to tell me her agent's on the manifest as well?'

'Actually not,' the Brigadier said with pleasure, passing another paper to Caspasian. 'But *he* is.' He watched Caspasian as he scanned the information and the small photograph. 'Lionel B. Domain.'

'The mogul?'

Percival shrugged. 'Producer, though with ambitions to become a mogul. Like Miss Lavelle's, his career hit the doldrums when the talkies arrived and he hasn't quite managed to pick up his old stride since. It might have something to do with the fact that they're actually both English, in spite of all the fuss. Lavelle's accent came as a shock to the preconceptions of her fans. Domain followed in her wake, though with him, I'm told, it was more the fact that he failed to grasp the impact of the new technology.'

'But he's fighting back I suppose,' Caspasian said, observing the face grimacing confidently, almost threateningly, out at him from the photograph.

'Oh yes. You don't succeed in that business unless you've got skin like a rhino and clout like Jack Dempsey. He'll be back all right, even if he was a Londoner once upon a time. Miss Lavelle's another matter though. A sweet girl, but completely at sea in her first film with sound. The audience booed, I believe, when they heard her speak on screen. They'd grown too used to their own image of her as an all-American sweetheart. She hasn't made a successful film since.'

'Then why's Domain holding on to her? He doesn't look like the merciful type.'

The Brigadier smiled ruefully. 'Come, come, Caspasian. The oldest reason of them all.'

'Ah. He loves her.'

'I wouldn't put it as nobly as that. I suspect he'll tire of her in time, but for the moment he's trying to restart her flagging career and persuade her to have one more shot at it. The flight's intended to put her back in the public eye. Prepare the way, if you like.'

Caspasian handed back the forms. 'Is that the lot?'

The Brigadier reached into his brief case, paused a moment, and then shut it. 'Yes.' He looked up and smiled. 'Now let's go and eat.'

The Brigadier had ensured that their table in the dining room was equally private and as they took their seats, ushered into them by an ingratiating waiter, he noticed how Caspasian moved to position himself with his back to a wall giving him a clear view of the room and of everyone in it. Whether he had done so from old habits of vigilance or to annoy the Brigadier by denying him the seat that he also preferred, Percival could not say.

The menus and wine list were presented and studied, selections announced, suitably rewarded with compliments by the waiter, and they were again left alone. They sat in silence for a while as other diners drifted in. The hotel appeared to be busy.

People had come to watch the departure of the *D200* the following morning, but apart from himself Caspasian had not so far detected anyone else from the passenger manifest.

'One thought, Brigadier,' he said when their meals were in front of them and two glasses had been charged with a rich claret. 'The press are going to focus a great deal of attention on the passengers. If my mission is clandestine, it's hardly going to suit our purposes if I'm included under that spotlight.'

'Not really,' the Brigadier replied through a mouthful of rather stringy pheasant. 'You'll be an observer on behalf of the Indian Army evaluating the use of airships for reconnaissance operations or some such. Seconded by the headquarters in Delhi. I've jacked up the necessary clearances and so forth. If anyone takes the trouble to check, they'll receive all the appropriate answers to corroborate your story.'

Caspasian was about to reply when there was a flurry of activity in the reception area beyond the bar as if a door had been flung open to admit a passing hurricane. Around the dining room conversations stopped in midstream, restarting seconds later as the news filtered through.

'Emma Lavelle,' someone said loudly.

'It's Emma Lavelle! Look, it's her!'

'There she is!'

People rose from their tables and craned to catch sight of the film star. Brigadier Percival put down his cutlery and looked round, searching this way and that through the standing diners now thronging towards the entrance. Caspasian glanced once and then returned to his jugged hare.

A light ripple of applause passed through the hotel guests like wind through corn and an elderly gentleman in the heaviest tweeds Caspasian had seen since arriving in England, blew her a kiss and shouted 'Bravo! I say, bravo!'

Brigadier Percival returned to his food, sneering at Caspasian. 'Looks like you'll have a lively old time.'

Caspasian was stoical. 'At least she'll distract attention from whatever I'm doing.'

'That's the spirit,' the Brigadier said, raising his glass and thinking of proposing another toast but then giving up on the idea. He put it to his lips, realized it was empty and poured himself a refill, helping Caspasian to more as an afterthought. Sediment dribbled out of the bottle and it expired. Neither of them moved to order a replacement, Caspasian because he had been unimpressed by the vintage and the Brigadier because he had been even more unimpressed by the outrageously inflated price. Whilst he knew he would be able to submit a claim for expenses, he had never been able to shake off the habits of thrift bequeathed to him by his vicarage-reared mother who had suffered at the hands of the young James Percival's profligate father.

'Pudding?' the Brigadier suggested hopefully. To his disappointment Caspasian shook his head. 'No, I suppose not. Probably just stodge,' he conceded. He perused the menu with a manufactured indifference. 'Might try some Stilton, though,' he mused. He glanced at Caspasian. 'Perhaps not. Port?'

Caspasian realized that this time a negative response would be highly inappropriate. 'Fine, thank you. Why don't we have it in the drawing room?'

'Good idea.' The Brigadier ordered accordingly and rose to lead the way. The other diners had returned to their meals, buzzing excitedly about the celebrity arrival who had now disappeared to the suite of rooms reserved for her. However, half an hour later, when Caspasian and the brigadier were sitting by an open but empty fireplace pretending to be relaxed in each other's company, the door to the drawing room opened with a silent fanfare and Miss Emma Lavelle entered sweepingly. Positioned commandingly and possessively at her elbow, a man whom Caspasian took to be Lionel Domain steered her towards the centre, only considering where they might occupy seats when he had reached the highly visible epicentre of the large and formally decorated room.

There was an audible intake of breath from the room's handful of other occupants, and Caspasian thought that even the Brigadier looked inspired by the spectacle. Caspasian leaned towards him and whispered, 'Lights! Camera! Action!'

The spell broken, Percival scowled at him. 'Is nothing sacred?'

Caspasian smiled. 'Certainly not pomposity.'

Only just achieving medium height, Domain had dressed in a cream tuxedo. Savagely pressed black trousers culminated in black patent leather shoes and when he withdrew a silver cigarette case from his dinner jacket's inside pocket, he revealed a cummerbund of imperial purple. Everyone waited while he lit a cigarette, holding it between rigid fore and middle fingers and turning his head through ninety degrees to the right in order to inhale. His groomed hair, oiled flat against his narrow skull, had been allowed to grey at the temples, but Caspasian suspected that, left to its own devices, the grey would have long since taken the high ground.

Such had been the impression created by Domain that contemplation of Miss Lavelle only came a second later. Caspasian had seen two of her silent films and was struck by how little difference there was between her screen presence and the reality now standing some ten yards away from him. He did not doubt that she had prepared herself for this public airing, but there was nevertheless a quality about her that marked her out as extraordinary.

Short-cut blonde hair framed a face that Caspasian could only describe as lovely. There were few other words for it. Long-lashed blue eyes sparkled and Caspasian reckoned that her skin appeared paler in the artificial light than it probably was in the day. A dress of cream silk covered in sequins hung straight from her bare shoulders, and matching stockings and shoes presented her to all observers as a beautifully matching companion to Lionel B. Domain.

'Over here, honey.' Domain deftly engineered their further progress towards an unoccupied clutch of armchairs in one corner of the room where large closed doors were capable, in finer weather, of opening onto a patio. Two waiters rushed to attend to them, competing for the prize of an order. Miss Lavelle looked from one to the other, preparing to speak and with the slenderest thread of admiration, Caspasian understood that she was trying to honour them equally, unwilling to dismiss either. Domain cut through her considerations.

'Miss Lavelle will have a glass of champagne and I'll have a Bourbon. On the rocks.'

He had addressed his order to the more aggressively forward of the two, and again Caspasian was struck by Miss Lavelle's kindness as she rewarded the other waiter with a smile whose radiance far outweighed the value of Domain's order.

The waiters sped from the room as fast as mere walking would allow, and at that moment, while Domain was reaching for an ashtray from a neighbouring table, Emma Lavelle cast her gaze around the room, smiling with the grace of a princess born to the role. When her eyes fell upon Brigadier Percival and Caspasian, the Brigadier saluted with the slightest bow of his close-cropped head. Caspasian looked levelly back, unsmiling.

Unperturbed, Emma Lavelle returned the Brigadier's acknowledgment, and with the tiniest of smiling frowns, made Caspasian agonizingly aware that he had been chided in the gentlest of manners by a thorough professional.

3

The *Grenadine Quest* was a ship that even its own captain was ashamed of. Any vestige of its once bright covering of red paint had long since succumbed to rust which now pitted every area of the vessel like the very worst case of smallpox. For many years there had been no attempt to dry dock the ship and repaint it. It was being run until it fell apart and at the outset of every voyage Captain Planer crossed himself and hoped that it would not be on this trip that the inevitable happened. It was a strange and rather pathetic exercise, this burying of his head in metaphorical sand. Rationally, he knew that one day the disaster must happen, but always he found himself thinking, not yet, not on this trip, not now. Please.

The reason for this was that he was coming up for retirement. A race had therefore developed, his own sprint towards his personal finishing line, and the *Quest*'s equally desperate dash into oblivion. The ship was owned by a small company working out of Martinique and it was for them that Planer had worked these last few, washed-up years of his life. Prior to that his career, which had started with promise, presented a sorry tale whose downward trend had acquired the inevitability of Greek tragedy, at least in his own eyes.

He stood in the fresh air beside the bridge, the muffled sound of a jazz tune coming through the open doorway where one of the hands was sprawled in a much-repaired chair reading a book, an ancient phonograph crackling out the music at his elbow. From time to time the man would glance up and stare past the Captain out across the calm surface of the sea. Captain Planer smiled whenever the man did this but the sailor ignored him. Amongst the crew the Captain was viewed with contempt, or at best indifference. To them he cut a ridiculous figure, for while he insisted on high personal standards from himself in both dress and general behaviour, he lacked the authority to impose similar standards upon those supposedly under his command. Hence the path his career had taken. An absence of willpower had left this intelligent and well-meaning being adrift in a business for which his weak character was wholly unsuited. Furthermore, the same weakness of character had kept him firmly entrenched in the seafarer's life, unable to break out and try anything new.

The ship had cut through the Guadeloupe Passage at daybreak and now, after a day's ponderous sailing and as the light began to fade, it was well past Montserrat and heading south-west into the heart of the Caribbean Sea. The latest reports received over the radio-telegraph predicted fair weather all the way to their destination at Cartagena in Colombia. A routine trip. This time their cargo was scrap iron, and the holds were crammed full of the stuff making the ship sluggish and un-responsive. It sat low in the water, the engines chugging tiredly like the heartbeat of a dying man, pushing the vessel slowly through the waves.

Dolphins appeared out of nowhere and skipped and bucketed alongside the *Quest* for several minutes, weaving in and out of the foam like curved suture needles stitching the waves together. Planer watched them, his eyes becoming alive for the first time that day. But eventually the creatures veered away and went in search of something that was more fun than the shuddering old steamer. In the gathering darkness, Planer strained after them, following the shiny boomerangs of their wet backs for as long as he could.

When they were finally out of sight and Planer had been

fruitlessly observing their last point of visibility for some moments, a great sigh broke from him as his previous melancholy flooded back with a vengeance. He was about to turn aside, suddenly angry with the inanity of the jazz music at his back, when something caught his eye. His brow furrowed as he squinted towards the source, trying to make out what it was. It looked like a low cloud, vast and grey, but against the heavy dusk it was difficult to tell. Normally Planer would have turned away, but something about the vague shape hovering above the distant seascape held his attention. It was the regularity of the shape. It had to be an object, something material, but what?

He wondered if it might be a giant shoal of fish on the surface of the sea, reflected on the underside of a cloud. Possibly it was a whale, similarly reflected. Tricks of light were commonplace at sea.

He decided to go and fetch some binoculars. Stepping onto the bridge, he apologized as he caused the seaman to move his outstretched legs, retrieved his binoculars from the desk on which charts were spread haphazardly and returned to his observation point. He looped the strap around his neck and raised the eyepieces, twisting the focus onto the object. Beneath the binoculars his mouth fell open.

'Well I'll be damned.'

The seaman looked up and stared slack-jawed at the Captain. He blinked once and then returned to his book.

'Hobbs, call Mr Tyler.'

The seaman finished the sentence he was on, looked up but did not move.

The Captain stared mesmerized at the distant shape, turning his binoculars this way and that to search for other ships in the vicinity. There were none. He looked round after a while to find the seaman's dull eyes still upon him.

'I thought I told you to go and get Mr Tyler?' he said irritably.

The seaman slammed his book shut and tossed it aside. With

a purposely audible sigh he gathered up his long legs and pushed himself to his feet. He stood there a second, scowling at the Captain's back before lumbering off towards the companion-way, hands in pockets and shoulders hunched.

Planer was now certain that the object that had caught his attention was an airship. Although he had never seen one before, he had seen enough pictures of them to recognize the lozenge shape and tail fins. It was still several miles distant and in the gathering darkness Planer estimated that it would soon be invisible.

'You rang, sir?' Mr Tyler said, his voice heavy with sarcasm.

Planer turned to see his first officer standing there scratching himself. He had obviously just tumbled out of his bunk and had made no effort to try to hide the fact. He was dressed in baggy creased trousers and soiled string vest through which a vast pendulous gut sagged like a catch of fish writhing in a net. His feet were splayed inside rope-soled canvas shoes, the heels trod flat, big toes protruding through holes. Fate had played with him, stripping his head bald while covering the rest of his face in a savage stubble that rasped beneath his searching fingers, nails ingrained with oil.

'An airship, Mr Tyler! Look!' Planer freed himself from his binocular straps and handed them to his colleague.

Tyler did not reach for them. He stared at his superior officer as if he had been addressed in a foreign language.

'Quickly man, or you'll miss it!'

Unconsciously, Tyler calculated the number of seconds he could wait without insulting his Captain in front of the seaman, and then doubled it. At last he roughly took hold of the binoculars and shuffled to the railing to follow the direction the Captain indicated.

'Well, bugger me,' Tyler said, wholly unimpressed. The seaman sniggered.

Captain Planer smiled nervously but his excitement at the

prospect of seeing an airship for the first time got the better of his embarrassment. 'Perhaps we should alter course to have a better look at it,' he suggested, stiffening his voice in an attempt at authority.

Tyler stood with the binoculars stuck to his heavy-lidded eyes. 'No need. It's heading straight for us.' Against his natural inclination for sloth, he too was becoming interested.

'I wonder whether it wants to communicate with us?' the Captain asked no one in particular. He turned to the seaman. 'Hobbs, go to the radio room and see if they've received anything.'

Hobbs looked slowly from the Captain to Tyler. Tyler jerked his head in the direction of the bridge, binoculars still in place, and Hobbs slunk away. Apart from anything else, he was disgruntled because the radio room was usually unmanned which meant he would have to trawl the bowels of the ship in search of the signaller who was probably either asleep, drunk or most likely both.

The airship was now plainly visible without the aid of binoculars and down on the deck of the *Grenadine Quest*, a little clutch of sailors had gathered to watch its steady approach. Captain Planer stared at it in wonder, Tyler beside him similarly mesmerized.

'It's absolutely huge!' Planer said.

Still some distance away, the airship was already filling the night sky and yet it continued to grow bigger and bigger. On the *Quest*, the men stood as if hypnotized.

Hobbs reappeared from the bridge. 'Nothing on the radio,' he said. 'Dead as a doornail.'

Planer was about to suggest they try signalling it with a light when Tyler said, 'Hobbs, get my torch.'

Once again Hobbs descended into the ship's innards. By now, word had spread of the airship's arrival and the entire crew had congregated on deck to spectate. Hobbs returned a minute later and handed Tyler the torch which he began to flash on and off. His signals knowledge was less than rudimentary but he continued nonetheless, waving the pencil-thin beam into the darkness. The airship loomed ever closer, unresponding.

'That's odd,' Planer said after a while.

'What?' Tyler grunted, growing tired of his efforts and flicking his torch off.

'The whole thing's in darkness. I mean, there aren't even any lights from the bridge, the control gondola or whatever it is.'

Tyler shrugged. 'Perhaps they're asleep.'

'Even so, there must be an officer of the watch. Most odd.'

'Not really. A light would spoil his night vision. They'll probably hail us at any moment.'

But the airship remained in complete darkness. It now lay alongside the ship and parallel with it, sitting about three hundred feet to port and suspended some five hundred feet in the air, utterly dwarfing the *Grenadine Quest* which continued chugging on its course, a long triangular tendril of foam expanding in its wake across the wide dark sea.

'There must be some sort of identification mark on it,' Planer said. 'A flag or number or something.'

'We've got a handheld searchlight in one of the lifeboats,' Tyler replied, and shouted down to one of the sailors to set it up and bring it to bear on the flanks of the airship. 'It's like they're all bloody dead up there,' he concluded, speaking more to himself than to the Captain who was also becoming unsettled.

Four powerful motors, each in its own gondola, idled gently as the airship effortlessly kept station alongside the *Quest*. Planer noticed that ever so gently the airship was edging closer and for the first time he considered giving instructions for the *Quest* to alter course in order to flee from the hovering monstrosity looming over them. He knew it would be futile however as the airship could outstrip his vessel with ease and if its intention was to keep pace with the *Quest* then there was nothing Captain Planer could do to prevent it. It really was most odd, he pondered, gazing up at the darkened airship. He glanced at Tyler who returned his look, uneasy.

'What do you suppose they want?' Planer asked.

Tyler shrugged, rubbing his bristly chin. He leaned over the railing and shouted to the men below. 'Where's that blasted searchlight?'

'Just a minute!' someone shouted back from the darkness. There were mutters and curses as sailors fumbled with the equipment and then a moment later a beam shot skywards as the powerful handheld light was successfully wired to a battery.

Careening across the heavens the beam was brought to bear on the airship, hitting it with almost physical force.

'It must be an American naval Zeppelin,' Planer suggested. 'But where the hell are the crew? If this is some kind of joke it's not very funny.'

Bigger than the *Titanic*, the airship completely dwarfed the *Grenadine Quest*. Its presence so close created a feeling of claustrophobia amongst everyone on board the old steamer as if they were about to be sat on and squashed. From beneath the airship, streams of water tumbled down into the sea as from a huge fish that has just been hauled out of the deep.

'The gondola!' Tyler shouted to the sailor handling the light. 'Shine it on that!'

Obediently the beam swung quickly towards the control car slung beneath the prow of the airship. But as it did so it slid smoothly across some giant numbers. All muttering and chatter amongst the sailors stopped. Everyone fell silent. Slowly, the beam was brought back towards the identification markings emblazoned across the huge flank of the airship. There, held fast in the silver beam and plain for all to see, was the designation *D100*.

'Oh my God,' Captain Planer said quietly, his flesh creeping.

Hobbs stared. 'But it can't be. It was lost with all hands. They found the wreckage.'

On the deck below the crew gazed up, transfixed, all of them staring in mute horror, too terrified even to scream.

Quietly, as if afraid of waking a slumbering monster, Captain Planer turned to his first officer. 'Hard to port, Mr Tyler. Take us away from this infernal thing.'

For the first time in his life Tyler was grateful for the Captain's order. He managed three steps towards the bridge when there was a cry from the deck.

'There's a man! Look!'

Two hundred yards distant and framed in the control gondola window high above them, Captain Planer, Tyler and his men saw a lone figure standing at the gondola window, looking back at them. He was too far away to make out anything but the outline of his features, but they could see that he was wearing the cap of an airship officer.

'It must be the captain,' Hobbs whispered, his terror audible.

Then, on either side of the single figure, others moved up to flank him, coming from the depths of the gondola until the windows were filled with the blank silhouettes of men, all of them dressed in the uniforms of airship officers.

'There, look!' one of the steamer's crew shouted, and snatched the searchlight, directing it back towards the phalanx of windows from the passenger compartments. Each window, previously blank, was now filled with a single staring face, ghostly pale in the silver light of the beam.

'It's the passengers,' Hobbs said, starting to whimper. 'The passengers and crew of the old *D100*. They've come back.'

Caspasian was up early the next morning. Light pushed through the curtains and woke him from a long and restful sleep. He stretched and reluctantly sat up. The mattress was far softer than he liked so rather than sit and muse for a while, he threw back the eiderdown and blankets and stepped onto the floor. He went across to the window and looked out. The sky was grey and it had been raining in the night, but the clouds were breaking up, giving way to a watery sunlight and growing patches of vivid blue. From the courtyard below a delicious smell of frying bacon arose out of the kitchens where breakfast was being prepared.

Resisting the temptation to shave, bath, dress and go straight to the dining room and eat, Caspasian changed into shorts, running vest and pumps and went down the back stairs to the tradesmen's entrance near the laundry. A young housemaid looked up, startled, until she realized he was one of the guests. Caspasian smiled brightly. The maid blushed and curtsied.

Out in the open, the air greeted him, fresh and clean, a welcome change after his days in London. He shook his limbs free of sleep and performed a couple of simple stretches to prepare his tendons and muscles for work, and then set off at a gentle pace along a road leading away from the town and out into the countryside. Farmland bordered the road on both sides, the neat fields covering the landscape in a patchwork quilt all the way to the horizon. For most of the way tall hedges impaired his view but every so often the vista opened out and then he was able to run with head erect, taking in the modest sights.

He could feel his heart and lungs starting to work so gently lengthened his stride and accelerated the pace. The perfectly flat road presented nothing by way of challenge so Caspasian increased his speed to compensate. On a whim he halted, dropped to the ground and did forty push-ups, then sprinted on again, repeating the exercise every hundred yards for the next half mile or so. When his lungs and arm muscles screamed for a rest, he slowed to a jog, but lifted his knees chest-high at every step. Finally, when he could do no more, he slowed to a walk, coming to rest beside a gate that barred the entrance into a grassy field from which a herd of Friesian cows gazed back at him, jaws working contentedly.

Caspasian leaned heavily on the gate, head hanging forward, watching the beads of perspiration crash into the hard dry folds of a tractor's tyre marks.

'Nice morning,' said a woman's voice from behind him.

Still leaning on the gate he twisted his head round. Perched on a stile set into the hedge opposite him was Miss Emma Lavelle. She was dressed in pale grey tracksuit bottoms and a cream cotton top with a coral-coloured silk scarf loosely around her neck. A neat pair of white tennis shoes were lightly dusted with dried mud, evidence of similar, if less strenuous, exercise.

Seeing who it was, Caspasian swivelled round to face her, running a hand through his wet, unkempt hair. 'Indeed. It's the best time of day.'

Emma Lavelle nodded agreement. 'You're staying at the Carlton, aren't you?'

Flattered, Caspasian said that he was. He smiled. 'You too, I believe. It would have been difficult to miss your arrival.'

Emma Lavelle laughed good-naturedly. 'I'm sorry if it interrupted your otherwise peaceful evening. Lionel does enjoy creating a stir.'

'I suppose it goes with the job.'

She tilted her head to one side, agreeing. 'It certainly does.'

'How do you cope?' Caspasian asked. 'I mean, it must all get a bit much at times.'

She seemed at first not to understand his question, and when she did, Caspasian felt he could detect a slight withdrawal, a defensive posture as if she feared she had already conceded too much to a complete stranger.

'Don't worry,' he added quickly. 'I'm not a journalist or anything like that.'

His reassurance worked a little, but no more.

'One learns to cope with the pressures.' And then, feeling a more positive approach was required she added, 'Actually I enjoy it.'

Caspasian smiled kindly, not believing her but tactful enough not to say so.

'So what brings you out here at this unearthly hour?' he asked.

'Much the same as you probably. And also, perhaps, a last long walk before we board the *D200*.' She regarded him. 'Are you a passenger, or here to see someone off?'

'A passenger,' Caspasian answered. 'Well, a member of the crew actually. Sort of.'

'Sort of? Either you are or you aren't, surely?'

Caspasian regretted the direction the conversation had taken but supposed the matter had to be tackled sooner or later. 'I'm an observer. For the army, that is. We're evaluating the *D200* model.'

'Oh I see,' Emma Lavelle said, pivoting back on the stile, hands around her knees as she contemplated his answer. 'You mean, to see how many bombs you can cram on board?'

'Not really. Long-range reconnaissance is a more likely use, particularly at sea.'

'But I thought you said you were from the army?' she commented reasonably.

Caspasian laughed, feeling completely at sea himself. 'That was just an example. Actually I'm Indian Army.'

'Oh, so there are seas in India, are there?' she said, playing with him.

'Very funny. What I mean is, the airship has a reconnaissance role over remote, inaccessible areas. The North-west Frontier Provinces, for example. Possibly the Himalayas, even.'

'That makes a bit more sense.' She eyed him shrewdly. 'So you're really a sort of spy.'

Caspasian laughed. 'Well if I am you can hardly expect me to admit it.'

'True.'

'Anyway, I'm nothing so grand. More of a humble liaison officer.'

She screwed up her nose, disbelieving. 'Humble? That's funny, you don't look the type.'

'Thank you.'

'You're welcome.'

Caspasian looked back down the road in the direction he had come. 'You should probably be starting back. It's quite a way to the hotel and . . .'

'And I obviously won't be able to make it back as fast as you? Is that it?' She noted his discomfort with satisfaction and got to her feet, shaking loose her leg muscles, which had started to go to sleep. 'Don't patronize me, Mister . . . ?'

'Caspasian. John Caspasian.' He crossed the intervening space of road and they shook hands. She grimaced at the touch of his wet hand and inspected her palm once she had got it back.

'Sorry,' he added as she wiped her hand on her cream-coloured top leaving a grubby smear. Before he could say any more she had set off down the road in the direction of the town, jogging at a very respectable pace. He started after her, falling in alongside. 'So why the *D200* trip?' he asked.

She glanced at him sternly. 'I'd rather not talk while I run, if you don't mind. But since you ask, it was Lionel's idea of a career refit.'

Caspasian remembered from her entry in Percival's passenger brief that she was twenty-nine. 'Is a refit really necessary?'

'You obviously don't follow the movie business very closely.'

'I don't.'

'Well even you must have heard about the reception of my last movie.'

'*The Lights of Damascus*?'

She swept back a strand of hair, the gesture charged with anger. 'They booed it off the screen in New York.'

'What the devil for?'

'My voice didn't match the image they'd formed of me.'

'You mean being English was not exotic enough for them?'

'I'm still trying to figure it out. I think they were more disappointed to hear that I wasn't one of them at all. A dream can be a perverse thing. Anyway, theirs crumbled.'

Now it was Caspasian's turn to compliment her. 'Then they were unworthy of you.'

'Kind of you to say so, but unfortunately you're in a minority of one. The public couldn't accept that the star of *Eastern Princess* and *Slave Girl of Zanzibar* was plain old English Emma. Somehow, a homegrown Lavelle would have been acceptable. At least that's what Lionel reckons. See what I mean by perverse?'

'So the *D200* flight is going to reinvest you with cinematic presence?' Caspasian thought about it for a moment. 'Not a bad idea, actually.'

'Lionel hopes so.'

'And you?'

'I wish people could accept me as I am.'

'Then perhaps an actress wasn't the best choice of career.'

She laughed, mopping her brow with the back of one hand. 'Don't get me wrong. I love acting. It's just . . .'

'You want to have your cake and eat it.' Caspasian shrugged. 'I don't have any difficulty with that. Who doesn't want the same? But what I'd like to know is . . . !'

'Look,' she said, out of breath. 'Can we talk about all this some other time?'

'I'm sorry. Of course we can. Forgive me. It's not every day I get to chat to a world-famous star.'

She glanced at him to see if he was being sarcastic. Seeing that he was sincere she smiled. 'We'll continue the discourse on board.'

Caspasian nodded. 'I'll look forward to it.'

In the hotel lobby, Brigadier Percival was pacing anxiously in search of Caspasian. 'I thought you'd done a runner.'

Fresh from his bath, Caspasian came quickly down the stairs, straightening his tie as he went. 'Sorry if I've kept you from your breakfast.'

'Damn right you have. Come on, man.'

Caspasian watched amazed as the Brigadier's heaped plateful of bacon and eggs disappeared into his lean frame. Morning papers had been provided at the entrance to the dining room and the meal passed in silence until the plates had been cleared away, toast and marmalade consumed, and the two men sat in front of cups of steaming coffee.

The Brigadier checked his watch. 'We must be off shortly. I want to introduce you to the captain. He's been briefed on your role and will assist in any way he can.'

'And the rest of the crew?'

'Must remain in ignorance. If too many people know what you're up to word will leak out and the saboteur, if there is one, will be warned.'

Half an hour later they rendezvoused in the lobby to settle their accounts. A taxi had been ordered to take them the short drive to Cardington and the airship embarkation point. As their luggage was loaded into the boot, Brigadier Percival took his briefing folder out of his briefcase and handed it over to Caspasian.

'Put this somewhere safe. I suggest you lock it away in your bag and don't take it out until you're on board, and only then in the privacy of your own cabin.'

'Very well.' Under Percival's watchful eye Caspasian set about doing as he was instructed.

By the time he had finished, the Brigadier was already settling himself comfortably on the red leather seat in the back of the taxi, leaving it to Caspasian to tip the hotel porter.

4

Lying east of Bedford, the inconsequential red-brick hamlet of Cardington was surrounded by flat open farmland. Slender roads threaded the dull landscape of hedge-bordered fields, the overall mundaneness of the setting emphasizing the other-worldliness of the two giant airship hangars rising out of the plain. They stood side by side like the houses of giants, vast rectangular structures whose arched rooves projected towards the leaden clouds overhanging the extraordinary scene. Off to one side, a tower had been erected to which an airship could be secured by the nose like a bull with a ring. Once stable, the dirigible could be serviced. Gas cells could be replenished with hydrogen, cargo loaded or offloaded and passengers would embark or disembark. For now however, the tower remained unoccupied, standing like a lone sentry on watch over the twin chambers of the slumbering leviathan.

The doors to only one of the hangars were shut, that which had once housed the ill-fated *D100*. Its neighbour's stood open and out of them protruded the silver-coloured nose cone of the *D200*, bigger and better in every way than its lost sister ship.

Driving towards it Caspasian felt a bolt of excitement as the taxi neared. The thing was large even at a distance, but as they got closer, the hangar towered higher and higher until, by the time they drew to a halt at the barrier permitting entrance to the airfield, the hangars had grown into the most monstrous edifices Caspasian had ever seen. They were by no stretch of the imagination beautiful, but they were spectacular. Of that there was no doubt.

It seemed, from the choked roads approaching the airfield, that Bedford had disgorged most of its population to spectate at the event shortly to take place. In addition to crowds of people and cars thronging the grass verges, many of them equipped with picnics and binoculars, there was also considerable representation from the press. Reporters clustered like flies around anyone who seemed to be in authority, notebooks and pencil stubs poised to scribble down any useful fact or opinion.

'What a bloody mess,' Brigadier Percival sneered looking out of the car window.

'Where to now, guv'nor?' the taxi driver asked.

'The passenger reception area. It's over there I think,' the Brigadier replied tersely, waving a gloved hand vaguely in the direction of the *D200*'s hangar.

The taxi made its way slowly through the milling crowds of people towards a wooden hut where a man in cap and uniform was inspecting a pile of suitcases and bags of various descriptions. After each check of a name tag he ticked the corresponding entry on a clipboard with an elaborate flourish.

Brigadier Percival wound down the window and shouted to him. 'Captain Harrison?'

The man jerked his head in the direction of the hut door. 'Inside.'

Brigadier Percival slumped back into the leather car seat. 'Seems to me they could do with a tad more respect around here.'

Caspasian smiled, knowing that what the Brigadier really desired was servility.

They got out of the taxi and the Brigadier directed the driver to wait.

'I'll have to keep the clock running, mate.'

Brigadier Percival muttered under his breath but nodded agreement. Caspasian retrieved his valise from the boot and dropped it with the rest of the luggage just as a team of porters arrived to start loading it aboard.

'Just a minute,' the man in the uniform called across to him as he began to walk away. 'The contents have to be inspected.'

'What for?'

'Anything flammable. Cigarette lighters, matches, anything like that.' He pointed with his clipboard to the airship hangar. 'Hydrogen gas, you know.'

Caspasian sighed and went to open his valise. The inspector crouched down beside it and rummaged amongst the folded clothes and toiletries. Finding nothing to alert him he zipped the bag closed and put it on the trolley which the porters were now loading. 'It'll be waiting for you in your cabin on board, sir.'

Caspasian nodded and went in search of the Brigadier. He found him talking to a small, wiry man with greying hair, wearing a dark blue uniform and hat similar to the man who had been inspecting the luggage, but distinguished from him by the addition of gold braid around the cuffs and on the cap's peak. Gold-coloured buttons shone on the front of his double-breasted jacket and from his mien as well as his dress Caspasian deduced correctly that here was the captain of the *D200*.

Brigadier Percival broke off from his conversation with the man to introduce him to Caspasian. Captain Harrison's smiling eyes did a thorough search of Caspasian's, giving no sign of what he had found there. He held out his hand and Caspasian shook it formally.

'Pleased to have you along for the ride,' Harrison said cheerily. He lowered his voice, yet without any unnecessary sense of drama. 'I've been briefed on your role. Let me know if there's anything I can do once we're aboard. Anything at all.'

'Thank you, sir,' Caspasian answered, liking the man.

'In fact, once we're aloft and away from all of this hullabaloo,' he said, waving a hand at the crowds of reporters and spectators, 'come to the control gondola and I'll give you a tour of the ship. Point out all the key features. All right?'

'I'd appreciate that. Thanks.'

The noise level suddenly surged. They looked towards the source and saw a limousine with whitewall tyres pull up at the air-field entrance. Lionel B. Domain leaned out of the window, cigarette holder in hand, and acknowledged the applause of the crowd with a circular motion of his gloved hand as if stirring the air, regardless of the fact that it was Emma Lavelle everyone had really wanted to see.

Captain Harrison sighed heavily. 'And now, if you gentlemen will excuse me I had better welcome my passengers.'

Brigadier Percival said goodbye and together with Caspasian watched him go. 'Harrison's a fine man. A bit too trusting, perhaps, but otherwise quite sound.'

Caspasian glanced at the Brigadier's profile. Trust, he suspected, had probably not featured greatly in the Brigadier's relationships.

The passengers had now begun to separate from the on-lookers and from those who had accompanied them for the grand send-off. A band materialized and struck up a robust tune as the ground crew took hold of the securing ropes trailing earth-wards from the flanks of the *D200* and, with a concerted effort, started to draw the giant airship out of the hangar. Suspended just off the ground, the vast beast slid easily from its lair, the relatively paltry energy expended by the ground crew belying the weight of the colossus. There was a collective gasp from the watching crowds who broke into spontaneous applause as the full extent of the airship came inexorably into view.

'Great heavens above!' the Brigadier murmured beside Caspasian.

Caspasian stared up at the silver-coloured airship, eyes wide. As if in recognition of the moment, a shaft of sunlight penetrated the clouds making the *D200* sparkle. People cheered and the band increased in volume to be heard above the din.

'Best get aboard then,' the Brigadier said to Caspasian. 'Find your cabin, and all that.'

'Don't tell me you're going to miss me?' Caspasian asked mischievously.

Brigadier Percival scowled at him. 'Just get aboard, Caspasian.' Then, as an afterthought he added, 'And don't muck it up this time. I'm a forgiving man, but cross me again and I'll see you broken.'

Caspasian smiled. 'Well that's plain enough.' He considered offering to shake hands but instead turned towards the tower where preparations were being made to embark the passengers. 'I'll be in touch,' he called back to the Brigadier.

'You'd damned well better be. And with something decisive too.'

Very well, Caspasian thought. He wants something decisive. I'll see what I can manage for the old bastard.

With the nose of the airship secured to the tower, a retractable metal stairway was lowered from the bowels of the ship leading directly into the passenger accommodation, main saloon and observation decks. An officer positioned himself at the bottom and, assisted by a clerk and two crewmen, called for the passengers to come forward so he could begin checking documents. Against their natural inclination to rush aboard, the passengers formed an orderly queue and shuffled eagerly towards the base of the stairway, heads jockeying to left and right to see how much longer the process was going to take. Caspasian hung back, observing the people who were shortly to become his travelling companions on an extraordinary voyage, the like of which few, if any, of them would have undertaken before.

He noticed how Lionel Domain and Miss Emma Lavelle were similarly maintaining a distance from the crush, leaving their embarkation to the last in the hope of creating the bigger impact with the assembled press. Domain was giving a few last-minute interviews and, when he looked her way, Caspasian saw that Miss Lavelle was also busy with the public relations stunt. However, as one journalist completed his questions and another leapt into the breach with his own, Emma glanced briefly in Caspasian's direction and met his gaze. Her smile, polite for the journalists, broadened into something even more attractive, and she tilted her head ever so slightly in acknowledgement before turning once again to her interrogator.

Caspasian recognized most of the passengers from their photographs in the brief that Brigadier Percival had left with him. However, others were still peeling themselves away from relatives and friends, bidding ever hastening goodbyes before joining the tail of the line. In all, Caspasian understood that there would be some fifteen passengers, including himself. Added to eighteen crewmen, the figure reached the overall complement of thirty-three.

Unable to think of any further reason for delay, he moved across to join the queue which by now had shrunk considerably. A few minutes later he reached the officer at the foot of the steps and gave his name. The officer ran his finger down the list on his clipboard, identified Caspasian's entry, checked the identity documents that Caspasian offered and, with a polite smile, handed him to one of the crewmen who ushered him onto the stairway. Caspasian took one last fond look at terra firma and stepped off the ground. He could not help wondering when he would touch down again.

Inside the airship, he entered a cosy little world that might well have been the interior of a comfortably sized sailing vessel. It was somehow both compact and roomy at the same time. Everything had been constructed with the weight factor being a prime consideration. Partitions were such that Caspasian was confident he could punch his way through them with relative ease, not that he anticipated having to do so.

The top of the staircase opened into a corridor at the end of which lay the large, elegant saloon which, together with the dining room, was the main passenger living space on the vessel. Running the full length of either side of the saloon was a viewing gallery with downward-angled windows giving stunning views of whatever lay beneath the cruising airship. Easy chairs and occasional tables made this the most popular area with passengers, the place where they would spend most of the daylight hours while aloft.

Leading from the dining room was the galley kitchen, all of whose cooking implements were electric, naked flames being strictly forbidden on board. There was also a small bar next to the saloon and the whole compact effect was such that the chef and stewards could move with ease between the various facilities.

A flight of steps led up to the passenger accommodation situated on an upper floor. Here cabins flanked either side of a second longer corridor. Each cabin was tidily furnished, mostly with fitted furniture, and a window was once again angled outwards and downwards permitting spectacular views. Beds came in the form of bunks, and the whole feel was of a train's sleeper compartment. A small sink and wall mirror, table, chair and wardrobe completed the fittings.

For the moment, this was all of the airship that Caspasian could explore, and this he did in the space of several interesting minutes. His tour complete, and further exploration of the wider facilities of the vessel having to wait until after take-off, he located his cabin where, as promised, he found his valise waiting for him on the bunk. He locked the cabin door and, once alone, removed the .38 calibre Webley pocket revolver from the inside of his jacket where he had secreted it to avoid the inspection of the ship's officers. A box of ammunition was similarly conjured and the two were placed in a lockable drawer beside

Caspasian's bed. He turned the key, removed it and popped it in his trouser pocket. He severely missed a more comprehensive armoury but for now this would have to suffice. He did not doubt that the captain and crew possessed a handful of similar items and he resolved to locate these at the earliest opportunity. There was unlikely to be anything too aggressive on board for the simple reason that the slightest spark risked an instant and fiery death for everyone, passengers and crew alike. Weapons, such as they were, would mostly be intended for survival on the ground should the airship be forced down in some remote area.

Unpacking his valise was Caspasian's next task. Clothes that needed hanging in the wardrobe were stored away on hangers, shirts and other items slotted neatly into the trim drawers, shoes slipped under the bed and Caspasian's washing and shaving implements deployed to the shelf above the basin. One item remained in the valise. Brigadier Percival's briefing folder. Caspasian took it out and weighed it in his hand, pondering. Deciding to review the contents later, he unlocked the revolver drawer, slipped the folder inside, locked it again and returned the key to his pocket. Of course it was far from secure there, but he hoped that for now nothing more extreme was necessary. He judged that the simple device of the lock and key should at least keep the folder and gun safe from the steward's casual interest.

Locking his cabin behind him, Caspasian made his way back down the stairs and into the saloon. His fellow passengers were milling around, mostly along the two observation decks from where they were busily waving farewells at the bystanders. The slanting windows had been opened and through them a great cacophony rose up. From the cheers Caspasian deduced that Domain and Miss Lavelle were at last embarking and, sure enough, a moment later they appeared at the saloon entrance, flushed with the excitement of it all.

'Good morning everyone!' Domain said grandly, raising a

hand in salute. 'I hope you'll forgive our exuberance. This is the trip of a lifetime.'

There were good-natured calls of agreement and approval, and a ripple of applause greeted the starry-eyed couple.

Domain surveyed his fellow passengers. 'Has anyone seen the Captain?'

'He'll be in the control gondola in the prow, Mr Domain,' the chief steward said with an obsequious bow.

'Can I go and take a look?'

The steward giggled uneasily. 'I'm afraid not, sir. Access is strictly controlled and involves a laborious venture through the very heart of the airship. However I am sure he will be willing to arrange a trip for you and Madam once we are airborne and his immediate duties have been executed.'

Domain conceded generously and helped himself to a glass of champagne from a laden tray being passed around the guests. He raised it to the room in general. 'Here's to the maiden voyage of the *D200*. May we all reach South America without getting fried!'

He guffawed at his jest which was met with a combination of uncomfortable silence from some and embarrassed titters from the less bold.

Caspasian took a glass from the tray. 'To the *D200*,' he said loudly. Others gratefully took up his toast.

'To the *D200*!'

Emma Lavelle raised her glass in his direction. 'The *D200*.'

From the windows flanking the saloon a cry went up, partly from the crowd outside and partly from the passengers ranged along the viewing promenade. 'She's lifting off!'

Instinctively Emma Lavelle seized hold of the table nearest to her. The steward laughed good-naturedly. 'Madam, there is no need. Watch the champagne in your glass. You will not see so much as a ripple.'

Tentatively she let go of the table and raised her glass to

study the contents. Sure enough, there was not the barest movement of the pale golden liquid, only the streams of bubbles rising to the lightly foaming surface. Caspasian became aware of a motion similar to being in a slow-moving lift, and went across to the windows to peer out. He was surprised to see that the *D200* was already about a hundred feet in the air. It had risen completely without him knowing. Down below, the men in the crowd removed their hats and threw them in the air as the band continued to play, the musicians trying simultaneously to read their music and look up at the ascending airship.

The huts and cars were increasingly becoming like toys, and to one side, standing aloof from the throng of celebrating spectators, Caspasian saw the stern figure of Brigadier Percival. He appeared to be looking straight at Caspasian. Because of the height, the Brigadier's face had been robbed of expression. It presented to Caspasian only a void, inscrutable. It was a canvas onto which Caspasian could paint whatever he chose. Knowing the Brigadier as he did, he could picture the lie of the harsh, angular features. Mirthless. Severe. Demanding.

But the man was walking away now. Alone of the crowd, he had turned his back on the airship and was striding towards his waiting taxi. He would be making his way to the station and then back to London and whichever of his plots required his own very particular attention.

Caspasian sipped his champagne. It was decent enough but he had never really liked the stuff. Soon, Bedford appeared across the lie of the fields and then, when the airship had attained a certain altitude, the passengers heard the sound of the ship's four giant engines starting up, each sitting squatly in its own gondola, two on each side of the vessel, and the airship began to turn and move away from the Cardington airfield. Even at this height the two giant hangars were still impressive, dwarfing everything around them, but soon even they had melted from view, becoming part of the rolling patchwork of the English countryside spread out below.

While most of the passengers had enjoyed the take-off from the saloon, some had remained in their cabins, preferring a more private experience of such a unique event. Caspasian returned to his own berth, feeling at a bit of a loss. Lunch would not be served for an hour or more, and then the afternoon would provide ample opportunity for a delicate survey of his fellow travellers. He would have to get to know everyone on board in person, a prospect that hardly delighted him. Socializing was one of the aspects of Mess life that he liked the least. It was not that he was a particularly natural loner, rather that he had found few others who shared his tastes. Military men seemed to possess either strident opinions or none at all. Caspasian fitted into neither category.

He stretched out on the bed, bouncing on the mattress to test it. Firm and supportive. Just right. Lying back with hands behind his head, he contemplated the ceiling, listening to the throaty hum of the motors further down the airship's exterior, and tried not to think about the gigantic gas cells bulging with highly flammable hydrogen suspended above the passenger compartment in the body of the *D200*.

He had only been resting for several minutes when there was a knock at his cabin door. He invited the caller to enter and a steward popped his head in.

'Captain Harrison asks if you would like to join him in the control car, sir.'

Caspasian swung his legs off the bunk and stood up. 'I'd love to.'

'If you'd care to follow me, then, sir.'

Instead of going back down the stairs to the saloon and bar, the steward turned in the opposite direction and made for a locked door at the far end that bore a large 'Keep Out' sign in bold red letters. It opened onto another narrow flight of steps that ascended towards a trapdoor at the top. It swung open easily, being constructed of a light alloy like most other metallic objects on board. Caspasian climbed after the steward and found himself in a darker corridor that stretched to both left and right.

'This way, sir,' the steward said, indicating the front of the airship.

'Where does that lead?' Caspasian asked, pointing the other way.

'That goes to the cargo areas, sir. I expect Captain Harrison will include that in your tour of the ship.'

It was a surprisingly long walk to the front of the airship, bringing home once again to Caspasian the impressive size of the dirigible. Just before they got there they encountered a room off to the right. The door stood open and Caspasian saw two signallers at work in front of the latest radio-telegraph equipment.

'The radio room,' the steward said unnecessarily.

Caspasian peered over the shoulders of one of the signallers and saw that he was in the process of receiving the latest weather reports.

'Everything all right?' Caspasian asked.

The signaller turned round. 'Just a bit of a squall out at sea. Nothing to worry about though, sir. You shouldn't even feel it.'

Eventually they reached another trapdoor. The steward bent down and opened it. 'After you, sir.'

Caspasian lowered himself onto the ladder and climbed down.

'There you are. Welcome to the control car!'

He turned round to find Captain Harrison waiting for him. The steward was dismissed. 'Everything all right so far?' the Captain asked.

'Very impressive,' Caspasian answered. 'I can't get over the size of the thing and the fact that it flies.'

Captain Harrison held up a finger in correction. 'Not quite true. You see, you don't really fly an airship. You sail it. In effect. Of course it's a combination of both activities, but that's how I like to think of it. Sailing.'

He moved to one side in the cramped gondola to provide a clear view of the main controls and operators. Two crewmen stood side by side, each manning a large wheel. 'This chap here,' the Captain said clamping a hand on the shoulder of the left-hand man, 'is the elevator operator. And this,' he continued placing the same hand now on the shoulder of the right-hand man, 'is the rudder operator. Adjustments to these two wheels manoeuvre the elevators and rudders respectively.'

'You mean they make the ship go up and down, and to left and right?'

Captain Harrison smiled. 'Port and starboard, yes. Think sailing.'

Caspasian nodded, getting the hang of it. Harrison continued, 'A watch officer is always on station here to oversee the general operation of the controls, two watch officers in stormy weather. In particularly rough conditions, and for take-offs and landings, I will always be in here as well. Gets a bit cramped,' he laughed.

He studied Caspasian's face and then moved across to a chart table, took out a blank sheet of white paper and a pencil and began to draw. 'You see, an airship is a rigid structure of vertical rings held in place by longitudinal girders with a row of some eighteen separate gas cells between the rings, the whole thing covered by a fabric outer cover.'

Under his pencil point a sketch unfolded illustrating the Captain's explanation.

'The early models used a sliding weight to alter pitch and attitude. Basically a huge chunk of metal on a long rail. If the captain wanted the ship's nose to go up for a climb, he'd slide the weight down the rail towards the stern of the vessel and the nose would go up. But it was fraught with problems. The rails would warp and bend, the weight would jam in place. All sorts of trouble. So . . .' he continued, working on his sketch, 'the weight system was replaced with elevators, in effect horizontal tilting vanes like the flaps of an aeroplane.' He sketched them in. 'Then, to control the violent pitching they put huge stabilizing fins at the stern, and for steering there were rudders. See?' he said, looking up from his sketch.

'Very clever,' Caspasian said, finding the Captain's enthusiasm infectious.

'Remember, a heavier-than-air aeroplane flies because of aerodynamic lift, the effect of airflow over the wings caused by the plane being propelled forward by the engines. But an airship, on the other hand, flies because of aerostatic lift provided by a lighter-than-air gas like hydrogen.' His pencil tapped the part of his diagram where the huge gas cells had been shaded in. 'It can generate aerodynamic lift if the captain wants it to, and can also take off and land like a plane at the appropriate speed in a nose-up attitude using the elevators. That is, the engines drive the ship forward and the elevators convert that forward motion into aerodynamic lift. It's especially useful if the ship's carrying a heavy load.

In normal flight when in equilibrium, altitude is controlled by the elevators operated by that wheel there,' he said pointing to the relevant control. 'Direction is controlled by the rudder, the wheel to the right of it. But the important thing to remember is that an airship is an aerostat. It can stay in the sky if the engines stop.'

'That's a relief,' Caspasian said.

'Flying an airship depends on constantly adjusting its buoyancy. The ship is either light or heavy or in equilibrium, depending on a number of variables such as the temperature of the gas inside the hull, the temperature of the air outside, the weight of the load, the amount of fuel consumed or gas vented, altitude, atmospheric pressure, or the weight of snow, ice or rain picked up on the outer cover. So, if the ship's heavy I've got several options. I can either release ballast through those levers there,' he said indicating row upon row of levers at head height in front of the elevator wheel, 'to lighten the load aerostatically or I can create aerodynamic lift by flying in a nose-up attitude or, indeed, employ a combination of the two. On the other hand, if the ship's too light, I can release gas through vents in the top,' he said pointing to rows of levers also at head height, 'or I can take on sea or rain water. Alternatively I can fly in a nose-down attitude or employ a combination of any or all of these.' He tossed his pencil onto the chart table where it rolled back and forth until achieving an equilibrium of its own.

'That's basically the art of an airship captain. Constantly juggling all these different factors. Then there's the weather and that's probably the most crucial factor of the lot. You have to have a keen eye for it, which is why I equate captaining an airship more to sailing than to flying. Understand?'

Caspasian scratched his head. 'I'm starting to.'

'Right then,' Captain Harrison said, making for the ladder. 'Time for a tour of the airship proper. You've seen the passenger quarters and the control car. Now it's time to see the lungs and heart of the creature itself. Follow me.'

He led the way up the ladder out of the control gondola. They made their way back along the corridor past the radio room and instead of returning to the passenger compartment, they continued on until they reached a door at the end of the passage. Captain Harrison opened it and stood to one side to let Caspasian pass. He found himself on a narrow gantry and looking up he stared in amazement at the sight before him. Stretching into the murky distance was the voluminous interior of the airship. It was like a cross between a cathedral and the most enormous warehouse. Caspasian felt utterly dwarfed. There was an eerie whistling sound of wind in the metal girders and the vast gas cells towered overhead, giant-sized sacks extending all the way to the top of the airship, billowing like the sails of a galleon, except that the element causing the disturbance was not air but the hydrogen contained within them.

Captain Harrison watched the effect on his guest with satisfaction. The airship never failed to impress.

'I suppose I expected them to be taut like a balloon,' Caspasian said.

'Everyone does,' Captain Harrison answered smiling. Instead the bags looked almost empty towards the bottom. The gas within seemed to be moving like something alive. Alive and very dangerous. A slumbering, invisible spirit, but one capable of the greatest malevolence.

'Come on,' the Captain urged happily. 'Let's see more.'

Proceeding carefully along the gantry, Harrison pointed out the ballast tanks on either side, full of water. But Caspasian was staring intently at the skin of the airship, taut like the canvas flooring of a boxing ring.

Captain Harrison saw where he was looking. 'The outer cover is coated with a solution of cellulose nitrate in acetone. Aluminium powder is mixed with it and that gives the airship its silver sheen.'

'Presumably not just for aesthetic purposes?'

'Not at all. It tautens the cover and also waterproofs it.'

'Could I stand on it?' Caspasian asked.

'Yes, but bearing in mind there's nothing outside except thousands of feet of empty space, I wouldn't advise it. My men do actually walk on the top,' he said looking up into the vastness above. 'They go outside to service the gas vents, but they're belayed securely with ropes.'

'Like mountaineers.'

'Exactly.'

'How do they get access to the roof?'

'There are several ladders. We'll see one just ahead. Come on.'

They continued on their tour, and as they went the Captain pointed out the crew's quarters, the fuel tanks, the cargo rooms, and, right at the stern, the auxiliary steering station. Off to either side, he showed Caspasian the gangways leading out to the engine gondolas.

'Can I have a look at one?' Caspasian asked eagerly.

'I'm afraid not. It would be much too dangerous. The engine gondola sits outside the hull and can only be accessed by the narrowest of horizontal ladders. It really isn't a place for tourists.'

When the tour was over, they returned along the axial gangway to the door leading back towards the radio room and the passenger compartments below.

'You're finding the accommodation comfortable, I hope?' the Captain asked.

'Very, thank you. But after this it'll feel a bit cramped, I suspect. Still, the capacity is . . . what?'

'Oh, we can accommodate about thirty passengers altogether,' the Captain answered. 'Far more than the sixteen currently on the manifest.'

Caspasian was halfway down the corridor. He stopped. 'You mean fifteen.'

'No,' the Captain said confidently. He smiled. 'Believe me, I know to the last pound of weight exactly what is on board my ship.'

'You're saying there are sixteen passengers?' Caspasian said, wondering where he had gone wrong and knowing in his heart that he had not made an error. The Brigadier's folder, when he had inspected it at the Carlton hotel had contained fifteen entries.

'Most definitely. Sixteen, Captain Caspasian.'

'Did someone join at the last minute then?'

The Captain frowned. 'No. You can't just hop aboard an airship as casually as that. These things take a great deal of planning. Weights have to be carefully measured and gas and ballast loaded accordingly. We were booked to take sixteen passengers some time ago. There should be a passenger manifest in the radio room. It's kept there in case messages come for anyone on board. Would you like to see it?'

'Very much.'

The Captain led the way to the radio room and located the manifest tucked away safely in a drawer. 'Here we are,' he said, handing it over to Caspasian.

Caspasian quickly ran his finger down the list of names. He knew them pretty much by heart following his study of the forms in the Brigadier's brief. His finger stopped at one name and he read it again carefully. He looked up, pondering.

'Is anything the matter?' the Captain asked.

Caspasian forced a smile to hide his discomfort and confusion. He handed back the list. 'No. I must have made a mistake, that's all. Never could count.'

He took his leave from the Captain, thanking him for the tour, and made his way rapidly back to his cabin. When inside, he locked the door behind him, took another key from his pocket and opened the bedside drawer. He took out the Brigadier's folder and sat on the bed to open it. The forms were all there, just as they had been when the folder had last been opened, by the Brigadier at the Carlton. Caspasian thumbed through them, his eyes racing ahead. This time he counted sixteen. But he knew he had made no mistake.

More cautiously, he leafed through the forms one by one, the procession of passport photographs in the top corners winking at him in succession as he made his way through. Suddenly, one leapt out and he felt himself start as if scalded. It was the same name that had stopped him in his tracks when reading the passenger manifest. The Brigadier had not included it in his brief to Caspasian and now Caspasian could imagine why.

A confident, keen young man stared boldly out of the

photograph directly into Caspasian's eyes. A challenge. Perhaps a dare. Certainly a confrontation of some uncertain sort. Just as the Brigadier would have known. A confrontation that Caspasian would have gone to some considerable lengths to avoid. Beneath the photograph, the young man's name had been inserted in bold type. The entry read, Richard David Edward, and both the features in the picture and the further details contained elsewhere on the form confirmed to Caspasian that his fellow passenger on the *D200* was the half-brother he had never met.

5

Known to his mates as Scratch, Private Harvey's real Christian name had long since fallen into disuse. He had attracted the unfortunate tag of Scratch during recruit training at the regimental depot back in England when he had been afflicted with a nasty but unidentifiable skin condition that the regimental medical officer had attributed to poor personal hygiene. The name, like his clothing, had stuck.

Although not on sentry duty, he stalked the battlements of the old eighteenth-century fort that faced west over the Demerara river, the sluggish brown ooze that slithered along the edge of Georgetown. Scratch hated Guiana. The military cemetery was full of men just like him. Men who had run to the army to escape from poverty only to end up confronted with something worse. A malarial tropical hell. Nothing happened there. Nothing except the annual arrival and departure of the wet season when rains drenched the rotting buildings of the town, leaving them after each downpour to steam like washing.

At the moment the place was just bearable, The wet season had gone, at least until it made a brief return in December, and breezes blew pleasantly from the sea just north of the town. Occasionally the wind direction would change and then a fetid stink would wash up the river from the jungle hinterland like a foul-smelling belch, but right now Scratch was enjoying the best weather that British Guiana had to offer.

The fort had been built by the Dutch just before the British had thrown them out and taken the place over for their own ends, although the Dutch remained in neighbouring Suriname, and the French even further along the coast to the east in French Guiana. While the French used their own colony as a cesspit in which to offload their more hardened convicts, the British, ever more enlightened, sent instead to their own Guiana men like Sergeant Major Horner and Major Westacott. As far as Scratch could see, there was little to choose between the lot of them.

At the thought of them, Scratch turned quickly to check he remained unobserved. Loitering, Major Westacott would call it. Sergeant Major Horner would accuse him of idling. It all came to the same thing. A thrashing. Of course, strictly speaking it was completely illegal, the thrashing that is, but who was there to enforce the law in this godforsaken hole? He sighed and raised his face to make the most of a sudden upsurge in the breeze. Lovely.

Things had gone from bad to worse since Lieutenant-Colonel Martin had been taken ill and sent back to England. The official line had been that he was stricken with malaria. Everyone knew the truth though. Syphilis and alcohol. Georgetown had done that to many a man over the years. Martin was merely the latest in a long line of weak-willed feeblings. How on earth he had ever risen to such an elevated position, Scratch would never know. Westacott, the second-in-command, had run rings around the man from the beginning, and together with the evil Sergeant Major Horner, the two of them now had a completely free hand to do as they pleased. Decimated by disease, the regiment had been reduced to the point where Sergeant Major Horner was the most senior non-commissioned officer on the post, and by God he made sure that everyone beneath him knew it.

Amongst the few other officers there were one or two who would have liked to rein in his excesses, but they were kept firmly in check by Westacott whose purpose it served to have such a bully and lout as his lackey. There was simply nothing that anyone could do about it. While Martin had been around

Westacott had at least paid lip-service to the King's Regulations, but now it was open season. Martin had been loaded onto a tramp steamer bound for Southampton, gibbering and jabbering, saliva, pus and cankers bejewelling his slack-jawed face, and Westacott had taken command. With officer recruitment in the home country in the state it was, no one existed to replace Martin. Indeed, on hearing of the vacancy, the only eligible contenders had gone to all manner of extremities to avoid the posting. Westacott was in charge, secure on the throne and with Horner at his side.

'Harvey, you idle bastard!'

Scratch spun round at the sound of Horner's gravelly bellow and almost lost his balance. Seeing the Sergeant Major approaching at the swagger, pace stick under his arm, Scratch braced to attention, sweat breaking from him that had nothing to do with the heat.

'Well, well, well. What have we here?' Horner crooned as he closed the last yards between the two of them. 'Caught you red-handed, haven't I?'

'What's that, Sergeant Major?'

Horner's face screwed up like paper. 'Deaf, are we?'

'No, Sergeant Major.'

'Well that's something.' Horner jabbed Private Harvey in the stomach with his pace stick. 'What do you mean by lurking up here when there's jobs to be done?'

'I'm off duty, Sergeant Major,' Scratch mumbled. Once again he felt the savage jab of the brass-tipped pace stick.

'Off duty? There's no such thing, my lad. Not now I'm in charge.'

Scratch searched for a response but could not think of one. He remained silent, eyes fixed on a point above the Sergeant Major's head. His subservience made Horner all the more irate. He hefted the weighty pace stick in his hands, considering where to plant it, like a golfer evaluating his next stroke. There was a

shout from the courtyard below and the two men looked down
to see another soldier, Private Merritt, staring anxiously at them.

'What's that?' Horner shouted down to him.

'Major Westacott wants to see you in his office, Sergeant
Major.'

Horner glared at the man for a long moment. Reluctantly he
replaced the pace stick under his arm and sighed. 'Lucky little
sod, aren't you, Harvey?'

'Yes, Sergeant Major. I mean no . . . I mean . . .'

'Shut up.' Horner took a step backwards and fixed Scratch
with the most contemptuous scowl he was capable of summoning. 'I'll be watching you, my lad. By Christ I will. And don't
you forget it.' And then he was gone.

Scratch heaved the biggest sigh of relief and was consumed
by the need to urinate. He hurtled down to the latrines and
passed Private Merritt on the way.

'Thanks, mate,' he whispered as he hustled past.

Merritt smiled. 'Yeah, you owe me.'

'Was it pukka?'

' 'Course it was. You don't think I'd make up something like
that, do you? Not with old Horny.'

'Then how's it I owe you?'

Merritt shrugged. 'I could have waited till he'd beaten the shit
out of you before calling him.'

Scratch had to concede that he had a point, but rather than
debate the matter further, he broke into a run, reaching the
lavatories just in time.

In Lieutenant-Colonel Martin's vacated office, Major
Westacott was musing over something he had unearthed
amongst the chaotic morass of unfiled paperwork cluttering the
drawers, cabinets and desk top. He only took his eyes off it when
Sergeant Major Horner knocked and entered, the pause
between the two actions truncated to the point of rudeness.

'Sir!' the Sergeant Major barked, slamming his feet to

attention and saluting, his body quivering with the shock waves.

'At ease, Sergeant Major,' Westacott drawled. Unlike the Sergeant Major, Westacott had physically let himself go. The process was not as far advanced as it would obviously one day become, but the trend had been set, the corner turned, the die cast. He was a man in decline. His waistline, which had become slack before he even arrived in British Guiana, had developed comfortably into a belly that was starting to loll on top of his belt which was increasingly required to hold everything together. As if in compensation his backside was becoming smaller by the day, to the point where his trousers' seat hung like peeling wall-paper. It would not be long before neither belt nor buttocks would suffice to hold his trousers aloft.

But if there was an air of dilapidation about his physical appearance, there was nothing slack in his manner which was caustic at the best of times. He was more cunning than clever, and a lifetime of underachievement, due largely to his own lack of drive and application, had left him embittered. It was his habit to vent this bitterness on those beneath him. This gave him a certain relief, much like the sea breezes from the Atlantic following the rains. For like all ill-willed weak men who also possess a little, but not quite enough self-awareness, he enjoyed spreading his inner misery around.

'Did Martin ever mention anything to you about this?' He waved a piece of paper at him. Horner could see that it bore strips of signal type but nothing else.

'What is it, sir?' He kept his tone respectful. As far as he was concerned, Westacott was just another loathsome officer, like all the rest of them. But he was useful. With the instinct of a torn-eared fighting dog, Horner could recognize a whip hand. He might not like the structure of the world he found himself in, but he knew its rules. He had learned them the hard way. In his youth he had teetered on the brink of a life of crime. More by chance than design he had tumbled into the army instead and had been delighted to discover how little he had to adapt his old ways in order to survive. Now, with the cretinous Lieutenant-Colonel Martin out of the way and the malicious Westacott in charge, Horner's time had come. The two of them were made for each other. Westacott had the authority and Horner had the brute muscle.

Westacott studied the signal again, brow furrowed. 'It says here that we've got to render assistance to some berk from London who's coming in on the *D200*.' He looked up and smirked. 'Render assistance. How bloody pompous. Why not just say we've got to help the blighter?'

Horner smiled. Like all his smiles it was a harsh expression, devoid of mirth.

Westacott passed the signal across. Horner accepted it and read the text, disguising the difficulty with which he did so. 'Captain Casp . . . What kind of a bloody name's that?'

Westacott chortled. 'Caspasian, you idiot,' he said fondly. The Sergeant Major was the one person Westacott viewed with a certain respect. He had seen what Horner could do to a man and although his rank protected him from the NCO's physical violence, he knew that in the final analysis Horner was the harder man. In an outback hole like Guiana the final analysis had a nasty way of turning up.

'Didn't the Colonel mention it to you, sir?' Horner asked.

'Ha! You must be joking.' He gestured to the mess of strewn papers. 'I don't think he knew himself half of what was here.' He took the signal back and studied it again. 'This could be awkward, though.'

'Why's that, sir?' Horner said, ears pricking at the hint of a threat.

'Don't be daft, man. Someone poking their nose in? Of course it's bad news.'

Horner nodded, light dawning. The equilibrium was in danger of being upset. 'What kind of help?'

'Doesn't elaborate. But it seems to give the bloke a blank cheque. What a bloody nerve! Who the devil does this man think he is? A damned captain at that.'

Horner shifted, stretching his neck out of his sweat-smeared collar. 'Like you say, sir, he's only a captain. I don't think we'll have any trouble dealing with him. If he wants a helping hand, I'll be only too happy to give it to him. If you know what I mean.'

Westacott grinned. 'Now, now, Sergeant Major. Let's see that the fellow has to say first. He might not need our help at all. With any luck he'll just bugger off and leave us alone.'

'Whatever you say, sir.' Horner returned to a rigid position of attention, eyes fixed on the wall opposite his hard, flattened face. 'Will there be anything else, sir?'

'Not for now. Thank you, Sergeant Major.'

'Sir!' Sergeant Major Horner saluted again, spun on his heel and marched out of the office, the frail door providing only the slightest of inconveniences on the way. Left alone, Major Westacott continued to puzzle over the future arrival of the unknown captain aboard the *D200*. Caspasian. He pondered. He was sure he would have recognized a name like that if he had ever met the fellow before. He had not. Why then did he feel an unaccountable disquiet? The outside world was intruding into his affairs and he did not like it. He did not like it at all. Here at the fort he had managed at last to carve out a comfortable little niche for himself. Very comfortable. All sorts of prospects had unexpectedly opened before him since arriving in British Guiana, prospects that had caused an otherwise miserable future to take on an altogether rosier hue. Perhaps he was exaggerating the threat posed by the impending arrival of this outsider, but there was too much at stake. This troublesome captain would have to be dealt with.

Occupied with his thoughts, Caspasian had taken a light lunch in his cabin and then spent the afternoon studying the

Brigadier's folder. But always he kept coming back to the same piece of paper and the same photograph. The same smiling young face. He was alarmed to discover that he was starting to loathe the chap even though he had never met him.

It was towards evening when he dropped the folder on the bed and went across to lean out of the window. The airship was well out at sea. Far below the waves were visible only by the fragile streaks of white foam capping them. From this height it looked calm but it was hard to tell. Certainly there was little or no movement of the vessel. It hummed smoothly through the heavens living up to the publicity literature's most favourable claims.

Caspasian's watch showed that it was nearly time for dinner. He would have liked a shower, but with strict water rationing on board, the best he could manage was a wash in his small basin. It was a bit fiddly but not unworkable. Combing back his wet hair, the colour darkened from fair by the water, he stared back at his reflection, wondering at the coming ordeal. The other's photograph gave little away about the young man's character. What would he be? Braggart or wimp? Villain or fool? But Caspasian had never been able to deceive himself for long. He possessed an innate honesty that quickly forced him to accept that his half-brother just might turn out to be perfectly decent and principled. Balanced against that was the fact of the fellow's parentage. Of the mother Caspasian knew nothing. The father, on the other hand . . . well. Principles had hardly loomed large in his life, it seemed. He had been content to cheat his absent young wife whilst he had been overseas and then desert the girl he had impregnated in Yokohama. It had often been a cause of concern to Caspasian that he might have inherited some of the man's character traits, but time had consoled him. Time and the careful tutelage of his grandfather. He was his own man, his grandfather had said. Free to carve a path for himself. To make his own name. The young John had borne his mother's name of

Caspasian with pride, spurning that of his unmet father. The spurning had been applauded by Grandfather Caspasian while not fooling him for one minute. He recognized it for what it was. An act of bravado by a youngster cast adrift.

Caspasian straightened his tie and marched from his cabin, ensuring first that his folder was securely locked away in his bedside drawer. He decided to go first to the saloon but when he got there he saw that everyone else had done likewise, electing to have a pre-dinner drink before proceeding to the dining room. A steward met him by the door and took his order.

'Scotch and ice, please,' Caspasian ordered. The steward nodded and retired to fetch it. Caspasian's fellow passengers had congregated along the observation windows of the port side promenade. A ship had been spotted below and was sending up flares in greeting for the airship. The 'oohs' and 'aahs' of the passengers told Caspasian all he needed to know about the firework display. His interest was elsewhere.

Lionel Domain and Miss Lavelle were central to the crowd, as was to be expected, and were being engaged in conversation by several of the reporters on board. Then there were the officials, men from the various ministries and departments involved with the airship programme, a scattering of grey business types, moneyed men who demonstrated their wealth more soberly than Lionel Domain but perhaps less honestly.

There was a small, wizened old man who was tattily dressed in a dinner jacket that looked far too big for him. His back was to Caspasian and he was trying to make himself part of a conversation whose other participants clearly had little intention of allowing him to do so.

There was a tall, straight-backed man of a similar age to Caspasian and for a moment Caspasian felt his heart stop, thinking it was Richard Edward. But the next moment the man turned his way and Caspasian saw that it was not him. The Brigadier's file identified him as a German observer sent by the

Zeppelin company, a man by the name of Gustav Wolter. As he turned he revealed several severe facial scars. At first Caspasian thought they were duelling scars such as might be inflicted by a sabre, but a second inspection showed them to be the result of burns, the irregular and discoloured crimping evidence of some painful past episode. His records showed that he had served in Zeppelins during the war and Brigadier Percival had cautioned Caspasian to be particularly alert when investigating this gentleman.

And that was it. He had counted sixteen individuals and his half-brother was not one of them. Caspasian's head was spinning. What the devil was going on?

Before he could do a recount, working through everyone milling on the promenade walk individually, Captain Harrison and two of his officers appeared to welcome the passengers. He was greeted with a light round of applause as the fireworks petered out below and the darkness outside intensified.

'Ladies and Gentlemen,' the Captain began. 'If you would care to move through to the dining room, dinner is now being served.' He held his hand out towards Miss Lavelle. 'And Miss Lavelle, I would be honoured if you and Mr Domain would join me at my table.'

Emma Lavelle smiled radiantly and accepted the offer, although it was Lionel Domain who was first at the table in the adjoining dining room. The tables were laid out in rows and in the absence of a seating plan, Caspasian selected a chair from which he could observe the rest of the passengers with ease. As he drew the wicker chair from underneath the table and prepared to sit down, he was aware of a tall figure worrying at the seat next to him. He looked up into the severe face of Gustav Wolter.

'Do you mind if I join you, Mr . . . ?'

'Caspasian. John Caspasian.'

'Gustav Wolter,' the newcomer said, holding out his hand.

They took their seats. 'This wicker furniture is all very well as regards weight, but it is hardly intended for comfort, is it?' Wolter said pleasantly.

Caspasian smiled. 'A bit hard, perhaps.' He could not avoid the feeling that he was being evaluated. Perhaps the Brigadier had hit upon the right man for his suspicions.

'Have you flown in one of these before, Mr Wolter?' He asked.

Gustav Wolter laughed. 'Many times, unfortunately.'

'Oh?' Caspasian answered, trying to make his surprise sound genuine.

Wolter eyed him shrewdly. 'I was in Zeppelins during the war,' he said. He made the slightest bow of the head. 'I regret to say that I had cause to overfly your country on more than one occasion.'

'Overfly?' Caspasian repeated sternly.

'Bomb.'

'Ah.'

Wolter held out his hands palm-up. 'What can I say? I apologize. In war one often does things that one regrets later on.'

Caspasian smiled. 'Indeed one does.'

'You were in the war too?'

'Infantry,' Caspasian said.

'So. There we are,' Wolter responded, indicating that between two such veterans, nothing more need be said. At least for the moment.

A steward passed along the rows taking their orders. A quick study of the menu by the two men resulted in a choice of duck for Caspasian and pork cutlets for Gustav Wolter.

'Will you join me in a bottle of wine?' Wolter asked.

'That's very kind. I would love to,' Caspasian answered.

'Of course, that means I get to choose!' Wolter laughed.

He ran his finger down the contents of the wine list, necessarily brief due to weight restrictions on board, and selected a pleasant Burgundy. 'Personally I never care what colour of wine they say I am supposed to choose with this food or that. When you have survived a war such as ours, things like that matter little.'

Caspasian smiled, twirling his empty wine glass by the delicate stem. 'They matter not at all.'

'So,' Wolter said once again. He craned round in his seat to observe their fellow diners. The last people were just arriving from the saloon. 'The interior of the passenger accommodation,' he said looking around him, 'is much more spacious than on the *Graf Zeppelin*. In our newer models we will also go for such an area.'

'I think you'll have to if you're going to wrest the transoceanic passenger business from the steamer companies,' Caspasian replied.

Wolter looked interested. 'Is that your purpose on this trip? Are you involved in the dirigible business, Mr Caspasian?'

Caspasian admired the German's directness. If he really was Brigadier Percival's saboteur, he was hardly going out of his way to remain discreet. 'Only in a manner of speaking. Actually I am a captain in the army. We are evaluating the airships for possible military application.'

Wolter laughed. 'Then you need only speak to me. I can save you time. Militarily they are a complete waste of money. Too vulnerable.'

'And for reconnaissance purposes?'

'Ah,' Wolter conceded. 'There they might have a role. But personally I think that the aeroplane is the vessel of tomorrow. Even for long-range reconnaissance. It is only a matter of time before they can achieve the same endurance as the airship.'

'So you think the airship has only peacetime applications?'

'Absolutely. Believe me, Captain Caspasian. I know what I am talking about.'

Caspasian was intrigued. He was about to pursue the matter

when he saw the small old man coming towards them. He cursed silently. Interruption was just what he did not need. Not now he had successfully engaged the German in conversation. Out of the corner of his eye he followed the old man's progress, noticing that he moved with a limp. The poor old fellow was lame. He appeared to be quite lost. The individuals with whom he had been attempting to converse had successfully repulsed him, and now he roamed the dining room, friendless and in search of somewhere to set himself down.

Gustav Wolter became aware of Caspasian's distraction and followed the direction of his surreptitious glances. His face brightened and, to Caspasian's surprise and dissatisfaction, he shifted sideways in his seat to open its neighbour to the newcomer.

'Now here's a fine chap you must meet, Caspasian,' he said purposely loud enough for the old man to hear. Caspasian noticed how the fellow's face brightened at the welcome, and with difficulty he quickened his uneven step towards the offered wicker chair. As he did so, and as Caspasian looked grumpily at the pathetically grateful smile, he felt himself shudder. Recognition struck Caspasian in the midriff, knocking the breath clean out of him.

'There you are,' Wolter said, rising out of his chair to assist the new arrival into his. 'Caspasian, I must introduce you to Richard Edward.' He clapped a friendly hand on the man's narrow shoulders. 'The two of you will like each other. I am sure.'

Richard Edward reached across eagerly, his pale, thin hand open and waiting. Frozen in place, Caspasian stared at it stupidly. In the split second before his hesitation became a slight, habit took command and he shook his brother's hand. It was a surprisingly firm grip that met his own, but Caspasian was shocked to recognise the young man from the photograph, encased in such a physical frame. The picture had given no hint of his disability. Indeed, it was hard to identify exactly where the disability lay. He was lame, to be sure, but aside from that, it appeared simply that he was slight of build. But there was something more that was hard to define. It was as if a large man had been condensed into too small a frame, and his limbs rebelled against the confinement. He was not old at all. It was the sheer effort of existing that had cast the unfortunate young man in such a disguise.

He surveyed Caspasian with wide blue eyes, his smile speaking of nothing but openness and a generous spirit behind it. But the shock of the unexpected meeting had registered on Caspasian's face and was misinterpreted by the young man watching him. Seeing the reaction, and being well used to it, the smile slid from his face, becoming polite rather than friendly, and Richard Edward withdrew into a study of the menu.

Caspasian realised straight away what had happened but, awash with conflicting emotions, was unable and, to a degree, unwilling to disabuse the other man of his false assumptions. Gustav Wolter appeared not to have noticed anything untoward and turned to gaze out of the window at the passing clouds, incongruously level with the dining room.

'Quite spectacular, isn't it Edward?' He said to his neighbour.

'Please, call me Richard.' He gave a small laugh. 'When people use my surname it sounds as if they are calling me by my Christian name. So, that being the case, I'd prefer they at least use my correct Christian name.'

Wolter chuckled. 'It must be very confusing.'

'It can be.'

'In that case, feel free to call me Gustav.'

They agreed on the new arrangement but neither was sufficiently comfortable to invite Caspasian to join the alliance. Conveniently he was leaning to one side to allow the steward to pour his wine so was able to pretend he had not heard the exchange, albeit with some regret.

'So what brings you on board the *D200*?' Richard Edward persevered bravely, fixing Caspasian firmly with an uncomplicated stare.

Gustav Wolter answered for him. 'He's a spy for the army,' he joked.

Richard widened his eyes dramatically. 'A spy? How exciting!'

Caspasian laughed uneasily. 'I'm a liaison officer. We're evaluating the airship for military usage.'

'Oh,' Richard said, sounding disappointed.

'And you?' Caspasian countered speedily, shifting in his chair whose lack of comfort was only partly due to the unyielding wicker seat.

'I have family business interests in South America to see to.'

'Oh? And what might those be?' Caspasian asked, only realising a moment later how intrusive his question must have sounded.

Richard smiled, giving only the slightest sign that he had found Caspasian rude. 'Mining mostly. But my father also has dealings in coffee, sugar and tobacco.'

'My, my,' Caspasian said, unable to keep the sarcasm from his voice. 'He must be a very important man, your father.'

This time he saw his tone register on his brother's face.

'I wouldn't say that,' he replied, stumbling over the words, unsettled by the aggression that was coming from this unpleasant new acquaintance. He was beginning to wish he had dined on his own.

Gustav Wolter glanced uneasily at Caspasian. 'So, are you travelling all the way with us?'

'That depends,' Caspasian answered, drinking deeply from his wine glass.

'On what?' Richard asked, fighting back with a tone equal to Caspasian's.

'On whether we all get blown up first.' He forced a laugh.

'Only joking. Didn't mean to be offensive. No, I'm only going as far as Georgetown.'

Wolter fixed him with a harsh stare. 'Sir, if you had seen Zeppelins going down in flames as I have, you would not make a joke of it.'

Caspasian felt instantly chastened. But Wolter was not going to let him off lightly. 'I have heard the screams of men as they plummeted earthwards, some of them as flaming torches. Their comrades had to decide whether to become incendiaries themselves by remaining aboard the stricken airship, or dive out into space and fall to their deaths. No sir, it is not funny at all.'

'I am sorry,' Caspasian said lamely. 'I didn't mean to . . .'

Ironically it was Richard Edward who came to Caspasian's rescue. 'Didn't they have parachutes?' he asked, diverting the conversation, although whether to save Caspasian's face or purely out of interest, Caspasian was unable to tell.

Wolter shook his head gravely. 'To save weight parachutes were never carried. Bombs, bullets and fuel were the priorities.'

'That's terrible,' Richard said. Caspasian had taken the opportunity to observe his half-brother and was struck by the sincerity of the fellow's dismay. He truly was distressed by Wolter's tale and was not merely pretending.

'And you, Gustav,' he continued. 'How did you fare?'

Gustav Wolter shrugged. 'My time came too, eventually.'

'You were shot down?' Richard asked, amazed.

Wolter nodded.

'But you survived,' Caspasian said, suddenly alert to the story.

'Yes, I did . . .' Suddenly they were stopped in their tracks by the sound of someone tapping loudly on the side of a wine glass with a spoon. They all looked round to see Captain Harrison on his feet and on the brink of an address.

'Ladies and gentlemen . . .' he began.

Wolter leaned across to Richard and Caspasian. 'Captains always love a captive audience,' he whispered, winking.

Reluctantly Caspasian put Gustav Wolter's story to the back of his mind and turned his attention to Captain Harrison who was giving a report on the airship's progress. Stewards stood on the sidelines, ready to serve dinner as soon as the Captain had finished. Outside, far away in the night sky there was the ominous flicker of lightning and then, moments later, the first gentle spots of rain began to drum ever so lightly on the window panes.

6

That night Caspasian lay in his bed listening to the unsettling noise of thunder. It was still some distance away as the Captain had managed to steer the airship around the outer edges of the storm. Harrison had left the table soon after his truncated speech and had spent the remainder of the night in the control car overseeing the watch himself. The meal had resumed in the dining room, but Wolter had been commandeered by someone else and Richard Edward had gone with him, leaving Caspasian to dine in the company of two journalists. Tired of their probing questions, he had left the table early, retiring to his cabin and, soon after, to his bed.

Winds buffeted the airship but by an expert use of the rudders and elevators, Captain Harrison and his crew maintained an admirable stability. The gentle rocking motion was not as bad as a ship at sea, nor as regular, which seemed strange at first. It was more like the disturbance of a train carriage, though considerably less violent.

Staring up at the ceiling, Caspasian imagined the vast gas cells overhead, the giant lungs of the airship that kept it afloat. If only one could eradicate the unpleasant thought of the hydrogen from one's mind, then airship travel really was the way to move between continents. Fast and stately.

At last he slept. Dreams came fitfully, but in one of them he was in Kensington Gardens, although now it bore a resemblance to the wooded bluff above Yokohama where his grandfather's house had been. Caspasian was playing there, a boy once more and quite young. His mother was in the house. He could not see her but he knew she was there. He could hear her singing. Then, on a bench, he saw Richard watching him. But it was only partly Richard. Something about the young man hinted at another. He was accompanied by a dog. A spaniel that also observed the playing boy.

The young Caspasian stopped playing, got up and went to walk towards the seated man resembling Richard. As he did so, the man quickly held up his hand, signalling the child to stay where he was. The smile on his face remained as pleasant as before, but while friendly, it was unreadable. Perturbed, the young Caspasian could not understand why he was not allowed to join the seated man. Suddenly his mother called from the house. Caspasian looked round and saw her standing in the doorway. Her expression was alarmed. Gravely so. Her father appeared at her side, Caspasian's grandfather, and together they beckoned to the young boy to return to them. He could not understand why they did not come and fetch him. They remained rooted in the doorway as if to venture away from the threshold was dangerous in some way.

When Caspasian looked back at the bench, the man had gone. Only the spaniel remained, but that too began to walk away. Caspasian was filled with an overpowering sense of loss and felt himself shudder. It was absurd. He had not even seen the dog before. He steadied himself and made to walk back to his mother and grandfather, but as he did so he became aware of girls laughing. Three of them were playing in the woods. Although he could not see them, he knew there were three. Their voices were carried to him on the wind coming across an expanse of water. He wanted to join them.

He awoke to an urgent knocking on his cabin door. Light flooded through the window's open curtains. The storm was nowhere in sight.

'Coffee, sir,' a voice called from the corridor.

Caspasian sat up, running a hand through his dishevelled hair. 'Come in.'

While the steward positioned the cup and saucer on the bedside table, pouring the coffee from a pewter pot emblazoned with the logo of the airship company, Caspasian could hear the noise of the trolley and another steward in the corridor outside as other guests were similarly woken for the day.

'Breakfast is served in the dining room when you're ready, sir,' the steward said, turning to go.

Filling the basin with cold water, Caspasian splashed it over his face. He felt out of sorts. He was used to unsettling dreams. What veteran of the trenches was not, he wondered as he took out razor and soap and began to shave. But coming after the unexpected meeting with Richard Edward it filled Caspasian with a sense of unease. He felt a vulnerability and that was something he was not used to. The task set by Brigadier Percival had become complicated by personal issues and Caspasian knew that such interference always led to no good. He would just have to shake it off. Ignore the fellow and the relationship that connected them. Clearly Richard knew nothing of Caspasian's identity. But why should he? Sir David would have had no reason to brief his family on past indiscretions.

The cold water focused Caspasian's mind on the business of shaving, mercifully freeing him from thoughts of family, and by the time he emerged dressed and groomed from his cabin and made his way to the dining room, he felt he had successfully exorcised the whole damnable business from his thoughts. His spirits rose and when he took a seat at the window and ordered kippers, toast and a pot of tea, he found that he was humming to himself.

'You're happy this morning.'

He turned in his seat to see Emma Lavelle passing close to him. He rose to greet her and she diverted to join him at his table, to the poorly disguised annoyance of Lionel Domain.

'Good morning, Captain Caspasian,' Domain said in his affected drawl. Caspasian put the man's irritability down to the inability to smoke on board except under the strictest supervision in a sealed room next to the bar. Cigarette lighters, matches and all such equipment had been removed from everyone's luggage before departure, and only a single electric lighter existed, to be used on specific request. Even then it was only operated by one of the ship's officers. All of the cooking equipment in the small galley was electric, naked flames being forbidden. Nonetheless, it had not so far had any noticeable effect on the high standard of the cuisine. Caspasian's kippers were excellent when they were placed before him, together with a rack of toast, condiments and his pot of steaming tea.

Domain helped Emma Lavelle to her seat and then took his place next to Caspasian who noted his extravagant outfit. A maroon velvet jacket was cut tight to his shoulders, and a square cut ruby winked immodestly from the centre of an exotically fastened cravat in a slightly paler shade of maroon. Dark trousers were immaculately pressed and the uppers of his patent leather shoes were hidden by fawn spats. To complete the picture of studied elegance, a large silk handkerchief sprouted vivaciously from his breast pocket.

He retrieved the breakfast menu from the centre of the table, drawing back his cuffs as he did so to reveal diamond-studded links and a gold Cartier watch with crocodile strap. Had he not found the whole impression claustrophobically vulgar, Caspasian would have felt underdressed.

The exotic couple gave their order to the overawed steward, and as Domain gazed out of the window studiedly ignoring Caspasian, Emma Lavelle did her best to be polite.

They were interrupted halfway through their meal by the officer of the watch who came discreetly to Caspasian's side.

'I'm sorry to disturb you, sir, but Captain Harrison asks if you wouldn't mind joining him?'

He had spoken softly so as not to alert the others to his purpose. Caspasian replied in kind, draining his cup of tea and wiping the corners of his mouth with his napkin before taking his leave. Once out of the dining room, the officer led the way through the passenger accommodation to the step ladder leading up into the airship's interior. However, once there, Caspasian was surprised to be taken in the opposite direction to the control car, back towards the heart of the airship. They found the Captain waiting for them by the door leading onto the axial gangway that stretched the length of the vessel. Caspasian was struck instantly by Harrison's appearance. He looked exhausted, his face haggard from the night's wrestling with the storm, but that aside, Caspasian could tell that there was something else. The Captain wore an expression of deep worry. Furthermore he was accompanied by another of the ship's officers and two crewmen, each of whom carried a short wooden stave.

The Captain saw Caspasian's eyebrows rise at the sight of the improvised weaponry.

'Trouble?' Caspasian asked.

'Can't say,' Harrison replied. 'I thought it best to be prepared. I think we might have a stowaway on board. Possibly several.'

Caspasian stared. 'I thought you said you could account for every pound of weight on board?'

'I can,' Harrison said. 'I mean, normally I can. If we were over our pre-planned weight I would be able to tell from the way the airship handled. That's why I've only just been alerted. Everything's handled exactly according to my expectations. Until now.'

'So what's happened?'

'During the storm we took on a large amount of extra water. That's perfectly normal. The hull's outer covering repels most of the rainwater but inevitably it soaks up quite a bit which adds to the airship's weight. To compensate we release ballast, making it up later if necessary, as the rain water's channeled into the empty tanks.'

'And?'

'And we've released ballast as normal but there's something wrong. We're still overweight and according to my calculations we shouldn't be.'

'Could it be that we've just taken on more rainwater than usual.'

The Captain frowned. 'Not really. As a matter of fact, the storm last night was not particularly bad. There were some nasty high winds, but as regards water it was relatively kind to us.' He shook his head. 'No. Our normal post-storm procedures have revealed an anomaly. Without the storm it would probably have gone unnoticed.'

The officer accompanying the Captain smiled, 'Any other airship captain would have missed it. Not Captain Harrison though. Personally I don't think it's anything to worry about but . . .'

'Thank you, Lieutenant Davies. That will do.'

Caspasian thought. 'But why do you jump to the assumption that it must be stowaways?'

'I can't think what else it could be. I checked the cargo myself as it was loaded. I wondered at first if we might have accidentally vented some gas during the storm, but the valves were checked and found to be in good order, and we were at too low an altitude for the automatic release procedure to take over.' He pointed to one of the crewmen. 'To cap it all, Jones here said yesterday that he thought he had heard something from inside one of the aft ballast tanks. He'd investigated but had found them secure. However, now I'm not so sure. If anyone wanted to stow away, the inside of an empty ballast tank would be ideal. It could be made quite cozy in fact.'

He regarded Caspasian and, so that only the two of them could hear, quietly added, 'Bearing in mind your role on board,

I thought it appropriate that you should accompany us.' He offered Caspasian a stave.

Caspasian declined. 'I suppose firearms are out of order?'

The Captain looked horrified. 'Most certainly. One shot is all it would take to ignite the whole vessel. I'm concerned enough at the prospect of even a scuffle. There mustn't be so much as a spark. Particularly as we'll be right in amongst the gas cells!'

Caspasian removed his jacket and tie and laid them aside, unfastened his cuffs and rolled up his sleeves. 'Better lead on then.'

Lieutenant Davies let them in through the door and closed it behind them. He detailed one of the crewmen to remain on guard beside it to ensure no one escaped into the passenger accommodation or towards the control car and radio room.

The little group moved along the narrow gangway, the huge gas cells billowing above them, the hydrogen rippling inside like a caged animal pacing. From port and starboard, the noise of the mid ship engines suspended outside in their gondolas powered through the fragile material coating the hull. Frail overhead lights illuminated the voluminous interior, the glare from the morning sun beyond the hull adding an ethereal glow as it worked through the material.

'It was just along here, sir,' Jones whispered as they approached the after sections of the ship. In between the gas cells Caspasian could see the complicated criss-cross structure of duraluminium girders that formed the vessel's framework, the skeleton to which everything else was attached. A web of cables and wires held the gas cells in place and there, beneath the axial gangway and running along both sides of the airship, the lines of ballast tanks came into view, long cigar-shaped steel cylinders, whose outlet valves were controlled by the levers in the control car near the ship's prow.

As they approached the end of a run of ballast tanks, Jones slowed his step and pointed to the last tank in the line.

'How can we get access to it?' Caspasian whispered, placing his mouth beside Captain Harrison's ear.

'There's a watertight hatch in the top.'

'Right, let's have a look then.' Caspasian tapped the wooden stave in the Lieutenant's hand. 'Best keep those at the ready. If there is someone inside they could be armed.'

They moved along the gangway until they were over the suspect ballast tank, and then Caspasian and Lieutenant Davies eased themselves through the railings and lowered themselves down beside it, being careful to move soundlessly. Lieutenant Davies pointed to the hatch. Caspasian inspected it and frowned. It had been opened recently and scuff marks had scored the highly-polished steel. Using sign language, he indicated to the Lieutenant that he should stand ready to use his stave while Caspasian himself pulled open the hatch.

Taking a firm grip on the handle, he waited until Lieutenant Davies signed that he was ready, wooden stave raised overhead, and then Caspasian tugged hard. The hatch swung open with ease, clanging down noisily onto the outer skin of the tank. Davies braced himself for attack, eyes searching the dark interior.

'It's empty.'

'Any sign of water?' Captain Harrison called down.

'Dry as a bone. Just a minute!' Davies peered deeper inside. 'There's a bedroll here. And a pack or something.'

'Is there anyone inside?'

'Not that I can see,' Davies replied. 'But there has been. Two, by the look of it.'

Caspasian checked to confirm for himself. 'Whoever it is, they've only just left.' He held the palm of his hand against the rolled blanket. 'Still warm.'

He stood up, alert, eyes scanning the depths of the voluminous airship. 'Somehow they found out you were on to them.'

Captain Harrison cursed, searching around in the hope of

spying the intruders. 'Who the devil could it be? And what the hell are they doing aboard my ship?'

Lieutenant Davies scrambled back onto the gangway to join the others. Caspasian was about to follow suit when he decided to try another tack. He looked down below the ballast tanks. Several yards down he saw one of the encircling girders. Taut against it, the outer skin of the airship thrummed with the wind from outside, a muted daylight penetrating through.

'Captain, you say the skin should take my weight?' he called up to Harrison.

'I wouldn't risk it. If you're going that way, try and stick to one of the longitudinal girders. Can you see anything?'

'Not yet, but if I were trying to evade a search party, I'd steer clear of the gangway. I'd keep low. Find somewhere else to hide.'

'All right. But be careful. I don't want to have to explain to Brigadier Percival that you fell to your death.'

Caspasian grinned. 'Don't worry about that. The old bastard would give you a medal.'

The Captain shook his head, not wanting to listen. 'That's not for me to comment on. We'll search up here while you take the underside. Jones will go with you. We'll rendezvous at the aft fuel tanks.'

Caspasian worked his way down until he was standing on the main keel. To left and right of him, the interior surface of the airship's canvas cover curved gently upwards. Suspended above him, the gas cells moved gently against their restraining wires, but beneath them, a gloomy underworld extended the length of the vessel.

Suddenly there was a cry from the gangway overhead. 'There's one!'

Lieutenant Davies set off in pursuit, footsteps pounding down the gangway, closely followed by the Captain. Down on the keel, Jones made a move to join them but Caspasian held him back.

'Just a minute. We've got our own fish to fry.'

Reluctantly, Jones stayed where he was, listening to the sounds of the chase above. Together with Caspasian he continued the sweep along the bottom of the airship, sidling gingerly along the thick metal girder, stepping over the framework of the vertical rings whenever they encountered them. In the gloomy distance they could see the keel starting to rise as it neared the tail section. In this part of the airship, piles of rolled material for the gas cells had been stored, secured to the framework by ropes to prevent it from shifting in flight.

Caspasian turned to speak to Jones next to one such giant bundle, but as he did so he caught a flash of movement out of the corner of his eye. Instinctively he ducked, feeling a rush of air caress his face. Jones cried out a warning as the two-handed wrench swung past. Caspasian leapt away, rolling out of harm's reach. But the only place he could do so was off the girder and onto the canvas of the outer skin. It held his weight but he could feel it strain under him, the silver-coloured coating on the outer surface crackling ominously.

Coming up onto his feet, he turned to confront his opponent. He found himself facing a tall man with blond hair and angular features. Jones braced himself to attack.

'Steady, Jones,' Caspasian shouted. 'We'll take him together.'

Walking on the canvas was like being on a trampoline. Each step was larger than intended and the whole effect was ungainly. The man looked from Jones to Caspasian and smiled, hefting the wrench in his hands. In a flash he had reversed his grip on the handle and with a savage stabbing motion, slashed downwards at Caspasian's canvas floor with the sharpest part of his weapon. Helpless, Caspasian saw the material rip, knowing what was about to happen. As if in slow motion, the edges of the rip held for a full second, and then gave way, tearing in several directions at once, the most dramatic being directly towards the point of greatest tension beneath Caspasian's feet.

Caspasian managed two giant strides before the tear reached him, throwing himself towards the nearest of the girders as it did so. He was too late. While his hands were just able to scrabble hold of the metal, his body plummeted down through the gaping hole that had opened in the airship's fabric and he found himself swinging in thin air, hanging underneath the *D200*.

He looked down and his head swam with vertigo. There was nothing between himself and the sea several thousand feet below. His legs swung frantically in the icy air and he felt his arms strain under the weight. His fingers gripped the metal girder for all they were worth. The airship was making good progress, a tail wind adding to the power of its own engines, scudding it along with an extra boost. But the increased speed made it all the more difficult for Caspasian to maintain his grip. The wind rushed into him, pounding his body with physical force, seeking to pry his fingers loose, pluck him from the vessel and hurl him out into space.

He lifted his head and looked up through the rip into the interior of the airship which suddenly seemed a very long way away. To his alarm, he saw Jones struggling with their assailant. The wrench was poised above their heads and all four hands were clasped around its shaft, each man trying to wrestle it free from the other. Left to his own devices, Caspasian tried to pull himself up. His fingers screamed with the effort, the metal girder biting into his flesh, hard against the bone. All the while, the wind hammered into him. He had fallen with his back to the airship's direction of travel so the wind was working against him, seeking to pluck him off the airship as if he was some un-welcome parasite. With an agonizing effort, Caspasian slowly managed to lift himself towards the girder. Loose strips of torn canvas flapped and slapped in his face. One thrashed into his gasping mouth. He spat it out viciously, anger getting the better of his fear. He focused his whole strength into his arms, imag-ining the rest of his body weightless. His eyes clenched shut and he pulled. Ever so slowly his body rose towards the tear. His fingers screamed for release but he had to hang on. The only alternative was to plunge to his death.

At last he managed to hook his right forearm over the girder. Then the left. He hung there gasping for breath, his chest aching, shoulders burning. Suddenly someone was grappling at his arms. He looked up in alarm, wondering whether he had enough fight left in him to resist. With a flood of relief he saw that it was Jones.

'Come on, sir. Let me give you a hand.'

With Jones' help, he hauled himself into the airship and rolled onto the girder, the gaping rent in the canvas cover yawning at his side, cold air rushing in and buffeting the two men.

'Where is he?' Caspasian gasped.

'He took off. I got the wrench away from him and he legged it. I was going to go after him but I couldn't leave you hanging there.'

'Much appreciated,' Caspasian panted. He sat up, rubbing his arms and massaging his stiff fingers. Red weals were scored into them, perfectly reproducing the outline of the girder's edge. 'We'd best get after him before he does any damage.' He looked at the hole in the canvas, the sea visible far below them. 'What about that?'

The crewman examined the edges of the tear. 'It's all right for now. We can stitch it shut and patch it later.'

Jones helped him to his feet and they set off along the keel. 'Did you see which way he went?' Caspasian asked.

'He seemed to be heading for the aft storeroom. I wouldn't be surprised if he's got a parachute stored there or something, to make his escape that way.'

Caspasian thought of the vast seascape below. 'What's he going to escape to?'

Jones was about to answer but something caught his eye. 'Look,' he said, pointing to a narrow walkway that led off at a tangent. 'The door to the engine gondola's been left open.'

Before Caspasian could stop him, Jones had jumped up onto the walkway and edged his way towards the opening. From outside they could hear the noise of the engine and as Caspasian approached behind him he could see that outside the door, the slenderest of ladders extended across the abyss to the engine gondola itself.

'Better wait a minute,' he cautioned. But it was too late. In his eagerness, Jones passed through the low doorway and began to edge his way across to the engine car. Caspasian reached the doorway at the same moment as Jones arrived beside the engine. The gondola was shaped like a giant egg, both of whose ends had been cut away to allow a free flow of air through the centre, cooling the engine secured inside. It was suspended outside the hull of the airship on stalks, and to the rear of the egg, giant whirring propellers powered the airship, driving it through the air.

'There's no sign of him!' Jones shouted back, pitching his voice above the roar of the engine.

'Look out!' Caspasian's warning came too late. Rising out of the gondola itself, the stowaway seized Jones by the shoulders, swung him round and punched him on the jaw. Jones staggered back, hands coming up to protect his face, but not in time to avoid the blow. A second punch sent him reeling. The man checked over his shoulder, took a firm grip on Jones' overalls, and then threw him out into space, back towards the propellers.

Caspasian screamed. 'No!'

The propellers barely faltered as the crewman's body flew into and through them. The pitch lowered a fraction and the engine surged to compensate. The next moment it was over. A scarlet stream fired out to the rear and Jones was gone.

Caspasian rushed across the ladder to the engine gondola before Jones' assailant could turn to face him. Arms outstretched for balance like a tightrope walker, he forced from his mind the image of the drop beneath his feet. The stowaway had anticipated his arrival by switching to the opposite side of the gondola so that when Caspasian reached the relative security of the car, he found himself separated from the man by the body of the roaring engine. The noise was deafening and thrummed painfully in Caspasian's ears until he felt as if his head was about to split open.

Slowly he edged towards the front of the engine, sidling around it. The stowaway came to meet him and as he neared, Caspasian saw that he carried a long-bladed knife in one hand. The man brought the point up menacingly, directing it at Caspasian's throat. The vibrations of the engine shuddered through the gondola making it difficult to maintain a balanced stance, but Caspasian had to let go his handhold to use both arms to counter the attack he knew would come. Sure enough, the man lunged suddenly. The speed of it caught Caspasian by surprise and he dodged to the side, the blade slicing close to his cheek.

As he dodged, he counterattacked, using a rapid gyaku-tsuki reverse punch to the man's side, aiming for the base of the ribcage. His knuckles grazed the target, lacking the penetrating power that a better stance would have allowed. Forewarned that he was confronted by someone who knew how to handle himself, the man took a step backwards, away from Caspasian. Behind him, only another yard or two of the gondola's floor remained. Then nothing until the blur of the propellers that had consumed Jones only moments before.

The man glanced uncertainly back at them, then regarded Caspasian again. Caspasian smiled.

'See how you like it,' he said, but his words were drowned by the engine noise. There was a shout from the airship's door and both Caspasian and his opponent saw Captain Harrison and Lieutenant Davies standing in the doorway. Seeing his only avenue of escape now severed, the stowaway straightened up.

He held out the knife towards Caspasian. Caspasian indicated that he should reverse the blade. The man did so, offering it to Caspasian handle first.

Caspasian reached towards it. Instead of allowing him to take hold of the weapon, the man let it tumble from his fingers. It fell over the side of the engine car and disappeared into space. Caspasian looked at the man, braced for some new ploy. To his surprise the man was smiling. By now Harrison and Davies were almost across. In another few seconds they would lay hold of the stowaway and he would be their prisoner.

The man suddenly braced to attention, saluted, and with an agile grace vaulted over the side of the engine gondola and launched himself into the air. His manner of doing so seemed to indicate to Caspasian that the man half expected to be able to fly. Instead he shot downwards with outspread limbs, falling freely towards the distant ocean. Caspasian knew that whether he remained conscious or not all the way to the point of impact, the result would be the same. Every bone in the man's body would shatter instantly in a thousand breaks. The skin casing holding him together would split asunder like a piece of fruit hurled at a wall. The waves would bear up the bloody remnants for some minutes, and then they would be gone. He had knowingly hurled himself to his death. And as he had done so he had screamed something at his pursuers. Before Caspasian could grasp its meaning, Captain Harrison had taken hold of his sleeve and was pulling him back into the airship.

'Come on, man. Tread carefully.'

Caspasian had every intention of doing so.

They retraced their steps across the ladder and closed the door behind them.

'This way,' Captain Harrison urged, making quickly for the axial gangway. 'We've got the other chap. But there's something wrong.'

They found the other stowaway lying beneath one of the huge

gas cells, his body supported by the intersection of two girders. His eyes were closed. Someone had made a crude attempt to secure his limbs with a leather belt.

'That's mine,' Davies explained. 'He simply dropped in front of us. Didn't put up a fight. Nothing.'

Caspasian stooped to check the stowaway's pulse. He was dead. He inspected the lips, gently prizing open the mouth. Suddenly Caspasian tore his fingers away as if scalded.

'What is it?' Harrison asked.

'Cyanide,' Caspasian answered sombrely.

'You mean he killed himself?'

'Just the same as if he'd jumped over the edge like his companion,' Caspasian said, wondering. He stood up. 'Did you find anything on him?'

'Nothing,' Davies replied. 'I'll go and have a look at their kit in the ballast tank. See if I can find anything there.'

'Do that,' Caspasian agreed, trying to fight off an uneasy feeling that the Lieutenant would be wasting his time.

When Davies had gone, Caspasian told Captain Harrison about Jones.

'He was a damned fine man. How the devil am I going to explain this to the company?'

But that was the least of Caspasian's worries. For he was mulling over the last words of the man as he had vaulted over the side and plunged to his death. Something about someone waiting to see them. It had sounded like the Baron.

7

They had waited for night to fall, just as in the plan that had absorbed their every spare moment for the past few weeks. They knew the times the guards changed over and they had noted how each one patrolled. Where they started and where they finished. It was impossible to be precise because the guards themselves were not. As often as not they were drunk or half asleep, but that did not mean they were any less dangerous. The bullet from a rifle fired by a drunk was just as lethal if it hit you as one fired by a marksman.

Ramos stared out through the wooden slats of his shelter, checked that the courtyard was clear, and nudged Pecanha hard in the chest. The old Indian had begun to doze in the stifling heat of the jungle night but at the jab from Ramos' elbow he was instantly alert, eyes wild with fear.

'It is time,' Ramos whispered into the old man's ear. He could smell his terror, even through the rank stench filling the accommodation sheds where Colonel Delgado kept his workforce of labourers. Slaves, in effect. Their snores crowded the heavy air, rising from the exhausted sleep into which everyone had tumbled at the end of the day. No one bothered to chain them any more. Where was there to run to, after all? Deep in the jungle, anyone escaping was sure to perish away from the camp, and if a fugitive was recaptured then their fate would be even worse.

But for Ramos even the fears of the jungle and recapture had been subjugated to his desire to be free. Existence in the camp had become a living death. Ramos could not understand why more of the labourers were unable to see that. Hope had died for most of them. Colonel Delgado and his thugs had slaughtered it over the weeks and months with their brutality.

To survive in the jungle, Ramos had realized that he would have to persuade a native Indian to accompany him. Someone like Pecanha. Someone who knew the ways of the bush. How to track, how to hunt and fish, how to navigate and move. Ultimately, how to evade the pursuers that he knew Delgado would send after them. Persuasion had been no easy task. He had been working on Pecanha for days. Now, as he closely watched the old man's face in the gloom, he wondered if he was about to renege on his promise.

Pecanha blinked away the sweat running into his eyes and wiped the back of a grubby hand across his mouth. To Ramos' relief, he sat up, seeming to come alive. 'All right. We'd better go quickly,' he said, his voice gruff with anxiety.

Together they slithered off the rush sleeping mat, being careful not to disturb their slumbering neighbours. Old Pecanha moved stiffly, doubled over to keep below the level of the sills. Around them the mass of men lay unmoving, limbs glistening with sweat and grime. Scrawny beyond imagining, their physical state was another reason Ramos was anxious to escape now, before it was too late. Soon, he knew, he too would have passed beyond the point where he had enough energy for flight. As it was he was far from confident. His muscles were accustomed to hard physical labour, but each day there were diminishing returns. It was a one-way journey with a mass grave yawning at the other end of it. Delgado would see to that.

The courtyard was poorly lit. Behind the guardhouse a single generator rumbled discontentedly, but after powering the lights for the guards' accommodation and Colonel Delgado's quarters, there was little left for the three or four bulbs that had been strung at points along the perimeter fence. They pulsated

with a sickly yellow glow, sensitive to the slightest falter in the
generator's ancient motor.

'Any minute now,' Ramos said as the two men crouched in
the shadows. He had been listening to the engine carefully,
waiting. It was almost time.

The next second, it happened. The motor coughed, bulbs
fading proportionately, and then died, whirring feebly into
silence. From inside the guardhouse came a burst of invective
as one of their number was sent out to refuel the tank. Someone
lit a paraffin lamp, the light of a match flaring in the sudden
darkness. Elsewhere, nothing moved. It was the same at about
this time every night, as Ramos had eventually noted with
interest.

'Come!' he hissed to Pecanha.

They sprinted along the route that Ramos had recced time
and time again over the past days and weeks. He knew every
inch of it by heart, not needing to see every bump and pitfall.
His footing was sure, driven by a heady cocktail of fear and
hope.

Following in his wake came Pecanha, less sure-footed but
equally eager now that he was away from the stifling atmosphere
of the hut and able to sense the jungle only minutes in front of
them.

They rounded the latrine block, the deep trenches
announcing their presence with a foul-smelling odour and the
ever-present hum and buzz of mosquitos which flocked around
the interior in thick clouds. Ramos covered his nose and mouth
with one hand, pinching his nostrils shut. A few yards further
on and they came to the rubbish tip at the back of the kitchens.
Here the piles of refuse backed right up to the walls surrounding
the camp. Ramos had engineered a stint of cookhouse duty to
enable him to recce a possible escape route up and over the wall
and, to his delight, had found one. He had even been able to

stack a number of old boxes in readiness. To his relief he saw now that they were still there.

'This way,' he whispered, his confidence growing with every minute. But he knew that they had only moments of darkness left. It would not take the guard long to remove the cap from the generator tank, empty the contents of his jerrycan into it and then restart the motor. Then the lights would splutter back into life and his chances of making a clean break would diminish considerably.

Gingerly he mounted the first few boxes, steadying himself as he climbed. Halfway to the top he braced himself in order to reach down for Pecanha's outstretched hand. The old Indian's fingers felt gnarled in his grip as Ramos hauled him up alongside.

'Not far to go now,' he said, eyes flitting across every angle of approach to their position. He reached up and his hands were on top of the wall. A walkway extended around most of it, but here it had crumbled, eaten by termites and eroded over the years by the incessant tropical rain. It was hard to say how old the fort was. Someone had told Ramos it had been built hundreds of years before by the Dutch. What did it matter? He longed only to be rid of it. To confine it to the realm of frightening but harmless nightmare.

Ramos eased himself up to squat between two of the battlements' crenellations. 'Quick!' He waved his open hand impatiently at Pecanha. The old man was fumbling with something. Searching. 'What is it?' Ramos said.

'My pendant,' the old man answered, distracted, hands still searching his ragged clothing. 'I've lost my pendant.'

Ramos stared in disbelief. 'Don't be stupid! What the devil does it matter? Come on! Now!'

Pecanha looked up at him. 'But . . .' He was mumbling, starting to panic.

Ramos waved for him to come up. He looked over the wall towards the jungle. There it was. A dark, brooding mass only yards away. He could jump down and be gone. But what good would that do him without the Indian?

He looked back to Pecanha, trying to instill patience into his tone. 'Whatever it is, I will replace it. I promise you.'

Pecanha's face was a mask of sadness. 'No one can replace it. It was given to me by the gods themselves.'

'Please,' Ramos begged, 'Come on. It will have to stay here. There is no more time. Now climb!'

With one final backwards glance, the old man reached up and seized Ramos' hand. At that moment they heard the unmistakable splutter of a motor from behind the guardhouse. Inside someone drunkenly cheered. The next second the engine coughed and fired, purring back into life and, with it, came the yellow pallor of the lights, leaking back into the fetid night air of the jungle fort.

Ramos scanned the surrounding walls. No guards were in sight. He and Pecanha were lucky, but he knew it could not last forever. He pulled Pecanha up beside him. This time he decided to make sure the old man went first. He did not want to leave him alone on top of the wall to have any more doubts. If Ramos jumped first he would never be able to climb back up. He would then have to face the jungle alone.

'Ready?'

Pecanha nodded, preparing himself for the drop. The ground was invisible below the wall. Pecanha spread his arms and jumped. The sound of him landing was appallingly loud to Ramos. He crouched lower and searched the courtyard to see if anyone had heard. There was nothing. From Colonel Delgado's quarters in the distance the faint sound of a gramophone player drifted intermittently between the closed shutters and from the guardhouse only the occasional curse could be heard as someone or other lost at cards.

'Is it all right?' Ramos called quietly into the darkness.

'Yes. Jump,' came Pecanha's reply.

Ramos braced himself, letting go his handhold on the battlements.

'Hey! You!'

The cry shattered the peace of the fort and the next second a shot cracked out, the bullet whipping past Ramos. While the miss had been harmless enough, its significance was disastrous. They had been spotted.

'What's up?' Pecanha called to his friend.

'Out of the way.' Ramos launched himself off the wall. The ground appeared out of the gloom in the split second before his feet touched ground. He was more tense than intended, panicked by the rifle shot. Nonetheless, he landed without a sprain.

'Which way?'

Instinctively, with the jungle in sight, Pecanha reacted as Ramos had hoped. 'There!' he said, setting off at a shambling run for the nearest of the trees. 'Once we're into cover they won't find us.'

Ramos prayed that his companion was right. They were committed to their escape now. No other course was open. It would be freedom or death. At their backs they could hear shouts, muffled by the high walls that stood in between them and their captors. They were almost at the trees when further shots rang out.

'There they go! Get after them!'

Ramos glanced over his shoulder and saw several heads poking over the battlements, bobbing this way and that, silhouetted against the glow from the pale yellow lights. There was a ferocity in their shouts, like dogs scenting quarry, full of excitement as well as the urgency of the chase. Life had suddenly become more interesting than just a card game for them. There were men to be hunted. There was sport to be had.

The jungle enveloped Ramos and Pecanha like a blanket. Nearest to the fort it was dense, saplings having grown thickly where earlier growth had been cleared. The two men forced their way through it, ignoring the cuts to their limbs. Already Ramos could feel his lungs working to keep pace with the effort. Sweat poured into his eyes.

From behind they heard the sound of the fort's gates being opened. Then dogs were barking. Ramos shuddered. He knew them well. Colonel Delgado kept a brace of big attack dogs outside his quarters. Obviously these had been brought and were now part of the pursuit force.

'Quick!' he urged Pecanha. 'Get us away from here!'

But Pecanha was having trouble. 'It's all so different. I'm not sure of my direction.'

'Well you'd better pick it up fast!'

The old man stopped for a moment, sniffing the air like an animal. Ramos was almost exploding with the tension. The sound of the dogs and the shouting of the hunters was louder every minute. 'Come on,' he hissed, one hand on Pecanha's shoulder, pushing him. As he did so, his hand touched something metallic. Pecanha felt it too and reached round behind his neck. He smiled broadly.

'My pendant,' he said happily, producing the small charm threaded on a leather thong and showing it to his friend. Suddenly confident, Pecanha was off.

'This way,' he said. His pace quickened and he began to pull away. Ramos resisted the urge to shout for him to slow down. They would only have this one chance. The hunters seemed to be going in another direction and Ramos' spirits picked up. The night enfolded them comfortingly, concealing them from their enemies. The air was stiflingly humid and sweat soon soaked their clothes, but still they pushed on, putting as much distance as they could between themselves and the fort.

Suddenly they tumbled out of the trees onto the edge of a

clearing. They recognized it as an extensive area of farmland where they had sometimes been ordered to work in the past.

'We have to cross it,' Pecanha said. 'We will meet the river on the far side and can take a boat from there. It will be quicker. We have to get into deep jungle until they call off the search. The river will take us there.'

Ramos nodded, eyes attempting to penetrate the darkness that covered all but the closest of the cultivated plots. Pecanha set off, but as he went, his pace slowed. Again he sniffed the air.

'What is it?' Ramos whispered.

Pecanha shook his head. 'There's something wrong.'

Ramos listened intently. All he could hear was the sound of the hunters blundering now in the wrong direction altogether. The dogs were going mad but fortunately had missed the trail completely being more used to intimidating subservient labourers than the subtleties of tracking.

Slowly, Pecanha looked up, staring into the dark sky. He was puzzled.

Ramos' impatience got the better of him. 'What is . . . ?'

The next instant, a beam of light struck them, coming out of the heavens as if some god had reached down and torn the night wide open, allowing the sun to stream into the vacuum. But unlike the sun, this light was cold and deathly, silvery white in colour. Pecanha fell to his knees trembling and jabbering, burying his face in his hands.

'I am dead! I am dead!' he cried out.

Ramos likewise dropped to the ground as if physically struck down, but unlike the old Indian, curiosity got the better of superstition. He tried to examine the beam, shielding his eyes towards it, squinting furiously through the harsh glare. In the background he detected a strange noise. There were other men in the field with them. Ramos looked away from the light and stared hard into the corrupted darkness around its edges. Figures were looming towards them. At first he thought they were the guards from the fort, but then, as they came closer, he saw that they were dressed in a uniform of some kind. They were tall men, and they walked slowly towards the two cowering prisoners like sleepwalkers. Pecanha caught sight of them and screamed.

Ramos snatched at his shirt and tried to haul him to his feet. 'Come! We have to run. Now!' He felt something snap and found the old Indian's pendant in his hand.

On the ground, Pecanha was transfixed by terror. He would never move again. A gun fired and the bullet struck him in the chest, killing him outright.

Ramos sprinted away as another bullet snapped at him, then another and another, missing by inches. He had no idea where he was headed. His one urge was to put distance between himself and the ghostly figures. To his dismay, the beam of light followed him, but in doing so it also illuminated his path. Some distance in front of him he spied the outline of trees again and surged towards them. The firing intensified, bullets pocking the earth at his feet and crackling around his head like fireworks. The next moment he reached the tree line and plunged into the welcome cover. The light was unable to penetrate the dense foliage although bullets continued to seek him out.

All of a sudden Ramos became aware of a new sound. His heart leapt at the recognition of water and he altered his direction towards it. It was closer than he had imagined, for a few seconds later he almost fell headlong into the turbulent swirling currents that appeared at his feet. It was fast-flowing, alarmingly so. He hunted around for a boat but he had struck the river bank far from Pecanha's intended location. Somewhere behind him he heard dogs barking. Colonel Delgado's attack dogs. Alerted by the light and the firing, the fort guards had caught up with him and were closing fast.

Desperately Ramos searched for a way across the river.

Tentatively he put one foot down into the water. It was as if a hand had snatched at his ankle, almost sweeping him off balance. The current was ferocious. Panic swamped him. The dogs were ever closer, and with them came the shouts and taunts of the guards, shouting to their fleeing prey what they would do to him when they caught him.

Ramos strained to see across to the far bank of the river but it was hidden by the night. The river was too broad. One of the dogs bayed, a terrifying sound signalling to all that it had stumbled upon Ramos' scent. Its companion picked up the trail a second later and then both of them were howling for blood. A sudden surge in their barking indicated that their handlers had let them off the leash. They were running free now and would be upon their quarry in seconds.

Terror surged through Ramos' body. Despite the heat he trembled, muttering a prayer. Then, as the dogs closed upon him, slashing their way through the last of the undergrowth in a frenzy of teeth, claws and jowls, Ramos plunged headlong into the river and surrendered himself to the powerful current.

It was not until the day after the discovery of the two stowaways that Captain Harrison was content that no further individuals had secreted themselves aboard the *D200*. By then, a thorough search had been conducted by all members of the crew, assisted by Caspasian who had wanted to satisfy himself that the threat had been eradicated.

'So that's that,' Captain Harrison said with evident relief as he and Caspasian sat in Harrison's spacious cabin enjoying a glass of Scotch. 'The danger has passed.'

Caspasian twirled his cut glass tumbler in his hands, staring distractedly out of the window at the passing cloud formations. He was still overawed by seeing them daily at eye level. 'I wish I shared your confidence,' he said. He took a sip of his whisky. He had allowed the ice cubes ample time to chill it.

'But we've searched the ship from stem to stern and found absolutely nothing. Even you've admitted that none of my crew or even the passengers is suspect any more. Gustav Wolter appears to be exactly what he says he is. The signal from Brigadier Percival has cleared him. He checks out as a member of the Zeppelin company.'

'It doesn't make sense, though,' Caspasian said. 'Why would both stowaways kill themselves rather than fall into our hands? They obviously didn't intend to destroy the ship. They'd had ample opportunity to do that. All they had to do was make a small hole in one of the gas cells and strike a match next to it. Couldn't be easier. Instead they chose to sacrifice themselves.'

'Why do you think they did that?' Captain Harrison asked, puzzled.

'It takes a certain kind of dedication and commitment.'

'Fanaticism, if you ask me.'

'Yes, that too,' Caspasian conceded. 'Devotion as well.'

'To some cause, you mean?'

'Yes. To a cause. Or to a person.'

'You're thinking of that Baron fellow you heard the chap shout about.'

'I'm sure that's what he said.'

'And London's produced nothing so far?' Harrison asked.

Caspasian shook his head. 'Nothing. I checked with the radio room only an hour ago. Still no word.'

'It could have meant anything.'

'Yes, but whatever it was, it was enough to send two men voluntarily to their deaths.' Caspasian drained his glass, declined the offer of more and stood up, stretching. 'Anyway, we arrive in Georgetown tomorrow and I'm to continue my search there.' He looked out of the window once more. 'I'll be sorry to leave the airship. It's a wonderful way to travel.'

'The way of the future,' Captain Harrison said, flattered by his passenger's compliment. 'Soon there'll be whole fleets of airships criss-crossing the globe. Vessels of every nation ferrying cargo and passengers. Bigger and better ones than this,' he said, looking around at his comfortably proportioned cabin. 'With better communications, national barriers will be broken down. Old suspicions will erode and people will come to realize that everyone's pretty much the same as everyone else.'

Caspasian smiled sadly. 'I'd love to believe you were right, Captain. Personally I think Utopia will take a bit longer to reach.' He shrugged. 'But who knows?'

Afternoon tea was being served in the saloon. Tables had been spread with white cloths and stewards moved between them helping the seated passengers to a choice of Darjeeling, Assam or Earl Grey, and a generous selection of cakes. The chefs had excelled themselves, given the limited cooking facilities. Several large sponge cakes vied for attention on the trolley's various shelves, together with scones, strawberry jam and clotted cream specially packaged in Devon for the *D200*.

'Captain Caspasian, come and join us!'

Caspasian had sauntered in unawares and looked up as he was hailed from across the room. Seated together round a table, Gustav Wolter, Lionel Domain and Emma Lavelle were enjoying a close inspection of the trolley's contents. Caspasian smiled and moved towards them, noticing only when halfway there that Richard Edward also sat deeply in one of the wicker chairs. Their eyes met briefly and Richard flashed an embarrassed smile. He seemed to half-rise as if considering whether to abandon the little group, but then thought better of it and remained where he was.

Pulling up a chair, Caspasian lightly punched the chintz seat cushion into shape and sat down.

'Well I never,' Lionel Domain began, looking severely impressed. 'Captain Harrison has told us of your encounter with stowaways yesterday. Sounded like quite a party. The very stuff of movies, Mr Caspasian.' He leaned closer until

Caspasian caught a sickly odour of lavender. 'Tell me, sir, have you ever considered a career on the screen?'

Caspasian was not sure whether Domain had just cracked a joke, but the conscientious expression advised against it.

'I have to say that no, I haven't,' Caspasian replied, resisting the urge to laugh out loud.

'Are you about to make him an offer?' Gustav Wolter suggested, similarly amused.

Domain sucked in his cheeks, considering, until his narrowed eyes caught the shared joke between the two military men. 'Go ahead and laugh,' he said grandly. 'But I'll wager that Miss Lavelle here has earned more on one of her movies than the two of you together will earn in your lifetime . . .'

'Lionel, please!' Emma Lavelle interrupted.

He waved a chamois-gloved hand. 'Oh I know, my dear. To you, talk of money is all a bit vulgar.'

'I hope I am big enough to appreciate that there are other things besides the contents of one's bank balance,' she protested. She turned her beautiful eyes on Caspasian and raised them to the heavens.

Once tea, slices of cake and scones were in front of them, the trolley moved on, leaving them to manoeuvre the *D200*'s fine bone china around the confines of the small tabletop. Domain allowed Emma to serve him tea with lemon, while Wolter and Caspasian assisted each other to milk and sugar respectively. Richard Edward waited until the others had what they needed before reaching for his own cup. It reminded Caspasian of the wounded animal that waits on the fringe of the kill until the big cats have finished feeding. He felt a surge of regret and sympathy. As Richard silently retrieved his cup and saucer from the table, positioning it on his lap, Caspasian tried to smile. He handed his half-brother the sugar bowl.

'No thank you. I don't,' Richard replied. But he suddenly

seemed to understand the sentiment behind Caspasian's gesture and quickly added, 'I've only just been advised to give it up.' He chuckled at the tediousness of it all. Caspasian smiled and returned the bowl to the table.

'I hear you are in the Indian Army,' Richard pursued, unwilling to sever the new contact.

Caspasian, aware that all eyes were upon him and never comfortable as the centre of attention, acknowledged the fact.

'Which regiment?' Richard continued, interpreting Caspasian's curt gesture more generously than it really allowed.

'Twelfth Gurkhas.'

'Oh how splendid.'

'You know someone in them?' Caspasian asked, alarmed at the prospect.

'No,' Richard conceded regretfully. 'But I know their reputation,' he added quickly. 'My father has always spoken highly of the Gurkhas and the Twelfth has a particularly distinguished reputation. Beyond that,' he said with disarming honesty, 'I am completely ignorant.'

Caspasian stirred his tea thoughtfully. He waited until the others were distracted by a conversation of their own before continuing. 'You sound close to your father,' he said, keeping his voice low so as to confine the exchange to the two of them.

Richard observed him. 'Why do you say that?'

'You're conducting business on his behalf. You exchange views.' Caspasian shrugged, not sure why he had voluntarily entered a potential minefield.

'Don't you?' Richard asked. 'Exchange views, I mean?' He caught himself quickly. 'Assuming your father's still alive, that is,' he stammered, embarrassed.

'Oh, he's alive all right.'

'But there's an estrangement, then?'

Caspasian smiled. 'You could say that.'

Richard nodded, thinking he understood. 'Actually you're quite wrong. My relationship with my father is . . . distant. Businesslike, in fact.' He was surprised at Caspasian's close attention to his response. He chuckled. 'You know what I used to think? When I was younger and less worldly-wise? That I'd love to have met my father and somehow for us to have been the same age. Then I think we could have been friends. When he was a young man. I feel I'd have been able to understand him then. His hopes. His fears. As children we never really get that level of insight into our parents' natures. Somehow it's always scrambled by the age difference. Odd things get in the way and obscure the truth of the man.'

He laughed, looking at Caspasian as if wondering whether to venture the next step. 'I sometimes wonder if the next life is like that. We all meet up, children, parents, grandparents, generations further back even, and we're all the same age, able to communicate properly for the first time. Discover the truth of it all. Discover where things went wrong.'

'Your paradise sounds a bit crowded,' Caspasian said.

Richard looked at him seriously. 'You have to see your father, Caspasian. You have to speak to him. Before it's too late.'

'Have you spoken to your father?' he countered.

'I've tried,' Richard admitted.

'And?'

He sat back and smiled, but sadly. 'All right. Perhaps I'm a bit of an idealist. It doesn't always work. But my failure shouldn't stop you from trying.'

Caspasian shook his head. 'There are complications.' He considered going further but decided against it. Instead he changed tack slightly. 'I was brought up by my grandfather. My mother's father.'

'Oh. I see. And were you close to him?'

'Yes.' Caspasian nodded. 'Yes, I was. He was a good man. A man of honour. My father was not.'

Richard hesitated a moment and then said, 'Presumably your grandfather's now dead?'

Caspasian nodded. 'Oh yes. Some time ago. We lived in Yokohama. I remember the last time I saw him. I was about to leave for the other side of the world and I think we both knew we'd never see each other again. I remember how subdued and serious he was. His mind was somehow preoccupied, and yet at the same time absolutely focused on me and my questions. It was odd. I was about to depart, and yet he was the one like a man about to embark on some perilous undertaking, off to climb a mountain or cross an unexplored continent. And I knew I'd never see my grandfather again.' He stared out of the promenade window. 'In a way I suppose he was on the brink of something. I remember meeting Mallory as he was preparing for the ascent of Everest that killed him. He was the same. Present and distant, and both at the same time.'

Richard shook his head. 'Well, personally I think you should visit your father and have it out with him.'

Caspasian eyed him shrewdly and smiled. 'Perhaps you're right. Maybe one day I'll do just that.'

There was a burst of laughter from the others as Wolter took issue with Lionel Domain. Caspasian and Richard looked up.

'Well I've never been of the military orientation myself,' Domain was saying loudly. 'All that stamping about and saluting and "yes sir, no sir" nonsense. That's not for me.'

Emma Lavelle stared at him. 'Lionel, how can you sit there and say that? You absolutely love it!'

He regarded her, affronted.

'Go on, admit it,' she continued. 'You've just given the most perfect description of life on one of your productions.'

He smiled, somewhere between embarrassment and anger. 'My dear, you forget yourself. If we didn't have order on the set and someone in charge, then where would we be with our schedules and budgets?'

'Exactly,' Emma said, triumphant. 'So you can hardly accuse Captain Caspasian of stamping and saluting with quite such a disapproving tone.'

Caspasian, Wolter and Richard shared the same fleeting smile, but behind it, all three recognized that Emma was in severe danger of biting the hand that fed her. As the gentlemen they were, all three conspired to dig her out of the hole.

The conversation therefore veered away from the Indian Army, which admirably suited Caspasian, and instead focused on the film world and, especially, on Lionel Domain himself. He leaned back in his wicker chair and held forth about the business which absorbed him. As he did so, Caspasian observed Emma as closely as discretion allowed. She sat smiling graciously, but he felt that it was for public consumption only. Behind it Caspasian felt he could detect something far more genuine. In the company of Lionel Domain, she struck him as a princess in the custody of an ogre, albeit a strangely effete one, if such a thing was possible. Nonetheless, she seemed like a princess in a tower, awaiting rescue. He was only sorry that, as a lowly army Captain, such a task would never fall to him.

He sighed and sipped his cup of Darjeeling. He knew the place well. A beautiful spot. He loved the hill station and pictured the little square at the top of the town, a horizon full of white-capped mountains for perpetual entertainment across the distant valleys. The Windermere Hotel with its open fires and afternoon teas, and then warm brandy as the sun went down, the bells from the Anglican church mingling with the tinkling of Buddhist wind chimes.

Someone was observing him. He felt it like a true soldier, as surely as the drumming of rain on a hat. He turned to find Richard Edward contemplating him with a questioning frown. He blanched and quickly looked away. But for a moment Caspasian felt he had noted recognition there. He hoped not.

Why the devil had he pursued that stupid conversation with the fellow? It never did to rake up the past. Never. So what if they were related? Best leave it a secret. The following day would see their arrival in Georgetown. For Caspasian it could not come a moment too soon.

8

Georgetown had cloaked itself in sunshine for the arrival of the *D200*. A fresh wind scudding in off the sea amused the palm trees in the botanical gardens but presented Captain Harrison with an array of handling problems as he negotiated the final approach to the landing ground on the eastern outskirts of the town.

'Hard rudder to port,' he snapped at the helmsman. 'Aft engines full astern.'

His commands were executed with critical precision although there was an agonizingly long pause before the vast creature sluggishly responded.

Lieutenant Davies removed his cap and stuck his head out of the control car window to observe back along the hull. 'Ship's in trim, Captain, but descending slightly.'

'Drop ballast aft, six hundred pounds,' the Captain ordered, and the crewman controlling the elevator wheel reached up to the relevant knobs at head height and opened the valves. A cascade of water poured from the rear of the airship causing it to rise gently.

'How many degrees out of trim now, Lieutenant Davies?'

Davies studied his instruments. 'Nil, sir. A fraction light in the bow but negligible.'

A moment later, just as the airship was nearing the mooring mast, Davies barked out, 'Wind's shifted direction, sir!'

'Bloody hell!' Harrison muttered. 'Rudder hard to starboard.' He leaned out of the window himself and studied the ground.

'Stand by to drop the lines. Bring us down, Stevens,' he said to the elevator crewman. A moment later he added, 'Cut all engines.'

Everyone in the control car held their breath as the airship sank peacefully towards the mooring mast. 'Drop the lines.'

From the length of the hull, ropes unfurled, tumbling towards the ground where the waiting ground crew rushed to grab hold of them. Scores of men attached themselves to the ropes like some grossly unequal tug of war between Gulliver and the inhabitants of Lilliput. Steadily the descending airship was brought under control by its ground handlers who steered its blunt nose towards the mooring mast where a team of men waited on a platform to lay hold of the giant ring.

To the watching passengers lining the promenade windows it looked as if the whole of Georgetown had disgorged from their offices and houses to come and witness the arrival of the *D200*. The breeze continued to snatch at hats and whisk them into the air but nothing could dampen the enthusiasm of the crowd. As at the send-off a band played, though slightly less in tune. Dogs strained at their leashes, yapping maniacally at the monstrosity looming over them. It was so big that it darkened the sky. To those immediately underneath, it blocked out the sun as effectively as an eclipse.

With his ship securely tethered and all ropes fastened to their moorings, Captain Harrison heaved a sigh of relief. 'Lieutenant Davies, prepare to disembark the passengers.' He consulted his watch. 'I believe I've got to attend some blasted reception at the Governor's residence tonight, but I want to get under way as soon after first light tomorrow as possible. Understood?'

'Yes, sir,' Lieutenant Davies grinned. The Captain's dislike of formal functions was legendary amongst the crew.

In the passenger accommodation, everyone was preparing for a tour of Georgetown. Although there had been ample invitations for them to stay in the various hotels, Captain Harrison had directed that they should sleep the night on board to ensure a speedy departure the following morning. The last thing he needed was to find himself with a passenger adrift when the critical moment came for take-off. He had encountered such problems before and did not intend to repeat the experience.

So it was, that the only person who joined the queue beside the exit gangway clutching their luggage was Caspasian. Gustav Wolter briskly wished him farewell, Lionel Domain ignored him as a person of no consequence and Richard Edward was nowhere to be seen. Emma Lavelle was the only one who seemed genuinely sorry to see him go, although on this occasion Caspasian found it strangely difficult to ascertain where her public personality ended and sincerity began. Nonetheless, she looped her arm through his as he dumped his valise in the corridor outside the saloon.

'Have you seen the town before?' she asked, her eyes searching his with such an intensity that he found it impossible to break the contact. Not that he wanted to.

'No. You?'

She shook her head. 'Lionel has promised me a tour. I'd love to invite you to join us but . . .'

Caspasian waved the suggestion aside. 'Don't worry. I don't think Mr Domain has much interest in soldiers.'

She smiled and Caspasian felt as if he was being bathed with sunlight. He could understand the camera's love of her. 'I will follow your future career with the greatest of interest, Miss Lavelle,' he said.

'Please, call me Emma.'

'Emma, then.'

'It remains to be seen whether I'll have a career at all.'

'Now that's one subject upon which I'm in complete agreement with Mr Domain,' Caspasian said confidently. 'If he is lending his weight to your success then I wish him well.'

Emma was delighted, genuinely so. 'Well, thank you. And I

hope you too have a successful life in the army, ending up as a general or major or whatever they call them.'

Oddly, Caspasian felt his whole enthusiasm suddenly drain from him. The thought of ending up as some beribboned grandee with greying temples, moist eyes and gout was an appalling prospect. Compared to Emma Lavelle's potential future it appeared shabby by comparison. But then he conceded that perhaps he was being swept along by the moment. With such a beautiful woman on his arm, any alternative that did not involve her could only ever be tawdry. The truth was that she belonged to a different world altogether, a different species even, one that Caspasian had been allowed to glimpse for an instant only. To make long-term forecasts based upon such a vision would be rash in the extreme. Even so, it did not prevent him from regretting his imminent return to earth.

Reluctantly he disengaged himself from Emma's arm and, in a moment of uncharacteristic exuberance, raised her hand and kissed it. A shout from the lowered steps announced that passengers were now able to disembark and with a final glance back at the interior of the *D200*, Caspasian stepped out of the airship.

He was met at the bottom of the steps by a junior official called Sanders from the Governor's office who informed Caspasian that he was to accompany him to a meeting with one Frederick Giles, head of security at the High Commission. Brigadier Percival had briefed him on Giles who was to be Caspasian's liaison with the authorities, including the military garrison.

Leaving the airship behind, Caspasian got into the waiting car and drove into the centre of town. Built on a grid pattern, the streets were pleasantly wide and tree-lined. Many of the white-painted houses were raised on stilts, and amongst them he noted a splendidly Gothic city hall and, to the north, St George's Anglican Cathedral. Further north still, the car arrived at the

Governor's Residence and turned into the drive which was flanked by flowering trees and shrubs.

'Attractive, isn't it?' Sanders offered, turning round from his seat in the front. Caspasian nodded, dutifully adding a smile, his mind still with Emma Lavelle.

Frederick Giles was waiting for him in his office and rose to lean across his desk and shake hands. He was a vast man, his several bellies encased with difficulty inside an unruly shirt and trousers. Indeed, he was the fattest man Caspasian had ever seen.

'Captain Caspasian,' he said, matter-of-fact, as if reading from the seating plan at a dinner party. Small eyes worked their way through layers of flushed, sweating skin to fix Caspasian with a lizard's utter indifference. The observed could not be certain whether they were seen or unseen, despite the direct gaze. 'Be seated, please.' He gestured to a green leather chair into which Caspasian lowered himself.

'Snuff?' He pushed a small silver box across the desk towards his guest. Caught unawares by the invitation at such a time of day, Caspasian declined politely. Frederick Giles showed neither approval nor disapproval, maintaining the reptile's absence of moral judgement. 'I want our relationship to proceed without misunderstanding,' Giles stated. He redirected his eyes towards an area of his stomach which had settled itself in his lap now that he had resumed his seat. 'So I will tell you at the outset that I find Percival's intrusion into our affairs here offensive and unnecessary.'

The statement was made without malice or even, it appeared, displeasure. The words were left to inflict whatever discomfort Caspasian chose. He was a little surprised to find himself smiling.

'You find that amusing.' Giles proclaimed it as a self-evident fact. His fingers kneaded the worn arms of his enormous chair with the alternating rhythm of a cat but the appearance of enlivened sausages. Caspasian suspected that Frederick Giles would have been incapable of interlacing them across his middle.

'No, not at all.' Caspasian declined to add 'Sir' as he was far from sure whereabouts in the rank structure Giles existed. He did not much care, either.

'Your facial expression is evidence to the contrary.' He exhaled, bored. 'Be that as it may, you know where I stand. The French have a saying for it but I couldn't give a damn what it is.' His body shifted and Caspasian realized that Frederick Giles was leaning forward. The sausages followed a moment later and played silent tunes on the two extreme ends of an imaginary keyboard halfway across the desk's nearly bare surface.

When he inhaled, it was as if he had suddenly remembered to do so. 'I understand that the good Brigadier wants you to swan up the river in search of Atlantis?' It was the first identifiable question he had addressed to Caspasian.

Caspasian smiled, this time genuinely amused by Giles' sarcasm. 'The Brigadier thinks it is worth pursuing the inquiries of his late operative into the reported sightings of the *D100*. He places some faith in the man's word. Says he was reliable. One of the best.'

'Yes. One of the best asses this side of Palestine.'

'Excuse me?'

'The fellow was an ass. Right down to his braying hee-haw laugh. Deserved what he got, if you ask me.'

'And what exactly did he get?'

Unperturbed, Frederick Giles halted his fingers in mid-chord. 'His comeuppance.'

'So you're discounting all possibility of the sightings being correct?'

'I'm discounting nothing of the sort.' He leaned closer still, the action translating into a single inch of territory gained. 'Don't try and play games with me, Captain Caspasian. I've been at it for longer than you've . . .' His sentence petered out, not, Caspasian realized, because Giles lacked a suitable conclusion, but rather because he had lost interest in extending his point unnecessarily.

Giles sat back, surrendering in a single move the inches previously advanced. It reminded Caspasian of Captain Harrison's airship being manoeuvred towards its mooring. His fingers resumed their kneading of the chair arms, elbows bent, or apparently so. He was starting to irritate Caspasian.

'Frankly, Captain, if the *D100* alighted in my back garden tomorrow morning, I wouldn't come out of the lavatory to witness the event.'

Caspasian was appalled at the image just conjured. 'And why is that, Mr Giles? I wouldn't describe myself as a convert to the airship programme, but certainly the Air Ministry considers this whole business a matter of national importance.'

Caspasian thought that Giles had sneezed, comprehending a moment later that the snort was a derisive one. It nonetheless ejected something from Giles' nostril which Caspasian did not wish to dwell on.

'Believe me, Captain, the airship programme, as you call it, will be dead within a decade. It is a . . .' His face tilted sideways as he searched the air as if for a troublesome mosquito, ' . . . fad. A mere taste of the moment. It will not last.'

'Why?'

Giles regarded him in the manner of an undiscovered genius faced with his dullest apprentice. 'Because they explode, Captain Caspasian. They are the most highly flammable objects on the planet. It is a mercy that so few souls perished on the *D100*.'

'If they did indeed perish,' Caspasian persisted.

'Perish, survive, what does it matter? The whole thing is a diversion from the real march forward of civilization. The sooner the airship is consigned to the scrap heap, the better. I just wonder how many more people will have to die before governments come to their senses.'

'So you don't like airships?'

Giles noted the twinkle in Caspasian's eye but if he was amused his features betrayed no hint of it. 'Flying incendiary devices navigating the circumambient ether.' He held up one finger after careful selection. 'But an incendiary device, nonetheless. To me the logic screams aloud. Or rather, the illogicality.'

'But aeroplanes . . .'

'Will get bigger and faster and safer,' Giles interrupted. 'The payload's smaller, but they're cheaper to build so you make more of them and do more trips. The mathematics are not difficult, Captain.'

Caspasian refused to be cowed. 'Have you ever been on an airship, Mr Giles?'

Giles smiled for the first time. 'And now you're going to tell me about the stately facilities.' He shook a finger in front of his face like an oversized metronome that continued wagging as he spoke. 'Save your breath, Captain. Crematoriums are always decorously furnished.'

'And helium?'

'Is only manufactured in sufficient quantities by the Americans and who can rely on them? They'd shanghai our empire as soon as whistle Dixie.' He shook his head. 'Cads, the lot of them. Cads, sir. Mark my word.'

He consulted the clock on the wall at Caspasian's back. 'I can't say I've enjoyed our chat, Captain, but I will take no pleasure in identifying your corpse when it is fished out of the Demerara like Percival's other lickspittle.' With gargantuan effort, Giles levered himself upright and held out a hand for Caspasian to shake. 'Everyone's down at the field watching that absurd contraption. The whole place is empty so I can't offer you tea, even if I was moved to do so. Which I am not.'

Caspasian had to concede that the man was direct. He shook the offered hand, managing to close his own around most of it, and was halfway to the door when Giles spoke again.

'You haven't asked anything of me, Captain.'

'Asked anything?'

'Help,' Giles said.

'Do you have any to offer?' Caspasian asked doubtfully.

Giles studied him. 'If you are intending to venture upriver, you will have been directed to the garrison.'

'That's correct,' Caspasian admitted. 'Brigadier Percival signalled ahead.'

Giles looked mildly troubled. 'A pity. You may not have heard but that wastrel of a Colonel – Martin was the idiot's name – got himself evacuated on medical grounds. Severe dose of the clap. Went to his brain, though how they can tell beats me. Anyway, you'll be met by his second-in-command.' He paused, and Caspasian wondered whether he was being weighed before being entrusted with a confidence. 'Watch him. He's a viper.'

'Oh?'

But Giles had said all he intended. For whatever reason, his mouth had closed and was going to remain so. He lowered himself into his chair, waving his guest out of his presence, and as Caspasian exited the room, closing the door behind him, his last view of Frederick Giles was of fingers kneading the arms of the vast chair, and of a terraced face observing nothing in particular.

A room had been reserved for Caspasian at the Atlantic Club. Sanders had him driven over in the same car that had met him at the landing ground, but did not escort him, much to Caspasian's relief. He had had enough of Georgetown hospitality for one day. Heeding Giles' warning he decided to put off his meeting with the acting garrison commander until the following morning when, he hoped, he would feel refreshed and ready to entertain the prospect of a new start. Until then all he wanted was a comfortable room, a bath, and perhaps a stroll around the town before an early supper and bed.

To his delight the room was more than adequate. It did not have any view to speak of, but was quiet, spacious and clean. He dropped his valise on the floor beside the large bed, and went through to the bathroom to start the taps running. After the water rationing on the *D200* he was looking forward to the luxury of a plentiful supply.

Later, his bathing complete, he spent the early part of the afternoon napping on the bed, the windows open and a vigorous breeze alternately bullying and consoling the curtains. By the time he ventured out into the streets, he found the town as busy as he imagined it normally was. He was starting to wonder how the novelty of the visiting airship had worn off so quickly when he overheard a comment from one disgruntled passerby to another. He stopped them to confirm what he thought he had heard.

The man looked him up and down angrily. 'That's what I said, wasn't it? The *D200* had to leave. Something about a report of bad weather moving in. Captain Harrison decided he had to continue his journey at noon today instead of waiting for tomorrow morning. He was afraid he might get stuck here if the weather changed.'

'Thank you,' Caspasian said, smiling to himself when the men had moved on. So Captain Harrison had found the excuse he needed to escape the Governor's reception. A weather report. 'Well done,' Caspasian said, congratulating the absent captain. No one could object. It was well known that an airship's captain had the last say in all matters relating to the safety of his vessel. By now, Caspasian judged, the *D200* would be well over the Amazonian jungle and on its way south to Rio De Janeiro.

Reflecting on it, he was struck by a sudden melancholy. He

had enjoyed the company of the people on board and had unwittingly drawn some comfort from the thought that he had not
really parted from them. They were still in Georgetown with
him, albeit elsewhere. Now the fiction was untenable. He was
alone. And he felt it.

He returned to his room soon afterwards and lay down on the
bed waiting for supper time. The dining room, when he later
went in search of it, was a dismal affair and he could not help
thinking about the sparkle that Emma Lavelle had brought to
the Carlton in Bedford. He also found himself thinking of their
chance meeting the next morning, until he had to drag his mind
away because he was making himself thoroughly miserable.

That night he was awoken by the bad weather which had duly
arrived, as predicted in the forecast that had sent Captain
Harrison scurrying on his way. It came in the form of a squall
and hardly appeared serious enough to have put the *D200* at
risk. By first light it had blown itself out and a watery sunlight
flooded the town, bold slashes of fast-moving white clouds
daubing the sky.

Caspasian decided on some exercise before his visit to the
garrison, so put on his running clothes and went out. The air
had been freshened by the rain, but so had the drains. The
sudden flush of water had stirred up the rotting vegetation and
its rank smell lay in wait at unpredictable points along
Caspasian's course. At last he came across a small park, kept
private by a ring of trees which were thickened around the
trunks by a lively growth of bushes. The centre consisted of an
ample lawn, the broad-bladed grass cut short, and pleasantly
cool to his bare feet once he removed his shoes and socks.

After he had stretched out the tensions of the brief run,
Caspasian slipped into a balanced fighting stance and worked
his way through a selection of punches and open hand blows,
increasing the speed as his muscles became reacquainted with
the moves. Next, he executed several *kata*, the prearranged

sequences of movements that brought together attacks and defences, both static and mobile.

By the time he had finished his breathing had quickened and beads of perspiration ran down into his eyes from his wet hair. He left his warm down exercises until he had jogged back to the hotel and then sank into a hot bath to let the water soak his aching muscles. A hearty breakfast followed, taking advantage of an array of exotic fruits that he had missed while in London. As he drained his last cup of coffee, he felt ready for his next meeting.

A taxi deposited him at the gates of the garrison cantonment where two sentries noticed him with reluctance.

'What d'ye want, mate?'

Caspasian felt himself bridle. Any Gurkha acting in a similar manner would have spent the next month in the guardroom, not that it would ever occur to any Gurkha soldier to behave in such a slapdash fashion.

'I'm here to see the CO,' he said.

'That'll be old Westy.'

'Who?'

The sentry eyed him sullenly, resenting his presence. 'Major Westacott.' A malicious grin severed his face. 'The Colonel was taken ill. Evacuated back to Blighty.'

'Could you show me to Battalion Headquarters?'

'Who are you?'

'Captain Caspasian. To see Major Westacott.'

The mention of Caspasian's rank did nothing to amend the sentry's attitude. 'Better come with me, then.' He glanced at his mate. 'You all right on your own?'

The other half of the miserable duo shrugged. 'This way,' the sentry said, indicating that Caspasian should follow him.

Caspasian's instant reaction to the headquarters building was that it cried out for the attentions of a stiff broom. A fresh coat of paint would not have gone amiss either.

'Wait in here,' the sentry drawled.

'Wait in here, sir,' Caspasian suggested, his expression making it clear that it was not a suggestion at all.

The sentry blinked, paused a moment and then added 'Sir,' as lugubriously as he was able without making it a direct insult. He obviously fancied himself as a master of brinkmanship. To Caspasian he had overstepped the mark in the first second of their meeting.

The office where he had been left bore a vague resemblance to an orderly room, but the mess cluttering the desk tops was a wonder to behold. If a chief clerk existed, Caspasian would have had him taken straight to the rifle range, tied up in the butts and used for target practice. A single typist hammered away at the keys of a dusty typewriter, a cigarette dangling from his lips. An inch of ash teetered at the end of the glowing stub.

The door to an adjoining office opened and a uniformed officer wearing the rank badges of a major poked head and shoulders round the frame.

'Are you Caspasian?' His tone was unfriendly but for a major in a British regiment addressing a more junior officer, it was not unexpected.

'Yes sir.' Caspasian braced to attention, an action that brought a sneer to the major's face.

'Better come in, then.' The head and shoulders disappeared and when Caspasian entered the room, it was only to find the remainder of the man equally disagreeable.

'I know why you're here,' Major Westacott said. He felt no need for introductory small talk. 'And I'm afraid I'm unable to help you.'

Caspasian smiled, forcing himself to relax. 'I believe a signal was sent . . .'

'From London. Yes. It said I was to help you but, you see, I simply don't have the resources.' He smiled. A waste of facial effort, as far as Caspasian was concerned.

'Do you mind me asking what other duties are occupying the entire battalion?'

Major Westacott's face reddened. 'Yes, I bloody well do.' He had been bristling for a fight and now Caspasian had opened the doors allowing the bull into the ring. In he charged. 'You come here, a jumped-up little captain from God-knows what regiment, and expect me to lay my whole command at your disposal.' He pushed his face unpleasantly close to Caspasian's which did not move, but set in lean, firm lines. 'Well let me tell you that you can forget it.'

'And London?'

'Is a long, long way from Georgetown, Captain.'

Coming after the meeting of the previous day with Frederick Giles, Major Westacott's manner made Caspasian grateful that he had not wound up in British Guiana before.

Caspasian paused to consider his options and how best to continue the meeting. 'Major Westacott,' he began as reasonably as possible. 'I have been tasked with carrying out an expedition upriver to investigate claims of airship sightings . . .'

'Stuff and nonsense.'

Caspasian held up one hand. 'That may well be, but the fact remains that I am under orders.' He braced himself. 'And so are you.' He saw the Major's chest start to swell in preparation for an onslaught and cut in quickly before the storm could break. 'Now you can order me off your camp and tell me to go to hell – although frankly I'm starting to think that I'm already there – and I will obey and go quietly. However, I will then be obliged to contact London for guidance and they, in turn, will seek an explanation from you.'

He saw his words sink in like stones cast on top of thick liquid mud. 'You see, we are both servants of the Crown. Whether we like all of its orders, or not, is immaterial.' He could not believe that he, of all people, was giving a lecture on the necessity for obedience to orders. The irony almost made him smile.

When Major Westacott spoke again it took the form of a hissing sound. Caspasian's lecture had changed the manner of delivery of Westacott's reply, though not its substance.

'Get out of here, Captain. Get out and do not return. You will get nothing from me. Nothing. Do you understand?' He turned to the door and bellowed. 'Sergeant Major Horner!'

The door burst open and a fierce, fit-looking individual with the bludgeoned features of an old boxer entered, slamming to attention in the middle of the room. 'Sir!' he barked. His eyes swivelled onto Caspasian whom he evaluated scathingly, content that his loathing should be noted.

'This is Captain Caspasian. He is just leaving. Kindly escort him to the front gate and see him off the premises. There's a good fellow.'

Caspasian smiled. 'That won't be necessary.'

Westacott ignored him. 'Sergeant Major?'

'Sir!' Horner acknowledged. He turned about, slamming his booted feet into the floor again. His eyes bore down on Caspasian again. 'This way . . . sir,' he said in threatening tones.

Seeing that any further conversation was useless, Caspasian braced to attention to give the Major due recognition for his rank, turned and exited, followed closely by Sergeant Major Horner. As they made their way to the gate, the Sergeant Major marched hard on Caspasian's heels, attempting without success to get him to accelerate his pace.

'Your commanding officer has a novel way of conducting himself,' Caspasian said.

'Maybe that's because we don't like people interrupting routine battalion business. Sir.'

'Indeed?'

'Like I said. Sir. We're kept busy here. Don't have time for loafing. If you know what I mean. Sir.'

When they arrived at the gate Caspasian continued walking out into the street, looking for a taxi as he went. He would have to get to the High Commission and signal Percival for instructions. He did not bother to say goodbye to the Sergeant Major who halted noisily at the camp's entrance. All the way down the road Caspasian could feel the man's eyes boring into the back of his head like two blunt nails. The man could go to hell. In fact, Caspasian resolved, he would take great pleasure helping him on his way. But for that he would need help, however reluctant he was to ask for it.

Back in the battalion headquarters, Major Westacott was also watching Caspasian's departure. He waited until Sergeant Major Horner returned before leaving his place by the window. He paced the room, hands clasped in the small of his back, the outermost one tapping irritably against its partner.

'Nicely handled, sir,' Horner said.

'Don't be stupid, Sergeant Major. That man's trouble. I know the type.'

'But what can he do?'

Westacott spun round, waving one finger towards the window and, Horner presumed, Caspasian beyond it. 'That holier-than-thou type can do plenty, believe me.' He thought. 'Given time,' he said, considering, weighing his words and thoughts carefully. He brightened. 'And that's exactly what we can't afford to give him, Sergeant Major. Time.'

In Horner's brain, a light went on. Dimly, but nonetheless on. He smiled. 'Leave it to me, sir.'

9

Caspasian decided to delay his visit to the High Commission until later in the afternoon to give himself time to think. He did not like having to appeal to anyone for help, Brigadier Percival least of all. In this situation, though, it could not be avoided. If Caspasian was going to get upriver he was going to need the assistance of the garrison commander and the resources at his disposal. There were no funds for a private expedition, so, with Westacott having made his opinion crystal clear, an appeal to Percival was the only option left.

His mind was preoccupied during an early lunch in the hotel. The service was so slow that he felt like complaining to the manager, and when the waitress finally took his order, Caspasian had to repeat himself several times as her mind was very obviously elsewhere. At one point she broke off to blow her nose, snivelling over some personal tragedy or other.

By the time he exited the hotel and started on the walk to the High Commission, taxis being inexplicably absent from the streets, Caspasian was in an evil temper. The pavements were deserted except for the occasional small group of people huddled in tight conversations on street corners as if some dastardly conspiracy was being hatched. Indeed, the trend became so pronounced that if Caspasian's mind had not been occupied with Westacott and Percival, he would have interrupted one of the conversations to discover what was going on.

The gates to the High Commission stood open and to Caspasian's amazement, the sentry was absent from his post.

Walking through the entrance into the hall, Caspasian was completely ignored by the first clutch of people he came across, who hurried past clutching files and note pads. A clerk came bolting down the stairs, blind to his presence until Caspasian grabbed hold of his sleeve,

'Is Frederick Giles in?' he asked.

The man stared at him, barely noticing the restraining hand fastened to his jacket.

'Who?'

'Giles, man. Frederick Giles?'

'Oh.' Recognition fought its way through the muddle cluttering the man's brain. 'In his office. He's just finished with the Governor.'

In Caspasian's head, an alarm began to sound. He took the stairs two at a time and rushed to Giles' office. The door stood ajar but he knocked all the same. Silence. He knocked again.

'Enter.'

Frederick Giles was standing with his back to the room, staring out of the window, his vast frame blotting out the sun. When he turned to identify his visitor, he did so in a series of small shuffling steps.

'Ah, Caspasian.'

'Well you were right about Westacott,' Caspasian began.

'Westacott?' Giles said. Caspasian realised that Giles' thoughts were miles away. 'The least of my concerns now.'

'Why's that?'

Giles stared at him, suddenly understanding. 'You mean you haven't heard?'

'Heard?' Caspasian was beginning to feel very stupid.

'Good God, man. You must be the only person in Georgetown not to have heard the news.'

'News?'

'About the *D200*!'

Caspasian went cold. 'What about it?'

'Lost with all hands. In the early hours of this morning. While we were all still abed.' Giles' tone was business-like but with the slightest edge to it that, Caspasian suspected, was the closest he ever came to showing emotion.

Uninvited, Caspasian pulled a chair in front of Giles' desk and sat down. A torrent of jumbled feelings hammered at him, coming from every direction like an enemy force in the final stages of an assault. With them came glimpse after glimpse of the faces. Harrison, Wolter, Richard Edward, and chief amongst them, Emma Lavelle. Caspasian could feel her arm upon his, see her eyes looking up at him as they said goodbye only the day before.

'What happened?'

'Bit sketchy,' Giles replied. He positioned his own chair and once it was secure, lowered himself into it. It was not easy to tell exactly when the process had been completed but gradually the folds of his body settled like billowing parachute silk, though less graceful.

'There were two signals. The first was received at about zero two hundred hours this morning and said that they had encountered a squall that was intensifying. Then, barely thirty minutes later, part of a second signal was transmitted by the airship.' He opened a drawer, took out a slip of paper and thought about skimming it across the desktop to Caspasian. Instead he read it himself. 'Fire in the galley. Spreading. Fighting to bring it under control.'

Seeing that the text ended there, Caspasian reached across and took the paper, studying the terse message.

'Nothing was heard thereafter and no response was received to any of our calls.' Giles retrieved a second piece of paper from the drawer. 'Then shortly before zero three hundred hours we intercepted this from a fishing vessel off the Brazilian coast.' He angled the paper to the light and read. 'Long tongue of flame seen streaking down into the sea near Recife.'

He deposited it on the desk. 'It goes on to speculate about it being the *D200*, but until the Brazilian authorities come up with any wreckage we won't know for certain. Personally I don't think there can be any doubt. It all ties in.'

Caspasian's mind was racing. 'Yes. It all ties in very conveniently. Very nicely indeed.'

Giles narrowed his eyes. 'What are you insinuating?'

'Have you got a map?'

Giles glanced at the wall behind Caspasian. Caspasian got up and went quickly over to it, searching along the coast. Giles joined him at a more stately pace. 'Look, Recife's here,' Caspasian said, planting a finger on the spot. He looked at Giles as if his point should be self-evident. 'What the devil was the airship doing off Recife? It was bound for Rio. Recife's hundreds of miles out of its way.'

Giles looked thoroughly unimpressed. 'Perhaps Captain Harrison was trying to avoid the squall.'

'Then he'd hardly head out to sea. Squalls die out once they hit land. It would have been safer to head across country, letting the squall lose its force as it followed. Harrison had ample warning of the storm and left here in good time. Everyone in town was complaining about it.'

Still Giles refused to be swayed. 'The coastal route might be longer but navigation would be easy. Just follow it until you hit Rio. Why make life difficult by going over the jungle? Furthermore, if anything untoward should happen over the bush, what chance do you think anyone would have of surviving even if the airship could be brought down intact? By the coastal route, they could set down at any one of a number of settlements.' He studied Caspasian before deciding to head back to his desk and chair.

'I can appreciate how you must feel, but clutching at straws won't help anyone.'

Caspasian paced the room. For a second he pictured the

scene as it must have unfolded in the final moments of the airship's life. The panic as the passengers and crew attempted to bring the fire under control, the terror as it spread, and the final flash and explosion as its outermost tongues ignited the hydrogen. The fiery plunge into the sea. He wondered whether Emma would have been consumed by flames before the airship crashed, or might she have jumped, preferring a terrifying but less painful end?

His body prickled with cold beads of perspiration and he shuddered, cold despite the heat of the day. This could not be happening. Unbidden, an image of his half-brother entered his mind. Oddly, the expression on Richard's face was peaceful acceptance. There was an air of noble tragedy in his bearing and again Caspasian had to shrug away from the haunting vision.

'I don't believe it,' he said firmly, gritting his teeth. 'I won't believe it.'

'It's not a matter of what you do or don't believe, Caspasian. It's a simple question of facts.'

Caspasian rounded on him. 'Then I don't accept the facts. I don't believe those are the facts.'

Giles sighed. Fittingly it was like a balloon deflating. 'Have it your way. It's nothing to do with you in any case. Your mission, as I understand it, is to investigate the sighting of the *D100*. As I presume Westacott's told you where to go, you'll be wanting to signal London.'

Before Caspasian could answer, Giles continued, holding out yet another signal. 'Before you do, you'll need to read this. When we received news of Harrison's disaster we informed London straight away. This was the reply.'

Warily Caspasian accepted the signal and read it. It informed him that Brigadier Percival himself was coming to Georgetown to take command of the investigation. It also ordered Caspasian to do nothing further until the Brigadier's arrival.

He stared at it dumbfounded. 'You mean I'm supposed to sit here kicking my heels for . . . How long? A fortnight?'

Giles held up a hand and closed his eyes momentarily against the tirade. 'Nothing of the sort. Apparently the Brigadier's flying to North Africa, hopping down the coast by mail plane and will catch a fast steamer across to Georgetown from there. He'll be here in about four days. Maybe less.' He studied Caspasian to gauge the effect of his statement. 'In the meantime, the search will continue for wreckage . . . Or survivors,' he added hastily.

'And I do what?' Caspasian fumed.

Giles shrugged. 'You do all any of us can. Wait and hope.'

'Well that's not good enough. I want that arsehole Westacott brought to book. The Governor . . .'

'The Governor wants no part of it,' Giles said, interrupting. 'If Westacott has a problem with his military superiors in London that's for them to sort out. And I'm sure Percival will do just that.' He sighed, bellows blowing ineffectually on slumbering embers. 'Caspasian, you have to realize that Georgetown is not London. It is not even Delhi.' He shifted his weight with several miniature convulsions and his fingers recommenced their kneading of the chair arms. 'Think more of a tropical Eastbourne.' He paused, a smile spreading. 'Without the summer rush.'

Caspasian glared at him, the extent of his powerlessness making him want to scream. He rose to go.

'One last thing.' Giles' voice pursued him to the door. 'I would stay away from Westacott if I were you. Leave him for Percival. No point aggravating the man.'

Without replying, Caspasian left the room, neglecting to close the door behind him. He knew that Giles was right. He would indeed leave Westacott alone. But he promised himself that in due course he would do far more than merely aggravate the good major.

★

High up in the clouds, Emma Lavelle was wondering if she was dead. It was strange, she thought, to find herself considering the matter, as she had always supposed that, when the time came, there would be nothing to doubt. Instead, doubt was just about all there was.

She had woken with a splitting headache. Her temples thundered and drums beat a furious rhythm in her head. She looked around and discovered that she was lying on the floor of the cargo section of the *D200*. Memory returned in pieces, the various bits gradually fitting together to form a coherent picture. There had been a squall. Nothing to worry about, Captain Harrison had assured the passengers. All quite routine.

A short while later Lieutenant Davies had urged everyone to return to their cabins and remain there throughout the rough weather, although Emma remembered Gustav Wolter commenting that it did not seem particularly rough to him. She remembered Lionel bemoaning his lack of a smoking jacket and, to put a stop to his continual whining, she had gone in search of someone to guide her to the cargo hold where their larger items of luggage were stored. A steward had succumbed to her persuasiveness but had sworn her to secrecy. He would lose his job, he told her, if the officers knew he had given a passenger access to the cargo hold, especially during a storm.

Once there, he had left her to hunt for Lionel's trunk, promising that he would return to fetch her shortly. He had never done so. The airship had been bucketed about, the gyrations becoming increasingly violent. She could hear the rain pounding on the outer side of the airship's skin and in the background the noise of thunder crashed terrifyingly close. The next thing Emma could remember was waking up and wondering whether she was dead.

She felt her limbs to check that nothing was broken, and then inspected her face delicately with her fingers, feeling for bruises lest she had been thrown by the storm and had struck something, knocking her unconscious. There did not appear to be any bumps, lumps or anything else. Puzzled, she got to her feet. The airship was perfectly stable now and all sounds of the storm had vanished. In fact, there were no sounds to speak of at all. The engines were silent and all Emma could hear was an eerie sighing of wind in the rigging.

She opened her mouth to call out and see if anyone was within earshot but stopped herself, although without knowing why. Something seemed not quite right. She went across to the doorway and peered outside. The axial gangway ran in front of her, stretching in either direction into the bowels of the airship. Overhead the gas cells creaked gently within their restraining wires. The brightness penetrating the hull's silver-toned skin told her that it was daylight, but the complete absence of movement was remarkable. It felt as though the vessel was floating in a vacuum.

The fine blonde hairs at the nape of her neck bristled at the silence. She shivered. Hugging herself, Emma moved out onto the gangway and began to walk slowly back towards the passenger accommodation towards the prow. As she went she came in line with one of the narrow walkways leading off to either side where doors in the outer hull gave access to the engine gondolas. On an impulse, she turned right and, at an even slower pace, edged towards the end. The door in front of her was small and shut. From outside the hull she could see the shapes of clouds waving as the sun played on them, altering their patterns against the airship's taut skin. It was mesmerising and she almost strayed off the walkway and tripped, grabbing a handhold at the last moment to steady herself.

But something else had entered her consciousness. Something she could not quite believe. As she approached the door and reached towards the handle, turning it and pushing the door open, she could distinctly hear birdsong. And the motions of the clouds against the outer skin were not clouds at all, for the door swung open and to her amazement, Emma found herself looking out over mile upon mile of jungle canopy.

Her mouth fell open. 'Oh my God,' she said quietly, reverently. The spectacle was awe-inspiring. As far as she could see, an undulating green blanket had been spread across the world and for a moment Emma felt that if an angel had appeared to her at that moment she could have believed that she really had perished in the storm. And given her current perspective, she would not have been overly concerned.

The sense of security lasted only a handful of seconds. Then she became aware of the heat. It rose out of the forest floor scores of feet below and with it came the birdsong that had teased her a moment ago. Now, with the door cast open, it found her more clearly. It was beautiful but wholly alien to her everyday experience. And suddenly she felt very alone.

She took a step forward and peered down outside the hull. Below her the drop made her head swim. She clutched at the handrail but forced herself to inspect her surroundings more closely. The ground was so far down it disappeared into the dark gloom of the jungle interior which was in stark contrast to the brightness of her vantage point above the canopy. By taking a couple of steps out onto the ladder that extended towards the engine gondola, she was able to view the greater part of the airship's length from stem to stern. At first sight it looked as if it was resting on top of the canopy itself, but a closer inspection showed that ropes had been lowered down into the jungle itself and the airship was in fact tethered.

The realisation that the ship had not been wrecked but had obviously been brought down under control sent waves of relief flooding through her. A smile broke across her face and she let out a huge sigh. Turning back into the hull, she made her way to the axial gangway and headed as quickly as she could for the passenger accommodation. Presumably the Captain would have signalled their position to Georgetown and a rescue mission would be on its way to them at that very moment. She reached the door and descended the ladder into the sleeping cabin area, making for her own quarters. Some of the other doors stood open and although the cabins she passed were all empty, she assumed that everyone had probably gathered in the saloon.

Arriving at her cabin, she burst open the door. 'Lionel! I'm back.'

The cabin was empty. Her face fell. Disquiet registered a second later as she took in the spectacle of clothing and other personal articles strewn around the floor. Drawers had been emptied and the whole cabin was in an appalling mess. Still, she reasoned, at least they were alive. The storm had obviously wrought havoc but clutter could be tidied.

Out in the corridor, she went through the rest of the passenger sleeping accommodation, noting similar wreckage everywhere. When she reached the saloon, she stood in the doorway staring at the overturned chairs and tables, the broken crockery and the scattered articles littering the floor. She popped her head into the galley, the bar and the smoking room only to find all of them wrecked and, what was more alarming, all of them empty.

At that point she finally called out. 'Hello!'

Her voice sounded frail in her ears. A little pathetic. She cleared her throat and tried again, bolder than before. More in control. 'Hello!'

Silence.

'Is anybody there?'

The caw and scream of parrots entered through the open promenade windows. One of the panes was broken. Emma walked across to it. Halfway there she stopped. Lying on the floor was Lionel's cigarette holder. She stooped to pick it up. As she did so, she noticed something else. Lying amongst a pile of strewn papers was a single empty cartridge case from a gun. She did not know much about firearms but by the size of it she judged it to be from a pistol or revolver. Her hand started to shake as she reached towards it and picked it up. It was cold but when she put it to her nose she smelt a pungent odour that was similar to the smell put out by the pyrotechnics she had experienced on film sets in the past.

She looked back to the broken pane and saw that the cracks originated from a neat hole that had been punched through the glass. It must have been where the bullet exited. Feeling sick, she wondered if it had passed through any of her travelling companions on its way out. There was no sign of blood anywhere on the saloon floor so she presumed that it had probably been fired as a warning. But by whom? And what for?

At the open promenade windows she leaned out and peered down through the jungle canopy trying to catch sight of the floor beneath. The undergrowth at treetop level was so dense that only in one small spot was the light able to penetrate. It revealed a small clearing, although it appeared to be empty. But as she watched, Emma saw figures moving in the shadows. She was about to reach out and wave and shout when she noticed that one of them was carrying a gun. A rifle. He was pointing it at the others. The man looked up.

Emma jerked her head back inside and tensed, waiting for a cry of alarm or a bullet. There was silence. She had not been seen. Carefully, she angled the window pane so that she could see the clearing's reflection in the glass while herself remaining hidden. It cranked into view, still clear enough to make out the distant figures. She could see a whole line of people now, although it was impossible to distinguish individuals. But then suddenly she recognized one by his gait. It was Richard Edward. She was sure of it. Behind him another man with a rifle was goading him on, forcing him to walk. Someone appeared to be protesting on Richard's behalf. It might have been Gustav Wolter. Emma caught her breath and clasped her hand to her mouth as the man was clubbed to the ground with the rifle butts.

Shouts rose up to her, muffled but, amongst them, she thought she heard Lionel's. Then a shot rang out and all was silent again. When she looked back at the window pane the figures had all disappeared. She tried to angle it differently but there was no one to be seen. Tentatively she put her head out of the window again and studied the ground wherever she could in between the overarching canopy of foliage. All was silence. The gunshot had stilled the animal and bird noise, but slowly even that returned to normal.

She strode back into the saloon, hugging her arms about her, wondering what was going on and what on earth she should do. The control car! Perhaps there she would find a clue as to what was happening. Or the radio room perhaps. There would be maps, a log, messages. Perhaps those would give her some idea. At the very least they might indicate where the airship now was. Thinking about it filled her with apprehension. The jungle seemed to extend as far as the eye could see. How she was ever going to get away was anybody's guess.

She had just started on her way to the control car when she heard voices. Instantly she froze. They were some way off, although it was hard to pinpoint where they were coming from. But they were heading her way. Of that she was certain.

Trying to remain calm, she hunted for somewhere to hide. The saloon was altogether too open and the dining room offered little more hope. There, too, tables and chairs had been over-turned and oddly the chaos made hiding places harder to find. Emma quickly looked into the galley and the bar but both were small, cramped rooms, so with mounting alarm, she found herself tearing back towards the passenger sleeping quarters.

The voices were becoming louder by the second. She heard footsteps coming down the ladder from the axial gangway. They would be on to her within moments. Trying one door after another, Emma darted into the first one she found to be unlocked. To her horror it was tiny and dark, the curtains being drawn closed. There was an unpleasant musty smell. With the voices now outside the door, she backed into the gloom and bumped straight into someone. She gasped, catching the scream in her throat, hands clamped across her mouth, eyes wide. Behind her, the body of a man sat slumped in a chair facing the door. He had been shot through the forehead. Dried blood caked his face, the open eyes frozen and staring sightlessly through Emma. She recognized him as one of the reporters who had been interviewing her only a couple of days previously. A lamp lay at his feet, the bulb smashed. The shade had been removed and stood on the bedside table. She assumed he had been trying to use it as a weapon in the unequal fight.

She stood rooted to the spot, ears straining towards the voices outside, wondering if they had heard her. Without faltering they continued on their way. Only then did it strike her that they were not the voices of anyone she recognized. She guessed that there had been two, possibly three people. Men. The language had been English, but one of the men's voices was heavily accented. European rather than Latin American.

Without looking again at the dead man behind her, Emma slid towards the door and pressed her ear against it. Silence. She turned the handle and opened the door a crack, peering out into the corridor. It was empty. She could feel the panic rising in her. Her legs became weak and she felt as if she was about to faint. She gripped the door tightly, forcing herself to keep hold of her senses.

'Come on,' she said in a loud whisper. 'Come on, Emma!' The sound of her voice in the silent cabin was comforting. Little by little her strength returned. The faintness passed.

'You've handled pressure before.' She smiled ruefully. 'I'll just have to imagine it's a film set.'

Firmly in control of herself, she slipped into the corridor and made her way to the steps leading into the heart of the airship.

She was torn between finding a way out of the vessel, making her way down to the ground and following her companions, or remaining on board and seeking a more secure hiding place. The problem was, as the airship had obviously been taken over by someone or other, what did they intend doing with it? She remembered that it was filled with hydrogen. Bullets had already been fired so the thought of setting foot on firm land was attractive. But then she considered her options if she made it down to the jungle floor. What then? She had never been alone in the jungle before, she had no survival equipment or food, and as far as she could tell, she was miles away from civilization. How long would she last? Surely she would do better to remain where she was. She even considered giving herself up to the men, whoever they were, but the image of the murdered reporter dissuaded her from that course of action.

The question was decided for her a moment later when the silence of the airship was broken by the unmistakable sound of an engine firing. With a distant roar, it coughed into life, followed by another, and then another, as, one by one, all the engines were powered up. The *D200* vibrated gently and suddenly Emma was seized by the conviction that she had to get off the airship, come what may. Wherever it was bound, she was certain it would be nowhere she would want to go. She could hide for a while but eventually she would be found. And then what?

Some way in front of her, a shaft of light penetrated into the hull from an open hatch down beside the keel. Before she went to explore, however, she hurried stealthily back to the passenger accommodation and located her cabin. Snatching a valise from the top of the cupboard, she hastily stuffed it full of articles of clothing that she thought might come in handy. She clutched it tight and, checking that the corridor was still clear, darted back for the steps. The gangway above was empty. Hurrying towards the open hatch, she hefted the bag onto her shoulder to make quicker time. Steps led down to the hatchway. She edged down them one by one, careful not to lose her footing. As she let herself down onto the small wooden platform beside the hatch, she peered over the edge and saw the long slender thread of a rope ladder snaking down through the canopy towards the ground. The sight of the drop made her dizzy. She sat back on her heels, breathing hard, fighting to remain calm.

A sudden surge in the pitch of the engines brought her to her senses. The next second she heard someone calling from the passenger's corridor she had just left. They were coming in her direction. She glanced again the length of the rope ladder. Even if she started to climb down it now, she knew she would not be able to reach the bottom before the approaching man arrived at the hatch. Then she would be trapped, like the Grand Old Duke of York. Neither up nor down.

Cursing herself for having taken so long to come to a decision, she ducked behind a ballast tank that lay to one side. The man was on the gangway above her now, but his footsteps carried on past her hiding place. He was whistling. Walking briskly, he continued towards the stern. Emma waited until the sound had died away and then moved. She was not going to be caught out again.

Looping an arm through her bag's carrying handles, she shifted the weight of it onto her shoulders, took a deep breath, and worked her way out onto the rope ladder. Its considerable length worked in her favour, the sheer weight of it keeping it relatively straight and rigid. With rope sides, the rungs were of aluminium. Step by cautious step, Emma began the long descent towards the jungle floor. After a few yards she looked up at the underside of the giant airship. The next moment she entered the upper reaches of the jungle canopy and the vessel shrank out of sight, only the hatchway immediately above remaining visible.

Halfway down she paused for a rest, hooking one leg and an arm behind the ladder and bracing herself against it for safety.

She was breathing hard and perspiration poured into her eyes. She blinked it away and shook her head, watching the fine droplets fly away, down through the branches and into the darkness below. Something caught her attention and she looked up to find herself being studied minutely by a small furry creature. Huge eyes roamed across her, its head tilting in wonder. In spite of her dire predicament, Emma smiled at it.

'Don't suppose you've got a glass of champagne?' she said softly.

The animal cocked its head the other way and then, losing interest, turned and scurried away down the branch, leaving Emma to envy the ease with which it inhabited its environment.

The lower she descended the gloomier it became. She leaned to one side and looked down. The ground was visible now, although she still had some way to go. Suddenly there was a tug on the ladder and it jerked violently. She looked up. The hatch had been obscured by a large branch and foliage mercifully hid her from whoever was trying to raise the ladder.

'Johann, is that you?' a voice called from above her. Emma quickened her pace, removing her feet from the rungs altogether and lowering herself hand over hand instead, going faster and faster.

'Johann?' The voice was more urgent now. Suspicious. Again the ladder jarred in her hands, almost shaking her off it. The man above had assumed the ladder had snagged on a branch and he was trying to free it from the obstruction. Emma knew she had only seconds before she was discovered.

In one final burst, she lowered herself the remaining distance, dropping the last few feet. She landed with a thud, the bag hitting her on the head and bursting open. She cursed. Above her, the ladder quickly began to ascend into the trees, up into the airship from which the sound of the engines now roared out over the jungle. Animals and birds screamed in response, the air filling with noise. Through the cacophony, Emma just managed to hear a shout. It was from someone nearby at ground level.

Irritation at her burst bag and spilt clothing turned instantly to panic. She scrabbled to stuff the clothes back into the bag, got shakily to her feet and hunted around for somewhere to hide. Towering trees extended in every direction, but here and there, in the few places where sunlight managed to penetrate, thicker undergrowth flourished. She selected the nearest clump and ran towards it, picking her feet high to avoid cracking twigs. There was another shout and just as she dived into the bushes, a man appeared about fifty yards distant. Emma wriggled deeper on her stomach, turning so she could observe him. She was surprised how far it was possible to see in the jungle. It was rather like a North American forest only much hotter.

The man stopped where the ladder had hung moments before. He looked up into the canopy, shaded his eyes, and waved to someone overhead who was invisible to Emma. The engines surged and she became aware of a subtle change in the lighting around her as if an eclipse was drawing to a close. The cathedral gloom of the jungle began to brighten. She looked up and in between the treetops caught glimpses of the *D200* pulling away.

'Well, that's that,' she thought. To her alarm the man sat down with his back against a tree trunk and took out a pouch of tobacco and began to roll a cigarette. His rifle lay to one side. He was scruffily dressed in what Emma could only describe as a piratical fashion. Indeed, she half expected to hear Lionel shouting 'Cut!' and to see the camera and lighting crews emerge from the undergrowth. Instead, a further three men, similarly dressed like pirates or screen vagabonds of some description, came to join him. All four gathered to share the one cigarette, talking quietly. They were relaxed and clearly did not suspect that they were being watched.

Emma shifted deeper into the undergrowth. She pushed her bag behind her, edging steadily backwards. Floods of panic vied for place with an irrational sense of triumph. She had evaded capture. But where was she and what on earth was she going to do now? She had no food and, she suddenly realized, no water. What was more, she had no knowledge of how to survive in a jungle. Perhaps she could try and follow the others, her companions who had been taken prisoner. Maybe she would be able to free them, or at least one of them. Yes! That was the answer! Gustav Wolter would know how to escape. Someone like him was bound to.

She relaxed a little, wiping her brow with one hand. At least she was free and so long as she remained so there was hope that she could do something to help the others and, by implication, herself. She watched the four men, all of them chatting amicably, heads wrapped in tendrils of tobacco smoke. She was so intent on her observations that she knew nothing of another human presence close beside her until a hand closed tightly across her mouth.

IO

Caspasian knew he was being followed. A sixth sense, honed over the years, had sounded the alarm several minutes earlier as he had turned away from the city centre and headed west towards the Demerara river. It was dark and the night was particularly sticky. He had dined early several hours ago and now thanked his lucky stars that he had decided against a drink with his light meal. Consequently his head was clear and his step light.

Whoever was tailing him was reasonably good because it was a while before he caught a first glimpse of the man. Two men, in fact, both tall and thickset like waterfront stevedores. He gently increased the pace. For a moment he considered making a run for it, confident that he could outrun them and make it back to the hotel and, presumably, safety. However, he decided to postpone flight for the moment, partly because he wanted to find out if they were simply thieves or something more sinister, and partly from a bloody-mindedness that disliked the image of a Twelfth Gurkha running from a fight. Any fight. Furthermore, the past few days had been infuriating, spent sitting on his hands waiting for the Brigadier to arrive. He felt like a caged tiger and the chance of burning off some energy was not altogether unwelcome. He had kept fit, running and exercising daily, usually at least twice, morning and evening when the temperature was at its most comfortable for exertion. Now, strolling through the quiet town, he clenched and unclenched his fists in readiness, flexing his fingers for action.

Approaching the river, he caught a whiff of it on the evening breeze, unpleasantly ripe at the end of a long hot day. The water itself came into view a couple of minutes later. A barge chugged past, heading upriver at an unhurried pace. A portly figure dressed in shorts and vest lounged at the stern, the glow of a cigarette at his lips. He looked idly in Caspasian's direction, his gaze shifting to the two men who had started to close the gap. He turned away, unconcerned.

To one side, a dog scratched at a pile of rubbish, hunting for food. It found something and its teeth bared as it chewed it sideways on, bony haunches thrusting towards the ground for purchase.

It was then that Caspasian caught sight of the other two men. He swore under his breath. How had he missed them? Now there were four of them he quickly recalculated. Fight or run? But it was too late. They had him boxed in. Two to the rear and the two newcomers appearing from behind some stacked packing cases fifty yards in front of him. A high wall ran along his left-hand side, and to his right the river slapped insolently against the wharf.

'That wasn't very clever, was it?' he muttered to himself crossly.

What about diving into the river and swimming out to the barge, he wondered briefly? But no. The barge was already out of range and moving quickly even more so. Besides, he suspected that the water would probably do more harm to his health than the four men starting to close upon him.

In an attempt to buy the tiniest element of surprise, Caspasian put into action a deception plan. He let his chin sink towards his chest and slipped into a less assertive stride. He staggered, stumbling with a loud curse at the imaginary object that had tripped him. He began to sing, breaking off to wave an arm towards the river as if conducting a conversation with himself, hoping to appear every inch a hopeless and defenceless drunk.

As he covered the final yards between himself and the two men to his front, they moved to block his path. From behind he heard the footsteps of the other pair, accelerating to join their comrades, although without any sense of urgency. Caspasian veered unsteadily towards the nearest of the two men, raising his eyes and pretending to find difficulty focusing. Privately, he deepened his breath, using his diaphragm to draw it into his body, extracting every bit of oxygen from it, preparing himself.

'We've been waiting for you,' the man said. 'My mates and . . .'

Before he could finish his sentence, Caspasian went into action. He covered the intervening ground between himself and the speaker with lightning speed. Gone was the drunk. In his place was a blur of fists and feet. First in was a *mae-geri* front kick. The ball of Caspasian's right foot shot into the man's stomach driving up and through the target area. Caspasian projected the blow to a point of focus back around the spine. The man's eyes bulged and his whole body lurched upwards. His feet were lifted clean off the ground as the air was pounded from him like a thunderously punched cushion. No follow-up was necessary.

Pivoting on his left leg, Caspasian shifted his hips, rotating them into a new line. Still using his right leg for attack he drew his knee back and shot out a side kick at the man's vacantly staring companion. It connected but without the full force intended. The distancing was all wrong and Caspasian cursed himself. Nevertheless, it had bought him time. The man was still bewildered by the conversion of their prey from a piece of meat ready for tenderising into this new and far less promising object.

A quick check over his shoulder showed the other two men closing fast. They had seen what was happening and were running to join in. There would be no surprise for them. It would get harder for Caspasian from now on. Every second counted.

Making use of the last instant of hesitation on behalf of the man on whom his *yoko-geri* side kick had just failed, Caspasian shifted his stance and fired in a series of punches. The man's hands came up in defence but Caspasian's opening shots had been feints. As his opponent wondered what was happening, the first real blows were powering into his midriff, knocking the wind out of him. A *de-ashi barai* foot sweep pulled the ground from under him and a drop punch to the point of the chin put him out of the fight.

Caspasian felt hands taking rough hold of his shoulders, trying to spin him round. The reinforcements had arrived. He pretended to go with the direction of the pull, but accelerated, dropping as he did so. The punch that had been intended for his face sailed harmlessly over his head, the knuckles skimming through his hair. He heard the attacker grunt with the effort of the blow. It would have hurt. Instead, it acted to draw Caspasian's new opponent off balance. His punching arm shot out into thin air and his body followed, with Caspasian helping the momentum with a shove of his own. In the way, he planted an elbow *empi* strike, the best blow for such a close range encounter. He drove it up into the rib cage, giving a *kiai* shout from deep in the gut as he delivered the strike. Again he felt the man lift off the ground. It would have to do for now as the last of the four men was upon him.

To buy some ground and achieve the best distance for his next defence, Caspasian went into a forward roll taking him out of immediate harm's way. He came up onto his feet, turning as he did so to face his next opponent. The man opposite him showed no sign of fear. He was either stupid, Caspasian reasoned, or he knew how to handle himself. When Caspasian's feint to the man's head failed to evoke the desired response, he knew it was the latter. He dodged aside easily. With interest Caspasian understood that the man had waited until last not because he had been the slowest and therefore the last to arrive on the scene, but because he had been content to leave his companions to soften up their prey while he took stock, evaluating Caspasian's capabilities. Clearly he meant business.

Caspasian moved forward and the man retreated, hands in a boxing guard, but moving constantly, fists circling like an old prize fighter, knuckles outermost. With a jolt Caspasian knew that he was facing an army boxer. He had seen the style before, added to which were two tattoos, one on the back of each fist. One was a regimental crest, the other was a heart with a dagger through it. Though the crest was not that of the garrison battalion, Caspasian could well imagine the man as a friend of Horner's, a sparring partner perhaps. He was not in the least surprised. In fact he drew a certain perverse comfort from the knowledge as it explained the reason behind the attack.

A left jab snapped out towards Caspasian's nose. Fast. Very fast. But the power behind it was all from the shoulders. While strong enough, it lacked the penetration that a twist of the hips and a proper follow-through would have delivered. But then that was the jab for you, Caspasian reflected clinically, despite the pressure of the moment. It was a door opener. The gateway to other things. And sure enough these followed. Two more jabs, a right and then another left, and then the big one, a right hook. Or rather an attempt at one. The boxer shuffled forward and this time he put the punch in with the hips behind it, a neat little twist. But for the twist to have its proper effect the blow would need to land, and Caspasian had no intention of allowing it to do so.

Slipping to his left into a *kokutsu-dachi* cat stance, his right hand used a *kake-uke* block to envelope the boxer's punching wrist. Once again Caspasian used his opponent's own momentum to lever him off balance. As he did so, he tightened his hold on the boxer's wrist, drawing it down, opening his opponent's flank to an open-handed *shuto* strike with his left, aimed at the bottom of the ribcage. It connected nicely and he saw the pain register on his opponent's face. But the boxer twisted savagely from the hips, jarring himself out of Caspasian's grasp and bringing himself round to face his attacker again. At the same time he levelled a left upper cut at Caspasian's jaw. It struck home.

Caspasian reeled back out of range, head swimming. The words 'this is bad' sang in his head. Stupid too. Anger at his own carelessness raged inside him, threatening to destroy his remaining calm. He had taken too much for granted. Arrogance and overconfidence had almost done for him. He had not given the boxer his due, assuming his own skills to be superior. They were, but not when watered down with pride.

Far from resting on his laurels, the boxer, like any professional, was pushing home his attack. He had seen the effect of his punch and knew that his window of opportunity would remain open for a second. Possibly two, but no more. He came in fast and low in a crouching stance, fists curled and angling for the best opening. And therein lay his error. For he did not know the man he was up against. The heart and focus of any other man would have blinked. Not this one.

Instead of retreating with a backward step, gathering his efforts for a renewed defence or attack, Caspasian advanced straight into the boxer. Leaving his repertoire of hand and foot blows momentarily behind, Caspasian laid firm hand grips on the boxer's sleeve and jacket lapels, turned his back into him, lowered his hips and went for a throw. The boxer sailed up and over, with Caspasian accelerating his fall using the hard ground as a weapon, flinging the man against it. The boxer fell badly but not trusting the fall itself to complete the job for him, Caspasian went in hard and fast, dropping two rapid punches with the right fist one after the other. Nose and jaw. Both connected. The boxer was out for the count.

Caspasian pulled back immediately, surveying his handiwork.

His eyes still watered from the upper cut and he could taste blood, but at least he was standing which was more than could be said for his four attackers. Two lay still, the others moaned and rolled on the ground. A quick check on the two silent bodies showed them to be basically all right. Neither would be going anywhere in a hurry but they were alive and would remain so. Of the other two, neither was in much of a position to talk. Both were spitting blood and Caspasian's questions met only with glazed, unfocused stares from rotating eyes. There would be a few sore heads in the morning.

The contents of their pockets revealed little more by way of information. They had clearly prepared for the fight by removing all means of identification. It had all the hallmarks of a professional job, except for the outcome. Caspasian was not going to shed any tears over that.

He straightened his clothes, cricked his neck and rubbed his jaw, mopped the blood from his shirt front as best he could, and left the scene. He considered summoning the police but decided against it. If Westacott and Horner had indeed been behind the attack, there was no saying who else among the local authorities were also in league with them. The last thing he needed was to find himself under arrest for causing an affray.

The walk back to the hotel gave him a chance to regain his equilibrium. The tension drained from his legs and arms, and he felt almost light-headed for a while as the adrenaline seeped away. By the time he arrived back he was calm, although the growing bruise on his face and his dishevelled and stained clothes gave away his recent activities. Walking in through the doorway he entered the reception hall and came face to face with Brigadier Percival. In an instant his calm vanished.

The Brigadier looked him up and down as if inspecting a wayward and unpromising recruit on the parade square. 'Been in the wars, have we? I might have guessed. A drunken brawl, I suppose?'

Coming so recently from a fight, Caspasian was half-minded to continue the motion with an uppercut of his own. Instead he smiled wearily. 'Good evening, Brigadier. Did you have a smooth crossing?'

'Bloody awful. The sea was as choppy as hell and I'm decidedly not a good sailor. I hate the blasted stuff.'

'Then I hope rivers don't have the same effect on you.'

The Brigadier scowled at him. 'What's all this nonsense about the garrison commander refusing to cooperate?'

Caspasian smiled with genuine pleasure. 'Hearing that makes the wait worthwhile. Westacott's a thoroughly unpleasant character . . .'

'Major Westacott to you, Caspasian. You might not like the man but I won't tolerate insubordination.'

'Then Major Westacott's your man, sir,' Caspasian said with heavy emphasis on the 'Major'.

Percival sighed and shook his head. 'A trip upriver with you and Westacott at each other's throats is just what I don't need. London's going mad over this airship business. First the *D100* and now the sister ship as well. News of these sightings is starting to leak out and the PM's given the Imperial Intelligence Service a direct order to get to the bottom of it.'

'So when do we leave, sir? It'll take Westa . . . Major Westacott time to get an expedition together.'

Percival smiled. 'No it won't.'

'Oh?'

'I've already seen him. We're leaving at first light tomorrow.'

Caspasian stared at the Brigadier who took transparent delight in his stupefaction. 'But his refusal . . . ?'

'He completely denied it. Said you failed to explain yourself clearly.'

'That's absolute rubbish! Surely you don't believe . . .'

The Brigadier held up his hand. 'Enough! I don't have time for this. I'll see you at first light.' He inspected Caspasian's dishevelled clothes once again. 'And I suggest you make sure you are suitably attired and equipped for the trip.'

'I can see to that myself but I'd be grateful for a few loans from the Major's armoury,' Caspasian said.

'Then I suggest you contact his Sergeant Major. Man by the name of . . .'

'Horner,' Caspasian said dryly.

'You've met him?'

'Yes. And a few of his chums, I think.'

'Well, be that as it may,' the Brigadier continued quickly, guessing the implication but refusing to dig deeper, 'he's your man. Seemed a good fellow to me,' he added brightly. 'In fact, he'll be coming with us.'

The rendezvous on the following morning was only about half a mile from the point where Caspasian had had his brush with the boxer and his friends. Together with Brigadier Percival, Caspasian arrived on the waterfront at first light, to find a moderately-sized diesel engined craft waiting for them. Milling around on the quayside were about half a dozen soldiers at whom Sergeant Major Horner was shouting. Caspasian and Percival swapped glances.

'Just leave the man to Westacott,' Percival said. 'We'll get upriver, carry out our investigation and return.'

'As you say, Brigadier,' Caspasian answered, feeling himself bridle at the sight and sound of Horner and his loudmouthed bullying.

When they drew near, Horner slammed to attention and saluted Brigadier Percival. 'Good morning, sir. Nice to see you, sir. Ready for our little jaunt, are you, sir?' he barked. His features did not seem used to the broad smile that he attempted to give.

Percival returned the salute with the usual lazy wave of a

senior officer. 'Good morning, Sergeant Major. Nice to see you're ready bright and early.'

Horner beamed. 'Punctual, sir. That's me, sir. Set your watch by me, sir.'

'Where's Major Westacott?' Percival asked.

'On board, sir. Stowing his bags.'

Percival turned to Caspasian. 'Did you liaise with the Sergeant Major about your requirements for the trip?'

The Sergeant Major answered for him. 'Stuff's already on board, sir. All of it that we could get, that is.' He fired a rapid glance at Caspasian. 'Expecting a war, are you, sir?'

'No harm in being prepared for the worst,' Caspasian said, forcing himself to relax. They were going to be confined together on the boat for several days at the least. It would not do to fall out in the first hour of the first day.

The boat was a flat-bottomed craft used for ferrying passengers and cargo upriver. Boasting a handful of cabins, it consisted of a wooden superstructure on a rusting metal hull. Two large deck areas, one fore and a larger one aft, were linked by a walkway down either side. Down in the engine room, someone was gunning the motor sending clouds of noisome black smoke from the single funnel into the early morning air.

A scruffy, furtive-looking man in vest, shorts and flip-flops appeared on the bridge wiping his oily hands on a large filthy rag. Major Westacott emerged on the deck below him. He saluted the Brigadier sloppily and jerked his head in the direction of the bridge. 'Our captain,' he said scathingly. 'Best we could do, given the short notice.'

'What's his name?' Percival asked.

'Jose Contreras,' Westacott answered. He eyed Caspasian suspiciously. 'Ah, Captain Caspasian. Good to see you again.' He held out his hand and Caspasian almost passed out with the shock. The two men shook hands warily. 'You should have explained what you were after.'

Deciding not to pursue the matter, Caspasian shrugged and forced a smile. Keeping his temper was going to be very difficult indeed.

Seeing that he was not going to get a rise out of Caspasian, Westacott mentally dismissed him and engaged the Brigadier in conversation about the mission. While the two of them talked and Horner continued the loading of the stores, Caspasian took his luggage and the Brigadier's on board, edging gingerly up the rotten gangplank.

Horner scurried after him. 'I've allocated you a cabin by the rear deck,' he said. 'Brigadier Percival's got one next to the Major's up behind the bridge.'

'That'll be fine, thank you,' Caspasian said, trying not to look at the man. 'How many men have you got?'

'The Major said to detail a section but I reckoned six ought to do the job.'

Two soldiers shuffled past carrying a crate between them. 'Scratch, you horrible little man!' Horner shouted unnecessarily loudly, seeing as the unfortunate private was right next to him at the time. 'Careful with those rifles!'

'Right you are, Sergeant Major. Right you are,' the miserable individual replied feebly.

His eyes still trying to ignite the soldier, Sergeant Major Horner twisted his mouth in Caspasian's direction. 'Nasty piece of work, that one, sir. Watch him like a hawk. His mate Smudger's not much better.' He raised his voice again. 'Are you, Smudger?'

'What's that, Sergeant Major?'

Horner laughed, enjoying his power over the two soldiers who scurried out of harm's way.

The sun had climbed well up in the sky by the time the boat got under way. Brigadier Percival fretted at the prow, frequently consulting his watch and glancing menacingly up towards the bridge where Captain Contreras seemed to spend a lot of time talking with Major Westacott. Caspasian could not help thinking that the two of them looked uncomfortably like partners in crime, but the Brigadier was running the show now so Caspasian decided to sit back and enjoy the excursion.

Georgetown was soon left behind, the last of the outskirts giving way to scattered farmsteads which stretched along the river banks for mile after mile. Caspasian joined the Brigadier and together they watched the sluggish waters slide by. Sergeant Major Horner materialised at Percival's elbow with a mug of tea.

'I had young Scratch put on a brew, sir,' he said, handing the mug to the pleasantly surprised Brigadier. He looked briefly at Caspasian. 'There's one for you in the galley.'

When he had gone, the Brigadier tried his tea and found it to be very palatable having been made in true army style, strong and with plenty of sugar. 'You see,' he said pompously. 'You were wrong about Horner. He's a good man, like any Sergeant Major in a decent county regiment. Backbone of the army.' He smirked. 'Don't take it too hard, just because he didn't bring you a mug.'

'Oh don't worry about that, Brigadier,' Caspasian replied. 'He must have known I wouldn't have fallen for an old trick like that.'

'What do you mean?' the Brigadier asked, taking another sip of his tea.

'I remember an old soldier telling me once how he got his revenge on the CO by spitting in his tea before giving it to him.'

The Brigadier sniggered. 'Nice try, Caspasian. Nice try.' Caspasian shrugged and walked away in search of his own mug which he would pour himself. Halfway along the deck he heard a splash in the water and looked round to see the last drops of the Brigadier's tea being dispatched overboard.

The rest of the day was spent with everyone trying to keep out of everyone else's way. Sergeant Major Horner's voice bellowed all over the small vessel, making it seem even smaller than it already was. Caspasian located the galley where he befriended the miserable Scratch who had been relegated to the position of expedition tea maker. In the late afternoon Caspasian made his way there for another mug of tea from the water boiler that Scratch kept constantly bubbling away. With his steaming mug in his hand he returned to his cabin and lay on his bunk with a copy of Buchan's *Greenmantle*, an enjoyably far-fetched tale which provided light relief from his other current read, Conrad's much darker *Victory*.

Supper was taken centrally and provided Caspasian with plenty of practice in the exercise of self-control. Major Westacott and the Brigadier chatted away merrily, Sergeant Major Horner clearly out of his depth and highly uncomfortable at the lower end of the table. At one point Captain Contreras popped in to see what was on offer but one look at the all-in stew was enough to send him muttering back to his bridge. None of the diners complained at his absence as he had not bothered to change out of the same oil-stained vest and shorts.

With conversation and food both drying up, the Brigadier rose from his chair. The others followed his lead, bade each other a good night and withdrew. As Caspasian made his way down to his deck, Major Westacott caught him up.

'I say, Caspasian. About the other day. No hard feelings, eh?'

Caspasian wondered whether he was referring to his outburst at the headquarters or the attack on the waterfront. Either way his answer was the same. 'Don't worry about it.'

Westacott eyed him suspiciously. 'That's the spirit, old man. Bit of a nuisance, all of this. You know how it is.'

Caspasian nodded, feeling his knuckles twitch with the desire to launch themselves into the Major's gut.

Almost at his cabin door, Caspasian heard a commotion in the nearby galley. He edged towards the entrance. Sergeant Major Horner had Scratch pressed up against the bulkhead.

'I told you to have them polished by sundown, you piece of filth,' he hissed in Scratch's ear. With one beefy hand, Horner was driving the soldier's face sideways into the closed porthole. In the other he hefted a pair of boots, the toe caps dull and scuffed.

'Sorry, Sergeant Major,' Scratch mumbled, his words muted thanks to the bulkhead.

'Sorry, Sergeant Major,' Horner mimicked savagely, whining Scratch's words back at him like a playground bully with a new boy.

Caspasian had had enough. An incandescent fury burned in him. He was going to dismantle the Sergeant Major piece by piece and feed him to the fish. He marched forward, prepared for battle.

Darting out of the shadows and barging in front of him, another one of the soldiers plunged into the galley and seized the boots out of the startled Sergeant Major's hand.

'Blimey, Scratch! There they are. I've been looking for these all over the bloody boat.' The wiry little soldier beamed at Horner, nonplussed at the spectacle of the bully pressing his friend into the porthole's brass frame. 'Don't mind me, Sergeant Major. I told Scratchy I'd do the boots if he'd take my stag on duty this evening. My fault. No harm done.' Like a professional stage actor he turned around and spoke into the shadows where Caspasian's outline was just visible. 'Oh, good evening there, sir. Nice night, isn't it?'

Sergeant Major Horner glanced up, squinting into the darkness outside the galley until Caspasian took a step forward. The two men sized each other up. Horner released his grip on Scratch who shrank away from him, rubbing his face where the porthole's outline had been temporarily branded.

'On your way to bed, sir?' the Sergeant Major said, uneasy at being caught.

Caspasian had to admire the deftness with which the new arrival had handled things. The man had presented all of them with an exit from an explosive situation. It was only fitting that they should all accept it with gratitude.

'Exactly, Sergeant Major,' he replied, keeping Horner fixed in his cold stare.

'I was just finishing here myself,' Horner said, smiling crookedly. 'Now Smudger's cleared up a little misunderstanding I'll be on my way.' He looked at each of the others in turn before wheeling about and leaving, drawing his pride behind him like a bridal train.

When he had gone and Caspasian was confident that they were alone, he cursorily inspected Scratch's face. 'Does this happen a lot?'

Scratch moved his head, halfway between a nod and a shake. His mate answered for him.

'All the bloody time, sir,' Smudger said. 'All the bloody time.' He turned to his friend. 'You all right, Scratchy?'

'Yeah,' Scratch replied unconvincingly.

'Someone's got to put a stop to him,' Smudger ventured, taking advantage of the promising situation. 'No one in the regiment dares. Not now the Colonel's gone. Someone's . . .'

'That'll do, Smudger,' Caspasian said smiling. 'I get the message.'

'Right you are, sir. Only saying my piece, like. I mean, a man's got to, hasn't he, sir?'

Caspasian sighed. 'Yes, Smudger. A man's got to.'

He left the two soldiers gossiping like a couple of maiden aunts and returned to his cabin, regretting his lost showdown with Horner. He undressed and got into bed. Lying in the dark, staring up at the ceiling, he could not help thinking of his fellow passengers on the *D200*. He had to know what had happened to them. Gustav Wolter, Harrison, Richard and, of course, Emma. His present company was hardly the most fitting for a mission into the depths of the South American jungle but he would play with the hand he had been dealt. Right now it was all he could do.

I I

The column had been marching for weeks, or so it seemed to Gustav Wolter. In truth, he recognized that it had only been a few days since they had been taken prisoner. But time had a way of extending itself in periods of fear and discomfort. He had noticed the same phenomenon during his service in Zeppelins in the war. A mission of a single night's duration could seem like a week or more if terror was the ruling emotion. Agony was always prolonged. Why was it not the same with joy? At times like that he felt he really had to question whether the God who governed the destiny of the world was indeed a benevolent one. His manipulation of time was hardly evidence of it.

Rain had just started to fall. The jungle had thinned considerably and clearings were now a frequent occurrence in the landscape of low undulating hills they had entered. Although the rain had come in the form of a fine drizzle, it still thoroughly soaked everyone. It simply took longer to do so. The guards, perverse as ever, had halted the column in the middle of an open space to ensure the greatest torment from the sudden shower. They themselves had grouped under cover some dozen or more yards away, keeping a lazy watch, rifles couched in their folded arms in a slovenly fashion. To Wolter they mostly looked to be Latins, though some were clearly of jungle Indian stock. To a man however, regardless of race, they were morose and mean-spirited.

Wolter and the others had sat down immediately on being told they could catch their breath for a few minutes. The instructions had not been as coherent as that. Instead, the grumpy leader of the guards, a man Wolter had deduced from overheard snippets was called Rodriguez, had simply pointed at the ground, waved his rifle barrel threateningly at Captain Harrison, and given vent to an outburst of shouted Spanish, none of which Wolter had understood. Harrison, whether out of understanding or just from sheer exhaustion, had sunk to the ground where he was. Rodriguez had grunted and walked away, obviously content with the result, so the rest of the captives had followed suit.

They were all in bad shape and the soaking was not helping. Far from being fresh and cooling, it further irritated their already sore limbs. Sweat-drenched clothing had rubbed and chafed, and branches and undergrowth had cut and scratched, until everyone was not only exhausted but also starting to resemble a ragtag assortment of scarecrows. The other passengers were dismayed to see how rapidly a band of well-heeled travellers in the modern age could so deteriorate the moment the mainstays of their support system had been removed. Wolter had not been so surprised, having seen such degradation before.

To someone like Lionel Domain, on the other hand, the experience had proved truly shocking. Of all the passengers Domain had fared the worst. Initially he had tried remonstrating with his captors, adopting the role of movie mogul in a display of bombast that, for a moment, Wolter had thought just might work. It had certainly impressed him. The next instant, Domain had been stopped in mid-sentence by a rifle butt in the stomach. Not content to leave it at that, the guard responsible had closed in to give his fallen captive several hearty kicks with the toe of his boot, while his companions had looked on approvingly. Captain Harrison had tried to intervene but had received similar treatment. After that, no one else had tried to stop the beating. They had guiltily looked away.

All except Richard Edward who had stared horrified and, the moment the guards had withdrawn, he had rushed up to administer what help he could to the two injured men. Indeed, as far as Wolter was concerned, Richard was turning out to be the hero of the whole dismal piece. It was almost possible to overlook his disability for everyone was hobbling now, and in fact Richard's energy more than compensated for any ungainliness of step. He was everywhere, hastening the others and encouraging.

Another thing that Wolter had noticed was how the guards themselves responded positively to Richard, to the point where, eventually, they used him as an intermediary. He had a smattering of Spanish, the result of past trade missions on behalf of his father. This, combined with his resilience and mind-over-matter attitude, impressed the guards.

Wolter shrugged down into his shirt. His sodden jacket lay crumpled in his lap. His shoes squelched water and a fine viscous mud. He looked up and found two of the guards observing him. They grinned. One pretended to offer him a lighted cigarette. Wolter did not respond, knowing the outcome if he showed an interest. Nothing. At best, a burst of mocking laughter. He was wise to that old trick. He had been a prisoner of the British after being shot down over England. Guards the world over probably acted in the same way. Given a modicum of control over other people's lives, they could not resist rubbing a captive's nose in it.

He raised his face to the rain just as it strengthened out of drizzle into a cascade of fat, warm drops. He ran his hand through his hair. He needed a shave. Not much chance of that, he thought ruefully. Strangest of all had been the disappearance of Emma Lavelle from their party. No one had seen her since the storm on board the *D200*. Domain had mumbled something about her still being on board. If she was, then good luck to her, Wolter reckoned. It could not be any worse than this torment in the jungle. He tried not to think of the alternatives if the guards had got hold of a woman like her.

'How's it going, then?'

He looked round to see Richard Edward settling down beside him. 'Absolutely marvellous,' Wolter said smiling. 'I'm having the time of my life.'

Richard's expression of good intent faltered until he saw that there was a complete absence of malice or sarcasm in Wolter's response. Just a dry Teutonic irony. 'Whatever do you think they want with us?'

'My dear fellow, I haven't the slightest idea. I'm just grateful that they didn't kill us out of hand.' He pondered for a second before adding, 'I think.'

Several yards away Captain Harrison and Lionel Domain sat side by side. Neither spoke.

'Harrison's taking it very badly,' Richard said. 'I think he sees it all as his fault.'

'Well, he needn't,' Wolter answered. 'No one could have countered the use of a knockout gas.'

'Is that what it was?'

Wolter nodded. 'Must have been. I thought I recognized the smell when I woke up, and the headache . . .' He rubbed his temples as he remembered.

'Me too,' Richard added. 'My head was splitting. But who? Especially as they scuppered the plan of the two stowaways.'

'I still think Lieutenant Davies was in on it. Harrison swears he wasn't, but if not, then where is he now?'

Apart from Emma Lavelle, Lieutenant Davies and the reporter who had been shot when the airship had been seized, everyone else was accounted for, present in the rainswept jungle clearing.

'And it was Davies who ordered us all to return to our cabins, don't forget. Harrison says he doesn't remember that. I reckon Davies gassed him first of all, probably in the control car, then gave the order to us. Once we were all conveniently out of the way, he turned on the gas, presumably wearing a mask himself, and then brought the airship down to a prearranged rendezvous.'

Richard stared at him in amazement. 'Could he have done that all by himself?'

'It wouldn't have been easy, but certainly possible. He was a very experienced airship pilot. It's possible to handle both elevator and rudder wheels together.'

'So where's the airship now?' Richard asked.

'Your guess is as good as mine.'

'And what on earth would he want it for?'

Wolter shrugged. 'I don't know. But an airship's worth a great deal of money, quite apart from the political implications of the theft.'

There was a shout from Rodriguez and he strode out from under the cover of the trees to level a savage kick at the nearest of the captives.

Richard sighed. 'I think our host wants us to be on our way again.'

Wolter got up quickly to help Richard to his feet. Richard thanked him. 'It's too bad that Caspasian fellow isn't here,' he said.

'Caspasian? Why?' Wolter asked, bemused. 'He'd just be another unfortunate in the same mess we're in.'

'Oh I don't know,' Richard said. 'He didn't seem the type to get himself in a fix like this. Or if he did, I somehow suspect he'd find a way out of it fairly quickly.'

Wolter laughed. 'Who knows?' He stretched his aching limbs and, together with Richard and the others, began to shuffle forwards again, herded like cattle by the guards. 'But he isn't here. The big question is, where are they taking us, and why? I'm afraid that neither Caspasian nor anyone else can help us. We're on our own. It's us, and the charming Rodriguez of course.'

★

The boat was making good progress. Each day had seen them penetrating ever deeper into the thickly forested landscape. Settlements and farmsteads had been left behind and, in their place, the lush green jungle had closed in on either bank. The river itself had narrowed and was continuing to do so, to the alarm of Major Westacott who had anticipated an easy jaunt all the way to Sansaka.

What alarmed Caspasian, on the other hand, was the attitude of Westacott and Horner. It was obvious that neither of them had ever ventured this far up-country. In fact, Caspasian doubted they had ever set foot outside Georgetown. In addition, their routine precautions were virtually nonexistent. It was only after Caspasian had suggested to Brigadier Percival that at least one sentry would be a good idea, that anything had happened. Percival had passed on the concern to Westacott as if it had stemmed from himself, and the basic procedure had been enacted. Caspasian was desperate to take charge of the whole operation but Percival was keeping him on a tight rein. For the moment at least, Percival said, it was diplomatic to leave things in Westacott's hands, although even the Brigadier himself was starting to notice that the cantankerous major had little idea how to acquit himself on operations.

Horner was proving little better now that he was away from the barracks environment. He compensated for his lack of field knowledge by an increasingly obstreperous manner. Despite being on a boat and headed into the jungle, he maintained a barrack-square rigidity which, Caspasian was certain, would eventually prove disastrous for everyone. Flexibility was unknown to him. He marched about the vessel with his pace stick under his arm, unless, of course, he was using the brass-tipped point to jab at some unwary soldier or offending piece of equipment that had caught his malicious eye.

Caspasian was not in the least surprised therefore, that it was left to him to detect that the boat was being watched from the banks. At first it was very hard to be certain. It came in the form of a vague suspicion. An uneasiness. Initially Caspasian discounted it as just an attack of the jitters. The jungle was renowned for playing tricks on people. But he had been in the jungle on numerous occasions before and was surprised that he should be feeling eyes upon him. And yet he did.

Then, at one particular bend in the river, he was convinced he had seen some foliage move, a branch springing back to shield watching eyes. Percival sneered at his suspicions. 'Probably a monkey. Don't be such a chump. Or should I say, chimp? Ha ha!'

Caspasian smiled, refraining from pointing out that chimpanzees did not live in the South American jungle. Horner overheard the Brigadier's repartee and used the opportunity to have a dig of his own at the despised Captain, pitching it so that it would have been churlish for Caspasian to respond. Caspasian bit his lip and forced another smile. But they were making his face ache, and his knuckles were itching to answer for him.

Finally, confirmation came that Caspasian's intuition had been sound. He was standing beside the Brigadier, Major Westacott and Sergeant Major Horner on the deck, each of them enjoying an enamel mug of hot sugary tea courtesy of Scratch, when the slenderest of arrows hummed clear through the centre of their well-spaced group and struck deftly into the wooden superstructure beside them with a loud thud. For a full second they stared at it, wide-eyed. The next instant, Westacott and Horner threw themselves flat, mugs clattering to the deck. Brigadier Percival ducked, tea slopping over his trousers as his eyes scanned the forest for signs of the firer. Only Caspasian remained at his post. Curious, he studied the arrow, sipping his tea and hugely enjoying the discomfort of the others.

'Get down, man!' Westacott bellowed at him. 'Sergeant Major, have the men stand to!'

'Sir!' Horner screamed in return. 'Stand to!' He slithered away on his belly, his sweat-creased shirt mopping up the spilt tea as he went.

'Caspasian! Get down, I said!' Westacott repeated.

Caspasian lightly fingered the arrow's delicate flights, marvelling at the brilliant green feathers. 'Not much point in that,' he said drily. 'If they'd wanted to hit us I'm sure they could have done so. If the Indians can knock a fleeing monkey out of the treetops with their first shot, I'm sure a tea-drinking Englishman would not have proved a problem.'

Westacott stared up at him, livid. His face became increasingly scarlet as the truth of Caspasian's observation sank in. Caspasian gripped the arrow's shaft and tugged it out of the woodwork. He inspected the tip, sniffing it.

'And if it had been meant for any of us the tip would have been coated with curare. That's strychnos toxifera to you, Major.'

Westacott started to work his way to his feet, brushing himself down as he did so. 'Thank you for the lecture, Captain,' he said crossly.

Caspasian decided not to add that if the Major had indeed been hit with a curare-tipped arrow, he would now be in the final spasms of a very unpleasant death, as opposed to merely hurt pride.

Brigadier Percival quickly reassumed his position, sipping the remnants of his tea. He stared steely-eyed at the wall of forest that lapped at the river's edge, long dangling fronds concealing the actual banks. Suddenly he pointed.

'There! Look!'

In a ragged window of vegetation, a single figure was boldly studying the boat. He stood unmoving, face devoid of expression. Nearly naked, the Indian wore a fan-shaped headdress of bright emerald-coloured feathers. Streaks of paint fashioned lightning shapes on his high cheekbones and across his chest.

He was powerfully built and in his right hand he held a bow. An arrow was in his left hand, at rest by his side.

'Sergeant Major!' Westacott bellowed.

'I'm onto him, sir!'

Before Caspasian could react, Horner burst out on deck wielding a Lewis gun, a drum magazine attached and ready.

'No!' Caspasian shouted.

Horner levelled it at the standing figure and pulled the trigger. There was a metallic clunk as the hammer slammed onto an empty breech. Horner cursed and snatched angrily at the cocking handle. Fortunately for Caspasian, the Sergeant Major's weapon-handling drills were abysmal. In four giant strides Caspasian reached him and swung the barrel into the air just as it fired. A stream of bullets stabbed harmlessly into the watery sky. The recoil took Horner completely by surprise and propelled him back into the bulkhead with a thud. He winced and dropped the big gun. It crashed to the deck.

Unable to stop himself, Horner growled and hurled himself at Caspasian. 'You little arse . . .'

But Caspasian was no longer there. He had moved. In his place was the waist-high bulwark at the edge of the deck over which the Sergeant Major pivoted and fell head first into the river. There was a stunned hush from the soldiers who had been lounging in the shadows, and then bursts of howling laughter interlaced with a couple of cheers.

One evil-eyed glare from Westacott was all it took to bring instant silence. 'Help him!' he shouted at Smudger and Scratch, the nearest of the group. Restraining their giggles with a transparently painful effort, they scuttled towards the side and peered over into the water where the Sergeant Major was thrashing noisily.

'Stop the bloody boat!' Westacott yelled up to the bridge. He swung to face Caspasian. 'You!' he said, firing a finger at him. 'You'll regret this. By God you will.'

Caspasian was in half a mind to throw the Major overboard as well. Percival read his intentions and stepped between the two men. 'That'll do, both of you,' he said calmly as if intervening in a playground squabble.

Westacott stared at him, outraged. 'That'll do? Aren't you going to discipline him? Put him under close arrest?'

For a moment Caspasian thought the idea might appeal to his old enemy, but to his relief the Brigadier shushed Westacott into silence.

'Caspasian was quite right. The last thing we need is a war with the locals.'

'The locals?' Westacott said staring dumbfounded. 'This isn't bloody Sevenoaks. They're savages. Headhunters, probably.'

'Exactly,' the Brigadier answered, maintaining an admirable calm. 'It's because they're savages that we don't want to antagonize them unnecessarily.' He glanced towards the jungle and saw that the Indian had disappeared. Percival frowned. 'I just hope they haven't already taken the Sergeant Major's lack of hospitality the wrong way.'

An exaggerated spluttering and violent curses announced the arrival of the Sergeant Major back on board. He slapped aside the helping hands of Smudger and Scratch and shot fiery daggers at Caspasian. Major Westacott left the Brigadier and Caspasian in disgust and went to minister to Horner's damaged pride.

'That was not very bright, Caspasian,' the Brigadier said in a low voice once Westacott was out of earshot. He held up a hand as Caspasian started to object. 'But you did exactly the right thing.' He grimaced. 'It's just a pity you couldn't have caught Horner instead of sending him over the side.'

Caspasian glanced back at the Sergeant Major who was viciously fending off Scratch's attempts to help.

'I'm just sorry there weren't any crocodiles around.'

The one positive effect of the arrow incident, as far as Caspasian could see, was that it caused Westacott and Horner to tighten up their security procedures. Sentries were doubled and everyone with a firearm was issued with extra ammunition. Caspasian's big fear now was that his escort would be overly trigger-happy and turn their weapons on the wrong people. He himself, in addition to his Webley revolver, had been given a Lee Enfield rifle, of the Short Mark IV variety. It was in lamentable condition so the first thing he did was to take it back to his cabin, strip it down and give it a thorough clean with rifle oil. Small patches of rust hid in amongst the working parts, any one of them capable of engineering a stoppage at a critical moment. It could mean the difference between life and death.

For his revolver he managed to acquire a small brown leather holster and also a pouch for the spare bullets. He looped them both onto his belt. The rifle came with an adjustable sling and a bandolier of spare ammunition clips, each of which held five .303 rounds. The rifle magazine held two such clips, a total of ten rounds available before a reload was necessary.

During his enforced wait in Georgetown, he had picked up a good pair of brown leather boots as well as a couple of changes of clothing suitable for the jungle. Other purchases included a decent pack, a mosquito net, hat and canvas hammock. He was determined to be beholden to Westacott for as little as possible. Items he could not avoid borrowing from the garrison were a prismatic compass, protractor and maps, essential navigation aids not readily available elsewhere. He was dismayed to find that the maps were rudimentary at best but they would have to do. The rivers, known settlements and the major mountain ranges were all marked, but the interior – which accounted for most of the space on the paper – was mostly blank. A complete unknown. He was reminded of explorers in past centuries blazing trails across the globe. Uncharted regions were full of dangers, sometimes imagined and sometimes real. For Caspasian though, they were the most exciting part of any expedition. Places of discovery.

It was two days after the sighting of the Indian that the boat arrived at Sansaka. One moment they were chugging idly in midstream, dense jungle on either bank, the next they rounded the slightest of bends and the jungle parted, giving way to a modest village on the left-hand side of the river. As always with such places, their arrival was announced to the world by the dogs and children, in that order. A scruffy barking yellow dog was soon joined by a host of others, followed quickly by a gang of youngsters who danced and gambolled knee-deep in the river water, waving stick thin limbs at the boat, glistening white teeth bared in the broadest of smiles.

Brigadier Percival, Caspasian and Westacott gathered in the prow to observe the place. Horner appeared at Westacott's elbow like a bad smell.

'No need to machine-gun them, Sergeant Major,' Caspasian said, unable to stop himself.

Brigadier Percival shot him a fiery glance. 'That'll do, Caspasian.'

'So what now?' Westacott asked.

'Now,' Percival replied, 'we make our inquiries and find out what they actually saw.'

A long narrow rickety pier extended from the shore into the water enabling the boat to tie up alongside. Captain Contreras examined it dubiously first and then edged his craft as close as he dared. Fortunately the gangplank was just long enough to bridge the gap and once the ropes had secured the vessel in place, the whole party made their way ashore, Brigadier Percival in the lead.

As the arrival of such a craft was a highly unusual event, the whole population of the village, alerted by dogs and children, had turned out to meet them. A reluctant village elder was pushed and jostled to the fore where he stood fingering his hat brim in his hands in front of his groin as if to shield his privates from some danger. Knock-kneed and round-shouldered, he did not exactly cut an authoritative figure with the Brigadier. None-theless, with an eye to protocol, Percival paid him due respect. Caspasian was impressed, although he realized that, as ever, the Brigadier's apparently generous behaviour was motivated solely by self-interest.

The village elder's command of English was surprisingly good and they soon learned that the report from Percival's agent had been correct. An airship had indeed been sighted by some villagers on a hunting trip a couple of days' march south of the village.

'Can we speak to them?' Brigadier Percival asked eagerly, eyes bright with anticipated triumph.

The elder solemnly shook his head. 'Not possible,' he said.

The Brigadier maintained his smile. 'Why?'

'They are on a hunting trip.'

'Another one?'

'Si.'

'All of them?'

'Si.'

Westacott could no longer contain his impatience. 'Well that's a blasted inconvenience. We come all the way up the god-forsaken river and the blighters have buggered off into the jungle.'

Percival waved aside his complaint and asked the elder when the hunting party was expected back. A muddled consultation followed before he replied, 'One week, señor. Maybe.'

Westacott cursed. Alarmed by the Major's anger, there was a further and more agitated consultation amongst the villagers after which the elder said, 'But there is another.'

'Another what?' Westacott snapped.

'Another man. Maybe he can help.'

Percival and Caspasian swapped glances. 'Take us to him,' Percival said quickly, his previous eagerness returning.

The crowd parted and the elder led the way into the heart of the settlement. It was a miserable place, the ramshackle houses mostly on stilts to lift them above the reach of snakes and flood water. Only the poorest dwellings sat on the hard earthen floor, resembling upturned conical wicker baskets with holes cut in the sides for door and windows.

Arriving at one of the grandest of the huts, the elder mounted a precarious-looking ladder and beckoned his guests to follow him. Percival, Caspasian and Westacott did so, Horner and the remainder of the escort remaining behind. The children were taking immense delight in taunting the Sergeant Major, running up and tugging at the hem of his bush shirt. The first few tugs were misinterpreted as flies and he swatted them irritably until he discovered their true source. When he did so, great hoots of laughter erupted from the children and the Sergeant Major treated them to his most evil of scowls, his fingers stroking his rifle's trigger guard, aching for the command to open fire.

The interior of the hut was gloomy, thickened by the smoke from a smouldering fire over which some fish were giving off a nauseating smell. It caught in the back of Westacott's throat and he covered his mouth and nose with his hand, being sure that the elder was made aware of his disgust.

In a back room, they found the body of a man lying on a straw mat. At first they thought he was dead, but a quick inspection showed him to be sleeping, although in a poor state of health.

'Who is he?' the Brigadier asked in a hushed voice.

'We do not know. He just says his name is Ramos. That is all. He was found on the edge of the village only yesterday.' The elder touched one finger tip to his temple and rolled his eyes. 'He is . . . you know.'

'And does he say he saw the airship, too?' Caspasian asked.

In reply the elder reached down to the sleeping man and pulled at a chain hanging round his neck. Out from inside his grubby sweat-soaked shirt, a small metallic representation of an airship emerged.

'Well I'll be . . . !' Westacott said staring.

The next second the man awoke, starting up in alarm from his mat. One hand grasped at the talisman and the other fended off the elder's wrist. His eyes were wide and filled with terror. They darted from one to another of the men grouped about him until Caspasian placed a hand on his shoulder and calmed him.

When he finally understood that they were not going to hurt him, he gabbled at them in Spanish.

'What's he saying?' Percival asked the elder.

Hearing the Brigadier's words, recognition dawned on the man's face and he said, 'English? You are English?'

Percival smiled with relief. 'Yes. Who are you and how did you come by that pendant?' He reached towards it, holding out his open hand. 'May I see it, please?'

For a moment the man hesitated, sizing up the request. At last he withdrew the chain from around his neck and handed it over. 'It was given to me by a friend.'

Percival, Caspasian and Westacott stooped over their treasure to examine it. Percival turned it over and over, studying every aspect of it. A smile slowly dawned. 'It's the *D100*,' he said. He looked at the man. 'You are Ramos, is that correct?'

'Sí,' the man nodded.

'I have come a long way to find out what happened to this airship. This friend of yours to whom this belonged, where is he and how did he get it?'

Ramos' face darkened. 'He is dead, señor. We were prisoners of Delgado. Many years.'

'Who is Delgado?'

'Colonel Delgado. He made us work. It was terrible, señor.'

'Yes, I understand,' Percival said as patiently as his nature allowed.

Caspasian leaned forward. 'And Delgado killed your friend?'

Ramos's eyes widened further still. 'No, señor.'

'Then who did?' Westacott interrupted.

'The men from the clouds.'

The three officers stared at one another.

Ramos looked past them, reliving some private torment. 'The men from the clouds killed my friend.'

12

Captain Contreras was impatient. He had either got out of bed on the wrong side, or was merely conducting business with a rudeness straight from the heart. Listening to the exchange between the boat's grubby Captain and the Brigadier, Caspasian knew which he thought it was.

'How long before I can return to Georgetown?' Contreras asked gruffly.

'You'll stay here until I say so.' Percival was in no mood for compromise. He could smell success. It was close. Just over the next jungle-covered range of hills perhaps.

The captain leaned over the bridge and spat into the water, projecting his gobbet of phlegm far out into the river. A fish, its body invisible beneath the thick brown surface, poked its head out to test the morsel.

'I have business to attend to,' Contreras went on in a whining tone. 'You do not know how hard it is to make a living on the river. I cannot stay moored up here indefinitely.'

Caspasian could see that Percival was close to breaking point and his heart rejoiced at the prospect.

'Captain Contreras,' the Brigadier said with dangerous emphasis. 'I have commissioned this vessel for as long as I need it. You are getting paid, so what the hell's the matter?'

Contreras's hands writhed in his pockets like snakes in a sack. 'I have a family, señor. I have duties.'

'This is your duty. For the moment. I'm not taking anything for free, dammit, man!'

Caspasian was interested to note that the Brigadier had

missed what he had not. Contreras was not worried about the money. The man was frightened. Caspasian's suspicion was confirmed the next moment.

'The river becomes too shallow from here on. I cannot navigate any further south.'

The Brigadier was busy over his map. 'What?' he said half-heartedly.

'I cannot navigate . . .'

'Oh that. I'm not asking you to. All I'm asking is that you remain here until I return.'

In an instant Contreras' face brightened as a worry lifted from his mind. 'You go on foot?'

'How else?' The Brigadier looked up, wondering at the man's stupidity. 'I'm going into the bloody jungle to the place that half-baked idiot Ramos mentioned.' He shook his head which Contreras took as a welcome sign that he had been dismissed. Before his streak of good luck expired, he tried to make himself scarce. Caspasian caught him by the arm.

'What do you know of Delgado?'

The captain grimaced, halfway between a smile and a sneer. 'Who?'

'You heard.'

'I have never heard of him, señor.'

'Colonel Delgado. Come on, Captain. Maybe you would like to accompany us?'

Fear was back on Contreras' face at the suggestion. 'But my boat . . . ?'

'Would be fine right here until you returned.'

'Please, señor, I have a family.'

The Brigadier looked up, becoming interested. He got to his feet and came across to tower over the captain. 'That's not a bad idea, Caspasian. We could use the extra man.'

Caspasian smiled at Contreras. 'You were telling us what you know about Delgado,' he prompted.

Captain Contreras located a stool and sank onto it miserably. He pulled a filthy handkerchief from his pocket and mopped his glistening brow. 'I have heard of him. That is all. I have heard that this . . . Colonel Delgado is a bandit of some kind.'

'Bandit?'

'Well, a ruler almost. He has a big gang of men. Lots of guns. They use forced labour to run his operations.'

'What kind of operations?' Caspasian asked.

Contreras shrugged, thrusting out his bottom lip. 'Smuggling, extortion,' he glanced nervously at the two men above him. 'And some mining.'

Percival nodded. 'What do they mine?'

'I don't know,' Contreras said quickly. Seeing Caspasian's mouth open for a protest he said, 'Honestly, señor, you have to believe me. I don't know. I only hear that he is a rich man.'

'And what do you know about the airship?'

Contreras shook his head. 'I have never heard of any airship, señor. All I know is that Delgado is a bad man. Very bad. You do not want to go near him, señor. And if you do, it would take a whole army to get to him.' He waved a hand dismissively at Westacott and Horner who were lounging on the lower deck after their breakfast. 'Not just a couple like them.'

Percival jerked his head in the direction of the bridge and Contreras, taking his cue, fled. When he had gone Percival said, 'Do you believe him?'

Caspasian weighed the question. 'I believe he knows more about Delgado than he's letting on. If a man like that exists, a riverboat captain would certainly know all about him. I wouldn't be surprised if Delgado's used this very boat before now. As for whatever he's mining . . .' he shrugged. 'The surest way to find out is to go and take a look.'

The Brigadier grimaced. 'My sentiments too. And the men from the clouds who Ramos mentioned? Do you think that refers to Delgado's men?'

'Doesn't sound like it. Delgado's probably some kind of jungle warlord. He just runs his own little fiefdom.'

'Perhaps it's not so little,' the Brigadier offered.

'Maybe, but it would take someone with global reach to organise the stealing of an airship. Two airships, if the *D200*'s gone the same way as her sister ship.'

'Then who else is involved?'

'I don't know. But like you, Brigadier, I believe the answer may lie with Delgado.' Caspasian smiled evenly at the Brigadier, working hard to conceal his deep mistrust of him. 'So that's where we have to go.'

Scratch, Smudger and the rest of the soldiers were swimming in the river, jumping off the pier and making as much noise as they possibly could. Down on the deck, Horner let out a sonorous belch. Westacott laughed gamely. His boots were off and he was examining his toes.

Caspasian considered them distastefully. 'And that's all we've got for company.'

At the Brigadier's insistence, a brief attempt was made to persuade Ramos to accompany the expedition. Caspasian tried to argue that in his present state of health, the man would be more of a hindrance than an asset. Eventually Percival agreed. So, in one of Ramos' more lucid moments, Percival, Caspasian and Westacott sat down with him and, with a map spread between them, they gleaned what information they could of Colonel Delgado's whereabouts.

'Don't worry, señor,' Ramos chuckled bitterly. 'You will not have to find Delgado. He will find you.'

Westacott was becoming worried. 'Look, Brigadier. Maybe we should get some more men. A company or two.'

'But I thought you said the garrison couldn't spare any more than this?' Caspasian responded pleasantly, enjoying the Major's fear.

Westacott ignored him. 'I could take the boat back to

Georgetown while you and Caspasian wait here. I'll come back
with the whole battalion. How's that?'

The Brigadier made a pretence of giving the suggestion
serious consideration before shaking his head. 'That's very
helpful of you Major, but we don't have the time. The passengers might still be alive. I can't allow the trail to go cold. We have
to press on.'

'But what can we do against Delgado?' Westacott pleaded
pathetically.

'You have a fully-armed section of British regular infantry,
Major,' Caspasian goaded. 'Do you know something about
Delgado's strengths that we don't?'

Westacott was about to round on him when the Brigadier
brought the discussion to a close. 'Gentlemen, I think we've
wasted enough time.' He consulted his watch. 'I'd like us to be
in a position to leave by midday. Major, see that the men take
an early lunch. We'll assemble on the other side of the village by
the main path.' He smiled brightly. 'That'll be all.'

Seeing that further protest was useless, Westacott went in
search of Horner to pass on the instructions.

In spite of the Brigadier's orders, it was well after noon that
the little column was finally ready to move out. The village elder
had agreed, under some duress, to provide a guide. Percival had
threatened him that, if he did not oblige, he would accompany
the column himself. Within minutes a gangly youth was being
introduced to them as Diaz. When the Brigadier had satisfied
himself to the best of his ability that the individual was not as
stupid as he looked, he agreed to the choice, much to the village
elder's relief, and shortly thereafter the column got under way.
The send off was spectacular. Once again the whole village
turned out for the occasion, and Caspasian was almost worried
that the population was going to follow them all the way to
Delgado's stronghold. However, as the pace increased and the
distance between the column and the settlement grew, one by

one the villagers peeled away until the last of the children and, finally, the dogs, abandoned them to the immensity of the jungle.

Major Westacott had made only a token protest when Percival had appointed Caspasian as column leader. Even Horner seemed a much reduced personality when confronted with the jungle. It rendered the individual irrelevant. A lone man became of absolutely no consequence at all, and try as he might, there was nothing he could do to influence this awe-inspiring environment. He could thrash at it with machete or rifle butt, claw at it with his fists, stamp on it with his boots or scream into its vast, dark heart. It did not even bother to echo his efforts back at him. It absorbed everything he was capable of throwing at it without so much as noticing.

It was no surprise to Caspasian therefore, when, barely an hour after the last of the villagers had left them, the banter amongst the soldiers ceased and everyone marched on in silence. They were like Hansel and Gretel being led ever deeper into the wild unforgiving forest without even the illusory comfort of a pocketful of bread crumbs.

As a consequence of the trepidation which had gripped the party, Caspasian decided to halt early in the evening, well before last light. Trepidation was only the shortest step from fear, and the last thing he wanted in the lead-up to a meeting with Delgado's men was for his own pitiful command to be unsettled and off balance. Knowing that darkness in the jungle fell quickly, often within minutes, he judged his halt nicely. He located a stream and selected a campsite close by. He was horrified at Westacott's men's complete lack of jungle lore, and wished, not for the first time, that he was at the head of a column of his own Gurkhas. But that would have to wait for another time. For now he would have to make do with the raw material at hand.

He appointed a place for each man, locating them in a rough circle for defensive purposes, adjusting the exact site of the positions to suit the folds of the ground. It then became obvious that hardly anyone knew how to make themselves comfortable in the jungle. So, once again, Caspasian went from man to man, helping them establish a shelter that would keep out the rain which he knew would come soon enough. Even Diaz seemed at a loss now that he was divorced from his home settlement. Westacott and Horner accepted Caspasian's advice with as bad a grace as was possible, even for them. But neither man was completely stupid. In each case, laziness and the desire for physical comfort got the better of pride, and Caspasian soon had them chopping wood and weaving fronds to fashion a water-resistant roof over their shelters.

He was not surprised to find that the Brigadier did not need his help. A fellow Indian Army officer, operations on the North-West Frontier and in the jungles of the subcontinent and of Burma had similarly equipped him for such an expedition as this.

By nightfall, campfires had been lit and meals cooked. Caspasian was all for dousing the flames and calling a stand-to at dusk, but the Brigadier quietly told him to give it a miss on this first night. It was a finely balanced decision, but he reckoned that, given the likely distance between themselves and Delgado, morale was the higher priority. And nothing so enhanced the spirits in the depths of the jungle at night as a good fire, a comfortable bed and a hot meal with a mug of sweet tea.

Reluctantly Caspasian agreed, but insisted that at the very least, two men should be on sentry duty at any one time throughout the night. He sited them himself, the two men together, covering the most likely approach into the column's leaguer position. Each man would do a two-hour stint of duty, changing at alternate hours. That way, at any one time, one would be fresh from his rest, and the other would be halfway through his duty and accustomed to the ground in front of them.

When he was content that all the men were in their correct positions, that shelters had been erected, that meals had been prepared and consumed, and that all the minutiae of a jungle night camp had been attended to, Caspasian retired to the spot he had selected for himself and sat down to drink the mug of tea prepared for him by Scratch. It was not nearly as vile as he had anticipated, although he attributed a good measure of his appreciation to the circumstances. Food and drink that would be scorned as mediocre in the mess had a way of tasting exquisite when taken in the field. Perspective, as ever, ruled.

He woke on the brink of first light. He had slept well, deciding to exclude himself from the sentry roster in order to save his energies for later when, he had no doubt, they would be needed. It was a magical time, when the night noises were transitioning into those of the day. One group of species was packing up to make way for the day shift. Insects, birds and mammals were sorting themselves out, reassigning duties and territories, and all without a Sergeant Major in sight.

Caspasian rolled onto his back and folded his arms behind his head. Above him, the interwoven atap leaves had done their job of keeping out the rain. It had thundered briefly at some point in the black early hours of the morning and he had woken momentarily to see a latticework of silver rain threads cascading from the edges of his shelter's roof. Now, as the surrounding trees slowly became visible in the strengthening light, the last heavy drops bulged on the atap's pointed ends, before tumbling into the soft, damp earth.

A little way from him, Brigadier Percival was still sleeping, curled on his side, rock still, silent, unfathomable. Elsewhere around the camp, Westacott's men were making their presence known with a medley of bodily noises particularly common to the soldier. Caspasian smiled and thought that a mug of tea would be nice.

He slid out of his makeshift bed and retrieved his boots. For storage during the night he had stuck each one like a head on a stick, upside down to prevent anything nasty from taking refuge in them. Just to make sure that they were still vacant, he shook them vigorously before putting them on and lacing them up. Easing out from beneath his shelter, he stood up, stretching. He arched backwards, hands on the base of his spine, and felt the joints and muscles acknowledge the start of a new day. He circled his arms, then tried a couple of gentle executions of mid-level punches. Yes, he was back in business.

He buckled on his holster and stooped to pick up his rifle. That was the moment he knew something was wrong. He froze, palm on the wooden stock of the Lee Enfield. Slowly he closed his fingers around it and drew it towards him. There was nothing in the sounds of the forest to indicate anything untoward. Nothing, in fact, to give cause for concern. But something inside Caspasian had sounded the alarm. The hair on the back of his neck bristled and he could feel himself tensing like a cat in alien territory.

The sentries. He should check on the sentries. Ensure they were alert and ready. As he made his way through the camp, he shook each man by the shoulder. One by one they stirred and blinked at him, saw his expression, and started to shuffle into some resemblance of a stand-to. Brigadier Percival had been his first stop, Westacott and Horner were last.

Caspasian lifted the rifle butt into his shoulder as he advanced down the trail towards the sentry post. He brought the barrel of the weapon up, and with his thumb, eased the safety catch to the fire position. His pace slowed the closer he got, until he reached the spot he had designated for the two sentries. It was deserted. At first he was flooded with an instant rage. They had gone to their shelters to sleep. They had sauntered into the bush to urinate. They had . . .

Percival was at his elbow, Westacott and a bleary-eyed

Horner behind him like two anxious children peering out from their mother's apron. Horner eventually read the situation.

'They're not in their beds. I checked on the way,' he said. 'It was Smudger and Scratch.'

Westacott opened his mouth to bellow their names into the jungle. Caspasian clasped a hand across it, sealing the cry inside. 'Shut up!' he hissed. 'Get the camp to stand-to. Sergeant Major, come with me.'

Horner stared at him in alarm.

'Come on, man! We're going to look for them.'

Leaving Percival and Westacott to sort out the rest of the men, Caspasian and Horner ventured out into the jungle leaving the perimeter of the encampment behind them. Half an hour later they returned with the news that the two sentries were nowhere to be found. Percival and Westacott met them in the centre of the camp and listened with long faces.

'But we did find this,' Caspasian said grimly. He produced a single green feather.

Percival held it in his fingers and studied it. 'It's like the flights of the arrow,' he observed.

'Oh shit.' Westacott ground the heel of one boot into the dirt. 'Well that's them buggered. Bloody Indians.' He glared at Caspasian. 'And you wanted the Sergeant Major to spare the old sod.'

Caspasian kept his calm. 'I don't think we should jump to conclusions.' He retrieved the feather from the Brigadier. 'The Indians aren't the sort to go around dropping feathers all over the place like slovenly chickens.' He held it up and viewed it from several angles. 'I'd say this was a calling card.'

Westacott snorted. 'Oh yes! And they've left their hats, gloves and capes in the cloakroom!'

'That'll do, Major,' Percival said. He frowned at Caspasian. 'What do you suggest we do now? Conduct a search?'

Caspasian slipped the feather into his top pocket. 'If the

Indians have taken them there'd be no point. We'd never find them.' He looked at the surrounding jungle. 'In fact, I'd say they are probably watching us at this very moment. Studying our reaction. Seeing which way we'll jump.'

Westacott and Horner shot panicked glances all around them, hunting for ghosts. Oddly, the small find had made Caspasian feel more confident. 'Look, if the Indians had meant them harm, we'd have found the bodies.'

'Then what the blazes are they up to?' Westacott stormed.

Caspasian shrugged, starting to enjoy himself. 'No idea. But we won't find out by standing here arguing.'

'So we go on?' Percival said.

'Not much else we can do,' Caspasian answered.

'Oh yes there is,' Westacott said. 'We can jolly well turn round and go back to the village. The boat's there. We get on it and bugger off back to Georgetown.' He started to walk back to the camp. Horner waited no more than a second before gathering up his pride and following.

'And your men?' Caspasian called.

'Stuff them. The Indians probably have.'

Percival intervened. 'Major Westacott, get back here now!'

Westacott faltered and slowly stopped. Like a skulking schoolboy he turned for his rebuke.

'This expedition is going on. We are going to find this Delgado and discover what happened to the airships. Is that clear?' He flicked up his wrist and glanced at his watch. 'I want us to be on our way in thirty minutes. That's just enough time to brew some tea and break camp. Is that understood?'

After a pause to consider his pitifully limited options, Major Westacott nodded and stalked off.

An hour later the reduced column snaked out of the camp-site and continued on its way. News of their missing comrades had spooked the soldiers who advanced with eyes darting every-where, rifles cocked and ready.

'Sergeant Major, tell your men not to bunch!' Caspasian ordered.

Horner scowled resentfully but did as he was told, relaying the command as if from himself, the old jungle hand. With Diaz in the lead, the march continued throughout the morning with only a couple of brief halts for rest, and when Caspasian gave the signal to stop for a longer break in order to eat, everyone was more than ready. He selected another spot near a stream so that there would be water for cooking, and himself moved to one side to study his map and compass.

A moment later he became aware of a muttering and looked up to see that the soldiers were standing around in a tight huddle, gesticulating and pointing in all directions. Percival and Westacott were sitting on a flat-topped rock, drinking from their flasks.

One of the soldiers caught Caspasian's eye. 'It's the Sergeant Major, sir,' the man said.

'What about him?' Caspasian replied, barely interested now that he knew the subject matter of their concerns.

'He's gone.'

From his eyrie up on the rock, Major Westacott overheard. He was down in a flash. 'Horner!' he screamed into the jungle, aiming his cry back along the track the column had just travelled. His shout sent a flock of birds screeching into the air, crashing out of the treetops like detonating explosives.

'Who saw him last?' Caspasian asked.

One of the soldiers held up his hand. 'I did, sir. He fell behind, saying he was going for a crap and that he'd catch us up.'

'And didn't you think to tell anyone when he didn't reappear?' Caspasian asked, incredulous.

The soldier looked back at him blankly. 'I didn't think the Sergeant Major would want me interfering like.'

'You positive arse!' Westacott stormed. 'I'll have you court-martialed for this.'

Caspasian had had enough. 'Will you shut your blasted mouth!' He stood up, laying his map aside, and advanced on the Major. Percival, still on his rock, decided to leave them to sort it out between themselves.

Westacott bristled. 'How dare you speak to me like that! You, a jumped-up little captain.' He hunted around for someone he could order to make an arrest on his behalf but, in Horner's absence, was met only by morose stares. After a fruitless search, his eyes found themselves back on the hated Caspasian. He raised his hand and pointed at his nemesis. 'You, sir, are . . .' Words failed him. Amongst the soldiers someone sniggered.

Caspasian felt the corner of his mouth twitch. His belly cried out to laugh. Finally Percival felt it was time to enter the ring.

'Gentlemen,' he said calmly, 'It appears to have escaped your notice, but we are no longer alone.'

Understanding dawned slowly but gathered speed as, one by one, the members of the expedition caught sight of the figures observing them from the furthermost patches of jungle.

'Can you please conduct yourselves in a manner befitting officers and men of His Majesty's army?'

Caspasian silently cursed himself for having missed them. They were Indians similar to the one he had seen by the river, the one who had fired the arrow. His holster flap was fastened, his rifle lay against a rock several yards distant. He knew that he would never reach it. Nor would his hand make it to his revolver. He counted at least a score of bows aimed at the little group of arguing soldiers, each bow charged with an arrow, and drawn.

'Nobody move,' Westacott said, his voice leaden.

'I don't think anyone was intending to,' Caspasian responded.

'I wouldn't be so high and mighty if I were you, Caspasian. You got us into this mess.'

The temptation to fell the Major with a single punch was

almost more than Caspasian could bear, but he feared that if he did, the next second he would be a pin cushion, easy target practice for their new visitors.

'Scratch!' one of the soldiers shouted, pointing. On the edge of their range of visibility, two figures were hustled into sight, each one held fast by Indians, arms pinioned behind their backs. Scratch and, beside him, Smudger. A moment later, violent scuffles announced the presentation to the spectating expedition members of Sergeant Major Horner. Trussed like a chicken in the market place, he was carried on by six Indians who laboured under the weight. Only the vine clenched tightly between his teeth and secured at the back of his head contained the string of vitriolic curses that everyone knew lurked with explosive force inside him.

'Horner!' Caspasian called across. 'Good of you to join us.'

The Sergeant Major writhed and struggled until one of the Indians jabbed him meaningfully in the ribs with a spear.

Scratch was shoved forward. He looked to his captors for permission and then shouted. 'It's all right, sir. They're not going to hurt us.'

Westacott edged closer to Caspasian and whispered. 'If you believe that then you're a turkey looking forward to Christmas.'

'Then break out the crackers, because I do.'

Caspasian took a step forward and held his arms out at his sides. He shouted back to Scratch. 'Who's in charge and what do they want?'

Scratch listened to his question and then consulted with the men around him. They seemed to be searching for someone who was deeper in the jungle. A moment later, a single Indian stepped forward. It was difficult to be sure, but Caspasian felt it was the same man who had observed them by the river. The one he had prevented Horner from shooting with the Lewis gun. The Indian regarded Caspasian for a long time. Finally he nodded, an almost imperceptible movement of his head. The crown of feathers dipped like a peacock's fan.

The next second, Caspasian felt the breath knocked out of him. For stepping out of the jungle next to the Indian, was none other than Miss Emma Lavelle.

13

Caspasian advanced towards her with outstretched hand. 'I didn't realise you were filming here?'

Emma smiled as she shook his hand, relief flooding through her. 'Believe me, Caspasian, this is not my idea of a comfortable location shoot. Not a dressing room or make-up artist in sight.' Her eyes widened. 'I mean, how's a girl supposed to manage?'

Brigadier Percival descended from his rock and joined them, Westacott at his heels like a recalcitrant hound. 'Miss Lavelle, I'm delighted to see you safe and well.' Percival introduced himself and added, 'Now, perhaps, we can get to the bottom of this mystery.'

'If I am well, Brigadier, it's thanks to this gentleman here,' she said, indicating the Indian who stood observing the meeting with interest. 'He rescued me from the men who took over the *D200* and captured the other passengers.'

Before the Brigadier could press her for further details, the Indian said something to the little group. Westacott moved his hand to the gun at his hip and several of the Indian's companions jerked their bows in his direction.

'Diaz, do you understand what he's saying?' Caspasian called across to the villager who was trying hard to remain unnoticed. Reluctantly he came forward.

'Sí, señor. I think he is their chief. He says it is not safe to stay here. He wants us all to move.'

Caspasian regarded the Indian and acknowledged his

command. 'That sounds fair to me. Ask him where his village is?'

'I can tell you that,' Emma said. 'They took me there after they'd rescued me. I've been there ever since. As far as I can understand, the men who took Lionel and the others are also holding a large number of the Indians prisoner. I think they use them as some kind of slave labour.'

'That'll be Colonel Delgado,' Caspasian said. At the mention of the name the Indian chief started speaking very fast, his face suddenly ferocious. He peppered his speech with sharp stabbing motions of his spear.

Westacott rubbed his chin. 'I don't think he's a particular friend of this Delgado chappie.'

Caspasian looked at him. 'Brilliant.'

There was a howl of outrage as Horner was ungagged and released. When he had been calmed down, Brigadier Percival directed that everyone should collect their belongings and follow the Indians. 'Frankly,' he concluded, 'I don't think they're giving us much choice.'

It was a long journey to the Indian village, the route taking the expedition through ever denser jungle. The landscape became increasingly dramatic. Deep gorges appeared out of nowhere, sheer chasms opening in the ground with rapid flowing rivers tumbling over glistening rocks far below. Rope bridges enabled the column to cross except for the widest of them. Here, narrow paths wound precariously all the way down to the base of the gorge. It took a good hour to reach the torrent at the bottom. The noise of the water was deafening, and Caspasian had to shout to be heard above the roar and crash. A crossing was achieved by leaping from rock to rock, first removing packs and heavy equipment and throwing them over. Caspasian balanced himself on a rock in the centre of the maelstrom and clutched Emma's hand to help her reach the far bank.

Once across, it was a further two hours before the whole party reached the crest, clambering up an equally precipitous slope of rocks, scree and patchy scrub. By the time they cleared the top, they were exhausted and soaked with perspiration. Westacott begged for a rest but the Indian chief carried on, his men prodding rather than encouraging the crumpled Major.

The light was fading when Caspasian smelt woodsmoke. Amongst the warriors he detected a lightness of spirit. Their step hastened until in their eagerness they laid hands on the tired soldiers and pulled them along. One last crest was surmounted and then they saw it below them. The Indian village. As at the riverside settlement, dogs and children were first to greet the returning party. A stockade of wooden stakes surrounded the thatched huts. The youngest and oldest of the menfolk who had remained behind, surged out of the stockade and danced around Caspasian and the other soldiers who clustered warily in a tight group, clutching their rifles to them. Scratch marched boldly at the head of the party. Although it was his first visit to the village, apart from Emma he had been the longest in the Indians' custody and was the most confident that they meant the expedition no harm. Indeed, he had already decided that he would far rather entrust his well-being to their care than to that of Sergeant Major Horner whom he had secretly hoped they were going to leave tied up and later, with luck, boil in a pot with some potatoes and a few onions. To his great disappointment this had not been so, although he supposed there might still be time.

To Caspasian's surprise, the Indians made no attempt to remove the soldiers' weapons, a fact he brought to the attention of both Percival and the mournful Westacott who was lamenting his aching muscles and burning feet. Quarters were allocated to them and, after an hour or so, a meal was provided. Westacott and Horner stirred the proffered bowls suspiciously, staring into the dark swirling contents. Caspasian and Percival tucked in hungrily.

'What is it?' Westacott asked.

Caspasian chewed on a piece of meat. 'Not sure. Could be monkey. It's certainly not snake or lizard.'

Percival sighed. 'Give it a rest, Caspasian. It's jungle pig, Westacott. Boiled pork to you. It's delicious. Go ahead and try it.'

When the meal was over, Scratch and Smudger brewed some tea. The chief was offered a mug but one sip was enough to send him spitting the contents into the fire. Percival called for Diaz and, together with Emma, they began to unravel the story of Colonel Delgado and the missing airships.

'Before Delgado came,' Diaz explained after listening to a long speech by the chief, 'there was no stockade. The villagers lived in peace. Then one day, when the warriors were away on a hunting expedition, Delgado and his men came and raided the village. Many of the women and children managed to flee, but of those who stayed behind to defend their homes, Delgado seized most, taking them away as his slaves. They have been there ever since, working in his mines.'

'And what do they mine?' Caspasian asked.

Diaz relayed the question. The chief spoke quietly to one of his attendants who went away, returning a moment later with a leather pouch which he handed to the chief. The chief undid the thong fastening the mouth of it and tumbled the contents into the dirt beside the fire.

Emma studied the pile of grubby rocks. 'Is that salt?'

Percival picked one up, rotating it in the firelight. He smiled, a smile that Caspasian recognized with a feeling of disquiet.

'Not salt, my dear. Uncut diamond.'

Westacott put down his mug and took an instant interest. Horner likewise.

Percival replaced the stone on the ground. Caspasian noted his reluctance to release the object. 'Well that answers several questions,' the Brigadier said. 'But what about the airships?'

Diaz conducted a further conversation with the chief, nodding intermittently as the chief illustrated his story with large sweeping motions of his hands in the air. 'He has only ever seen one airship, señor. But maybe it was a different one on each occasion,' Diaz said, offering a suggestion of his own. Percival frowned impatience and Diaz continued. 'The chief describes it as a thunder cloud made of rock. It roars, he says.' Diaz laughed to distance himself from the chief's absurd story. His laughter lacked conviction. 'The chief says he has seen men descend from the cloud. Spirits, he calls them. He says he is not sure whether they are evil spirits or not, but he thinks they must be because they visit Delgado. He is very confused because of this. He and his ancestors had believed that the spirits were kind.'

Cross-legged by the fire, Caspasian leaned forward, elbows on knees. 'Tell the chief that these are not spirits. They are ordinary men, just like all of us here. Tell him that the cloud of rock is a special machine made by men. It is a boat that flies. No more.'

Diaz stared at him, hardly believing that the story was actually true. As he translated, the chief listened intently, but his eyes were on Caspasian.

Finally the chief nodded. He spoke again and Diaz took note. 'He says that he believes what you say. He can see that you do not lie.' Diaz glanced at Percival, Westacott and Horner before continuing. Caspasian wondered whether part of the translation had been omitted to avoid causing insult to others present.

'The chief says that if what you say is true, then he is no longer afraid of Delgado. He says that your men have guns like Delgado. With your help he will attack Delgado's stronghold, kill him and all his men, and rescue his people who are held captive.'

'Now just a minute!' Westacott was on his feet as if bitten by a scorpion. 'If he wants to wade in and get himself mown down that's his affair. But he needn't think I'm going to help him.'

Percival was eyeing the stones again. 'I hate to disabuse you, Westacott, but that's exactly what you're going to do. You, Sergeant Major Horner and the rest of your pathetic crew. Aren't they, Caspasian?' He looked across at Caspasian to find him watching his own close inspection of the uncut diamonds. Percival blushed, a child with his hand in the biscuit tin.

'We have a duty to rescue the passengers, Brigadier,' Caspasian said. The Brigadier nodded sagely, having quite forgotten about them.

Westacott looked from one to the other. 'You're both barking mad. Absolutely stark, staring lunatic. And I'm not sure you've got the authority to give me such an order.'

Percival stood and squared off in front of the Major. Horner took one look at him and remained where he was. Westacott could deal with it on his own.

'I do have the authority, Major. And I also have the authority to break you in two, militarily or any other way. Do I make myself clear?'

Westacott mouthed silently like a fish and then stormed away. Horner scuttled after him.

'More tea, gents?' Scratch offered.

The Brigadier declined the invitation and retired to his quarters leaving Caspasian and Emma to watch the firelight crackle and spit as the last of the wood burnt down.

'As a rescue team, your cohesion leaves something to be desired,' she said when she was sure the Brigadier could no longer hear her.

Caspasian laughed. 'It's the best we could cobble together, I'm afraid.'

'I suppose it will have to do then.' She looked at him. 'Did you know this was going to happen?' she asked eventually.

'No.' Then, feeling she deserved a better answer than

that, he added, 'I was put on the *D200* to keep an eye on you all.'

'Put there by the Brigadier?'

Caspasian nodded. 'It was just a precaution. No one foresaw any of this.'

'So all that stuff about being an observer for the Indian Army . . . ?'

'Cover, I'm afraid. If I'd known . . .'

'If we'd known what was going to happen I expect Lionel would still have wanted to come,' Emma said.

'You can't mean that?'

She smiled at him. 'You've no idea what a guy like Lionel will do for a bit of publicity.'

'And you?'

'I hope I don't seem as desperate as that?'

'You don't seem desperate at all,' Caspasian said. 'In fact, considering everything that's happened to you, I'm amazed at how well you are.'

Emma laughed. 'I've got the chief to thank for that. If he hadn't saved me I'd probably be dead by now. Dead or else captive of Delgado and his thugs which might just be worse.'

'Yes, but the fact you can even say that so lightly is quite remarkable.'

She eyed him suspiciously. 'For a woman, you mean?'

'For anyone.'

She grinned, pleased with herself. 'Thank you.' She stretched out her legs and waggled her feet beside the flames. 'It's odd, but I'm not scared. I know I should be, but I'm not.' She regarded him carefully. 'I think it's because of you.'

'Me?' he said astonished.

'You inspire confidence.' She saw him about to laugh. 'No, really. You do. I felt that the first time I saw you in the . . . what was it?'

'The Carlton?'

'Yes. Even then. There you were, so self-contained. A little bit formal, perhaps, but . . . in control.'

'Jesus,' Caspasian exclaimed. 'Most of the time I'm flying by the seat of my pants.' He laughed. 'Control has not featured large in my life. If it had, I wouldn't spend my time bouncing from one disaster to the next.'

'Yes, but I bet you survive them all and triumph.'

He shrugged. 'Muddle through, more like it.'

'That's a triumph in itself.'

The light shone on her skin and hair and Caspasian was struck again by how extraordinary she was. 'But look at you,' he said. 'Look at what you've achieved. Goodness, you're world-famous.'

She looked surprised, as if he had said something remarkably stupid. 'Do you think any of that matters? The fame is hardly an achievement.'

'Reaching the top of your career is.'

'You forget, I'm on the way down,' she said good-naturedly. 'In any case, my mother once told me, it's not what we achieve – it's what we do to others that defines us.'

An enormous fountain of sparks burst out of the heart of the fire. 'You've got a very wise mother,' Caspasian said after a while.

'Had,' Emma corrected.

'I'm sorry.'

She shrugged, watching the glowing patterns in the fire as a breath of wind fanned sudden life into the embers. For a moment she was far away. 'So I try my best to remember that. In my world it's not always easy to operate by such a principle.'

'It isn't easy in any world.'

'Indeed,' she said, and smiled at him, radiant and warm.

The following morning, Caspasian was up bright and early. He had slept well and was ravenously hungry. While the other members of the expedition prepared their own rations,

Caspasian sampled the Indians' food, which was fish and some sort of bread made from maize. As soon as they had eaten, he consulted with the Brigadier over the plans for the next stage of the mission. They quickly agreed that there was no point in trying to negotiate with Delgado. All they would achieve would be the surrender of the element of surprise, probably their only advantage.

'So it's to be a surprise attack, then?' the Brigadier said.

'That's what I think,' Caspasian answered. 'And if we're going to attack, we have to know what we're up against. I've got to carry out a recconnaisance.'

'Don't go and blow it, Caspasian,' Percival said doubtfully.

'I've no intention of doing so. I'd be grateful if, while I'm away, you ensure Westacott's crew clean their weapons thoroughly. I've never seen such a scruffy bunch.'

'They're not Indian Army,' the Brigadier said simply. 'What do you expect?' He thought a moment. 'Actually, I rather think I'd like a look at the objective myself.'

Caspasian shook his head adamantly. 'The moment we'd gone, Westacott would disappear, taking Horner and the rest with him. You have to stay here, sir. There's no other way.'

Reluctantly the Brigadier agreed. Caspasian went in search of Diaz and got him to explain his request to the chief.

'The chief says he will go with you himself,' Diaz translated merrily.

Caspasian smiled. 'As will you too, my friend.'

'Me?'

'You. How else am I going to communicate with him?'

Diaz tried to argue but soon realized his attempts were falling on deaf ears.

For the reconnaissance, the chief selected half a dozen warriors. Caspasian decided to leave his rifle behind and take only his revolver. He anticipated having to crawl in to close range of the target and the cumbersome Lee Enfield would only be a hindrance. As they prepared to leave the camp, the chief looked at Caspasian's face and then took a small pot from one of the warriors. Out of it he scooped a dark green paste which he then proceeded to smear on Caspasian's cheeks and forehead.

The rest of the expedition members had come to see them off. Emma could not resist a quiet chuckle. 'Warpaint suits you.'

Caspasian smiled. It was nothing new to him. Patrols into no man's land in the war had called for similar measures. Burnt cork, boot polish or other materials were applied to dull the skin's natural shine. The chief's own version would help him blend in.

The journey to Delgado's base took most of the day. In fact, Caspasian was horrified just how close the Indian village was to their antagonists. He had expected at least one night's halt, but as the light was thinning, the chief signalled that they were close. It was going to be possible to conduct the daylight reconnaissance straight away, followed by a closer inspection of Delgado's defences after dark had fallen.

The approach to the camp had brought them onto a high, densely forested ridge overlooking a valley. One moment they were moving through thick undergrowth, the next, the ground dropped away in front of them and there it was, the camp lying spread out below. Caspasian could see that it was actually an old fort – probably colonial, he reckoned. The walls were built of stone, but it was in a poor state of repair. There had probably been no requirement for a more robust upkeep, nor, indeed, the means. In places, the wall was lower than elsewhere. Most likely, stones had been removed over the years to build or repair the buildings inside the perimeter. One such, presumably Delgado's residence, stood out as the best of a bad bunch. Where the wall had been cannibalized in this fashion, a bamboo stockade had been erected to make good the losses. The whole effect was of a clumsily patched overcoat.

Further evidence of Delgado's slovenliness was the lack of proper clearance of the surrounding jungle. Once upon a time, the fort's occupiers had stripped back the trees for a good hundred yards from the walls to provide clear visibility and fields of fire for their weapons. Recently, however, the undergrowth had been allowed to creep back and fill the intervening space. As with all such secondary growth, it had done so with a vigour and a tangled density that presented any potential attacker with the means to approach to within close proximity of the walls and yet remain under cover. Clearly, Caspasian reckoned, Colonel Delgado was confident that he was not at risk of attack. He undoubtedly believed he had achieved dominance of the neighbourhood. To Caspasian a picture started to emerge. Delgado was a bully without brains.

The chief touched Caspasian's shoulder and indicated a rocky promontory some fifty yards to their right. Caspasian nodded and allowed him to lead the way. He noticed how, as the two of them edged forward onto it, crawling on their bellies, the accompanying tribesmen took up positions to watch the track along which they had come.

Caspasian took out a small pair of binoculars. To prevent the sun from glinting on the eyepieces and alerting the enemy to his presence, he wrapped a thin piece of gauze around them. Peering towards the fort, his view was only marginally obstructed by the cloth. He tightened the focus until presented with a sharp picture. The fort was only one part of Delgado's camp, the stronghold. Elsewhere around the valley, mine workings opened into the rock face where he could see the chief's villagers working under close guard from Delgado's men. He tried to identify the guards' weaponry. They mostly looked like German Mauser rifles. Not bad, although their maintenance was probably less than perfect. But then Westacott's men could hardly boast.

Taking out a notebook and pencil, Caspasian set about

sketching a diagram of the fort and other areas. He marked in distances and location of guard posts, where he could identify them. He sketched in the entrances to the fort, approaches to them, and any other tracks and trails he could see. He attempted to do a rough head count of Delgado's men and managed to pinpoint about twenty, but assumed that there were at least double that number. Many of them would have been inside the mines watching over the prisoners as they laboured. Others would have been off duty, temporarily out of the camp or engaged on various tasks that would have kept them out of sight.

Of Delgado himself Caspasian could see no sign. This unsettled him. If the Colonel was away from the fort, he would undoubtedly have a sizeable force with him. The last thing Caspasian wanted was for his own attack team to be surprised by Delgado's sudden return when they were halfway through the assault. It would spell disaster.

The chief seemed to read his thoughts, because the next second he nudged Caspasian and pointed to the building that Caspasian had assumed to be Delgado's residence. Caspasian trained his binoculars on it and steadied his aim. The sprawling building filled his vision. His eyes roamed across every part of it and then suddenly he detected movement. There was a courtyard in the centre. A door opened and a man came out. He was lean and thin. Caspasian turned to the chief but the Indian shook his head. He would not need binoculars to identify his arch-enemy.

Then, behind the first man, another stepped out into the daylight. He was stocky, strongly formed. His shoulders and arms were muscular and, to show them off, the man wore no shirt but only a waist length sleeveless jerkin fastened carelessly down the front by a row of silver buttons, the top three of which were undone. Tattoos liberally adorned both arms. Around his waist a purple sash supported a revolver that was stuffed into the top of it. For an instant Caspasian wondered if it was Lionel Domain's cummerbund, but this was more piratical, knotted at the right hip, the ends trailing down almost as far as the knee. A pair of black boots and a drooping moustache completed the image of a buccaneer incongruously deposited in the middle of the jungle.

'Delgado,' he said. No need for a question.

The chief grunted. No need for an answer.

At that moment the distant sound of a commotion rose up to them. Caspasian swung his binoculars onto one of the mine workings outside the fort. There was an altercation between one of the guards and some of the prisoners. The guard was quickly reinforced and the prisoners beaten back into line with rifle butts and barrels. With a shock Caspasian recognized Gustav Wolter and, on the ground beside him, the prone figure of Richard Edward. Wolter was helping Richard to his feet, holding off a remonstrating guard with his free hand. Caspasian felt the anger rising within him. He bit it back. Anger was a luxury he could not afford. Not yet. Suddenly he could imagine how the chief felt, seeing as how the majority of the other slaves were his own people. He turned and met the chief's eye. An understanding passed between them. Soon. Their moment would come soon.

They crawled back into the cover of the jungle and waited for darkness to fall. Through Diaz, Caspasian had told the chief that he wanted to have a closer look at the one approach that he had identified as a weak point. There would not be time to conduct a complete circuit of the objective as Caspasian would ideally have liked. This one close range foray would have to suffice.

As the light dwindled, in the valley below the workers were gathered in like cattle and herded back into the confines of the fort. The guards did a random sweep of the outlying areas to ensure no one had been overlooked, and then, in the last moments of daylight, the fort's giant gates were closed and

barred, locking everyone inside. Caspasian noted with interest
that no guards had been left to patrol the mine workings or other
sites lying outside the walls. In effect, each night Delgado
surrendered control of everything but the fort, taking it for
granted that the valley would still be his to control in the
morning.

With darkness complete, Caspasian allowed the chief to lead
him down to the valley floor. It was a clear and starlit night. The
moon would not rise until several hours later. The time for a
close recce was perfect. Leaving the other warriors behind,
Caspasian and the chief inched forwards once again. Much to
Diaz' relief, he was also left behind. Caspasian did not want to
risk it. He was confident of his own and the chief's jungle skills,
but Diaz would be well out of his depth. In any case, conversation would be impossible so close to the fort so there was no
need for the translator. Sign language and mime would do.

The approach to the fort was tortuous, the way being densely
overgrown. Unwilling to cut the undergrowth in case the marks
the following morning betray their recce, Caspasian and the
chief wove their way through the branches, manoeuvering
themselves ever closer to their objective as if they were needles
through cloth. It was an exhausting process and Caspasian was
soon soaked to the skin.

Suddenly, after what seemed like hours, he unexpectedly
reached the edge of the jungle and all but tumbled into the open.
The chief caught hold of his arm and held him back just as a
guard on top of the fort's surrounding wall, barely ten yards
away, leaned over the battlements to urinate down into the
bushes. It seemed to go on for ever, the thin stream spraying
down onto the leaves and grass. Further along the wall, one of
the guard's companions made some remark. They both
laughed. When he had finished relieving himself, the guard lit a
cigarette and his friend joined him. It was a quarter of an hour

before they moved away, idling slowly back into the fort's interior from where the sound of a phonograph invaded the insect buzzes and clicks and whirrs of the jungle night.

Caspasian moved stealthily across the open ground until he stood with his back to the wall. It was damp and surprisingly cool to the touch. He turned and hunted for hand- and footholds and, finding them, hauled himself up to the battlements some twenty feet above, his climb made all the easier by the badly eroded brickwork. He peered carefully over the top and his eyes swept the courtyard below, taking it all in. Satisfied, he let himself down again and gestured for the chief to follow him. They made their way around the walls until they came to the gates which they gave a wide berth, fearing lest guards were posted on the other side with slits to observe the ground outside the fort. Caspasian's intention now was to recce the outlying areas and the approaches to the mine workings.

Hour by hour the night passed, but gradually Caspasian built up a comprehensive picture of Delgado's little empire. Finally, when he was satisfied that he had seen everything possible, he and the chief returned to the place where they had left the others, and moving as fast as they could, they set out on their way back to the Indian village. Caspasian was exhausted, but the chief pressed the pace. He was clearly in no mood to delay.

Dawn was breaking by the time they approached the stockade. Warriors ran on ahead and when they entered the village they were met by the whole population, everyone anxious to hear news of their companions and family members held captive by Delgado. Scratch met Caspasian with a mug of tea that was the most welcome sight Caspasian had beheld in a very long time. Brigadier Percival was next on the scene, fresh and rested from his sleeping mat.

'Going for a spot of sleep, Caspasian?' he asked.

Caspasian shook his head. 'I'll brief you on the recce first, sir.

We can decide on a plan and then, if it's all right with you, I'll grab some shut-eye while you oversee preparations.'

'Fine.' The Brigadier led the way back to the open-sided hut where he was accommodated and they sat down in the shade to discuss the results of Caspasian's night's work.

First of all Caspasian drew a diagram in the dirt, using stones, twigs and other objects to represent the various landmarks and buildings of Delgado's stronghold. Fighting to keep his eyes open, he started on his briefing. Halfway through, he called for Scratch. 'Any chance of some coffee?'

Scratch appeared at the double. 'Major Westacott's got some, sir,' he whispered, holding his finger to his lips. 'Best in all Guiana. I don't suppose he'd miss a handful.' He jogged away on his mission.

'So what do you recommend?' the Brigadier asked thoughtfully, considering Caspasian's plan and diagram with care. 'A night assault over the wall? Catch them all in their beds?'

'I was thinking along those lines myself at first, sir,' Caspasian answered hesitantly. 'But now I'm not so sure.'

'Why's that?'

'There's every chance it could rapidly turn into chaos. For one thing, if the guards discovered us before we had a reasonable number of men over the walls, they could stop our attack dead before it had even got started. But more importantly, the fort's interior is badly lit as it is. If the generator failed or the lights were killed, the fight would become impossible to control. We wouldn't be able to distinguish friend from foe. I reckon we'd have double the casualties than in a daylight attack, mostly from our own fire.' Scratch arrived with the coffee and Caspasian paused to drink deeply, feeling it work on his system, bringing him more fully awake.

'Right now,' he continued, 'the chief's on our side. How long would that support continue once Westacott's crew started blatting away indiscriminately in the dark?'

The Brigadier had to agree. 'So what's your solution? Surely not a daylight assault? That would be far too costly!'

'Delgado doesn't bother to patrol the outlying areas at night. I propose that we move up under cover of darkness and lay a series of ambushes, then wait until daybreak when his men come out of the fort, bringing the prisoners with them, taking them back to the mines. That's when we strike. We'll catch them in the open, away from their defences. No need to assault the fort at all.'

He looked up from his plan to find the Brigadier watching him. After a moment Percival nodded. 'All right. Have you worked out any of the details yet?'

Caspasian smiled wearily. 'Funnily enough I have.'

It was an hour later that Caspasian made it back to his own quarters. It had been agreed that they would move into position that night, ready for an attack the following morning. The rest of this day would be taken up with preparations and liaison with the chief over the various tasks to be allocated to his men and to Westacott's. First of all however, for Caspasian there was rest. He took off his belt and gun and dropped them beside his bedroll. He sat down and eased off his boots, unbuttoned his shirt and lay back with a groan, luxuriating at the prospect of sleep.

There was a light cough from the doorway. He opened his eyes to find Emma Lavelle observing him. 'I'm sorry to bother you,' she said.

Caspasian sat up, leaning back on his hands. 'Not at all. Come in.' He looked around fruitlessly for something to offer her by way of a seat. 'It isn't much, but it's home,' he apologized, finding nothing.

She smiled and sat cross-legged in front of him. 'I was just wondering whether you saw Lionel.'

He saw the concern on her face and felt his heart lurch. But then what had he hoped for? What stupid hope had possessed him? Of course there was no chance for a man like him with a girl like the famous Miss Emma Lavelle. She was one of Lionel B. Domain's girls. Doubtless one of many.

'No, I didn't, I'm afraid,' he said, faltering, taking command of himself. 'Just Gustav and Richard. No sign of your Lionel, though.'

'Oh,' she said blankly, wondering at his brittle tone.

'But I'm sure he's all right,' he added quickly, trying to re-assure her but unable to keep the bitterness from his voice. 'Men like Lionel are always all right.'

To his surprise Emma laughed.

'Have I said anything funny?'

'Men like Lionel. That's all.'

Caspasian was confused. Angry too. He felt taunted by her presence in front of him, but knew it was wholly unreasonable of him. What could he possibly be to a woman like her? 'I can imagine this must be very distressing for you,' he said, again more curtly than he intended. 'But I'm sure that after tomorrow you and Lionel will be reunited.'

Emma eyed him shrewdly, a twinkle in her eye. 'You really don't get it, do you?'

Caspasian felt the tiredness wash over him. He longed for her to be gone so he could sleep. 'Suppose you tell me,' he said.

'Lionel is . . . How shall I put this?'

'You're not married, I know,' Caspasian said impatiently. 'But in your circles I imagine that's not an issue.'

Emma blanched. 'Oh, do you? I suppose you know all about things like that?'

It was on the tip of Caspasian's tongue to say that he knew all too well about matters like that. To his own personal cost. His own mother had been deceived and betrayed by a man like Lionel B. Domain. But he guarded his silence, locking it away with its dark secret.

Emma got up quickly to go. In the doorway she stopped, her

back to him, shoulders tense. Set to fight. She turned on her heel. 'Lionel has been very good to me. He says he is going to help my career get back into the swing.'

Once again, tiredness threatened to overcome Caspasian. But it was more a weariness with the world and its vicious ways. 'I'm sure he will, Emma. I meant no offence.'

'You insinuate that I'm a whore, Captain Caspasian, yet you say you don't mean to offend? Well you do. By God you do!'

She took two steps out of the doorway into the light before returning. 'What I had been going to say was that Lionel has no interest in women, Captain Caspasian. He . . . what's the phrase? He bats for the other team. Our relationship is about as Platonic as a relationship can get. Do I make myself clear?'

In her face and in her voice Caspasian could sense it all. The hurt, the embarrassment of the confession, the fear of failure, the degradation, even, as a woman, of having to do what she was doing to make her way in a cut-throat business. Lionel Domain's motivation was doubtless less than pure altruism. There would be pecuniary advantage were he to succeed in resurrecting Emma Lavelle's career, and, in the meantime, it enabled him to maintain the image of his own identity that he wished to project to the outside world. But the fact remained that the man was helping her, and without the immediate grati-fication that Caspasian had, he was ashamed to admit, assumed all too rapidly.

He started to get up. 'Emma, I'm sorry. I . . .'

But this time she was going, out into the bright sunshine that blazed down onto the village, her step brisk and resolute, deter-mined like her courage. Like the fists clenched at her sides.

He caught hold of her and pulled her back. She shrugged his hand off ferociously, then spun towards him, glaring up into his face. 'How dare you assume that . . .'

Exhausted beyond words, weary of struggle and fight, Caspasian gripped her shoulders and kissed her. Tight in his grasp Emma stood rigid, arms by her sides. He pulled back and looked at her. 'I'm sorry,' he said softly. 'I had absolutely no right. No right whatever to judge or to . . .'

She reached her arms behind his head and kissed him back, pulling him fiercely against her. Caspasian's head was swimming with the taste and the feel of her. Her lips brushed against his ear. 'Then you can damn well apologise.'

14

Colonel Delgado lay watching the light inflict patterns on the wall at the end of his bed. They grew in distinctness the more the day intensified. Right now, they were weak, as feeble as kittens. In due course they would carve their lines into the plaster and brickwork as strongly as if with hammer and chisel. And yet it would all be an illusion. Just light in another of its manifestations. As fragile and meaningless as . . . What?

His head turned on the pillow and he regarded the extinguished candle, the congealed wax set hard on the chipped porcelain of the holder. There was a moan next to him and a woman's arm flopped across his chest. He threw it off. It flopped back again.

'Guillermo, what is the matter?'

Annabella's voice was hoarse and sleepy. It rasped like an old axle. The back of her hand stroked his cheek. Her skin felt dry. He knew the palm was rougher still. Old leather, hardened by too much life. The wrong sort of life.

Once more he threw off her arm, this time flinging it away so the momentum rolled Annabella to the far edge of the large rumpled bed. She giggled and rolled back, her broad body slumping back into its hot rut like a prodded corpse. With boisterous effort, she rolled onto her stomach and propped her folded forearms on Delgado's chest. Her dark brown eyes stared down into his. Sleep crusted her eyelids and the corners of her mouth.

Delgado squinted up at her. 'Your hair's been blown by the winds of hell,' he said.

Annabella's laugh rumbled deep in her tobacco-corrupted chest. She arched back her neck and pushed a hand through her black dishevelled mane. The fingers snagged in the mats which she pushed against a couple of times before giving up and trying to smooth it down instead. 'You know the trouble with you, Guillermo?' she croaked. 'You love your Annabella.'

'Ha!'

'No, you do.' A thick brown finger wagged in his face, the scarlet nail polish chipped like the candlestick. Like everything in the whole godforsaken place, Delgado reflected. 'Why you not make an honest woman of her?'

Delgado scratched the thick hair of his chest. He was depressed to note the amount of white in it. 'I'd have as much chance of making you bearable to look at.'

Annabella pouted and for a moment Delgado delightedly thought he had really managed to hurt her feelings. She raised one gnarled fist and brought it down on his sternum with all her might. His eyes bulged and a racking cough erupted from him. He gasped, catching hold of her wrist as she raised it above him a second time. For a moment she pitted her strength against his, the two limbs engorged with energy. He was surprised at her resistance. Then it gave way and she allowed herself to be rolled onto her back, home again in her rut. Now it was his turn to survey her from above. He shifted closer, ignoring her smell, too familiar with it to care. He pushed her wrist back on the smashed and lifeless pillow, a single yellowing feather popping into the stale air and floating away.

'You should show more respect, woman.' He snarled it through gritted teeth. In response, Annabella snatched his lower lip between her teeth and bit hard. Delgado screamed and pulled away, tasting blood.

'Raddled dog!' He raised his open hand to strike her, releasing her wrist as he did so. Instinctively she covered her face to protect herself from the coming blow. Nothing happened. She peeped between parted fingers and saw Delgado's face cracking into a savage smile. His hand came down softly and ran itself across her breasts. 'Woman,' he said, as if he had just remembered the name for her part of the species.

Annabella freed her other wrist and spread herself, her flesh shuddering as she chuckled. 'See?' her voice rasped in his ear as he sank into her. 'You do love your Annabella.'

Delgado grunted. Rodriguez would be hammering on the door soon, announcing the start of the day's routine. For Delgado it had already begun.

On the far side of the fort, Rodriguez stared out towards the mine workings. He was chewing a mouthful of cold tortilla, the rest of which was gathering flies in a terracotta bowl sitting on the wall's verdigris covered battlements. The stumps of his rotten teeth encountered a piece of eggshell. He spat it over the wall, spraying a large portion of his half masticated food with it. He wiped his nose with the back of his hand, tore off another chunk of tortilla and stuffed it into his mouth. A substantial amount failed to make it past his generous moustache and was soon discovered by the more enterprising of the flies.

When his bowl was empty, his heavy-lidded eyes stared at it for a full five seconds before he sniffed deeply and turned to saunter back towards Colonel Delgado's residence. He passed one of the prisoners' accommodation shacks and hurled his bowl at it, hearing it smash.

'Get them moving!' he shouted to the guards who were starting to gather for the day's work.

His heels dragged in the dust, carving parallel trails like a sidewinder snake. Although there were only two shallow steps leading up to Delgado's front door, Rodriguez mounted them as if closing on a mountain peak without oxygen. He kicked the door open, knowing the handle mechanism to be absent, and barged through to the inner courtyard. Delgado's two attack dogs shot to their feet, tugging at the restraining chains that anchored them to a wall. Seeing Rodriguez they lowered their heads and wagged their tails like puppies. He hawked loudly and spat at them as he crossed towards Delgado's bedroom door to give prior warning of his approach. As he neared he could hear the bed inside rhythmically slamming against the wall, accompanied by various grunts and groans.

Rodriguez sighed, leaning impatiently beside the door to wait. He knew that Delgado knew he was there. He looked up at the sky. It was colourless. It would be hot today. A real scorcher. Already he itched with sweat.

Eventually the noise beyond the door subsided into silence, out of which Delgado's dry-throated voice started to speak, choked, coughed to clear itself and then spoke again.

'I'll be there in a minute.'

'Sí, señor,' Rodriguez called back.

Five minutes later, the door swung open and a foul-scented blast of hot air struck Rodriguez in the face. He screwed up his nose then quickly straightened his features before his boss noticed. No words of greeting were exchanged between them, just a cursory nod.

Delgado led the way back across the courtyard towards the outer door, buckling on a pistol belt as he went. A cutlass swung from the other side of it and banged and clanked against his legs as he walked. He fastened only the lower three buttons on his sleeveless jerkin, tucking the ends into his trousers.

'Everything went well last night, señor,' Rodriguez said.

Delgado nodded, agreeing. 'As usual.'

'He was pleased?'

'As usual.' Delgado glanced at his second in command and smiled. 'He is always pleased with what we do for him.'

By now the accommodation shacks had disgorged their miserable inhabitants into the square where armed guards stood watch over them, loaded rifles couched in folded arms after the fashion set by Rodriguez. Delgado cast his eye over the slaves as he passed by. None of them held his gaze. That was good, he thought. Lowered eyes indicate submission. Even the captured outsiders had been broken. Their clothes were reduced to rags, along with their wills.

'What are you waiting for?' he shouted ahead to the four guards standing watch over the main gates. 'Get them open. Get these monkeys to work!'

The guards acknowledged the order and started to draw back the wooden beam that bolted the doors shut. At the same time, their comrades lashed out with boots and rifle butts at the huddled workers, herding them into a column that shuffled towards the opening gates. Daylight cracked through the widening gap, the parched earth appearing on the outside, jungle rising in the distance beyond the area of the mine workings. Yard by yard, the column exited the fort, guards flanking both sides. Very occasionally one of the workers would make a break for freedom, dashing towards the jungle. They rarely made twenty yards before a volley of rifle fire cut them down. The guards liked it when this happened. It provided them with a bit of sport.

Delgado sauntered along beside one of his men, a fellow by the name of Manzini. Manzini was young and eager. Ruthless too. Delgado recognized the hunger. Manzini was after Rodriguez's job. Unfortunately he was too good. He was the sort of man who, given time, would not be satisfied even with that. Next he would want Delgado's position itself. He would have to go. Either that, or be slapped down. Delgado decided he would have to watch Manzini very carefully. He nodded a silent greeting at him as they walked. Manzini returned it with half a grin. His narrowed eyes squinted against the glare. He reached up to pull his hat lower. As his arm started to rise towards the brim, an arrow struck him sideways in the throat. The force of the shot drove the arrowhead clean through the cartilage so the shaft lodged fast behind the windpipe. Delgado stared at him in horror, feet stuck to the dirt floor. Manzini's rifle tumbled out of his arms and both hands took hold of the arrow shaft.

'Get back into the fort!' Delgado shouted at the top of his voice. He started to unfasten his holster. His fingers closed about the pommel of his revolver and drew it, thumb cocking the hammer as it came free. He took one more quick look at Manzini. He should still have been able to breathe. That was not the problem. The arrow had severed the jugular but as the wound's exit was securely stoppered by the slender wooden shaft like a cork in a bottle, the blood was pumping straight into Manzini's windpipe and down into his lungs. He was drowning in his own blood. Delgado could not avoid noticing with cold detachment that Manzini's eyes had lost their previous arrogance. Now they were brimful with terror. In the space of one second, a big, confident man had been reduced to a tiny animal on the brink of extinction. A rabbit in the jaws of a hound.

On the other side of the column a second guard had been struck, this time by a whole volley of arrows. As his feet tottered, gradually losing coherence, his hands slapped at the arrow shafts piercing his body in half a dozen places. He seemed not to know which to attend to first. His comrades had deserted him and, as his legs gave way and he sank to the ground looking around pathetically for help, death overtook him, rendering all his efforts useless.

Rodriguez appeared at Delgado's side. He was firing wildly, loosing off rounds into the jungle fringe. 'Can you see them?' he shouted.

'No, but by Christ they'll pay for this!' Delgado yelled in response. 'I'll torch their village and slaughter every last one of them.'

Delgado glanced over his shoulder. The fort was a hundred yards to his rear and his captives were fleeing in all directions. The guards did not know whether to try and cut down the slaves or to engage their attackers. In an instant Delgado knew that he had to impose some order if he was going to survive.

'Let them go!' he shouted. 'We can get them back later. Get back to the fort!' They would be safe once behind their walls. The Indians could fire all the arrows they wanted once Delgado and his men were safely inside. It would not matter. There he could regroup and then mount a proper attack on their village at a later date. A fierce anger burned in his heart. A thirst for revenge. How dare they think they could ruin his business with mere arrows! They were savages. Nothing more than that.

The sound of a single rifle shot struck Delgado like a bucket of cold water in the face. One of his men spun in a circle and dropped to the ground, stone dead.

'Where the hell did that come from?' Rodriguez shouted. 'Did anyone see?'

'Back to the fort! Run!' Delgado ordered, leading the race back to the gates himself. Other rifle fire crackled from elsewhere along the jungle fringe. It was poorly coordinated, the first shot having signalled the arrival of an enemy apart from just the Indians. For the first time in a long while Delgado felt the unfamiliar shiver of fear. This was a new and wholly unexpected threat. A force equal to his own, for once. He had an answer to it, but it was in the fort. If he could only get back there he would know how to deal with this new enemy, whoever it was.

On the edge of the jungle Caspasian was fuming. 'That arse Westacott! Where the hell did he get to?'

Caspasian's first shot, which had felled the guard, was supposed to have heralded a devastating volley of rifle fire which, together with the fire from the Lewis gun, was to have mown down Delgado's force before they could make it back to the safety of their fortress. Instead, his own round had been left in a vacuum for several seconds and by the time Westacott and Horner had brought their men into action, the element of surprise had been lost. Now, as he watched Delgado and his men sprinting back towards the open gates of the fort, Caspasian realized that the fight was not going to be the simple ambush he had planned. They were going to have to fight, and fight hard. Especially if the enemy made it back into cover.

Standing next to him, Brigadier Percival potted away with his revolver, regardless of the fact that at the range of two hundred yards its effect was next to useless. It had been his idea to allow Westacott some modicum of face-saving by letting him select his own fire positions, so long as they were within hailing distance of himself and Caspasian. The unfortunate result was that it released the Major from Caspasian's direct control.

Percival coughed to hide a mild regret, the closest he ever came to embarrassment. 'Too late for remonstrating, Caspasian. Time to close with the enemy.'

Caspasian knew that the Brigadier had no intention of closing with anyone. He would ensure that the messy work was left to the Indians and the lower ranks.

Fifty yards away, Caspasian could see Sergeant Major Horner messing with the Lewis gun which still had not been brought into action. Scratch, Smudger and the other privates were now firing at a reasonable rate, but the volley fire had totally failed. The chief and his tribesmen had positioned themselves closest to Delgado's men to make best use of the shorter range of their bows. Now they were advancing out of the cover of the jungle with a wholly misplaced confidence. The chief himself danced at their head, waving his men forward. The fleeing captives had reached the jungle fringes. Some were snatching up weapons from their comrades and returning to the attack, hungry for vengeance on the hated Colonel and his men. Caspasian had recognized several of the ex-crewmen and passengers of the *D200* by their clothes but they had fled in the opposite direction from him and were now well out of sight. He would have to wait till later before he could locate

Gustav Wolter and the others. First the battle had to be won.

Anger burning inside him, he dashed across to Sergeant Major Horner. 'What's the matter with that blasted gun?' he shouted as he ran.

'Bugger's jammed,' the Sergeant Major replied, red-faced with the exertion of trying to clear the blockage. Unexpectedly, it suddenly let out a burst of fire which tore narrowly past Caspasian.

'Get it onto the target, you bloody fool!'

Horner glowered at Caspasian but nestled down behind the gun and squeezed off a long burst, lifting his head to observe the effect of his fire at the target end. The shots hammered into the slowly closing doors of the fort. As the final round of the burst pounded home, splintering wood and sending shards flying into the air, they slammed shut. Delgado was home and dry. Barely half a dozen of his men lay unmoving in the dirt. The greater part of his force was safe.

Caspasian slumped down onto his knees beside Major Westacott. 'Great. That's just bloody terrific!'

'Don't blame me, Captain. If you hadn't fired before we were ready the ambush would have worked. You should have waited until they were further from the fort.'

'Any further and they'd have been stepping on the chief,' Caspasian spat back, longing to put a bullet straight between Westacott's eyes.

Several of the guards had made it onto the battlements and were bringing effective fire to bear on the Indians who were now horribly exposed in the open. They did not seem to notice that events had swung against them, at first, but gradually their headlong charge behind their chief began to falter as more and more of their number fell to Delgado's rifle fire.

Caspasian looked around for Diaz and found him cowering in terror behind a tree trunk. 'Go and tell the chief to get his men back into cover.'

Diaz stared at him with wide, fearful eyes. He shook his head defiantly. Caspasian grasped him by the shoulder and shoved him forward. 'Move!'

Diaz took two steps into the open, froze, and then turned and sprinted back behind the trees, falling onto his stomach and crawling under some bushes.

'Better go yourself,' Westacott said pleasantly, relishing Caspasian's predicament. 'Don't worry, old man. I'll keep you covered.'

Caspasian took one look at Westacott and Horner and saw the glint in their eyes. 'The hell you will,' he said. He seized Westacott by the scruff of the neck and yanked him to his feet. With one giant shove he propelled him into the open. 'You're coming with me. Move!'

Westacott stumbled and almost fell, but Caspasian had a firm grip of his elbow. 'Come on, granddad. Get out there,' Caspasian said, pushing him in front.

'You can't do this! Sergeant Major, stop him!'

But it was too late. Caspasian was on his way, dragging, pushing and kicking Westacott along with him. 'Personally, I don't reckon the Sergeant Major's got the marksmanship skills to hit me without taking you down as well,' Caspasian said coldly. 'What do you think?'

He saw the terror on Westacott's face. 'Sergeant Major! Don't shoot! Fire at the fort!'

'That's the ticket,' Caspasian said, pulling the Major after him. They reached the chief, who was trying to rally his men and encourage them on. Caspasian flung Westacott to the ground. The chief looked at him, puzzled at the turn of events. Caspasian pointed back towards the jungle.

'Get your men under cover,' he urged, trying to get his message across as best he could, waving his hand in the direction of the trees. The chief understood but shook his head and said something. His hand chopped resolutely towards the fort.

'You're wasting your time, Caspasian,' Westacott snarled from his position on the floor. 'The old fool wants to carry on.'

The chief met Caspasian eye to eye. He repeated his sentence and Caspasian read the meaning in his face. It was now or never. The fight had to be finished here, today. If not, Delgado would be back. The village would never know peace.

Cutting through the air, a livid burst of machine-gun fire cracked close over their heads. Westacott cursed the Sergeant Major, but Caspasian knew better, recognizing the distinctive hammering of a Vickers medium machine-gun. A cold shiver of dread ran down his spine. He dropped onto his stomach, pulling the chief after him and scanned the battlements. There, protruding from a hole in a stretch of wicker fencing that had been used to patch one of the damaged parts of the wall, he saw the chubby business end of the Vickers barrel, a blue cloud of cordite erupting from the muzzle.

He knew that the moment the firers got the range, everyone on the plain was doomed. The whole balance of power had shifted in that one instant. Flight and regrouping were now the only options. He turned again to the chief and urged him to pull his men back. This time the chief faltered. But a second burst of fire from the Vickers swung the argument in Caspasian's favour. The chief raised his head and shouted the commands to his men, projecting his orders to left and right across the battle-field. Gradually his men pulled back, firing arrows uselessly at the fortress walls, the few that made the distance rebounding harmlessly off the brickwork.

A great cheer from Delgado's men rang out at the sight of the Indians turning to run. The trick now, Caspasian knew, was to prevent the withdrawal becoming a rout. The chief was right. The fight had to be concluded today. They would not be able to surprise Delgado again. Somehow Caspasian had to turn the battle round. But how?

With Westacott eagerly leading the way, Caspasian and the

chief pulled back to the Lewis gun which Sergeant Major Horner was using to little effect, peppering the fortress walls at random.

'Engage the Vickers!' Caspasian shouted at him. 'Put them off their aim to let the Indians get away.'

Horner swore but did as he was told. The result was instant. The Vickers went silent as the Lewis bullets punched through the inadequate protection of the wicker and found the firers on the other side. For the moment the initiative had been seized back. Caspasian waved to Brigadier Percival telling him to come and join them and after a few moments he arrived on the scene, reloading his Webley as he went.

'Brigadier, can you take charge here?' Caspasian began. 'If you can keep Delgado's attention focused on this position, I'll try to work my way round the back of the fort and see if I can lead an assault over the wall.'

He grabbed the cowering Diaz and got him to translate his intention to the chief who gave his agreement. 'I'll take four of your riflemen, Major.'

Westacott considered opposing the plan but judged that if he gave way he might be left behind in safety with Horner and the Brigadier. 'Good idea, Caspasian.' He rubbed his calf. 'I think I've pulled a blasted muscle.' He winced.

'Don't worry. You can stay here. I can't afford to have this screwed up as well.'

Westacott left it at that. He had got what he wanted. He would be safe. Nothing else mattered.

'Keep your fire directed on the Vickers,' Caspasian told the Brigadier. 'You've got to make them think we're all still here.'

'Don't worry about us,' Percival said. 'You get on with it.'

Leaving the Brigadier and the others behind, Caspasian and the chief led the way back into the jungle, selecting a circuitous route that would keep them well out of sight to the fort's occupants. While the chief had chosen a force of some twenty of his best men, Caspasian, lacking the same choice, had settled for Scratch, Smudger and two others, Privates Donnelly and Roper. He let the chief lead the way, heading for the point that the two of them had identified on the recce where the jungle came closest to the rear of the fort. Advancing at a fast trot, the chief sped nimbly through the jungle, his warriors moving with equal ease and speed. Caspasian only managed to keep up with difficulty. For Scratch and the rest it was a hopeless task. They quickly started to fall behind and Caspasian had to persuade the chief to slow down for fear of losing contact with Westacott's soldiers.

Time passed and very quickly everyone was working hard. The intense heat of the day was exhausting. Private Roper called out for the others to wait for him. Caspasian hissed at him to shut up. They could not afford to compromise their attack plan a second time.

Finally they arrived at the chosen place. Caspasian dropped down on one knee beside the chief, breathing hard. One by one, the four riflemen arrived and collapsed behind him, their clothes drenched in sweat, all of them gasping for air.

'Can we just get our breath back, sir?' Scratch begged, leaning on his rifle.

'You've got three minutes,' Caspasian said. He regarded the little group. All of them looked back at him, fear in their eyes. 'Any of you lot been in action before?' he asked, dreading the reply.

They stared at him blankly, then shook their heads. 'Well, don't worry about it. They won't be expecting us to come at them from behind and they won't know that there are only five of us with rifles. Mark your man and shoot to kill. Whatever you do, don't hesitate. It's us or them. Once we're over the wall, the only way out is through the gates on the far side when the fight's over.'

'Either that or in a box,' Scratch added helpfully.

Caspasian smiled. 'Correct.'

The others chuckled nervously, trying to hide their fear. Caspasian signalled to the chief that they were ready to go. 'Fix bayonets, lads,' he ordered, regretting his own lack of one. The brass-plated butt would have to do.

The chief and his men surged forward and scaled the wall as easily as monkeys up a tree. Behind them, Caspasian and the others followed, pulling themselves up with much greater difficulty. One by one they cleared the top of the wall and dropped silently down onto the walkway on the inside. The pitched roof of Delgado's residence concealed them from the rest of the fort. Caspasian scanned to left and right. There was no one in sight. From the far side of the fort came the sound of heavy firing, the hammering noise of the Vickers and the accompanying shots of Delgado's rifles, and the answering calls of the Lewis light machine-gun and the handful of Lee Enfields.

The chief looked to Caspasian for the signal. He chopped his open hand towards the centre of the fort. Go. It would have been impossible to try and coordinate the assault in any detail. Language prevented it, apart from which time was of the essence. They would have to rely upon speed and the shock effect of the attack coming from an unexpected direction. The trick now would be to kill as many of the guards as necessary in order to force the remainder to throw down their weapons and give up.

The Indians surged down off the battlements and raced towards the sound of the firing, bows drawn and ready. Behind them, Caspasian pushed his four riflemen out in a skirmish line with himself in the centre and advanced at a fast walk. They held their rifles with the butt in the shoulder, ready to fire.

A cry sounded from their left. Caspasian and the others spun round to see a large woman duck back inside Delgado's house, screaming. The next second, two huge dogs erupted from the open door like fiery boulders and hurtled straight for Private

Donnelly, the nearest of the riflemen. He swung his rifle onto them and loosed off a shot. But panic had sent it wide and the dogs barely faltered in their pounding stride. Caspasian dropped to one knee, aimed, steadied his breathing, and fired. One of the dogs was stopped in its tracks as if an invisible giant hand had swatted it stone dead. But its companion was on top of Donnelly. The force of its huge body sent him flying. Its bared teeth went straight for his throat and before the others could react or Caspasian could reload, working the rifle bolt furiously, the dog had torn flesh and membrane asunder. There was not even time for Donnelly to scream.

Caspasian's rifle fired again and the dog was flung clear with a piercing yelp. Its lifeless corpse stopped twitching only one second before Donnelly's.

'The woman!' Scratch shouted.

'Leave her,' Caspasian ordered. He saw two of the Indians running for the entrance. They could take care of her.

From beyond the house, the sound of shouting announced that surprise had been lost. Alerted by Caspasian's rifle shots, Delgado had sent someone to investigate. He had run headlong into the Indians who had cut him down in a flurry of blows. But his comrades had seen and were now rushing to face this new threat.

From all sides, Delgado's guards appeared. Bullets snapped in the air and the Indians whooped and cried, flinging themselves into the attack.

'Fire, lads!' Caspasian shouted to his men. He advanced steadily, firing and reloading as he went, rattling off shots at any of Delgado's men on whom he could draw a bead. Roper, Scratch and Smudger rose to the occasion and charged forward, bayonets levelled. Smudger was the first to find his mark. One of the guards ran full pelt round the corner of an outhouse and straight onto the end of his bayonet. It was hard to tell who looked the more surprised. In horror, Smudger kicked out and forced the dying man off his rifle, tugging the weapon free.

Throughout the inside of the fort there was hand-to-hand fighting. Across the heads of the crowd, Caspasian caught sight of Colonel Delgado trying to rally his men.

'Scratch!' Caspasian yelled. 'Take the others and make for the gates. Get them open so the Brigadier and all the rest can come in. Go!'

Scratch nodded and went about his mission, Smudger and Roper with him. From Caspasian's right-hand side there was a shout. He turned to see a man rushing upon him. Caspasian knew all ten rounds in his magazine were expended. In the final fraction of a second, he reversed his grip on his rifle and swung the butt at his opponent. The man ducked under it. The blade of a knife glinted and Rodriguez brought it up in a savage thrust at Caspasian's stomach. Dropping his rifle, Caspasian flung himself out of harm's way, rolling aside and coming up on his feet to face the next attack. Sure enough it came in, hard and fast. Rodriguez slashed at Caspasian's face, the blade passing within a hair's breadth of the skin. But this time Caspasian was ready. His right leg shot out, the foot snapping upwards, the instep driving up between Rodriguez's legs in a perfect *kin-geri* kick. Rodriguez was knocked double, gasping for breath. With one hand he clutched his testicles. The other swung the knife again in an attempt to drive off his attacker. But the blow was slovenly, a desperate gamble that failed. Caspasian palmed it aside and fired his right fist into Rodriguez's jaw. He saw it tell, the effect registering in the man's eyes. With the same hand, he closed in for the kill, bringing down a devastating *shuto sakotsu-uchi* open hand strike onto the base of Rodriguez's skull. He felt the bone crack and Rodriguez keeled over, dead.

Retrieving his rifle, Caspasian snapped open the bolt exposing the empty breach. He took two fresh five-round clips of ammunition from his bandolier, put the first one in place and thumbed home the rounds, sliding them out of the clip and down into the magazine. Then the second clip. He tossed aside the empty clips, their job done, and slammed the bolt shut sending a live round into the chamber and cocking the firing pin. Now he was out for Delgado. The Colonel himself. If he could finish him, the fight would be over.

He found him attempting to rally his men. They were trying to manhandle the Vickers gun, lifting the tripod round so as to fire down into the fort where the desperate hand-to-hand fight with the Indians was taking place.

'The gate!' Caspasian heard Delgado yell at the top of his voice. 'Fire at the gate!'

He had seen Scratch, Smudger and Roper working their way towards it. They had just struck down the last of the guards there. Roper was tugging his bayonet from the body. At that moment, a burst of Vickers fire cut right through him. Roper seemed to dance on the spot as if electrified. His limbs jerked and twitched and then, the firing over, he fell dead in a heap. From his position on the far side of the courtyard, Caspasian braced himself against a wall and took careful aim. He squeezed off a round, reloading immediately. His first bullet struck the man next to Delgado and he fell off the battlements. Caspasian aimed again, but this time Delgado had been alerted and Caspasian found his target staring straight at him. The instant Caspasian fired, Delgado flung himself to the ground and scuttled away, leaving his men to operate the Vickers by themselves.

Two more rounds took care of them. The Vickers gun overbalanced and tumbled headlong from the wall. By the gates, Scratch and Smudger were drawing back the bolt. There was the sound of creaking hinges and then daylight appeared through a crack, broadening as the doors swung open. On the other side, Brigadier Percival, Westacott, Horner and the others were waiting. But two more of Westacott's men lay dead outside the fort, their bodies visible through the widening doors.

Locating Colonel Delgado, Caspasian hurtled after him.

Closing the final yards, he flung himself at Delgado's legs and the two men skidded into the dirt in a tangle of limbs. Caspasian grabbed hold of Delgado's jerkin and aimed a punch at his face, but the Colonel pulled aside and the fist sailed past, the knuckles just scraping his unshaven chin.

'You dog,' Delgado hissed. 'Who are you?' As he spoke, he brought his knee up into Caspasian's stomach, knocking the wind out of him. Caspasian doubled onto his side, gasping for breath. He lashed out with a *uraken* backfist strike, trying to ward off his opponent who was levering himself on top. The blow struck Delgado in the chest but did little damage. The Colonel wheezed and blinked away the pain. He reached down to his boot and whipped out a short-bladed knife, raising the point above Caspasian's throat in readiness for a thrust.

'Die.'

But before he could stab, an arrow smashed clean through his jaw from side to side. With a look of shock and outrage, Delgado dropped his knife and grappled at the arrow. Caspasian swung his right fist upwards, hitting him in the throat. Delgado coughed and rolled off him. With a superhuman effort, the Colonel drew the arrow swiftly from his jaw. But no sooner had he done so than a second arrow struck him in the chest. Caspasian glanced up and saw the chief standing some twenty yards away, putting a third arrow to his bow string.

It was not needed. Delgado's eyes were glazing over.

Brigadier Percival ran to join them. He stood looking down at the dying man. 'Some of the passengers are missing.'

Caspasian stared at him. The words made no sense. He was still focused on the battle.

'Caspasian,' the Brigadier said more urgently. 'There's no sign of Captain Harrison. Wolter, Domain and several others have gone too.'

Caspasian fought to clear his head. He got up. 'The jungle?'

The Brigadier shook his head. 'Just some of the crewmen and a few others. All the key personnel have been taken.'

'Who by?'

On the ground at his feet, there was a gurgling sound from the dying Colonel. Caspasian knelt beside him and realized that the man was laughing.

'You're too late,' he mumbled. 'They've gone.'

'Gone where?' Caspasian asked, keeping his voice calm and trying to project it into Delgado's fading consciousness.

'Gone. He needed more workers. Always he needs more. He came for them in the night.' He laughed again, blood flowing freely from his mouth. Death was very close.

'Who came for them?'

But Colonel Delgado was dead. His chest deflated like a balloon as his last breath left him, his eyes setting like stones staring up into the sky.

15

Gustav Wolter and Captain Harrison sat back to back, the ropes securing them to each other biting savagely into their arms. The ties fastening Wolter's wrists and ankles were so tight that his hands and feet had long since gone numb. It was aggravated by the cold which swept through the air in icy blasts.

'I must say, Captain,' he whispered over his shoulder, 'I thought I'd seen the last of airships.'

Captain Harrison looked up. He had been dozing, exhausted after the labours at Colonel Delgado's mines. His uniform was in tatters and no sign remained of his once proud bearing. Around him, the cargo hold of an airship swam into view. The next second he recognized it as his own *D200*. But since it had been seized it had undergone a variety of modifications. The cargo hold had been enlarged and, aside from the handful of prisoners crowded together in the middle, it contained numerous packing cases, most of which were laden with food. He could see maize, sacks of rice, salted beef and pork. There were crates of live chickens, cases of eggs packed in straw, tins of tobacco, tea, coffee and sugar, potatoes, cabbages, and all manner of other goods. Of particular interest were several boxes that had been manhandled aboard and stowed well away from the dozen or so prisoners.

Opposite them, Richard Edward groaned with the discomfort. 'Personally I'm going to write a letter of complaint to the line. I think the service has been disgraceful.'

Captain Harrison chuckled tiredly. 'Yes. I must apologize on behalf of the management. I promise you a full refund.'

'And compensation for the inconvenience?'

'Of course.'

Back to back with Richard, Lionel Domain shifted miserably. 'Why don't you just shut the hell up? My head's pounding as it is.' Adorned with a black eye and a split lip, he too was a shadow of his former self. Across the way from him, three Indians sat terrified, wide eyes staring about them. Next to them, a further six rocked together, eyes clenched shut, keening eerily. Domain glared at them. 'Look at those poor dumb bastards. At least we're not labouring under the impression that we've been seized by malevolent gods as they probably are.'

'Can you be so sure they're wrong?' Wolter asked. 'I'd say the past few days are a pretty fair approximation of hell.'

'Amen to that,' Richard piped up.

Domain went to reply but accidentally opened the cut on his lip again. He winced, sucking in cold air. When he could speak, he said, 'What I want to know is who the hell these guys are.' He kept his voice low. 'My lawyers are going to sue the pants off them.'

Richard swapped an amused grin with Wolter and Harrison. 'I promise to contribute to the costs of the action, Mr Domain,' he said. 'In fact, just get me to court in one piece and I'll finance it myself.'

Domain sneered. 'Yeah, yeah. Go ahead and laugh. You think you know it all.'

'Come on, old chap,' Richard said, worried that he had gone too far. 'I was only joking.'

Just then a man entered. 'Quiet! No talking.' He was dressed in a grey one piece tank suit fastened with buttons up the front. It was thickly padded with a brown fur collar against the cold. He wore special soft-soled boots for use in airships, designed to prevent sparks from static electricity. His leather belt held a small pistol holster that sat on his right hip. Wolter recognized the weapon as a Luger. A pair of folded leather gauntlets was tucked neatly into his belt next to the holster. On his head he wore a soft hat with warm ear flaps, though at the moment they were fastened above it in the Russian fashion. On the left side of his chest there was some sort of insignia which Wolter tried to get a better look at. He thought he recognized the design but, try as he might, he could not remember where he had seen it before. The man spoke English but although it was not his mother tongue, neither Wolter nor the others could identify his nationality.

Wolter looked at Domain, wondering whether he was going to give the guard a mouthful. The film producer remained sullenly quiet. He had been taught his lesson by Delgado's men.

The airship had been flying for several hours. It was hard to be certain of the exact time because the prisoners had been stripped of all their valuables at Delgado's fort, watches especially. Wolter reckoned it had been the early hours of the morning when they had been kicked awake by Rodriguez and taken out of the fort. They had then been led away from the mine workings and onto a bare-topped hill about half a mile from the fort. There they had found all the food crates ready and waiting. They had been ordered to sit down and some time later Wolter had heard the telltale drone of the airship's engines. They had all stared in astonishment as the *D200* had appeared over the treetops and come in to hover above them in a perfectly executed manoeuvre. Harrison had been impressed.

Herded aboard, carrying the cargo, they had been tied up and then the airship had taken off, taking them with it, bound no one knew where. It was the second time they had seen the crew in their distinctive uniforms. They were clearly well disciplined, but did not appear to belong to the forces of any nation that Wolter or Harrison recognized, unless it was a rogue state or an especially secretive part of the armed forces of one of the great powers.

The outer doors to the cargo bay had been left open. Domain insisted that their captors had done it on purpose. Wolter reckoned he was probably right. The cold air blasting in served to subdue the captives further, forcing them into shivering huddles. From his position on the floor, Wolter could see nothing of the land they were passing over. He could not even tell whether they were headed north, south, east or west. He thought they were probably cruising at anything between three and five thousand feet, judging by the type of cloud formation he was able to glimpse from time to time.

It had been dark when the airship had picked them up, but it had been a clear starlit night and Wolter thought he could make out one other modification. In several different places along the side of the hull visible to him, machine-gun nests had been built into the structure. The airship had been converted into a weapon of war. It was all horribly reminiscent of his wartime experiences.

He had an idea. 'Excuse me,' he called across to the guard.

'I said no talking!'

'Yes but you don't understand. My face is itching.' He smiled. 'It is driving me crazy. Just here.' He turned his right cheek towards the guard.

The guard grinned and sauntered over. 'Where did you say?' he asked nicely, looking concerned.

Wolter looked up at him, then turned his cheek again. 'Just there. In the centre.'

The guard drew back his fist and punched him hard in the side of the face sending both him and, because of the rope bindings, Captain Harrison toppling onto their sides. The guard howled with laughter and strode away. Wolter and Harrison worked their way upright again, Wolter tasting blood.

'You bloody fool,' Harrison whispered. 'You asked for that.'

But Wolter did not reply. His mind was racing, a hundred thoughts coursing through it, a hundred possibilities. For when the guard had stooped over him, as Wolter had known he would, he had presented a clear and close-up view of the small design fashioned on his chest. It had been just enough for Wolter to recognize it and know it for what it was. A family crest. One that he knew all too well.

Just at that moment voices sounded outside the cargo bay coming from the axial gangway running down the centre of the airship's vast interior.

'What's going on here? What are you doing?' said the man who entered. He was accompanied by three others. Two were junior officers, the other a crewman.

The guard sprang to attention. 'One of the prisoners was giving trouble, sir.'

'Then throw him overboard,' the man said casually. Wolter realized he was completely serious. At his back, he felt Captain Harrison sit up, ramrod straight. Harrison craned his head round to see the speaker.

'You!'

Lieutenant Davies laughed unpleasantly. 'Why if it isn't my old shipmate.'

He came across and stood over them, hands on hips, smiling down. Captain Harrison wriggled and tore at the ropes with his teeth. 'You bastard. I should have known you were behind all of this.' He tried to kick out but his ankles were held fast by the ropes.

Lieutenant Davies took a step backwards, moving himself out of range just in case. 'Now, now, Captain. That's hardly the behaviour of an officer and a gentleman.'

Davies spoke to the guard, waving him forward. 'Throw them both overboard.' He smiled at Harrison. 'You'll be dead by the time you hit the water, but just in case you're not, this part of the Caribbean boasts some of the most aggressive sharks known to man. I'm sure they'd be grateful for an easy meal, even one as stringy as you.'

He jerked his head at the guard who stepped forward and laid hold of their bindings.

'It was quite an inconvenience when you discovered my two assistants after the storm.' Davies nodded with grudging admiration. 'Only you would have detected the extra weight. No one else. I should have known. Luckily I managed the rest by myself.'

'What did you use?' Harrison asked, his eyes burning hatred at his captor.

'A simple knockout gas. You should congratulate me really, landing this thing at the rendezvous all by myself.'

'You were one of my officers, damn it!' Harrison stormed. 'How could you betray us all like this?'

'Not half as difficult as you might imagine,' Davies answered casually. 'Money can be a great persuader.' He indicated for the guard to continue.

Wolter and Harrison fought as best they could but the crewman dragged them with minimal effort across to the edge of the open cargo hatch. Cold air blasted into their faces and far below, white-crested waves appeared through the broken cloud like tiny shavings of ice.

'Stop!' The command froze everyone where they stood. The junior officers and crewmen braced to attention. Davies less quickly but with equal respect. Wolter looked up to see who had just saved their lives. The man who had spoken wore a similar one-piece tank suit to the others, but it was decorated with gold braid epaulettes and rings on the cuffs. Wolter stared at him dumbfounded. The man was bearded, but it was wispy and all wrong. Beneath it his face was badly scarred as if from fire. All the same, recognition was instant. The family crest and the other pieces of the puzzle started to fit.

'Baron von Staaden,' Wolter said quietly. The man looked at him, brow furrowed.

'Do I know you?'

Suddenly Wolter realized that it might have been in his best interest to remain anonymous. But it was too late. He should have known better. The Baron had always had an excellent memory for names and faces. Especially for his old crews. But his interest had always been that of the scientist, rather than the comrade in arms. He had prided himself on knowing the names of his crewmen in the way an entomologist knows the identities of the specimens transfixed beneath the glass.

He narrowed his eyes and Wolter could see the mind coldly working, thumbing through old pages, searching for the relevant entry. And then he reached it. A thin smile dawned, first in the eyes and then working down through the burnt, twisted cheeks to the hard, firm-lipped mouth.

'Wolter. Gustav Wolter.' The Baron pronounced the name almost with awe, part of which could have been at his own feat of memory. He came across and crouched beside the bound man, laying a gauntleted hand on his shoulder. The gesture was somehow devoid of human warmth. 'So you too came back from the dead. It's been a long time.' He eased himself stiffly to his feet. 'It is unexpected to see you, although I might have wished it could have been under other circumstances.'

He turned to Davies. 'Really, I do not think there is any need for further unpleasantness.'

'Do you know this man, Gustav?' Captain Harrison asked, incredulous.

The Baron answered for him. 'Gustav and I are old comrades in arms, aren't we, Gustav?' He was thoughtful. 'But tell me. How the devil did you survive? The last I saw of you you were hurtling towards dear old Merry England in the severed observation basket.'

Wolter shuddered. 'Have you never seen a sycamore seed? How the aerodynamics cause it to spin, hovering to the ground? That's what happened to the basket. I fastened myself to it and my body acted like the wing, slowing the descent. But it was too late for poor Dieter. He was thrown out and died.'

He was about to ask about the Captain's story when Lionel Domain decided he had had enough. 'Well this is real cosy!' he sneered. 'This is turning out to be quite a red letter day for reunions, isn't it? Gustav, just suppose you get your old war buddy to release us.'

The Baron seemed to give the matter genuine consideration and for a moment Wolter wondered whether they were about to be untied.

'I'm sorry,' he said at last. 'For now at least it is better if you remain secure.' He checked his watch. 'It won't be long, though. We'll be arriving soon.'

'Arriving? Where, in God's name?' Harrison stormed.

The Baron smiled his twisted smile again. 'It's a surprise. My little secret. You will have to wait and see.'

With Colonel Delgado dead, resistance in the fort crumbled. The surviving guards threw down their weapons and surrendered. The slave workforce drifted back from the jungle and gathered around them, the mood getting nasty. Several of the Indians picked up rocks and hurled them at their former captors. Brigadier Percival ordered Sergeant Major Horner and his two remaining men to lock the guards in one of the accommodation blocks previously occupied by their prisoners. He hoped that once out of sight they would, to an extent, be out of mind. Not surprisingly, the guards were all too eager to comply with his directions.

'Well, that's that, then,' Westacott said cheerfully. 'Delgado's dead. Let's pack up here and get back to Georgetown. Mission accomplished, I'd say.'

Caspasian stared at him in wonder. 'Delgado wasn't the mission. The airship was.'

Westacott looked disgruntled, clearly unused to being

contradicted by a captain. Before he could speak, Brigadier Percival took over. 'Caspasian's right. We've got to track down the airship and find out who's operating it. They can't be allowed simply to steal two of His Majesty's dirigibles and get away with it. Apart from which, Harrison and several others are still missing.'

'That's all very well, but how on earth do you intend to find them?' Westacott asked scornfully.

Caspasian was already walking towards the imprisoned guards. Westacott watched him go. 'Are we to take it you've got an idea?' he called after him sarcastically.

'The airship came here to drop off the prisoners for Delgado's mines, and it was here again last night for whatever reason. It's fair to assume it's coming back at some point. One of the guards might know when.'

The others came trotting at his heels. 'Why should they?' Westacott persisted.

'Has anyone found any wireless apparatus here?' Caspasian asked.

No one had.

'Well there you are, then,' he said triumphantly. 'Visits are probably prearranged. The airship wouldn't simply turn up. Cargos would have to be packed and prepared. That all takes time. No airship would want to hang around the jungle in-definitely. Weather conditions are too unpredictable, for one thing. And if there's no signals equipment, then they must follow some sort of pattern. At the very least, the airship must have told Delgado when the next visit was going to be.'

'And Delgado's dead,' Westacott pointed out unhelpfully.

'Yes, but plenty of his men are not,' Brigadier Percival con-cluded on Caspasian's behalf. 'Well done, Caspasian. It's certainly worth a try.'

The guards were initially sullen and tongue-tied. However, the moment Caspasian suggested handing over the interrogation to the Indians hovering outside the building, brandishing spears, bows and arrows, the spell was broken and offers of help tumbled forth. But when he had quietened them, listened to their various tales and sifted the information, he discovered that no one knew the single piece of information he was after.

Caspasian was just on the verge of becoming despondent when Diaz appeared in the doorway. 'You might want to come and look at this.'

'You've found something?' Westacott asked, trying to wrest back control of events.

Diaz grinned wickedly. 'Some*one*.'

He led the others out of the building and, pushing his way through the throng of Indians who were still hoping for blood, crossed the central courtyard in the direction of Delgado's residence. Just inside the doors they came upon the chief and four of his men attempting to quieten a large woman. Half of the Indians seemed to want to kill her to put an end to her ranting, but the chief was trying to restore order.

Diaz stood aside with a huge smile, presenting the spectacle to Caspasian and the others. 'Delgado's woman,' he announced proudly.

The chief looked at Caspasian, his eyes appealing for help. Caspasian stepped forward and the Indians moved aside, thankfully giving him the floor. The woman was dressed in billowing blouse and skirt, both of which mercifully served to disguise her true size and shape. She sat like a collapsed circus tent, her arms waving about her head like the tentacles of an octopus in a stiff current. Her fists were clenched and in one of them she clutched a piece of cloth that had once been a handkerchief, probably a white one. She beat her breast and wailed. Caspasian regarded her warily, wondering how best to approach.

'Her name is Annabella,' Diaz prompted helpfully. 'We got that much out of her.'

After several attempts, Caspasian managed to get the

woman's attention. She blinked up at him through a ragged screen of black hair, her face swollen and smudged with tears.

'What do I care for any of you?' she howled. 'Do what you want with me. Use me as you will.'

Caspasian was revolted at the thought of it. 'No one is going to harm you, Annabella.' He watched her, trying a smile. 'Is that your name?'

She sniffed and glanced at him again, moving a strand of hair aside to get a better view. 'Sí,' she said. Her lips pouted.

'Annabella, we need your help. We need some information. Will you do that for us?' Caspasian crouched down beside her, his eyes level with hers.

'Why should I? You kill my Guillermo. He was the only one who cared for me. Who will look after me now?'

'We will look after you,' Caspasian said. 'I will see you get safely to Georgetown and . . .' His promise petered out. He did not want to lie to her. He knew where a woman like her was likely to end up once back in the town and there would be little or nothing he could do to prevent it.

Unconstrained by conscience, Brigadier Percival intervened. 'You'll be well looked after, my dear. I guarantee it.'

Annabella observed him shrewdly, evaluating the offer. 'What do you want to know?' she said at last.

'When is the airship due to return?' Percival asked.

'How do you expect me to know that? Guillermo never tell me such things. Besides, I am not interested.' She folded her arms and turned her head away from them.

'We can pay you,' Percival said slyly.

In a flash he had her attention. 'Pay?'

'Pay.'

'How much?'

'Fifty pounds,' Percival said, standing back proudly to antici-pate victory.

'Ha!' Annabella burst out in peals of ringing laughter that

echoed round the courtyard walls. Her tears were forgotten.

Brigadier Percival stared at her pinch-faced. 'Have I said something funny?' he asked acidly.

When she had recovered herself, Annabella mopped her face and beamed up at him. 'Do you have any idea how much money Guillermo made here?'

'Clearly more than the fifty pounds I offered,' the Brigadier observed. 'All right then, suppose you tell me how much it will take to loosen your tongue?'

'This is a nonsense,' Westacott stormed. 'Give her to Horner for a couple of minutes. He'll beat it out of her.'

Annabella stared at him fearlessly. 'If you lay a finger on me, I will tell you nothing.'

'We'll see about that,' Westacott said. 'Come on Sergeant Major, give me a hand.' He reached towards Annabella who shrank away from the two men with a piercing shriek. Before they could touch her, Caspasian put himself in front of her. 'That'll do. No one's going to beat anyone.'

Annabella peered round from behind him, daring the aggressors. Westacott glared at Caspasian. 'Get out of the way, Captain. That's an order.'

'I'd tread carefully, if I were you, Major,' Percival said, bemused.

'Damn that!' Westacott took a single step forward, laid a hand on Caspasian's shoulder and shoved. The next second he was flying through the air, the result of a perfectly executed *ippon seoinage* shoulder throw. Annabella stared in admiring wonder at her new champion. Horner growled and swung. His fist sailed through the empty space where Caspasian's face had been. He swung in with a left uppercut, but again his target dodged effortlessly out of the way. He moved in, his guard high, and stabbed again, a right jab, fast and furious but well controlled. Caspasian was unconcerned. He pulled back and struck the side of Horner's advancing foot with his instep in a foot sweep. The ground rolled away from Horner. He staggered and fell straight into Caspasian's uppercut that caught him squarely on the chin. Darkness closed about him and Horner crumpled sweetly to the ground.

Westacott looked up winded and confused. Stunned from the hard landing, he counted his limbs, gathered them together and got shakily to his feet. He straightened up to find Caspasian's eyes fixed on him.

'You'll pay for this, Caspasian,' Westacott said, his voice quivering with shock. 'You can't just strike a superior officer like that.'

But Caspasian was no longer concerned with him. Annabella was on her feet too, fingering Caspasian's arm wonderingly, agog at her saviour. He removed her grip as politely as he could. 'Annabella, it would help . . .'

'Oh yes, yes, yes, that,' she said with a bored sigh. 'The airship. I will tell you whatever you want to know. Everyone is interested in the airship.' She rolled her eyes. 'Men and their toys.' She stared into his eyes as the Brigadier looked on, enjoying every moment of Caspasian's mounting discomfort. 'You promise you will see me safely to Georgetown? Away from this jungle?'

'I promise.' Caspasian swallowed. It was suddenly very hot in the courtyard.

'And will you . . .' Her fingers returned to his sleeve. 'Visit me there? Will you visit your Annabella?'

Caspasian heard a choked smirk from the Brigadier. 'One thing at a time,' Caspasian said, brushing some dust from his sleeve, Annabella's fingers with it. 'We have to get out alive first.'

She pouted again, sulking and thinking. Eventually she said, 'I heard my Guillermo saying that the airship would be returning the day after tomorrow. He told Rodriguez something about needing maize and chickens.'

'Chickens?' the Brigadier queried.

Annabella stared at him, defiant. 'Yes. Chickens. That's what I said. Feathers. Two legs. Chickens.' Her eyes twinkled. 'And more stones too. The Baron always loves to have his pretty stones.'

Caspasian and the Brigadier swapped glances. 'This Baron,' the Brigadier asked tentatively. 'What do you know about him?'

Annabella shrugged. 'Nothing. I hardly ever see him. He is cold as a fish. And . . .' her nose wrinkled, 'scarred. All over here.' A sweep of her hand encompassed her face.

'Do you know his name?'

She regarded Percival as if it had never occurred to her to ask. 'No,' she said simply. 'He is just known as the Baron. Everyone calls him that. The Baron.'

'When the airship comes, Annabella,' Caspasian said, 'what's the procedure? I mean, how does it all work?'

Again she shrugged, wondering that she had never considered it before. 'There is a clearing quite close by. The airship lands there, I think. I have not seen it myself, but I heard the men speak of it. I used to see the food and other boxes being prepared outside. Then the men came and took it away. Sometimes I would see the lights in the sky and hear the motors. Very loud. It was always at night.' She smiled at the memory. 'I would always be waiting for Guillermo to come back. He was always . . . You know, excited, afterwards.'

Her smile turned instantly to tears and fresh sobbing wracked her body.

Percival and Caspasian consulted. 'Well, that's that, then. We've got the approximate time and place of the next rendezvous,' Percival said quietly, leaving Annabella to her grief. 'Even if the guards didn't know when the airship was returning, they should at least know the details of the procedure for when it gets here. All we need now is a plan.'

Westacott and Horner had withdrawn to nurse their bruises

and hurt pride. 'What about them?' Caspasian asked, indicating the two scowling men.

'We need the extra guns,' Percival said. 'Now more than ever, I'd guess.'

Caspasian was not so sure, but he feared the Brigadier was right. He knew that the sooner he could be shot of Westacott and Horner, the happier he would be. But that time had not yet arrived. Ideas were running through his head.

'What we need is a Trojan horse,' he said at last.

The Brigadier smiled at him. 'Go on.'

As Annabella grieved, Westacott and Horner mused blackly, and the Indians set about looting the camp of the late Colonel Guillermo Delgado, Caspasian began to outline his plan.

16

As officer of the watch in the control car gondola, Lieutenant Davies scoured the night sky through his binoculars. He always found it remarkable how much could be seen even at such an hour. The moon had risen and cast a radiant glow across the jungle canopy, softly undulating like a vast quilt across the earth's surface. He was searching for Colonel Delgado's signal flares, to be fired when the airship was heard approaching. So far they had been flying on a compass bearing, but a strong wind from the south-west had corrupted Davies' readings and he was uncertain of the exact location of the rendezvous. Nonetheless, he was not concerned. Out here in the wilderness of jungle, he would be able to switch on the searchlight without fear of compromise. Delgado would be able to see it even at long range and then Davies would be able to home in on the flares that the Colonel would send up.

The Lieutenant was in sole charge this evening. The Baron had remained behind and Davies was enjoying the freedom. He lowered the binoculars and in answer to the helmsman's questioning stare, shook his head. 'Nothing yet.'

'The searchlight, sir?'

'A ten-second burst,' Davies said.

The helmsman spoke briefly into the communication tube beside him and a moment later a harsh beam of white light split the darkness in two, cleaving it open in front of the cruising airship. It swept in a broad arc, first to port and then to starboard, covering a full one hundred and eighty degrees. The beam was angled slightly downwards to the jungle canopy and reached out for several miles. From the distance, Davies knew that it would appear as the beam from a lighthouse, flashing clearly in the night, indicating to any human observer the position of the approaching airship.

Ten seconds later the beam was shut off and darkness returned to the hostile landscape. For several moments everything was pitch black, but slowly the crew's eyes readjusted to the absence of the beam and the moon and stars established themselves once more in the heavens.

'There, sir!' the helmsman said pointing. 'Flare at ten o'clock.'

Lieutenant Davies saw the distant rocket climb shakily into the night sky, a slender arching thread of silver quickly swallowed by the darkness. He smiled. The Colonel was awake after all. And expecting them. He had climbed off his fat whore and would be waiting in the clearing as arranged.

'Bring us round onto course,' Davies ordered.

The helmsman obeyed, turning the rudder wheel steadily until the airship's blunt nose swung in the direction where the flare had been. With perfect timing, a second flare rose into the sky and burst at the exact moment the nose touched the invisible point in the sky beneath which the rendezvous party was located.

'Delgado's excelling himself tonight,' Davies said with a sarcastic smirk. He checked his watch. They were in good time too. All things being equal, he would have the cargo loaded and they would be away, out over the sea, well before first light.

'Elevators set to take us to three hundred feet,' he commanded. The crewman instantly complied.

Davies braced himself as the airship's nose tilted downwards and it began a steady descent. Some minutes later a third signal flare rose into the night sky and burst over the jungle. Davies could imagine the cries of the parrots and monkeys, startled and outraged by the interruption to their night's routine. In every tree and on almost every branch, the nightly battle for survival would be going on, from the highest member of the animal kingdom down to the lowliest reptile and insect, predator hunting its prey. Across the seemingly peaceful jungle, he wondered how many millions of creatures of all shapes and sizes would be dead by morning. In comparison, it made his own progress through life stately in the extreme.

At three hundred feet the elevator crewman brought the airship level. 'Ship in trim, sir,' he reported.

'Stand by for line drop.'

'Aye, aye, sir.'

'All engines full astern.'

The order was telegraphed to the engine gondolas, the result coming within seconds. Davies could feel the giant beast slowing. 'Steady as she goes.'

'Wind's dropped away, sir,' the junior officer said with a relieved smile. 'It's as calm as a millpond out there.'

'Good.' Davies nodded with satisfaction. Everything was going like clockwork. The Baron would be pleased.

'Shall I order the landing party to stand ready?'

Davies smiled. 'Go ahead, Mr Quesada. We'll bring her in to ground level to assist the loading. I want to be away sharpish. I don't want anyone disappearing off into the jungle. If they do, they'll get left behind.'

'Understood, sir.'

'Mind you, I'm sure Delgado would find some use for them.'

Quesada chuckled nastily. 'That should be incentive enough to keep them close by.'

An area of jungle large enough to accommodate the airship had been cleared and marked with lanterns, one at each of the four corners and a straight row bisecting the centre to enable the helmsman to orientate the airship correctly.

'Ground party at six o'clock, sir,' Quesada reported. Davies put his binoculars onto them and registered a large group of Delgado's men, together with a number of their Indian slaves who would carry out the loading of the cargo. Boxes and bundles were piled up beside them ready for bringing on board. Davies felt that things were getting better and better. Usually they had to chivvy and bully Delgado to get a move on. He was obviously improving with age.

Slowly but surely the airship inched towards the ground. The mooring ropes were dropped. Delgado's ground crew seized hold of them and guided the vessel down until it was floating a mere six feet above the earth. A ramp was lowered from the cargo hold and Lieutenant Davies' landing party hurried down to rendezvous with Delgado's men and begin the loading of the cargo.

'Going ashore yourself, sir?' Quesada asked.

'What on earth for? To socialize with that villainous cretin?' Davies laughed. 'You go, I'll stay here. Report back the moment everything's securely aboard.'

Quesada saluted and left the control car. Rather than making his way back to the cargo hold by the laborious route through the ship's hull, he lifted a hatch in the control car's floor and lowered himself down through it, dropping to the ground visible just below. From there it was a long walk back towards where the cargo had already started loading, but he was grateful for the opportunity to stretch his legs.

Lieutenant Davies reached for a thermos and poured himself a cup of coffee, taking advantage of the break to relax for a while. Aloft, he had to remain vigilant constantly, alert to every shift in wind direction and speed, every air current and temperature change, all of which radically affected the airship's handling. Particularly at low level over the jungle, a sudden gust or squall could drive them into the treetops with disastrous consequences. Now however, safely moored in Delgado's clearing, Davies sipped his coffee and waited. The experience would have been completed by a nice pipe of tobacco but the Baron would have had him scalped if he found out and, knowing his control over all members of his crews, Davies knew that word would speedily reach him. It was not worth the risk.

At last he heard Quesada's voice calling up to him from the hatch below. He went across and peered down. 'All set?'

Quesada nodded. 'Everything's aboard, sir. The landing party's just closing up the ramp now.'

'Excellent. How's Delgado?'

He had swung down a short ladder to help Quesada aboard. He pulled himself up into the control car. 'No sign of him. He'd sent one of his lickspittles to oversee the operation. Ganglylooking youth. I heard one of the Indians call him Diaz.'

Davies frowned. 'Wasn't Rodriguez in charge?'

Quesada shrugged. 'Don't think so. To tell the truth it was all a bit of a shambles. Men all over the place. It was difficult to keep track of who was who in the dark. The fuel in the nearest of the landing lights ran out and they didn't have any spare with them.'

Davies grinned maliciously. 'That sounds more like the Delgado I know. I was getting worried for a minute. His procedure up until now had been far too slick. Not like him at all.'

'Oh, they were Delgado's men all right,' Quesada said. 'As surly as ever. They barely said a word to us. Kept their heads down and carried on working. Miserable sods.'

Davies screwed the cap back onto his thermos and stowed it away. 'Let me see the manifest.'

Quesada handed over a clipboard. Davies ran his finger down the list of items detailed on it. Beside each one Quesada had marked a tick. Davies grunted with satisfaction. 'Seems fine. Did you carry out all the usual checks.'

'Of course.'

'Good. Let's be going then.'

Quesada passed the word through the communication tubes to all parts of the vessel.

'Retract all lines and drop ballast fore and aft,' Davies ordered. The sound of water cascading out of the ballast tanks announced the start of the airship's ascent. Ever so gently, the vessel began to rise.

'Start all engines. Set elevators for ascent on my command.'

'Aye, aye, sir,' the elevator crewman responded.

The moment Davies was confident they were clear of the treetops he gave the order. 'Engines full ahead. Take her up.'

'Aye, aye, sir.'

When the altimeter showed the airship at five hundred feet, Davies said, 'Rudder hard to port. Bring us round, helmsman.'

He checked a large compass and when the needle showed the bearing for their home base the helmsman set the new course and the airship accelerated away from the jungle rendezvous. Davies leaned towards the gondola windows and looked out, surveying the sky. The heavens were beautifully clear and bright. There was now only the slightest cross wind and everything seemed fine for a speedy and trouble free return voyage. The Baron would be pleased. The rendezvous had gone like clockwork.

In the cargo hold, Caspasian shifted uncomfortably in the bottom of his crate. Squashed in beside him, Major Westacott muttered savagely.

'Stupid bloody idea. I should never have agreed.'

'Shut up,' Caspasian hissed.

In the pitch blackness Caspasian could feel Westacott's eyes boring their hatred into him. 'You'll cross me once too often, Captain.'

Caspasian and the Brigadier had agreed that it would be safest if Westacott and his Sergeant Major were split from one another. Otherwise there was no knowing what they might do. So, while Caspasian and Westacott shared one of the packing cases, Brigadier Percival had the dubious pleasure of Sergeant Major Horner's company in another. In a third packing case, Scratch and Smudger were similarly cramped. The chief had promised to see the rescued passengers and crew of the *D200* safely back to Sansaka, Emma Lavelle with them. There they would rendezvous with Captain Contreras and return down the Karanato to Georgetown.

Squashed in the bottom of the packing case, Caspasian and Westacott were covered with a canvas tarpaulin, on top of which Diaz, the chief and his men had heaped vegetables and fruit, bound for the Baron's lair. In still more crates, a priceless consignment of uncut diamonds had been prepared, mined by Delgado's workforce immediately before his overthrow.

As the hours passed, Caspasian could feel Westacott becoming more and more restive. They were all aboard the airship, so what now? Ideally he would have liked to get a message to Frederick Giles in Georgetown to ask for some form of reinforcements, but with no communications equipment, it had been an impossibility. He was flying by his wits. Planning was being done on the hoof as he went along. It was the best he could do.

'Right, let's get out of here,' he said at last, after Westacott had kicked him for the umpteenth time while trying to stretch his legs. Caspasian had hoped to remain in the packing cases all the way into the Baron's lair, but clearly this was not going to work. While his own self-discipline was equal to the task, Westacott's was not.

Pushing aside the canvas tarpaulin, he reached up through the heaped vegetables above him and felt for the roof of the packing case. In accordance with their arrangement with the chief, the lids had not been sealed. There was no reason for them to have been so. He pushed against the wooden planks and felt the lid give. Easing his head and shoulders upwards, Caspasian peered out and found himself looking across the cargo hold. Across the way from him he could see the Brigadier's case, and, to one side, Scratch and Smudger's.

There was not a guard in sight.

'Everyone all right?' he hissed, projecting his voice towards the others.

Silence. Then, a shuffle and a scrape announced the presence of someone else. The lid of one of the other boxes lifted and Scratch poked his head out.

'Blimey sir, it right stinks in here. The bananas are rotten, I reckon. Either that or Smudger needs a wash something awful.'

Beside him, Smudger came up for air, sucking it in deeply like a diver clean out of oxygen.

'All out,' Caspasian ordered. 'Quick now.'

He climbed out of his crate and rubbed and smacked his numb limbs, beating the blood back into them. Pins and needles rippled through his muscles, slowly subsiding as the blood found its way back. He clenched his fists and punched the air, squatting down to stretch his tendons and exercise his joints.

Westacott tumbled into sight, cursing and swearing. The lid of the Brigadier's crate burst open and Percival and Horner struggled up like corpses resurrected from the grave, competing for the available air.

'Check your weapons,' Caspasian said as quietly as possible, while pitching his voice above the noise of the nearest engines. Rifles were hauled out, and bolts and safety catches worked back and forth. 'By the way,' he added as an afterthought, 'don't shoot, if you can possibly avoid it. It's likely to ignite the hydrogen and fry us to a crisp.'

Scratch and Smudger stared at each other. Westacott blanched and looked up at the ominous gas cells, their sides rippling with gas.

They had just started to reseal their crates when there was a sound from the far side of the hold. Instantly everyone froze. Caspasian's eyes were fixed on the furthest crate which appeared to be the source of the disturbance. Stealthily he closed upon it, hands ready to punch the life out of anything that threatened danger. He saw the lid move. Suddenly it burst open and Emma Lavelle was blinking in the light and rubbing her eyes, head and shoulders protruding from the middle of piles of maize.

'What the devil do you think you're doing?' Caspasian stared at her, his anger seething. 'You're supposed to be on your way back to Georgetown with Contreras.'

Her eyes becoming accustomed to the light once again, she located him and smiled nervously. 'I couldn't,' she said simply.

'Couldn't what?'

She looked past him to the others and clearly decided to save them both the embarrassment of the confession she had been about to make. 'I couldn't leave you all. I thought you could use some help.'

'Help? You?' Caspasian could feel the emotions tearing away at his insides. The sight of her was wonderful and sent shivers down his spine, but in such a place as this, a place of the most extreme danger, his terror for her got the better of him and exploded in anger.

'You can't do this. You'll get yourself killed. You'll . . .'

Emma opened her mouth to shout back, but Brigadier Percival stepped into the breach. 'Stop arguing, the two of you. This instant. If the crew haven't already heard you, they will any minute now.' He turned on Caspasian. 'It's not ideal, I agree, but what's done is done. She can hardly go back now, can she?'

Caspasian furiously kicked the nearest packing case. The Brigadier was right, but his cold logic took no account of Caspasian's feelings for the woman. He glared at her. 'Stick right beside me, is that clear?'

She eased her legs over the side of the crate and stood up. 'Quite clear, thank you.'

'Right then,' Caspasian said, forcing himself to calm down. 'Let's get on.'

They resealed their crates, using bits of sacking and other materials to add bulk and make them look as undisturbed as possible.

'We need a hiding place,' the Brigadier said. 'You've been on one of these infernal things longer than any of us, Caspasian. Where do you suggest?'

Caspasian racked his brains.

'The passenger accommodation should be empty,' Emma said. 'We could easily hide in a couple of the berths.'

Caspasian glowered at her, reluctantly admitting to himself that she had hit upon a good idea. 'All right. Why not? I suppose it's so obvious that no one would think of looking there.'

Leading the way, Caspasian made for the axial gangway, every sense alert for the presence of one of the crew.

'Down here,' he whispered when they reached the trap door leading to the sleeping berths. He eased it open, listened intently, and then let himself down the step ladder and into the corridor below. One after another, the rest of the team followed him. He led the way forward. To either side of them the cabins stood vacant and ready. Some of the doors were open, swinging lightly on their hinges. The signs of past struggles had been removed and now the vessel's passenger accommodation resembled a ghost ship.

'These will do,' Caspasian said, indicating two of the larger cabins. He detailed persons to cabins, allocating one for himself, Emma, Westacott and Scratch, and the other for Percival, Horner and Smudger.

'What the devil do you intend to do when we get to wherever this thing's going?' Westacott asked scornfully when they were safely inside and the door was closed and locked.

'The airship's got a radio room,' Caspasian answered coolly.

'Once we know the location of the Baron's base, I'll telegraph it to London and they can take it from there.'

'And what do we do in the meantime?' Westacott asked, his expression incredulous. 'How long do you think it takes to arrange an expeditionary force?'

'It shouldn't take as long as you think. There's a frigate on stand-by in the Caribbean with a force of Royal Marines on board. It should be capable of being with us within a day or two.'

'A day or two? Are we supposed to sit in here until then? What about food? What about . . . ?' Westacott stammered into silence. 'You're mad. Absolutely bloody mad.'

In a flash Caspasian had him up against the wall. 'And what do you suggest, Major?'

He felt a restraining hand on his shoulder. It was Scratch. Behind him, Emma stared at them bewildered, realizing that she was the cause of at least part of Caspasian's anger. 'Steady on, sir. The Major's just a bit upset, like,' Scratch said. 'He ain't used to this sort of thing like you are.'

Pinioned to the cabin wall, Westacott grimaced at the private soldier with contempt. 'Keep your foul little mouth shut, Scratch. I don't need you or anyone else to make excuses for me.'

Scratch regarded him at length. 'Sod it, then,' he said at last. 'Thump him.' And as an afterthought he added, 'And give him one for me.'

'This is mutiny!' Westacott protested in an outraged squeal, Caspasian's hand tightening around his constricted windpipe.

Emma stood beside Caspasian. 'John, I don't think this is helping. Put him down.'

With a final squeeze of Westacott's throat, Caspasian released his grip. The Major slumped to the floor. He shook himself, dusting down his sleeves with disdain. 'How dare you . . .'

'Major Westacott,' Emma said, rounding on him. 'I have

come across some idiots in my time but you take the biscuit. For all our sakes, but mostly for your own, I really do suggest that you keep your thoughts to yourself. Next time, I won't trouble myself to intervene.'

Major Westacott looked from one to the other of them. Failing to find an ally he grunted in disgust and withdrew to the far corner of the cabin to enjoy his own company undisturbed.

'So now what?' Emma asked.

'We wait,' Caspasian answered. 'And try to remain undetected.'

No sooner had he spoken than they heard someone approaching. He was whistling merrily, clearly unaware that anyone was hiding nearby.

Caspasian was about to urge his comrades to hide but realised the futility of the directive. There was barely room for all of them to sit down, let alone conceal themselves in the confines of the berth. Instead he shouldered past Emma and Scratch and positioned himself by the cabin door. He cracked it open and found himself looking at Brigadier Percival, similarly watching the corridor from behind his own door. The next second they heard the man turn in their direction. Both Caspasian and Percival held their doors to, ready to take action should the crewman try to enter. The whistling grew louder. Caspasian braced himself, but the man walked straight past, continuing down the corridor and climbing the stairway heading for the radio room.

'Perhaps this wasn't such a good idea after all,' Emma whispered. 'Do you think we can stay here for any length of time?' Emma asked.

'We don't really have any alternative,' Caspasian answered, his back to the door.

There was a loud rumbling from Scratch's stomach. He looked up and blushed. 'Sorry.'

Emma smiled at him. 'We could certainly do with some food.' She looked at Caspasian. 'Any chance?'

He sighed. 'I suppose I could see if there's anything in the galley.' He turned to leave, opening the door again and checking the coast was clear. On an impulse he went quickly across to Westacott and hauled him to his feet. 'You'll come and help me.'

Westacott started to protest but Caspasian's iron grip allowed for no objections. As they left, Caspasian instructed Emma to lock the door behind him. He then informed the Brigadier what he intended doing.

To reach the galley, Caspasian had to cross the large, empty saloon. It was uncanny finding it so deserted. He stopped outside and listened intently before entering. He had brought his pocket Webley .38 revolver, but was resolved to use it only as a last resort. It was not just because of the proximity of the gas cells, but more because the sound of a shot was likely to alert the entire airship's crew. With this in mind, he kept it in his pocket, relying on his fists to counter any opposition encountered.

The saloon was clear. 'Come on,' he said quietly to a very pale-faced Major Westacott.

The dining room was similarly empty. The tables and chairs had been rearranged as if for a conference of some sort, being laid out in a hollow square. One chair was set apart from the rest at the head of the setting and in front of it, some papers remained. Unable to restrain his curiosity, Caspasian went across and inspected them briefly. There was a large map of the Chilean coastline with some markings on it. Arrows indicating the direction of some vessel or other. Caspasian saw a cross and assumed that it marked an interception point, or a rendezvous perhaps, but with whom he could not tell.

'Caspasian, the food!' Westacott whispered, his voice breaking with strain and fright.

Reluctantly Caspasian left the papers and made for the galley that stood to one side of the dining room. He would dearly have liked to take the papers and map back to his cabin to study them at greater length, but knew it would have been asking for trouble. They would probably be missed and the theft would prompt a search.

The galley had not fared well since the airship had been seized. What cooking had been done had been careless and messy. Captain Harrison would have been appalled to see the state it had been left in. Nevertheless, the wall cupboards remained stocked with a range of items.

'Here,' Caspasian said, throwing a canvas game bag at Westacott. 'Use this.' While Westacott held the bag's mouth open, Caspasian tossed in a selection of tins and packets. Corned beef, tinned sardines, several packets of hard German rye bread, a couple of sausages each over a foot in length, a block of rather dry uninteresting cheese and, to leaven the plain fare, two pots of best Russian caviar.

'I say, look at this,' Westacott enthused, crouching down to study the contents of one of the floor level cupboards. He held up a modest little container. 'Gentleman's Relish. My, my.' He smacked his lips.

Caspasian snatched it out of his fingers, tossed it back on its shelf and firmly closed the cupboard door. 'If you think you're going to eat that while sharing a cabin with me, you can think again. One breath and you'd ignite the hydrogen.'

To round off the hunt, Caspasian went to the drinks cabinet and removed two bottles of cognac. 'For the cold nights,' he reasoned. Westacott shrugged. At least the two of them could agree on one thing.

They were halfway across the lounge when they heard the return of the whistler. Caspasian cursed silently and hunted desperately for a hiding place. Nothing.

'Quick, over there!' He shoved Westacott towards the door. 'Get down behind the bureau.'

The Major complied, gratefully shrinking out of sight as best he could, the game bag clutched in his arms. Caspasian positioned himself on the door's other side, flattening his back against the wall. 'Leave him to me,' he said quietly.

Westacott nodded. 'If you're sure.'

The crewman marched boldly into the room. Caspasian took one noiseless step forward, raised his arm, and brought down the edge of his open right hand in a perfect *shuto sakotsu-uchi* blow to the right side of the man's neck. The crewman's momentum carried him on for half a step as the strength rushed out of his legs and he sank to the ground unconscious. Caspasian caught him under the arms to quieten his landing.

There was a startled cry from the corridor outside the saloon and Caspasian glanced back in alarm to see that the man had not been alone.

'Damn.' For a second he hoped that Westacott might take action but even as the hope formed in his mind he knew it to be futile. Caspasian dropped the body and rushed after the second crewman who had turned and run. As the man dashed away he screamed for help as loud as he could. After the silence and stealth of their mission to the galley, the shouting struck Caspasian with almost physical force. He closed on his quarry just as he entered the passenger corridors. The fleeing man ran headlong into Brigadier Percival's fist, rebounding off it, eyes rolling up in his head. Blood gushed from his smashed nose and he fell.

'What the devil happened?' Percival asked.

'There were two of them,' Caspasian stammered awkwardly. 'I didn't see the second one.'

'Well, that's done it.'

Sure enough, calls sounded from all sides. Above them they could hear running feet pounding down from the crew's quarters.

Major Westacott stared at them terrified. 'Where can we hide?'

Percival and Caspasian hunted for a solution. 'Back to the cabins,' Percival said.

'It's too late for that,' Caspasian argued. 'They'll search everywhere now. Especially once they find their comrades.'

Brigadier Percival glared at him. 'Then what the hell do you suggest?'

Caspasian forced a smile. He was about to reply but the footsteps were closing on them. The next second, crewmen burst down the corridor both in front and behind them, guns brandished in their fists. Slowly Caspasian raised his hands above his head. The Brigadier, his eyes fixed on Caspasian's, did likewise. Major Westacott, still clutching his bag, grinned stupidly at the nearest gun an inch before his nose.

'There's more of them in here!' a voice shouted as Sergeant Major Horner, Scratch, Smudger and Emma were discovered.

'Bring them into the saloon,' the senior crewman ordered. Barrels prodded into ribs and they were shepherded unceremoniously away from the cabins. 'Sit down,' he said to them, his gun adding emphasis to the instruction. With eyes still warily on his captives he said over his shoulder to his nearest companion, 'Fetch the lieutenant.'

Next to Caspasian, Brigadier Percival shifted in his seat, hands on his head. 'This is a right bloody to-do.'

Caspasian relaxed. 'I prefer to look upon it as a new opportunity, Brigadier.'

Percival stared at him bitterly. 'Oh do you now?'

'You know what they say. When one door closes, another . . .'

At that moment Lieutenant Davies entered. His eyes swiftly took in the scene before him, alighting on Caspasian with undisguised malice.

' . . . Opens?' Brigadier Percival said.

17

The captives looked down through the promenade windows at the opalescent sea below. For the last few hours it had stretched unbroken from horizon to horizon, but now, for the first time, they spied a smudge in the distance. Land.

Following capture they had been confined to the cargo hold, hands securely fastened, but to their surprise they had been returned to the lounge in time for their arrival at the airship's mysterious destination.

'You'll enjoy meeting the Baron,' Lieutenant Davies said cheerfully as he shoved Caspasian. Caspasian could feel the metal of handcuffs biting into his wrists. But his legs were free. It would have been the easiest thing in the world to have felled the arrogant, duplicitous Lieutenant with a kick. He knew it was not worth it, though. A brief moment's satisfaction would be followed, he was certain, by regret. Davies would have him thrown overboard and Caspasian was not ready for that. He had things to do.

'What does the Baron want with our airships?' the Brigadier asked.

'You'd better ask him that,' Davies replied. 'Look,' he said, pointing down towards the growing parcel of land. 'We'll be there in half an hour. I've already signalled ahead to warn him that we've got some unexpected visitors. He's looking forward to meeting you.'

From the evil glint in his eye, Caspasian could imagine the sort of reception being prepared for them. He would not have long to wait. The land mass was growing by the second as the airship closed with it at seventy or eighty miles an hour, all engines working at full power to get the vessel under cover before it could be spotted by any ships in the area. Caspasian studied their destination closely while the Brigadier futilely tried to coax more information out of Lieutenant Davies. They were now close enough to see that it was an island, the largest in a long chain, its fellows only just becoming visible behind it. It was hard to say, but from the approximate direction of travel and the time and speed flown, Caspasian estimated that the chain was somewhere west or south-west of the Windward Islands.

The island was volcanic, with several tall cones, long dead, now thickly forested with lush jungle. A beach of pale golden sand appeared to encircle it like a lifebelt, with palm trees crowding the jungle's edge, and coral reefs extending out into the extensive and transparent shallows. Davies had returned to the control car, leaving the captives in the sombre care of his second-in-command, Lieutenant Quesada. His tanned, leathery cheeks were deeply pockmarked, and black hooded eyes stared fixedly at his charges. Flanking him, half a dozen guards all held revolvers. They were taking no chances.

As the airship descended, Caspasian heard the engine note alter as they slowed in readiness for a landing. The cells were venting gas, coming in gently for a textbook approach. It was then that Caspasian was able to see more of the island and realized that it was a horseshoe rather than a circle. The vessel was now down to about two hundred feet and rounding a sheer-sided wooded bluff. As it did so, Caspasian was presented with a view that made him stare in wonder. Beside him, Brigadier Percival, Emma and the others were equally amazed.

'Will you look at that!' the Brigadier exclaimed.

Major Westacott gaped. 'Why, that's the *Grenadine Quest*,' he said. 'She was lost at sea weeks ago. Gone without a trace.'

Anchored in the natural harbour, a rusty old tramp steamer lay dejected and apparently deserted.

'What was its cargo?' Caspasian asked, thinking that he already knew the answer.

Westacott shrugged. 'Nothing much. Just scrap iron. That was all. No value whatsoever. That's why piracy was discounted. Who would want a worthless old rust-bucket laden to the gunwales with scrap iron?'

Caspasian smiled. 'Someone wanting to manufacture hydrogen on an industrial scale.'

Westacott stared at him, brow furrowed. 'What?'

'Scrap iron. It's the prime ingredient in the manufacture of hydrogen.'

Brigadier Percival was unconvinced. 'Yes, but you'd need to have the whole infrastructure. Furnaces, storage tanks, piping. It would be a huge undertaking.'

The next moment the trees parted to reveal a wide valley beyond the immediate harbour. A small township appeared and, close to the waterfront, a modest-sized industrial plant with all the ingredients just listed by the Brigadier. Central to it was a tall building made of corrugated iron whose chimneys indicated the presence a smelting facility. Safely isolated from it, four large storage tanks rose out of the jungle halfway up the side of the tallest peak. In the centre of the valley, well away from both plant and storage tanks, a second airship was moored against a mast fashioned of girders. A pipeline ran from the mast across the valley floor, and disappeared into the jungle at the foot of the slope, heading in the direction of the storage tanks.

'My God!' Brigadier Percival marvelled. 'That's the *D100*! I'm looking forward to meeting this Baron fellow. Whoever he is, this is one hell of an outfit. He doesn't just have the airships, but the whole infrastructure to manufacture his own fuel for them. His rations are supplied by Delgado whom he also uses to mine uncut diamonds which, I'll wager, finance the entire operation.' He chuckled. 'You've got to hand it to him. Very impressive.'

Caspasian was less moved. 'Yes, but why?'

Percival shrugged. 'He must be in thrall to some foreign power. Someone trying to establish hegemony over the Caribbean perhaps.'

'What makes you think he's not working for himself?'

'You mean some sort of latter-day pirate?'

'Why not? Airships instead of galleons.'

Brigadier Percival scoffed. 'Nonsense. He has to be the tool of some foreign state. No individual could mastermind all of this on his own.'

Noticing that they were approaching a vacant mooring tower adjacent to the *D100*'s, Caspasian said, 'Well, it looks as if we're about to find out.'

As gently as a falling leaf, the *D200* came in alongside its sister ship, sinking to the ground with barely a quiver. Ropes were dropped and the ground crew seized them to secure the vessel, anchoring the nose to the tower like a tethered bull. The engines were shut down and the airship was at rest.

Davies appeared in the saloon moments later, accompanied by a strong escort of guards to bolster those already in attendance. 'Gentlemen,' he said sarcastically. 'Welcome to James Island, named after Deuteronomy James, associate of the pirate Sir Henry Morgan.' He grinned savagely. 'The Spaniards were also thinking of the buccaneers when they called the island chain Los Hijos de Puta. The Sons of the Whore. Nice, eh?' He waved his hand. 'Now if you wouldn't mind, follow me please.' He turned briefly. 'Not forgetting the lovely Miss Lavelle, too, of course,' he added with a leer. 'The Baron will be particularly delighted to make your acquaintance. We don't see much cinema in these parts, but your reputation has preceded you nonetheless.'

Emma smiled sourly and moved closer to Caspasian.

Under close guard, the captives were led down the steps from the airship. More armed men waited at the bottom, sub-machine guns cradled in their arms.

'This way,' Lieutenant Quesada growled, jerking the barrel of his revolver in the direction of a concrete path. Still with hands bound, the captives fell into line and marched resolutely behind Davies and his men, with Quesada and his team bringing up the rear. The path led away from the landing area and wound between paddy fields towards a wooded slope several hundred yards away. When it reached the foot, it began to climb, the ascent rapidly becoming steeper. At times the path doubled back on itself in a series of hairpin bends and whenever it did, it presented the marchers with a magnificent view of the landing field, glimpsed between the thickening trees and undergrowth.

'Hurry!' Quesada snarled, prodding Westacott in the back with the muzzle of his gun.

Parrots shrieked from the branches as if mocking the prisoners who were soon sweating with the effort of the climb.

'Not far now,' Davies called over his shoulder with deceptive courtesy.

Sure enough, after a further hundred yards or so, the group emerged from the jungle-bordered path onto a paved terrace. Westacott stopped and gasped for breath, Sergeant Major Horner scowling furiously at the guards nearest him. Scratch and Smudger encouraged each other on, muttering about what they would do if they had their hands free. A curse and a kick from the nearest of the guards silenced them. Beside Caspasian, Emma looked out across the treetops at the spectacular vista that opened up before them. To one side, the airships sat like two vast swaddled babies, suckling at their masts. To the other, the ground dropped steeply away, falling down towards the beach and the sea. The sound of waves crashing against the shore rose up to them, and with it came a salty tang. But Caspasian's attention, like the Brigadier's, was fixed on the rock face before them, on the far side of the neatly paved terrace. What had once been the mouth of a large cave, had been converted into the front of an extraordinary house, large glass doors standing open at ground level, with windows above and a balcony with a spiral staircase leading up to it from the terrace. Hard against it, the first of the storage tanks reared above the treetops, the others close behind.

Percival screwed up his nose at the futuristic design of the balcony, windows and staircase. 'Ghastly. Bauhaus, wouldn't you say?'

Caspasian stared. 'Not really my thing, Brigadier.'

'Mine, either. Quite tasteless, if you ask me.'

They were herded together and surrounded with guns while Lieutenant Davies disappeared inside. Almost immediately he re-emerged, this time accompanied by a bearded man in a navy blue uniform. His scarred and bearded face smiled at them coldly.

'I am Baron von Staaden. You have no right to be here. But now that you are, you can expect to remain here. Forever. You will have seen the plant. It needs labourers. You will work there until you die. I hope you think your curiosity has been worth it.'

Brigadier Percival stepped forward and introduced himself. 'Those are His Majesty's airships,' he added, jerking his chin in the direction of the valley at his back. 'The *D100* and the *D200*. My government wants them back.'

The Baron smiled. 'Correction. They are the Fafner and the Siegfried. Siegfried the hero and Fafner the dragon. You are familiar with Wagner?'

The Brigadier looked affronted. 'Certainly not!'

'A pity. But then it is my experience that small-spirited men seldom are.'

Ignoring the insult, the Brigadier continued. 'You have stolen them, sir. We want them back.'

The Baron stared at him for a moment, the smile freezing over. 'And you and your comrades have eliminated Colonel Delgado, a close ally. It will cause me a considerable inconvenience to re-establish control over the mines. Make no mistake, I will do so, but I would rather you had not made such an action necessary.'

'And we, Baron, will have our airships back,' Caspasian said, 'and our liberty.'

The Baron scrutinized him and chuckled sourly. He pointed to the guards. 'It is a pity, then, that you have got yourself into such a predicament.' He regarded the other prisoners. 'And not come with a more imposing force.'

'I assure you that it is only a matter of time before such a force locates your hideaway. Just as we have found you, so will others.'

'Correction,' the Baron said. 'You did not find me. We found you.' He looked suddenly bored. 'In any case, you're all too late. In just a little while there will no longer be any need for secrecy. Everyone will know that the airships have a new master. And everyone will know to what use I intend to put them.'

He turned to Davies and Quesada. 'Show our guests to their quarters.' He waved a hand tiredly at the prisoners as he walked away. 'I hope you will be comfortable here. I appreciate the extra help. The workforce can always use fresh blood.'

Quesada and his men barked out orders and pushed and shoved the Brigadier, Caspasian and the others back down the path towards the landing field.

'Where are you taking us?' Westacott stammered, the fear transparent.

'You'll see,' Quesada said, rewarding him with a hearty kick.

Their destination turned out to be a row of wooden barrack

blocks surrounded with a barbed wire fence. Behind the wire, groups of wretched looking men and women stared forlornly at them as they approached.

'The workers' quarters,' Quesada explained as the gates opened to welcome the new arrivals. 'You'll find some people you might know,' he added.

The guards left them at the entrance, unfastening their hand-cuffs and ushering them roughly inside. The gates swung shut behind them, sentries standing alert on the outside and in a tall lookout tower overhead.

'Enjoy your stay,' Quesada said chuckling. 'It will be a long one.'

No sooner were they left to their own devices than they heard someone hailing them from the doorway of one of the huts. Caspasian and Emma looked up and saw Gustav Wolter striding towards them, hand outstretched. He greeted them warmly.

'So this is where you got to,' Caspasian said, shaking his hand.

'Some of the others are here, too,' Wolter said. 'Harrison, Domain, Edward. And some of Harrison's old crew as well.'

'How is Richard?' Caspasian asked instantly, surprised at the relief he felt on hearing that he was safe.

'Stronger in spirit than the rest of us put together, I'd say. Quite a remarkable young man.'

'And Lionel?' Emma added. 'Where is he?'

Wolter smiled. 'Follow me. They'll be amazed to see you.'

They followed him to his hut and found the others resting. All of them looked ragged and dejected, all except Richard Edward who sat up the moment he saw the newcomers.

'Why Miss Lavelle!' he exclaimed brightly. 'What a pleasure.'

At the mention of her name Lionel Domain sprung to his feet. 'Emma! Thank the Lord! You're safe. We thought you were dead.' His face darkened. 'These goddamned madmen have got us working in their factory. Working some furnace thing. Gustav says it's to manufacture hydrogen for their . . .'

'I know,' she said. 'Caspasian explained.' His previously impeccable dress was tattered beyond recognition and his hair, untinted for days, was virtually white. His cheeks were hollow and unshaven and his nails torn. Emma was shocked by the sight of him, but did her best to conceal it.

Brigadier Percival sought out Captain Harrison. 'Have you any idea what the Baron's up to?'

'Not really, but I overheard two of the guards talking about Panama.'

'The canal,' the Brigadier said, more to himself, musing. 'What could they want with that?'

Caspasian and Wolter had joined them. 'They could cut it. Aerial bombardment,' Caspasian suggested.

Wolter was doubtful. 'The Baron tried that on England in the war and failed.'

'But the canal's a very precise target, and easily blocked,' Caspasian argued. 'He'd only have to sink a single ship and he'd have achieved his aim.'

'True enough,' the Brigadier said. 'But why would he want to?'

'He might just want to threaten to bomb it,' Harrison offered. 'Demand some kind of ransom or something. Perhaps to control all the traffic using it.'

Caspasian thought it unlikely. 'To do that he'd have to maintain a presence over it. It would be too easy for the Americans to bring in fighter aircraft and shoot him down. Besides, we've all seen the uncut diamonds Delgado was mining. The Baron doesn't need the extra cash. He's got plenty as it is.'

Then something occurred to him. 'Just before we were captured I saw a chart on the dining room table in the *D200*. It was of the Chilean coastline. There were markings on it which seemed to indicate a route. It was as if he was tracking something.'

'You mean tracking a ship's progress, perhaps?' Harrison said.

'Possibly.' Caspasian racked his brains to recall the detail of the markings. But it was no use. He could only recall snatches of them, and those made little or no sense.

'So what now?' Major Westacott asked, standing on the fringe of the little group. Brigadier Percival introduced him to the others. Wolter and Harrison observed him dubiously.

'We have to find out what he's up to,' Caspasian said. He moved across to one of the windows and inspected the security arrangements outside. 'For the moment, I suggest we play his game. Feign resignation to our lot.'

'Good,' the Brigadier said. 'Get them to feel secure enough to take their eyes off us.'

'Exactly.'

'And then what?' Emma asked.

'And then we escape and sound the alarm,' Caspasian said.

'You make it sound as if it's the easiest thing in the world,' Westacott said scornfully.

'Do you have any other suggestions?'

'We could try and reason with him,' Westacott suggested hopefully. 'He seemed a decent enough sort to me. Maybe he just wants to be left alone.'

'In that case he should have left His Majesty's airships alone,' the Brigadier said tartly. 'No, Caspasian's right. For now we play the game.'

The following morning the guards came to the camp and assembled the workforce. The majority consisted of Indians captured in the past and sent by Delgado. But there was also a ramshackle group of seamen from various hijacked vessels such as the *Grenadine Quest* and others that, like her, had fallen foul of the rogue airship.

Conveyed under a close watch to the Baron's factory, they were set to work. The strongest of the men, Caspasian and his companions amongst them, were used to transport scrap iron from the stockpiles to the furnaces. Trackway had been laid for the purpose, but the carriages had to be loaded and then pushed by hand, a back-breaking task that was made all the harder by the intense heat.

At midday, a whistle blew for the lunch break. The work gangs collected by a field kitchen where they queued to receive bowls of rice, vegetables and a tiny amount of boiled fish. Westacott studied it mournfully. 'I can't eat this slop.'

Across from him, Caspasian caught an exchange of glances between the Major and Sergeant Major Horner. Some sort of unspoken communication had passed between them.

Richard and Emma, being unsuited to the hard physical labour, had been put to work in the kitchens. That night, when they were reunited with the others in the accommodation block, they had an idea.

'We think we might have found a way to discover what the Baron's up to,' Richard said quietly. 'Emma's been told she's going to work in the Baron's household from now on.'

'If that's the case,' she added, 'I might be able to get a glimpse of his maps or plans or something.'

Caspasian looked at their eager faces. 'It would be too dangerous for you. Besides, you wouldn't know what to look for.'

Emma stared at him. 'What a patronizing thing to say! I might not be a soldier, but I am quite capable of reading. Contrary to what you might think, I do actually have a brain in here.' She tapped her head.

The Brigadier was delighted. 'Capital, my dear. I think it's a brilliant opportunity.'

'But she could get herself killed,' Caspasian argued.

'Nonsense,' the Brigadier answered dismissively. 'It'll be fine. Besides,' he added coldly, 'she knew the risks when she stowed away on board.' He smiled at her, 'Didn't you, my dear?'

Sure enough, the following day Emma was taken under escort back up the path to the terrace and into the Baron's quarters. The moment she stepped inside she was amazed by the size of the place. A vast open sitting room greeted her, with corridors leading into the inner recesses of the hollow mountain.

'In here,' her guard said gruffly, shoving her into the kitchen. 'You'll be working with Jorgelina.'

An enormous woman glowered at her and grunted, drying her massive fists on her apron.

'The Baron wants you to work here from now on,' the guard said. 'One mistake and she'll whip you like cream.' Jorgelina got the gist and leered. 'Do you understand?'

Emma smiled sweetly. 'How could I not?'

The remainder of the day was spent on chores. Preparing food, laundry and cleaning. It had been many years since Emma had been obliged to busy herself with such things and every few minutes Jorgelina found an excuse to cuff her, the blow accompanied by a burst of invective. By the time she returned to the accommodation block in the evening she felt thoroughly dejected, fearing she had let the others down.

'Keep at it,' the Brigadier urged, showing signs of exhaustion himself. 'Maybe tomorrow will give you a chance.'

The next day started similarly, but as the hours wore on, Emma noticed that Jorgelina no longer watched her so closely. She had decided that the young girl was thoroughly browbeaten. She lowered her guard, satisfied that Emma was wholly incapable of causing trouble.

It was therefore no surprise to Emma when she found herself left temporarily unsupervised. She was midway between the Baron's personal accommodation and the kitchens, her arms bundled with laundry. Seizing the opportunity, she made her way to a door on the far side of the sitting room which had previously always remained closed. Today however, it stood ajar and inside she could see the edge of a desk. Pushing it open, she went inside, closing it swiftly behind her. Her pulse was racing and she flattened herself against the door while she steadied her nerves. She was starting to wish she had never volunteered herself for such a mission. It was all very well for the movies, but not in real life!

Charts were spread across the desk and she quickly cast her eyes over them. Sure enough, they covered the coastlines of Chile, Peru, Ecuador and Colombia, and markings outlined a course all the way north towards the Panama Canal. Caspasian had been right. It was a route map. At several places, the same two letters – VA – were marked and ringed together with a series of numbers, different every time. When the arrows and markings reached the canal they stopped. It made no sense to Emma but thinking that it might mean something to Caspasian and the Brigadier, she did her best to memorize as much of the detail as possible.

She was about to start going through the desk drawers, when she heard voices. Still clutching her bundle, she left the room and darted across the sitting room heading for the exit that she knew led to the kitchen. But the voices were coming from exactly that direction. Anyone discovering her would know she had been prying. She could try and bluff her way out but it would doubtless invite further blows from the graceless Jorgelina.

Hunting around for an escape, Emma rushed to the first door she could see. She opened it and went inside just as the voices closed on her, walking past along the corridor. With the immediate danger gone, she heaved a huge sigh. The room she had entered was in darkness. She felt on the wall for a light switch, found it and turned it on. To her surprise the room was a laboratory. Amongst the array of equipment on the worktops, were several microscopes. She stepped forward and inspected the closest piece of machinery. It was a drill with an exquisitely fine head. There was another device next to it, but she could not tell what it was for. She leaned closer for a better look.

'It's a diamond polisher.'

She spun round, dropping her bundle. The Baron stood in the doorway, appraising her. At his side, Major Westacott leered delightedly over his shoulder.

'You see?' the Major said, exulting. 'I told you so. She was sent here to spy on you. They're all in it.'

The Baron nodded thoughtfully. 'Do you have anything to say?'

Emma quickly stooped to retrieve her bundle. 'He's talking nonsense. I came in here by mistake.'

The Baron gave a tired smile. 'You must think me very foolish.' He turned to one of two guards who stood behind Westacott. 'Take her back to the others. She can work on the furnaces from now on. We'll see how she likes that.'

As she was led away, she glared at Westacott. Standing at his side, Sergeant Major Horner grinned. 'Thought you'd found a cushy little number, did you, darling?'

Emma thrust her laundry into Horner's arms as she passed. 'If you think you can trust these two, Baron, you're even more stupid than you look.'

The Baron smiled. 'You cannot rile me, Miss Lavelle. Trust has to be earned. For now, I'd say I am better off placing my trust in these two gentlemen than in you.' He raised his eyebrows. 'You can hardly argue with that?'

Caspasian and Domain rushed to her side when she was thrown into the accommodation block. 'Are you all right?' Domain fussed. 'The moment we saw those two bastards talking to the guards we knew what they were up to.'

Emma brushed herself down. She pushed back her hair, wiping the perspiration and dirt from her face. 'I'm fine. At least I don't have to do his goddamned washing any more. I'd rather stoke the furnaces than scrub another thing.'

The Brigadier slumped down onto the side of his bunk. 'Well that's that then. What now?'

'I did see a couple of things,' Emma said. 'He's got a laboratory up there for processing the uncut diamonds. I didn't see any but he's got all the equipment for polishing them. And I saw some maps.' She told them about the coastal charts and the route markings which terminated at the Panama canal.

'The numbers sound like date-time groups,' Caspasian said immediately.

Emma could only remember snatches of some of them, but Caspasian noted down the numbers and studied them for a moment. 'You say these were the southernmost?' he asked, indicating one of the groups of figures.

'Yes.'

'In that case, the vessel, or whatever it is, is heading from south to north.'

'But what about the two letters?' she asked.

Caspasian shook his head. The Brigadier thought hard but was unable to suggest anything.

'What did you say the letters were?' Richard asked, getting up from his bunk.

'VA.'

'What's the matter?' Caspasian asked, noting his worried expression.

'Well, it might just be a coincidence, but aren't those the initials of the Royal Yacht? The *Victoria and Albert*?'

The Brigadier was on his feet in a flash. 'Great heavens above! Of course! How can I have been so stupid?'

Caspasian and the others looked at him. Richard located a battered stool and sat down heavily. 'The Prince of Wales,' he said solemnly. 'He's on a tour of South America. He rendezvoused with the *Victoria and Albert* at Valparaiso in Chile and is making his way north.'

'And it passes through the Panama Canal en route for

Barbados,' the Brigadier added. He turned to his companions, ashen-faced. 'The heir to the throne. That madman's after our future king.'

'What for?' Emma asked.

'Yes, what for?' Wolter said. 'To assassinate? To capture?'

'It's almost irrelevant,' the Brigadier said.

Harrison got up. 'Imagine it. The Prince of Wales kidnapped and held hostage. The government wouldn't know where to look for him. The Baron could demand anything he wanted.'

They were silent for a while, each one considering the implications of the news. It would deliver a body blow to the Empire. At last the Brigadier spoke. 'If such an audacious plan were to work, we'd be a laughing stock. Who could say where it would lead. The Baron could lay the blame on another state. Germany, say. In all the excitement there'd be plenty of people ready to believe him. It could provoke a war.'

'That's exactly what he wants.' Wolter stood looking out of the window. 'I flew with him in the last war, don't forget. I know the man. He was fanatical even then. The destruction of his fleet deranged him and the final straw was his own brush with death. When I saw him in the *D200*, he told me how he'd survived. He'd been badly burnt and was hospitalized. He passed himself off as an ordinary crewman and, after the Armistice, while other prisoners of war were repatriated to a ruined and impoverished Germany, the Baron disappeared. He set out to get the revenge he had promised himself. Now we know how he intends to achieve it.' He turned to face them. 'Siegfried, the archetypal Germanic hero, and Fafner, the fire-breathing dragon. I'd say he intends to bomb the Royal Yacht. He means to kill everyone on board. He must be stopped.'

'That's all very well,' Captain Harrison said. 'But how?'

Caspasian was very still. He seemed to be miles away. The Brigadier scowled at him. 'You don't seem very concerned,' he said harshly. 'I hope we're not keeping you from your sleep.'

But Caspasian was no longer listening. An idea had formed.

'Richard,' he said at last. 'Are you in the kitchens tomorrow?'

'What's that?' He shrugged. 'I suppose so.'

'Right then. Here's what I'll need.'

18

When Caspasian and the others arrived at the trackway the following morning at the start of another day's hard labour, they were greeted by the unpleasant sight of Westacott and Horner amongst the Baron's guards.

'Well, well, well,' Westacott crooned nastily. 'Look who we have here, Sergeant Major. Our old friend and erstwhile comrade-in-arms, John Caspasian.'

Caspasian smiled icily. 'Those are smart new uniforms you're wearing,' he said. 'Perhaps you should wear the jackets back-to-front. Isn't that what the turncoats used to do in the old days?'

Safe in the company of his fellow guards, Westacott punched Caspasian hard in the stomach. 'I wouldn't be so cheeky if I were you, Captain. That old windbag of a Brigadier can't protect you now.'

Percival looked the other way, refusing to get involved lest he invite a beating himself. Horner guffawed. 'Look at the old buzzard. Scared of his own shadow.'

Caspasian sucked in the air to get his breath back. Slowly he straightened up. Gustav Wolter stepped in front of him. 'All right, Major. You've had your fun. Now leave us to get on with our job. We've got a lot of iron to move.'

Westacott stared at him for a moment and then backed away. 'Yes,' he said at last. 'And you'd better put your backs to it, or else. The Baron's watching me and Horner, you see. So we've got to prove ourselves.' He grinned. 'What better way to do that than coming down like a ton of bricks on you pathetic bunch?'

'You're the pathetic one,' Caspasian said, his voice low and dangerous. Horner stepped in like a shot. His fist powered out and caught Caspasian on the chin, sending him sprawling. Captain Harrison went to his aid. 'For God's sake, man,' he hissed at Caspasian. 'Keep your mouth shut.'

'That's right,' Westacott said happily. 'You keep him in order. Otherwise he's as good as dead. No one would so much as bat an eyelid if I shot him.'

Caspasian glanced up from the ground as he got to his feet and noticed that neither Westacott nor Horner had yet been entrusted with firearms.

Throughout the course of the day, Caspasian was alarmed to note that the level of activity had increased. Although the factory was sited some distance from the landing field, he had several opportunities to observe the comings and goings of the Baron's men. During the lunch break, Captain Harrison and Wolter came to sit beside Caspasian, Emma and the Brigadier. The two loyal privates, Scratch and Smudger, listened in discreetly behind them.

'They've started refuelling the gas cells,' Harrison said quietly, toying with the food in his lap.

'The airships are becoming buoyant. You can see the strain increasing on the mooring ropes,' Wolter added. 'They're getting lighter and lighter the more gas goes on board.'

'Then they obviously intend to depart any day now,' the Brigadier said.

'Or even sooner than that,' Harrison said. 'They wouldn't want to endanger the ships by keeping them tanked up for any length of time.'

Caspasian was concerned. 'How long do you think we've got?'

Wolter and Harrison consulted. 'The Baron could intend to depart as early as tomorrow, if he refuels throughout the night,' Harrison said.

The Brigadier looked at Caspasian. 'Ideas?'

'If Richard can get me what I need from the kitchens, I can take care of things after dark.'

'What do you mean, take care of things?' the Brigadier asked suspiciously.

Caspasian regarded him. 'Destroy the airships. What else?'

The Brigadier stared at him in horror. 'Are you barking mad? Have you any idea how much those things cost? Not to mention the effect on Britain's standing in the race to control the skies. At one stroke we'd be knocked to the bottom of the airship league.'

Caspasian was amazed. 'But the Prince of Wales? Surely he's the priority?'

'Indeed,' the Brigadier said unconvincingly. 'But we have to ensure his safety without endangering the airships.

'But . . .'

'The airships must not be destroyed, Caspasian. And that's final.'

Caspasian was about to protest again but saw that it would be useless. He thought for a moment. 'Then we're going to need reinforcements. The Baron's guards are everywhere. Even if we all managed to break out, they've got the guns, not us. And we're outnumbered at least ten to one. If we're going to have any chance of capturing the ships and preventing their departure I need to get to the radio room and send a signal.'

'That's all very well,' Harrison said. 'But in the meantime, while we're waiting to be rescued by the navy, the airships might already have gone. The Prince of Wales will be in dire peril.'

Caspasian smiled. 'Not if I can destroy the hydrogen tanks before the gas cells have been fully charged. Without fuel they won't be going anywhere.'

The Brigadier smiled, 'All right. And what do you need from us?'

'A diversion.'

Scratch grinned. 'Leave that to Smudger and me. We know just the thing, don't we Smudger?'

'Yeah. Leave it to us,' Smudger agreed slyly.

'But you'll need some back-up,' Wolter said to Caspasian. 'Let me come with you. I can watch your back.'

'Me, too,' Captain Harrison urged. 'Gustav and I both know all about hydrogen, and I can help with the signals transmission.'

'And you won't find the signals room without me,' Emma cut in.

'Out of the question,' Caspasian said instantly. 'Gustav and the Captain, yes, but not you, Emma. It's far too dangerous.'

'There you go again. Patronizing me,' Emma protested fierily. 'I've seen the radio room. I can lead you straight there. Without me to guide you, you'll be thrashing about in the dark and that could risk the whole mission. It could endanger all of us, and the Prince of Wales too.'

'She's right, Caspasian,' the Brigadier said. 'Emma goes. Myself, Richard, Scratch and Smudger will remain here to take care of the diversion. And that's that.'

Reluctantly Caspasian had to agree. That evening, at the end of their day's work, they were escorted back behind the wire fences of their encampment. There was no sign of either Westacott or Horner which suited Caspasian perfectly. The last thing he needed was the vindictive attention of those two. Richard had worked wonders. Being lame, he attracted considerably less attention than the others. The guards assumed him to be harmless and devoted their time to watching the rest of the workforce. When Caspasian and the others were in the hut and the door was closed, Wolter kept watch, while Richard brought out the goods he had been able to smuggle out of the kitchens.

'It's all I could manage,' he said apologetically.

Caspasian nodded contentedly. 'It'll do just fine,' he said, taking the bottle of liquid in his hands and removing the cork. He sniffed the fumes. 'Petrol,' he said, impressed. 'That's better than I'd hoped.'

'And I got these, too,' Richard said, handing him a nearly-empty box of matches.

The others looked at Caspasian expectantly. 'An improvised incendiary grenade,' he said, as if his plan should be obvious to all. He got up. 'Come on. We don't have much time.'

Tearing a strip of cloth from the bottom of his shirt, he soaked it in petrol and stuffed it tightly into the neck of the bottle. 'Ready?' he asked Emma, Wolter and Harrison.

'Ready.'

'Let's go then.'

Opening the door, Caspasian led the way into the darkness. The kitchens were at the rear of the compound but the building stood in isolation, surrounded by open space. The nearest other building came to within twenty metres of it. Caspasian and the others crept through the deepest shadows until they arrived on the edge of the clearing.

Caspasian hand signalled for them to wait. 'Won't be long,' he whispered.

Sure enough, a moment later a commotion could be heard in the hut they had left some minutes before. Rising to a shout, Scratch's voice could clearly be heard, Smudger answering with shouts and cries of his own. Caspasian smiled. It sounded convincingly like a brawl. The next second, their voices were joined by the shouts of the Brigadier and Richard, the fight escalating into a miniature riot.

Caspasian peered out and watched. Then, in response to the fight the guard force came storming in through the front entrance, guns and cudgels in hands. Caspasian waited until he heard the sounds of the guards bursting into the hut and then struck a match and lit the bottle's improvised cloth fuse. The flame caught readily. He took aim at the closest kitchen window he could see, drew back his arm and threw. The bottle sailed gracefully through the air, straight in through the open window and smashed against something inside. Instantly the petrol ignited and the entire room burst into flames.

'Go!' Caspasian ordered.

Together with Emma, Wolter and Harrison, he bolted for the far side of the compound. A cry went up from another of the guards as the fire was spotted and the remaining guards went to combat the spreading blaze. Shots were fired, but whether to warn the other workers to remain in their huts, or to cow his rioting companions, he could not tell. The wire was in front of him, at the point he had identified as the most secluded place on the entire perimeter. He skidded to a halt and dropped to the ground, Wolter at his side.

'You first,' he said to Emma.

He gripped the wire in between the barbs, and yanked the strand upwards with all his might, creating a gap between the wire and the ground. On her back, Emma wriggled under it. Then came Wolter's turn, followed by Captain Harrison. Finally, while Wolter and Harrison held the wire, Caspasian did likewise. A quick check showed that the guards were still fully occupied with both fight and fire. Caspasian smiled. So far so good.

Across from the prison camp, the factory was in darkness. On the hillside from the direction of the Baron's quarters, Caspasian could see lights coming down the path. The Baron was not taking any chances. He had obviously heard the shots and was sending reinforcements. All the better, Caspasian thought. There would be fewer men to guard the radio room and other facilities.

'We'll have to go through the bush,' he said as they ran for the nearest trees. The guards were streaming down the path. The last thing Caspasian needed was to clash with them.

The moment they entered the jungle, Caspasian knew it was going to be hard work. The slope climbed steeply and the undergrowth was dense. He had little difficulty maintaining his bearing as the ground converged naturally on the terrace above. All he had to do was keep moving. Thorns and branches tore at their clothes and flesh and he heard Wolter gasp as something cut him. They heard further shots but then there was silence. Looking back, Caspasian could no longer see any sign of the fire. He hoped that his absence would not be noted. With luck the guards would be happy enough to have averted trouble. But he had to act quickly.

They tumbled out onto the terrace before they realized they had arrived. One moment they were stumbling upwards through the dense undergrowth, and the next they had emerged into the open, the glass doors standing in front of them. To Caspasian's relief the interior was in darkness. He led the way across, his steps silent, ears straining into the quiet for the slightest sound that might indicate a trap. There was none. Inside, he checked that the first room was empty before waving the others in after him.

'It's this way,' Emma whispered, taking the lead. 'It's on the level below this,' she said as they entered a corridor and made their way stealthily along. Caspasian prayed that everyone was otherwise occupied because if they encountered anyone now there was nowhere to hide. Down a flight of steps, they found themselves in a deeper part of the cave. Emma pointed to some steps on the far side that led up to a small door.

'I think that leads outside to the storage tanks.' Caspasian noted it.

Emma put her finger to her lips. 'The radio room's just around the corner,' she whispered. Caspasian nodded and moved in front, signalling for the others to remain where they were. He slid silently forward, back against the cold wall, bracing himself for action. Sure enough, as he rounded the corner he heard someone humming to himself. Edging towards an open door, he steadied his breathing, cleared his mind, and then moved in. In four rapid steps he was inside. There were two men. One, the radio operator, sitting with his back to the door, hands behind his head, feet up on the desk, humming. To his right sat another, side on to Caspasian. He was leaning forward, fiddling with the laces of one boot. He looked up, startled. Before the man could utter a sound, Caspasian closed on him and fired out a *kin geri* kick, flicking his instep into the man's face. His head was knocked backwards and as he rose from the chair, Caspasian aimed and punched, hard and fast, a *chudan gyaku-tsuki* blow, his knuckles powering into the man's jaw.

The radio operator spun round in his chair, starting to rise. But he paid dearly for his relaxed position. He was only half out of his chair by the time Caspasian was onto him. A *mae geri* front kick caught him full in the chest and sent him flying backwards across the table at his back. Before he could recover, an open-handed *shuto* blow chopped savagely into his neck and he was out.

Caspasian checked them both. Neither would be causing any problems for some time. He darted back outside and signalled the others forward. Captain Harrison went straight to the radio equipment and inspected it. 'This seems all straightforward,' he said confidently, sounding more like his old self. 'Leave this to me.'

'Emma, you stay here and watch his back,' Caspasian ordered. He could see she was about to protest but then she nodded.

'All right,' she smiled. 'But don't be long.'

He stooped to the two unconscious radio operators and removed pistols and spare clips of ammunition from their holsters. He stuffed one pistol and both spare clips in his pocket and handed the other weapon to Emma. 'Do you know how to use this?'

She looked at it doubtfully, but then brightened. 'Yes, I think so.'

'That's the ticket. If anyone comes, just point and fire.'

Before she had time to change her mind, Caspasian and Wolter went quickly across to the steps and jogged up to the door. Opening it, they were met by a rush of warm, moist air from the jungle outside, just as Emma had predicted. Before them they could see the outline of the nearest of the tanks.

As they ran across to it, checking that there was no one around, Wolter panted, 'Blowing up the hydrogen will be the easy part. It doesn't matter that we don't have any explosives. It is one itself. All we have to do is ignite it. But how are we going to delay the bang so we can get clear? Any ideas?'

Caspasian located an outlet valve. He reached into his pocket and pulled out the two clips of ammunition. 'I'm working on it,' he said.

He put both hands to the valve, turned it, and heard the hiss of gas passing out of the tank and into the pipe that led away into the jungle and down the hillside towards the landing field. On the top of the valve, a needle jumped into life in the glass-fronted pressure gauge. Caspasian considered the gauge. 'That should do,' he said, tapping the glass to test its strength.

As quickly as he could, he emptied the bullets out of both clips. 'Here, give me a hand,' he said, passing half the bullets to Wolter. 'I need the gunpowder.'

Clenching the head of a bullet between his teeth, Caspasian winced as he turned the brass case until the bullet came loose. Gingerly he tipped out the charge into a neat little pile. Wolter saw what he was up to and copied him with his own handful of rounds. Slowly the pile of black powder grew. When he came to the last bullet, Caspasian put it to one side, saving it.

'How far away do you think we'll need to be?' he asked Wolter.

Wolter looked at the huge tank towering over them, and at its neighbours looming out of the darkness. He swallowed nervously. 'A lot further than I suspect we're going to be.'

Caspasian chuckled. 'Pretty much what I thought. Oh well. In for a penny, in for a pound,' and he tore a strip of cloth from his shirt tail, twirling it into a long length of material. 'Have you got a handkerchief?' he asked. Wolter dug into his pocket and produced one.

'Thanks.'

Caspasian placed the one remaining bullet in the centre and then wrapped the rest of the handkerchief tightly around it so that the bullet formed the core of the little bundle. He then placed it against the glass of the gauge and fastened it there securely with the ends of the handkerchief, testing it to ensure it held firm. With the strip of cloth he had torn from his shirt, he tied one end to the handkerchief, and let the other trail down to the ground. Then, he carefully scooped up the pile of black powder and sprinkled it in a fine trail leading away from the cloth. He was dismayed to find that even by using it sparingly, he could only make it stretch for a couple of yards.

Wolter stared at him, realizing what he was up to. 'It'll never work. What if the flame goes out, or the cloth fails to ignite?'

'Then I'll have to stand as far away as I can and fire a bullet into the tank with the pistol,' Caspasian said resolutely.

'But that would be suicide! You'd be blown to smithereens.'

'Do you have a better idea?' Caspasian asked, reaching for the remaining matches from the box Richard had given him.

Wolter did not.

'Once the flame burns its way from the trail of powder up the cloth, the handkerchief catches fire, the bullet inside it cooks off and fires. The blast will smash the glass on the front of the gauge, igniting the hydrogen inside. The chain reaction that sets off will explode the whole tank within seconds, and the other tanks next door should go up too.' He glanced over his shoulder towards the entrance to the cave complex, the door still standing open. 'With luck the force of the explosion will be enough to send the whole edifice sky high.'

Wolter looked again at the tanks. 'I'm sure it will.' He studied the crude array of powder trail, shirt cloth and handkerchief, the whole assemblage looking ridiculously harmless next to the mighty storage tanks. 'But how long do you think this arrangement is going to give us to get clear? As a timer it's hardly precise, is it?'

'Best I can do, I'm afraid, in the complete absence of any proper explosives, fuse or detonators.' He regarded the cloth and trail. 'I'd say it should give us about three minutes. Five at the absolute outside. Anything beyond that and we'll know it's gone out, or the round's failed to cook off.'

Wolter took a deep breath. 'And that's when you come back and blow yourself up?'

'Cheery bugger, aren't you?' Caspasian said grimly.

When everything was set, he sat back on his heels and looked calmly at Wolter. 'Better go and hurry the others. Someone might come along at any moment.'

Wolter nodded and jogged back towards the door, disappearing inside. Caspasian waited tensely, fingering the matchbox. It seemed an age before Wolter reappeared in the doorway and whistled lightly. Caspasian looked and saw Wolter's thumbs-up. Taking out a match, he struck it, cupping the fragile bouncing flame in his hands until it had taken hold and was burning strongly. With pounding heart, he touched it to the powder trail. For a moment nothing happened. The tiny flame started to die. Then, just when Caspasian was about to reach for a second match, the flame caught and the black powder began to fizz and spit.

Caspasian was on his feet and running, in through the door and hurtling down the steps. 'Go, go, go!' he barked at Wolter. They sprinted to the radio room where Captain Harrison had just tapped out the closing segment of his message, giving the final coordinates of the island's position.

'All set?' Caspasian said from the doorway.

'There wasn't enough time,' Harrison complained. 'I should have signalled them about the plot against the *Victoria and Albert*. I should . . .'

'Too late now,' Caspasian said. Without waiting for Harrison to finish, he grabbed Emma's arm and pulled her after him. 'Run like hell!'

They tore back up the steps and into the corridor, running straight into one of the Baron's guards. Before alarm could even register in the man's eyes, Caspasian had cut him down with two short, sharp blows to the face. There was a shout from behind them and a gun fired. The bullet smacked into the plaster beside Emma's face. She screamed. Caspasian twisted round, simultaneously pushing her down, drawing the pistol from his pocket and raising it. Taking rough aim, he squeezed off two shots. The second struck its target.

From somewhere in the depths of the complex a bell sounded. 'That's torn it,' Captain Harrison said.

They came to the expansive sitting room beyond which the dark night beckoned invitingly from outside the open glass doors. But their way was blocked. Two armed guards came racing across the terrace. Silhouetted against the night they presented easy targets. Caspasian aimed again and fired. His pistol jammed.

'Blast!' He snatched Emma's pistol from her. He fired again, but by now the guards had gone to ground. Bullets snapped around Caspasian and his companions.

'The time, Caspasian! Look at the time!' Wolter called.

Ignoring him, Caspasian took a deep breath and dived forward. Rounds spat and cracked at him. He found a clear line to one guard and fired. He heard the man grunt. Then he darted to one side, dived forward over a desk sending a lamp and papers flying in all directions, and came up in a kneeling position half a dozen yards from the second guard. The man was aiming straight at him. Caspasian fired first, blazing away until his bullets found their mark. The guard's arms flew out to his sides and he was knocked backwards.

Before the guard had even hit the floor, Caspasian was on his feet. 'Come on!' he yelled. In his mind's eye he could see the flame catching hold of the cloth and climbing towards the bullet secured hard against the gauge's thin film of glass.

The others raced after him. Out in the night, they tore across the terrace. The complex behind them was alive with shouts now and Caspasian's main fear was that his fuse might be discovered and extinguished before it had time to detonate the gas tanks. But there was nothing he could do about it. He would have to hope that when the bodies of the radio operators were found, the Baron's guards would assume that his only intention had been to transmit a signal for help.

'What's that?' Captain Harrison said suddenly, stopping in his tracks.

Caspasian crashed headlong into him, grunting as the breath was knocked from his lungs.

'What?'

'That noise?' Harrison answered. His head was raised like a tracker dog that has just acquired the scent.

The others stopped to listen. Caspasian felt his spine tingle. Through the noise of shouts and alarms he could just detect another sound. It was the sound of a distant engine. Several engines. Coming from the far side of the valley.

'The airships!' Wolter said. 'They're starting the motors!'

Without replying, Caspasian sprinted for the path. 'But the guards?' Emma queried.

'No time,' Caspasian called back over his shoulder. 'It'll take too long through the bush. We'll have to use the path. Otherwise we'll be too late.'

As quickly as they could, they hurtled down the path. Caspasian forced from his mind the strong chance that at any moment they might run headlong into more of the Baron's guards. Then, just when he estimated they were about to reach the valley he heard shouts and the sounds of people approaching. In a flash he weighed the pros and cons. He could either stop and prepare to engage them, or run right through and try to bluff it out, pretending he and the others were part of the Baron's force. In all the chaos he reckoned there was every chance that they might just get away with it. A fresh surge of noise from the distant engines helped him make up his mind.

'Keep going!' he called back to his comrades. Wolter stared at him but understood his intent.

However, as they closed with the oncoming group, Caspasian recognized one of the voices.

'Scratch!' he called as they neared.

Out of the darkness, Scratch appeared at the head of a group of some half dozen or more prisoners, Harrison's men. When they saw their Captain they cheered and slapped him on the back. Most of them were carrying staves but Caspasian noticed that at least two of them had managed to seize rifles.

'We broke out, sir,' Scratch said as he stood panting before Caspasian, Harrison and Wolter. 'Got away in the middle of the riot. Proper big one it was,' he added proudly. But then his face fell. 'They've taken Smudger, sir. And Mr Domain, Mr Edward and the Brigadier, sir.'

'What happened?' Emma asked.

'We was separated in the fight. The last I saw of them they was being hustled out of the camp by the guards.'

'Where did they take them?' Caspasian asked, dreading the answer.

'Off to the landing field, I think, sir.'

'Hostages,' Wolter said sternly. 'The Baron wants hostages. He knows that with them in his hands we won't try to shoot him down as he takes off.'

Caspasian could feel the hope draining from him but he had to try to reach the airship before it was able to make its getaway.

Reinforced with Scratch and Harrison's men, he led the way towards the landing field as fast as he could. But they had just reached the end of the path where it emerged from the jungle-covered slopes of the mountain, when they came under fire. There was a sporadic crackle of rifle shots and bullets snapped in the air around them. Caspasian and the others hit the ground. He wriggled forward to try and locate the reason for this latest delay. Some thirty yards in front he saw about four or five of the Baron's men. They had been pursuing Scratch and the other fugitives from the camp breakout.

'That's all we need,' Harrison said, crawling up alongside Caspasian. 'What the hell do we do now?'

Caspasian glanced at his watch, then looked up the path behind them. 'Perhaps nothing at all,' he said.

Harrison looked at him, puzzled. But the next moment, his answer came. From the area of the storage tanks came the single forlorn crack of a pistol shot. But the sound was unusual, the small detonation not confined within the chamber of a gun. For a second or two, Caspasian waited, every nerve alert.

'Damn,' he said, when nothing further appeared to be happening. The round had cooked off in the burning rags but the rest of his plan seemed to have failed. Suddenly the night tore open. A ferocious explosion rocked the ground where they lay and from overhead an enormous fireball erupted into the sky. All around him Caspasian could see the faces of his companions illuminated as if in broad daylight. All of them were staring mesmerised at the fireball. Beside him, Emma gazed in wonder like a child staring into firelight.

A couple of seconds later there was another explosion, equal to the first.

'There goes the next tank,' Wolter said triumphantly. He reached across and slapped Caspasian on the back. 'Well done! You did it!'

'Come on, lads!' Scratch shouted, and while the attention of the Baron's guards was distracted by the explosions, he leapt to his feet and, with Harrison's men beside him, charged forward and rushed their opponents, sweeping over them in a cascade of clubs, fists and boots. From the jungle mountain top, more explosions followed, each bigger than the last. Showers of debris began to tumble out of the livid orange sky.

'The whole complex is going up!' Harrison said, amazed. 'Look!'

From the terrace, the entire front of the Baron's headquarters exploded outwards, as the mountain's secret interior detonated. Shards of glass and concrete rained down upon them. Caspasian snatched Emma to him and shielded her with his body.

'The airship. We have to hurry,' Wolter prompted.

On their feet again, they raced across the open fields. Off to their right they could see the burning buildings of the prison camp which Scratch and the others had torched. Behind them the towering flames from the ruptured gas storage tanks billowed into the heavens, sparks shooting up to join the stars. The light from the fires illuminated the whole landscape and, looking towards the distant landing field, they saw to their horror that the first of the airships was already airborne.

'The *Fafner*,' Wolter said. The Baron had named the *D100* well, he thought, for the reflected flames made the silver-coloured hull shimmer like scales making it seem like a living thing. As they watched, the nose swung gracefully away from them and with a surge of power, the engines propelled it safely out of their reach, away from the island and out towards the sea.

19

Lieutenant Quesada clambered out of the control car of the *Siegfried* and edged along the narrow gangway onto the mooring tower. He leaned over the edge and sought out a member of the ground crew.

'Get those ropes cast off!' he yelled, livid that the airship was still not underway.

'Just a minute, sir,' one of the men shouted up at him. The individual was fumbling with one of the ropes, making a meal of what should have been a straightforward task.

'What the hell are you up to?' Quesada shouted. 'Just cut the bloody thing.'

Quesada stared, his eyes narrowing. There was something wrong. With a bolt of alarm he realized that the man was not one of his own. And far from untying the rope, he was securing it fast to the mooring ring set in concrete beneath the floating leviathan. He dug into his holster for his pistol. The man looked up just in time and dived aside as Quesada's bullet spat in the dirt where he had been standing only a second before.

Quesada shouted back to the control car where a single crewman stood ready at the elevator wheel. He was operating with barely even a skeleton crew, the rest having been caught up in the riot in the prison compound and then the explosions at the storage tank area. He himself was going to have to man the rudder wheel. Nevertheless, the Baron's parting instructions before he had left aboard the *Fafner* had been explicit. Take off and follow to the best of Quesada's ability. Quesada grimaced.

It was all very well for von Staaden to speak. The Baron had been accompanied by Lieutenant Davies, a full complement, that idiot Westacott, his brutish sidekick and the hostages. He, Quesada, was supposed to perform miracles all on his own.

He fired another shot to ward off a second man who was trying to get to the rope. Then, he looked down at the foot of the tower. Someone was trying to climb up it. Quesada could see him through the superstructure. The man was trying to remain inconspicuous. Quesada sought out a new angle that would present him with a clean shot. He fired. The bullet missed, striking an iron girder and ricocheting off into space. With a bolt of alarm he realized that further shots would risk hitting one of the airship's gas cells. Reluctantly he made his way to the ladder. He would only be able to fire again at the closest range, when there was no chance of another miss and ricochet.

At that moment, the man looked up. Quesada recognized him. It was the prisoner, the one they called Caspasian. Behind him, the fires still raged on the mountain top. The Baron's ruined headquarters blazed and fresh detonations could be heard deep inside the cave system. Quesada's lips tightened into a thin dangerous line. He holstered his pistol, drew a knife from his belt and made his way to intercept the troublesome Englishman.

Caspasian met him on the last flight of steps leading to the gangway. Quesada's foot flew out at him, narrowly missing his face. Caspasian's pistol was as useless as Quesada's. He desperately needed to seize the airship intact. He could not risk losing it.

When Quesada came at him again, Caspasian was ready. He swung himself out from the tower, hauling himself nimbly onto a level with Quesada. The two men faced each other on the gangway, each angling for an opening. Quesada's knife flicked out at Caspasian's face. He dodged aside, nearly losing his balance. Below him, the ground seemed a long way down.

Only the frailest of railings guarded the flanks of the gangway.

'Die, Englishman,' Quesada spat with hatred. He made a feint with his blade, and then lunged hard and fast at Caspasian's throat. Caspasian was ready for him. Sliding into a low *shiba-dachi* stance, he allowed the knife to sail harmlessly over his head. Quesada's own momentum brought him toppling forward straight into a powerful *tate-tsuki* punch in the ribs. In the same instant, Caspasian grabbed Quesada's arm pulling him further off-balance and executed a foot sweep knocking Quesada's feet from under him. As the horror appeared on Quesada's face, he went headlong over the railings and somersaulted to the ground. Caspasian looked down at the crumpled body. From the lie of the limbs he could tell that the man was dead.

'Come on,' he shouted to Emma, who was waiting below. He started across the gangway and saw that a struggle was already taking place in the control car. While he had been making his way up the mooring tower, Wolter and Harrison had entered the airship through the cargo hold amidships. Now, throughout the vessel, Harrison's men were seizing control, ejecting Quesada's skeleton crew from the airship.

Together with Emma, Caspasian stepped through the small hatch into the control car. Harrison and Wolter were already there, checking the elevator and rudder wheels.

'I've ordered my men to cast off,' Harrison snapped, his voice and manner brisk and businesslike now he was at the helm of his airship once again. 'I'm starting engines.' He thought for a moment. 'The *Siegfried*, eh? Not a bad name, come to think of it.'

Caspasian searched out of the gondola's windows for the *Fafner*. It was nowhere in sight. 'How are we going to find it in the dark?' he asked.

Harrison chuckled grimly. 'That's tomorrow's problem,' he answered. 'Right now I'm more concerned with getting away from here. Those flames are spreading,' he said pointing to the blazing tanks. He checked the gas pressure gauges. 'The cells have been charged almost to maximum capacity.'

'Can you vent some?' Caspasian suggested.

Harrison shook his head. 'Never! Not with the fires so close.'

'Why would they charge them up like that?' Caspasian asked.

'Can't say.'

Wolter looked thoughtful. 'It's as if the ship's been charged for high-altitude flying, as in the war. The Baron's rigged it like one of the old height-climbers.'

There was a scuffle behind them and Scratch burst into the gondola, a broad grin on his grubby face. 'That's the last of them,' he said proudly. 'The ship's all ours.'

'Well done,' Caspasian said.

'I told the Indians that His Majesty's navy would be here soon. Maybe as early as tomorrow. They said they'll have the place under control by then. Just in time to hand over the last of the Baron's guards.' He grinned. 'If they bother to take prisoners, that is.'

Looking out of the control gondola's windows, Caspasian and Emma could see groups of Indians hunting down their quarry. But of greater concern to them were the occasional outbursts of flame that erupted every so often from the ruptured tanks. They were all burning furiously and fire had also caught hold of the uppermost parts of the jungle. Tongues of fire were being snatched away by the wind from the sea, licking dangerously close to the airship.

'I hope we're going to be away from here soon,' Scratch said, his eyes wide with alarm.

Harrison concentrated on the controls, tight-lipped. Wolter smiled. 'Don't worry. That is our intention.' He had taken charge of the elevator wheel, leaving the rudder to Harrison who was swinging it hard over to bring the airship's nose round as fast as he could.

'Watch out for those trees,' Wolter cautioned.

'Don't worry. I've seen them,' Harrison said. 'Drop ballast fore and aft. A thousand pounds. Get us up, Herr Wolter.'

'I need maximum power for lift, Captain.'

Harrison signalled the engine gondolas on the ship's tele-graph. Caspasian and Emma grabbed hold of the window sills for balance as the airship surged forward in response. Wolter spun the elevator wheel and slowly but surely the nose began to rise. In front of them a line of tall palm trees loomed out of the firelight.

'Can you take us around them?' Wolter asked.

Harrison shook his head. 'I don't have the space to turn her. It's up and over, I'm afraid.'

'You're not the only one who's afraid,' Scratch mumbled as he stared in terror at the approaching tree line.

With inches to spare, the airship creased narrowly over the palms. Captain Harrison ran to the back of the gondola and peered out of the rear window to watch the whole huge length of the underside clear the obstacle. Far away at the stern, he stared at the main keel and rudder, the lowest points on the fuse-lage. With a sickening crash they ploughed into the topmost branches. Everyone in the gondola held their breath, waiting for the tell-tale thump that would signal an explosion and the cata-strophic fire that would inevitably follow. Nothing happened. The rudder dragged itself on through the branches until it broke clear of them.

'We're out! We've done it!' Harrison called, grinning from ear to ear.

There was one final blast from the mountain top as if the long dormant volcano had erupted and then the flames subsided into a furious glow. All eyes turned away from the burning island and looked towards the sea. In front of them lay mile upon mile of darkness stretching into the west. The airship continued to climb at a steep angle, all engines labouring to drive it up through the layers of low cloud that hung over the Caribbean.

At last they punctured the cloud base and were enveloped. Caspasian and Emma rushed around closing the windows and securing them. The temperature was dropping markedly. The minutes passed as they continued on through an eerie world of mist, completely blind. Then, just as suddenly as they had entered it, they burst from the roof into a clear night sky bedecked with stars.

'Take us up another thousand feet and then level off, Herr Wolter,' Captain Harrison ordered.

'Aye, aye, Captain,' Wolter said good-naturedly. It had been many years since he had stood at the controls of an airship and although he was facing the experience with mixed emotions, overall he was pleased to find that he was enjoying himself.

With a check of the altimeter, Wolter spun the elevator wheel again until the airship was once more in trim. Harrison signalled the engine gondolas to slow to cruising speed and the *D200*, the Baron's *Siegfried*, glided effortlessly through the night.

Harrison rummaged in a locker and found a pair of binoculars. Moving to the front of the car, he scanned the skies ahead of them for any sign of the *Fafner*.

Wolter chuckled. 'If you're looking for a light, don't bother,' he said. 'The Baron flew scores of missions over England in the war and had to contend with your fighters. They posed far more of a threat than we do.'

'Except that we can climb to the same height as he can,' Caspasian observed as he dug into the chart cupboard.

'Yes, but what can we do even if we catch up with him?' Emma asked. 'I mean, we can hardly shoot him down. He's got Lionel and the others on board.'

'No, but with luck we can prevent him from intercepting the *Victoria and Albert*,' Caspasian said.

'You mean, race him to the Panama Canal and get there first?' Wolter asked. 'We'd never do it. He's got too much of a head start and he knows these skies better than any of us.'

'He's also got a full crew,' Harrison observed. He smiled kindly. 'Bags of spirit is all very well, and you lot have got it in bucketloads, but at the end of the day it's cold professionalism that counts in this business.'

'Ah! Here we are.' Caspasian found the charts he had been looking for and pulled them out, spreading them on top of the case and switching on the table lamp. 'I'm not talking about the Panama Canal,' he said, running his finger across the chart's surface until he located what he was looking for. 'And nor's the Baron. Here, look at this.' He tapped his forefinger on the spot. Harrison, Emma and Scratch leaned over, Wolter managing the controls.

Harrison stared at the markings in disbelief. 'My God. It's his course. But where the devil's he going?' he asked, hardly daring to hear the answer.

Stretched out before them were the charts Caspasian had suspected would be there, all prepared for Quesada, the duplicate set that would lead him faithfully in the Baron's wake. The markings had been hastily done, but the essentials were all present. Bearings, altitudes, rendezvous.

Emma leaned forward and read the names on the map. 'But that's Peru,' she said hesitantly. 'What ever is he thinking of?'

'The Baron obviously had a change of plan,' Caspasian declared. 'He must have suspected we'd found out about the Panama Canal option, and he couldn't be sure we hadn't warned the Royal Navy when Harrison got to the radio room. So at the last minute he changed his plan. It looks like he means to intercept the Royal Yacht before it ever reaches the canal. Further south, along the coast of Peru.'

Wolter craned round and glanced at the chart. 'He's mad.'

'I don't think that's in dispute,' Caspasian observed dryly.

'No, I mean he's mad because he means to cross the Andes, one of the highest mountain ranges in the world. The winds would be treacherous, to say the least.' Wolter turned back to his wheel, muttering darkly in German. Then, in one final attempt to dissuade Caspasian, he said, 'It's impossible. We have to go to the canal and then head south from there. Even that'll be hard enough.'

'And what if the Baron makes it over the mountains?' Caspasian countered. 'He might do. We know the *Fafner*'s gas cells are charged to maximum capacity for high altitude flying.' He saw his point register with Wolter. 'What if we made it to the canal, and all the while the Baron had crossed the Andes, intercepted the Royal Yacht, and snatched or bombed the Prince of Wales?'

'Caspasian's got a point,' Harrison admitted. 'The Baron's familiar with the details of the yacht's entire route. He can choose his own place and time, once he's over the mountains.'

'Don't tell me you're going along with this lunatic idea?' Wolter stammered, aghast.

Harrison cocked his head on one side, studying the chart. 'I'm not sure we have a choice. If we just slavishly head for the canal, the Baron stands every chance of getting to the Royal Yacht ahead of us.'

'Unless the *Fafner*'s wrecked on a mountain side in the process,' Wolter added sombrely.

Harrison regarded him. 'Can we take that chance?'

Wolter considered the point. Caspasian stared resolutely out of the window. 'No,' Wolter said at last.

'We have to follow him by the same route,' Caspasian said. 'Just as he intended Quesada to do. What's more, if he sees us following, he might just think it's Quesada. If he does, it'll allow us to close the gap without the need for stealth.'

They were all silent for a while, each one locked into their own thoughts. Eventually Scratch heaved a gigantic sigh. 'Well, I've never seen the Andes. Is it true they've got this bloody great vulture thing?'

Emma smiled. 'The condor.'

'Yeah. That's it,' Scratch said. 'Just keep that thing away from me and I'll be fine.'

Captain Harrison laughed. 'You'll be fine indeed, Scratch. You'll be fine indeed.'

'So where does my dear old comrade in arms intend to make the crossing?' Wolter asked.

Harrison studied the map closely. 'He appears to be heading for a pass at Cajabamba.' He ran his fingers through his hair. 'God knows why. There are easier routes to the north, by the looks of it.'

'Yes, but they'll be more densely populated,' Caspasian said. 'There'd be more chance of a sighting, and word getting to the authorities. And don't forget,' he added, 'it's what's on the other side that matters. The Baron doesn't strike me as one to take the easy option.'

'That's true enough,' Wolter added.

'If it's the more direct route to his interception point with the *Victoria and Albert*, then that's the route he'll take. And,' he added, 'that's the route we'll have to take with him.'

They set a course heading southwest that would take them down the eastern side of the Andes in accordance with the route marked on the charts. Behind them, the horizon was starting to show the first signs of daybreak. The starlight was becoming dimmer by the minute and across the eastern skyline, a thin strip of grey began to separate itself from the darkness.

'I'm half-minded to try and signal the *Victoria and Albert* from the radio room,' Captain Harrison said.

'Don't risk it,' Wolter responded quickly. 'The Baron's an expert at radio interception. He'd pick up your transmission and know we've got control of the *Siegfried*.'

'Does it matter?' Harrison pondered. 'Surely the main thing's to get a warning to the Royal Yacht. They can then take evasive action. Either that, or the Chilean navy can get some assistance out to them.'

Caspasian pored over the chart, quickly estimating times and distances. 'Not before the Baron reached them,' he said. 'They're going to be a sitting duck, whatever we do. The best thing is to leave the Baron believing it's Quesada behind him. That way we can close on the *Fafner*.'

'And then what?' Emma asked.

Caspasian smiled. 'I'm working on it.' He stretched. 'Anyone for breakfast? What say I visit the galley and see what I can find?'

There was a chorus of approval.

'Come on, Scratch. Let's go hunting.'

'Me too,' Emma said. 'I'm not much use here.'

When they reached the galley, they found that it had been restocked for the journey, albeit with a more basic selection of items than when the ship had left Cardington all those days ago. Emma produced a loaf of corn bread and cut it into thick slices, while Scratch similarly carved up a salami. Caspasian tested the electricity supply and switched on the boiler to brew some coffee. When a tray of sandwiches and a thermos of coffee had been prepared for the control gondola's crew, Scratch took his leave, taking his own breakfast with him.

Left alone, Caspasian and Emma went through to the small bar. Caspasian placed a low table beside the promenade windows, pulled up a deeply cushioned sofa, and Emma set down her tray. They sat in silence to eat and watch the sun come up. The light found them long before it touched the ground below. Caspasian poured them both coffee while Emma opened a can of condensed milk.

'Are you all right?' Caspasian asked, watching her profile as she stared out of the window.

She smiled unconvincingly. 'As well as can be expected, I suppose.'

'No wonder you're a star,' he said. 'It takes courage to go through what you have and still be able to produce a smile at the end of it.'

'The end of it?' she said, bringing her beautiful eyes to bear.

'Very well, then. The penultimate scene.'

She laughed. 'What worries me is how I'm going to be left in the final scene.'

'Oh I'm sure there'll be a sequel for you.' He reached forward and clasped her hand gently. 'Don't worry. We're going to make it.' He sat back. 'I suppose we could just set a new course for somewhere safe and look to ourselves. There's absolutely nothing at all to stop us.'

She regarded him wryly. 'Don't tease me.'

He shrugged. 'Well, why shouldn't we?' he asked. 'Haven't we done enough? We've recovered one of the airships, destroyed Delgado's little operation, as well as the Baron's base. We could just signal a warning to the *Victoria and Albert* and have done with it.'

He stretched out his legs, crossing them at the ankles, and gazed wistfully out of the window. Emma watched him, wondering what was going on in his mind.

'Perhaps the Royal Yacht could defend itself. Forewarned is forearmed. To an extent.'

She smiled. 'You know that wouldn't work. What could it do against an airship? You've no intention of leaving them to their own devices.'

He sighed, feeling the dead weight of duty load itself on his shoulders. 'You're right, of course. But it's nice to dream.'

Emma studied him. 'Now dreams, John Caspasian, are what I do best.'

She moved to his side. He placed his arm around her shoulders, drew her close and kissed her.

'You see?' she smiled. 'No screen goddess. Just an ordinary woman.'

He chuckled. 'About as ordinary as riding in an airship towards the Andes in pursuit of a mad German Baron who's out to shanghai the Royal Yacht and kidnap the Prince of Wales.'

Emma laughed. 'When you put it like that . . .'

Caspasian kissed her again. She unfastened the front of his shirt and stroked his chest, but the strengthening light was harsh in the small room. They looked at each other and laughed, each having the same thought. Going quickly out of the bar, they made their way through to the passenger accommodation, seeking out Caspasian's old cabin. Closing and locking the door behind them, they kissed again. Emma locked her arms around his neck. Caspasian could feel her pressing her body against his.

Slipping out of their clothes, they wriggled between the sheets of the narrow bunk that creaked beneath them. Emma shivered and Caspasian smoothed away the goose bumps that covered her shoulders and arms. She moaned softly, biting her lip as he bent to kiss her breasts beneath the sheets. Far away, the sound of the engines had dimmed to the gentle purr of a pampered cat. It reverberated through the fabric of the airship.

Caspasian could hear Emma whispering his name, sampling it. She said it over and over again like an incantation. He took a nipple between his lips and felt her sharp intake of breath. She pushed herself under him, enveloping his hips with her legs. Her mouth was against his ear, still whispering his name. Daylight pressed into the cabin, harsh and dazzling. Emma reached down and pulled the sheet over the two of them, softening the light. Caspasian gazed at her wonderingly. She smiled up at him, then closed her eyes and hugged him tight.

For the rest of the day the airship sailed south-west and by evening a thin line of hills had appeared on the starboard side, growing rapidly into formidable snowcapped peaks. But of greater concern to Captain Harrison was a belt of grey cloud that stretched across the horizon in front of them.

'Is there any way around it?' Caspasian asked as he stood in the control gondola, one arm around Emma's shoulders. He had found a jacket for her although it was several sizes too big.

'Afraid not, old man,' Harrison answered, his expression one of alarming concern. 'Not if we're to make the crossing where the Baron intends.'

'We'll have to climb to our maximum ceiling,' Wolter said from his station in front of the elevator wheel where he had remained faithfully with only one short relief. 'Try to ride over the top of it. If we enter the mountains in that we'll be flying blind. We won't have a chance.'

'I agree,' Harrison said. He consulted the hydrogen gauges and frowned. 'We're carrying too much weight, even if I ditch all the ballast. And I can't do that. It would leave me no room for manoeuvre if we get into trouble later on.' He turned to Caspasian. 'John, get every spare man and strip out all non-essential furniture.'

'You mean chuck it out?'

'Overboard. I don't care how you do it. Through the cargo doors, the promenade windows. Whatever. We'll have to strip the airship down to the skeleton if necessary. Go through every berth, the dining room, saloon, bar, galley, then the crew quarters. The lot.'

'Got it.'

As he went, Harrison called after him. 'And you'd better hurry. We're closing on the storm fast and the mountains are only an hour or two away.'

Caspasian and Emma located Scratch in the galley where he was making more sandwiches.

'Forget that,' Caspasian said. 'Duty calls.'

Leaving the minimum number of crew to man the engine gondolas, he mustered his small workforce in the saloon and briefed them on the task. As he did so, he watched their faces turn pale.

'I'd like to say there's nothing to worry about,' he said smiling, 'but I think you'd all know I was lying.'

A nervous laughter rippled through the room. 'Any questions?' There were none. 'Let's go then.'

First to go overboard was all the loose furniture. Propping open the promenade windows, every table and chair, desk, divan, cabinet, stool and cupboard was heaved onto the sills and toppled out into space.

'I hope there's no one living underneath,' Scratch chuckled.

'Just monkeys, mate,' one of Harrison's crew called back, manhandling a crate full of wine bottles over the side. 'And they'll have the best furnished tree house in the whole flaming jungle.'

When the saloon had been stripped bare, they worked through the dining room. Then the bar and galley and stores. Caspasian set aside a small stock of food and drink, sufficient to keep them victualled for a further two days on minimum rations. The passenger accommodation took the longest time. Using the fire axes, Caspasian and the other men hacked loose bunks and cupboards, sinks and other fittings, hurling everything overboard out through the windows. When this was done, they set to work on the walls themselves. Constructed for lightness of weight, they were thankfully flimsy and yielded before the rain of blows with only token resistance.

Elsewhere throughout the vessel, in the crew's quarters and cargo holds, a similar frenzy of destruction took place, until, several hours later, Caspasian and his team returned to the place where the saloon had once been, exhausted but satisfied that they had stripped out everything possible.

Spare clothing had been put to one side, and as everyone cooled after the hard work, they started to wrap up, putting on layer upon layer.

Caspasian dispatched the crewmen back to their posts throughout the ship. Scratch went back to the remains of the galley to see what was left for him to fashion into a semblance of a meal, and Caspasian and Emma returned to the control gondola to find Captain Harrison and Wolter delighted with the results of Caspasian's labour, but increasingly concerned at the spectre rising before them. It was now pitch dark and the outer fringes of the storm were buffeting the fabric of the airship, drumming on the hull and singing through the wires tethering the gas cells in the depths of the huge vessel.

'I don't like the look of this,' Captain Harrison said dourly. 'Not one little bit. It looks a right stinker.'

'Ready to climb?' Wolter called across, pitching his voice above the mounting noise from the wind pounding against the window panes.

Harrison nodded. 'Let's see if we can get above it.' He signalled the engine gondolas to accelerate the motors to maximum power, and Wolter spun the elevator wheel. Almost immediately the nose reared up, everyone held on for balance, Caspasian clutching Emma to him. The airship started to power its way towards the heavens.

Captain Harrison positioned himself in front of the altimeter, eyes riveted to the needle. 'Too high and the crew will start to black out. What do you reckon, Gustav?'

Wolter frowned at the gauge, dark memories clouding his mind. 'Try around fifteen thousand, Captain. See if that's high enough.'

'Are you a mountaineer, Caspasian?' Harrison asked without taking his eyes off the slowly turning needle.

'I've done my bit.'

'What would you say?'

'You could try twenty. But you might find the cold gets to the men before the lack of oxygen.'

Harrison nodded, watching the needle climb inexorably up to and then through the ten thousand mark. A sudden gust of wind struck the nose of the airship like a physical blow, swinging the entire colossus to port.

'Rudder hard over, Captain!' Wolter shouted. Caspasian was

the closest and reacted instantly, seizing the wheel and spinning it round.

'How long to first light?' Caspasian asked.

Emma looked at her watch. 'A good two hours,' she said, fear catching at her voice. Caspasian drew her to him. She pressed her body against his back, encircling his waist with her arms, her face flattened on his shoulder blades. Through the layers of clothing he could feel her trembling. For just a moment he took one hand off the wheel and squeezed her arm. He felt her kiss the back of his coat, just as a second blast of wind struck them on the underside.

The airship's nose bucked furiously, and the whole vessel began to roll and pitch. Captain Harrison was sent flying. His head crashed against the bulwark and he sank to his knees, dazed. Scratch came tumbling down the ladder, a basket of sandwiches and thermos flasks spilling everywhere. He gripped the rungs, swinging like an ape.

'Scratch, get the Captain!' Caspasian shouted, fighting with the rudder wheel which had developed a life of its own.

Scratch darted to Harrison's side and helped him up. Harrison shook him off. 'I'm fine.' There was blood pouring from a gash in his head. He stared through the window, a thick mist swirling unbroken on the other side. Caspasian could see that he was blacking out.

'We're going to lose it!' Wolter mumbled, terrified. 'I've seen it before. No airship can withstand a storm like this.'

'Well, this one bloody well can,' Caspasian said firmly. Emma's arms were tight about his waist. He was damned if he was going to let anything happen to her. 'Get us higher, Gustav.'

'I can't.' He shot a glance at the altimeter. 'We're at twenty thousand already, for God's sake!'

The wind roared outside, deafening them. 'We don't have a choice,' Caspasian shouted. 'Either we climb out of it or we die.'

'The engines will freeze. They're not made for this. If that happens we'll lose all power and that'll be that. We'll be spun head over heels until the ship breaks up.'

'Do it!' Caspasian shouted. He reached across and cuffed him. 'Now!'

Wolter stared at him, eyes wide with terror. Caspasian could see his lips working but whatever he was saying was drowned by the raging storm. His hands moved on the elevator wheel and the airship rose. On the altimeter Caspasian watched the needle inch ever upwards. Ice was forming on the window panes and inside the gondola the bitter cold penetrated every layer of clothing. He could feel his fingers and feet going numb. Of greater concern was a slight buzzing in his head. Emma's arms went slack around his waist. He felt her sliding from him. He gripped her arm and let her gently down to the floor. Her eyes were on him. She smiled. Then she was sleeping, deceptively, dangerously peaceful.

'You're killing her!' Wolter screamed at him. 'You're going to kill us all!' Caspasian saw his hands move on the elevator wheel, starting to level out. But the storm still raged all about them, tossing the airship as if it was the flimsiest piece of driftwood. In a flash Caspasian's fist lashed out and struck Wolter square on the jaw. Wolter blinked and his knees gave way. Caspasian gripped Scratch's arm and dragged him towards the rudder wheel.

'Take this,' he commanded.

Seizing the elevator wheel, Caspasian held it fast, the airship continuing to climb, the altimeter needle quivering higher.

There was a resounding crack and one of the panes shattered, smashed with cold. Wind blasted in at them, so bitter it stung their faces like the lash of a whip.

Then, as suddenly as if someone had turned off a switch, the airship burst out of the storm. Instant calm enveloped them, and a silence as chilling as the grave. Caspasian spun the elevator wheel like a maniac, bringing the nose down until the vessel was in trim. With one hand he reached down and slapped Wolter awake, dragging him to his feet and standing him, doddering like a drunk, in front of the wheel again.

'Hold it there,' he ordered. He leapt to Emma's side and checked her pulse and breathing. She was slumbering deeply. He prayed that it was sleep and nothing more. He knew that at high altitude capillaries could burst in the brain. His own body was shaking, though whether with the intense cold or the terror at what might have happened to Emma, he was too dazed to consider.

Looking out of the window he saw that they were skimming the surface of the storm whose ceiling raged and crackled with lightning some hundred feet or more below them. He felt a hand on his arm and Captain Harrison struggled to his feet.

'We can't maintain this altitude for long,' he said, eyes struggling for focus.

Caspasian was all too aware of the fact. Above the storm, starlight enabled him to scan ahead for a break in the clouds, a window that might offer some hope of a descent.

There was another crack like a rifle shot, deafening in the enclosed space of the gondola and another pane shattered, shards of glass exploding across them. One of the crewmen called on the airship communication system and reported that his engine had just shut down. It was now frozen solid. Another rang in to report the first case of hypothermia. But still there was no sign of a break in the storm beneath them.

Then, in the distance, Caspasian thought he detected an edge to the lightning-charged clouds. 'There!' he shouted over the noise of the wind, pointing. Captain Harrison swung his binoculars onto it.

'I see it,' he said, tightening the focus and studying the spot carefully. 'I think . . . I think it's a break,' he said at last. The rudder wheel turned and the airship swung gently onto its new course. Caspasian crouched at Emma's side, checking the pulse

in her wrists and throat. It was alarmingly rapid. He willed the
airship on, urging it towards the break in the storm. At their
backs the sky was beginning to lighten once again, making it
easier to define the edge of the storm. The airship closed upon
it at full speed and then, all of a sudden, they were there. It was
as if the ground had opened up beneath them. One moment
they were riding on top of a mass of swirling cloud, and the
next, they could see thousands of feet down to the ground
below. Without needing to be told, Wolter turned the elevator
wheel and the ship descended.

'Steady there!' Harrison urged. 'The mountains can't be far
away. We don't want to fly into them.'

As the needle on the altimeter dropped rapidly, Caspasian
noticed Emma's eyelids flutter. The next moment she was
looking blearily at him. Recognition followed and she smiled
weakly. He retrieved one of Scratch's thermos flasks and poured
her a mug of coffee. She cupped it in her hands, warming them.

'My head feels fit to burst,' she said. 'I'm not sure coffee's the
best thing.' But she smiled and drank it all the same, grateful for
the warmth.

The daylight was intensifying fast and the stars began to
disappear in swathes. A livid orange gash split the eastern
horizon, spreading upwards. Caspasian helped Emma to her
feet and they huddled together shivering to watch it.

'It's beautiful,' Emma said, her voice trembling in the icy cold.
'But a bit terrible.'

'Just a bit,' Caspasian agreed.

Captain Harrison pointed ahead. 'Look! The mountains!'

There in front of them, the whole spectacular range of snow-
capped peaks reared up, towering heavenwards out of dark,
mist-shrouded earth.

Wolter peered at them, spying something. 'Is that the pass?'

Caspasian leapt to find the chart, flattened it on the table and
checked the bearings. 'I think so.'

'The morning star,' Emma said, entranced.

Everyone looked to where she was pointing. Wolter's jaw tightened. 'I don't think so, my dear.' He glanced at Harrison and Caspasian.

The point of light winked at them from the far distance. The movement at that distance was almost imperceptible, but not quite.

'The *Fafner*,' Wolter said grimly.

Caspasian shaded his eyes and saw that Wolter was right. The rising sun had picked out the silver-painted hull and was reflecting off it like a bright but terrible star.

'She's heading straight into the pass,' Harrison said. 'But my God, she's low.'

'Will she have seen us?' Emma asked nervously.

Wolter nodded. 'Oh yes. You can bet on it. The Baron will have seen us by now. The sun will be illuminating us, too.'

'Then take us in,' Caspasian said at last. His features were set with determination. 'Bring us as close as you can. It's time we paid the Baron a visit.'

20

'Baron, the stern lookout's sighted the *Siegfried*. Ten miles and closing.'

Baron von Staaden looked up from his chart table. 'Good old Quesada.' He eyed Lieutenant Davies who returned his appraising stare sheepishly. 'And you said he'd never make it.'

'I stand corrected,' Davies said reluctantly.

The Baron smiled coldly and pushed back his chair. 'You can relay that to Quesada himself when he comes alongside.'

Davies grimaced and returned to his watch. Before him, the crewmen at the elevator and rudder wheels stood attentively at their posts. The storm had given them quite a buffeting, but they had ridden the currents like the Wagnerian dragon whose name the airship bore.

'Engines slow to half speed,' the Baron ordered. 'We'll let the *Siegfried* close up. I'll take the helm myself and lead it through the pass.' He got to his feet and stretched. Davies moved aside to accommodate him. 'Lieutenant, check the bomb bays.'

Davies concealed his irritation. 'But sir, I have been over the mechanisms countless times already. The alterations were perfect. It will work, I assure you.'

'Just do it, Lieutenant. And please don't question my orders again.'

Realizing he had gone too far, Davies snapped smartly to attention and saluted. 'Yes sir. Of course, sir.' He turned and was gone, hoisting himself swiftly up the ladder and out of the gondola into the main body of the vessel.

Striding along the main axial gangway in the direction of the bomb bay, he bridled at the thought of Quesada. The man would be insufferable now. He struggled to put it from his mind and focus on the task in hand. The Baron was a perfectionist. Everybody knew that.

He hurried through the body of the airship, passing beneath the pendulous gas cells, their sides rippling with the hydrogen within. The drone of the engines was hypnotic, thrumming through the fabric of the hull and resonating along the broad radial girders. Arriving at the bomb bay, he let himself down through the hatch and acknowledged the salutes of the two crewmen on station there. He quickly went through the checks that he had already carried out and found everything as he knew it would be. Functioning perfectly to order. The *Victoria and Albert* would not stand a chance. She would be sent to the bottom of the sea and the heir to the British throne along with her. The Baron's revenge would be complete.

One of the men offered Davies a mug of coffee. He accepted it gratefully, glad to dawdle away from von Staaden's critical eye. He chatted for some time with the crew and was alarmed, when he checked his watch, to see how much time had passed.

He was just preparing to leave when the communication tube buzzed into life. One of the crewmen answered it. He listened for a second and then handed it to Davies. He put his ear to the tube and grimaced, trying to comprehend the muffled voice. It was the Baron.

'Say again,' Davies shouted into the tube when the Baron had fallen silent. He placed his ear to the tube again.

'. . . topside . . . Top Lookout reports . . . Quesada . . . proximity . . .'

Davies frowned, struggling to understand the Baron's meaning. He did not dare ask him to repeat it again. There would be hell to pay.

'I understand that I am to check the Top Lookout. Is that

correct?' Davies asked, tensing himself for a barrage of abuse.

It came. His ear burned from the torrent that blasted into his head. He held the tube at arm's length, fixing the crewmen with an icy stare, daring them to smirk. Neither of them did. As far as Davies could tell, the message ended with an imperative to act swiftly.

'Roger,' he shouted into it when the Baron's muffled, broken voice had fallen silent again. 'On my way. Out.'

To regain some measure of dignity in front of the men, he calmly finished his coffee, draining the cup to the dregs, then shaking it dry and screwing it back on top of the thermos.

'Thanks for that,' he said with a stiff smile. He turned and left. All the way back he felt the prickle of anger rising inside him. He was a good officer. He knew that. The Baron had no right speaking to him like that.

The series of ladders that climbed all the way to the Top Lookout's post started from the midships section of the *Fafner*. He paused at the bottom and looked up. The rungs disappeared high overhead, each segment climbing up between the gas cells to a dizzying height. He removed his jacket and draped it over the lowest rung to await his return. He shivered but knew that the climb would soon warm him up.

He had only been climbing for a couple of minutes when he heard someone hailing him from below. He looked down and his head spun when he saw how high he had already got. On the axial gangway someone was standing looking up at him. Davies shielded his eyes and squinted. His expression set hard. It was that cretin Sergeant Major Horner. The deserter. He was shouting something up to Davies. Something about Davies having to wait for him. Davies scoffed. How dare the Baron! Horner and the equally contemptible Major Westacott had been detailed to guard the prisoners and special cargo. Now, it seemed, the Baron was expecting Davies to subordinate himself to a deserter. Sending Horner, of all people, to accompany him.

As if he himself was incapable of carrying out a simple check on the Top Lookout. Well he would not have it.

'Can't hear!' he shouted back. He turned again to the ladder and hauled himself up, going faster than before. Horner shouted something. It sounded like an insult. Davies was not surprised. The man was a lout. A quick glance below showed Horner to be following him, but he was a big man. The going would be slow for him. Slow and hard. Davies would have made it to the top, carried out the check and would be on his way down again before Horner had even got halfway. He grinned. That would show the idiot!

He increased the pace, pulling himself up hand over hand, scampering up the rungs. He was nicely warm now and could feel the sweat breaking on his forehead. He glanced up and saw that he was nearing the inner side of the hull's top cover. The metal framework of a thick radial girder arched majestically overhead. A narrow walkway was suspended there at the very top of the gas cells. Davies did not dare look down for fear of vertigo. He should really have brought a harness so he could belay onto something.

He reached the gantry, breathing hard. He looked down. Horner was far below, the top of his fat head bobbing from side to side as he hauled his gross carcass up the ladders.

The gantry was so narrow Davies had to shuffle sideways along it. He had not been up here for some time. Peering through the gloom he could see the back of the Top Lookout's cupola about twenty yards away. It would be freezing cold inside but the crewman on duty would be heavily swathed in fleece-lined flying leathers. Davies resolved just to pop his head in, check that everything was all right, and then be gone.

He arrived at the tiny door and tried the handle. It appeared to be jammed. He shouted for the crewman to open it from the inside. There was no response. The wind was howling outside the hull. No doubt the fellow had been deafened by it. Davies set his back to the door and tried the handle again. The mechanism had probably frozen when the airship had been flying at altitude. With a sudden jolt the door gave way and swung wide open on its hinges. Davies stooped to look inside. An icy blast of wind struck him in the face. It was absolutely perishing. But the cupola was empty. Davies frowned, puzzled. The communication tube dangled to the floor, swinging uselessly from side to side. Beside it, the lockout's belay harness sat on its hook, unused. If he had ventured out onto the hull's exterior surface without it, he must have gone completely off his head. In conditions like this he would almost certainly have been blown over the side.

Davies ducked under the lintel and entered the cupola. It was so cramped he was virtually doubled over. With an effort he straightened up, and as he did so the sky went dark. Puzzled, he looked up and nearly fainted. Barely yards overhead, the underside of the *Siegfried* loomed perilously close. For a moment Davies was convinced it was going to land on top of the *Fafner*. Quesada must have gone stark staring mad. He was going to collide. Both Zeppelins were about to be wrecked.

With eyes still fixed on the looming colossus, Davies scrabbled after the communication tube. As his rapidly numbing hands fumbled with it, the thought of the lookout returned to his mind. Where had the fellow gone? In an attempt to answer the question, Davies stood on the small stool and pushed his head and shoulders clear of the hull. Facing the stern of the airship he could see nothing. Just the broad acres of canvas stretching away on either side, sloping towards the rear, and overhead the long dark shadow of the *Siegfried*.

He swivelled round to face the prow. His jaw fell open. Standing there, facing him was a man. A familiar face, balanced on the outer hull, legs braced against the rushing wind that must have threatened to pluck him off and hurl him out into space.

'Hello there,' the man said, just as Davies recognized him as Captain John Caspasian.

Before Davies could react, Caspasian had gripped him by the shoulders and lifted him bodily out of the cupola until he too stood on the top of the airship. The wind that hit him full in the face sent him staggering. He clenched his fist and swung viciously at Caspasian. But suddenly Caspasian's face was no longer there. He had ducked clean under Davies' arm which sailed overhead. Davies could feel himself overbalancing. Caspasian drove his shoulder into Davies' stomach and pushed himself upright, lifting Davies bodily off the airship. The next second, Davies felt Caspasian take two strides away from the central spine of the vessel. Beneath him, he could see the broad back of the airship starting to angle downwards. With a sickening jolt he realized what his attacker intended and began to struggle furiously.

It was too late. Caspasian launched him into the air. Davies landed a couple of yards away but the momentum had him in its grip, combining with the rush of the wind and the ever steepening gradient of the canvas sides. He hit the surface hard and began to roll. His fingers scrabbled at the smooth sides for purchase, for anything to grasp. There was nothing. He could feel himself accelerating. His nails scratched and tore at the silver-coated material. He opened his mouth and was alarmed by the animal scream that burst from him. It terrified him and brought home the full horror that he was about to die. And then the airship's flank dropped away, sheer. And Davies was falling. He found himself looking up at the rapidly diminishing underside of the *Fafner*. He knew he must be cold but he felt nothing. He struggled for a thought, but found nothing. Just a blank terror as he plummeted to his death.

Caspasian braced himself and waved the *Siegfried* closer. Leaning out of the control car window, Captain Harrison's ashen face stared down at him, measuring the distance and shouting back instructions to Gustav Wolter at the elevator wheel and Scratch manning the rudder controls.

When the distance was as close as he dared, Caspasian gave the thumbs-up and Harrison heaved a giant bundle out of the gondola's side door. It fell neatly to within six feet of Caspasian who dived onto it to stop it rolling off the top. Heaving with all his might, he wrestled it back towards the cupola and, using the lookout's belay harness, secured it firmly to the hull. He would need its contents later.

He looked back at Harrison to give him the signal to move his airship clear. But the Captain was screaming at him and, behind him, Emma screamed too. Caspasian could hear nothing from either of them. The wind snatched away their words the moment they shouted them. But just as he realized it was a warning, Horner's boot crashed into his back sending him sprawling across the canvas. He was tumbling along the vessel's spine towards the distant stern. He could feel the wind trying to hurry him along to his death. Instead, Caspasian rolled onto his stomach and flattened himself against the taut canvas, slowing himself until he gradually came to a complete stop. But he had gone at least thirty yards and was now dangerously far from the cupola, the only entrance apart from the gas vents on the whole topside that led back to the interior of the airship.

He got shakily to his feet, the icy wind blasting into his face and chest, filling his jacket like a sail. He looked up and saw Horner belaying himself to the metal ring that surrounded the cupola's opening like a necklace. Horner shook out a generous length of rope and Caspasian saw that he had attached himself to it using a spring-loaded carabiner. By sliding the carabiner along the rope, Horner would be able to move as far away from the cupola as he wished, but with the security and extra balance of a taut rope at his back. He slowly stood upright, testing the belay for strength. Liking what he found, he looked for Caspasian, found him and grinned. This was going to be fun.

From the top of his boot, Horner drew a long-bladed knife. One step at a time, he moved away from the cupola, knife in his right hand, carabiner in the left, unfurling the rope as he went. Caspasian lowered himself into the *sancin-dachi* stance, knees bent, thigh muscles braced, abdomen as taut as the canvas surface he stood on. The wind pounded into him, pummelling against his stomach and chest like enraged fists. He fought to clear his mind in preparation for Horner's attack which was closing on him step by measured step. When Horner was within striking range he lashed out with his knife. Caspasian turned his shoulders side on and pulled his face out of the way, avoiding the swipe. His open hands swept the blow aside and he tried to fire out a *kin-geri* kick aimed at Horner's groin. But the wind was too strong and the moment he lifted his right foot from the canvas, Caspasian felt himself start to go over. Instantly he slammed it down again, his whole body wobbling for balance.

He sucked in a deep breath and exhaled, projecting it out through his throat with the hard rasping sound of the *ibuki* breathing technique. He felt the strength anchor him once more to the surface. His torso became solid and immovable, his arms flexing to meet Horner's next attack.

Horner crouched into a boxing stance, taking his left hand off the carabiner to let his weight bear confidently against the taut rope, trusting the belay to hold him. He leaned forward and swung again, this time feinting first to Caspasian's face and then sweeping in low for a stab at the stomach. In response, Caspasian first sidestepped and then darted backwards, out of range. Once again he found himself having to fight both Horner and the wind. It was hard to tell which was the more lethal opponent. Before he could regain his balance, Horner had released his carabiner and slid himself forward right onto Caspasian. His large body crashed into Caspasian's fragile stance and sent him flying onto his back. Caspasian scrabbled at the canvas for a hand hold, clawing his way into a sitting position.

But Horner was on to him again with another forward slide. This time he levelled a savage kick at Caspasian's face, and the toe of his boot caught Caspasian on the jaw, sending him spinning. His head reeled with the shock and he felt his sight clouding over. He shook himself like a dog. He was struggling for clarity. He rolled onto his hands and knees just in time to receive a second kick in the gut. It lifted him clean off the canvas. He skidded towards the sloping edge of the hull. There was a brief glimpse of the drop beneath, unimaginable miles of emptiness down to the snow-capped peaks beneath.

Suddenly Horner crashed on top of Caspasian with a grunt. The wind was knocked out of both of them. Caspasian twisted round and looked up to see Horner's puzzled eyes staring past him. He had lost his footing. But there was someone else with them now. Caspasian could see arms locked about Horner's neck. The frail arms of a woman. With gut-wrenching horror, Caspasian saw Emma's face behind Horner, grimacing with the effort of hanging on and trying to haul him off Caspasian. Through the haze of pain he understood that she must have launched herself from the *Siegfried* in an attempt to save him.

Using the slender breathing space, Caspasian jerked one arm free and landed an *empi* elbow strike onto Horner's jaw. Horner's face went red with pain and rage. He struggled to free his arms from under him but they were pinioned to his sides by Emma's fierce grip. He howled with rage and thrust his head backwards, driving the back of it into Emma's face. It knocked her clean off him. She began to roll away but Caspasian saw her grab hold of Horner's rope, hanging on for dear life.

Horner's knife had gone, lost in his fall. His hands were at Caspasian's throat, fingers tightening in an iron grip. Caspasian drove his hands into Horner's rock-solid forearms. They did not budge. He drew back and tried a second time with the same result. He could feel the breath being squeezed out of him. Blood pounded in his head. He was losing consciousness. With one last gigantic effort, Caspasian managed to draw up his knees under him and project them into Horner's stomach. The big man was lifted bodily off him. Caspasian rubbed his throat and gasped for air. Instinctively he rolled out of Horner's reach, coming up onto his knees facing his opponent, ready for the next assault.

Horner was on his feet and coming for him. But his rope snagged taut, the forgotten carabiner doing its job. With a curse, Horner snatched at it, sliding it forward until he was within striking distance of the kneeling Caspasian. He leaned forward to kick, his face set with an evil smile, putting his whole weight against the rope to use it as a brace. Suddenly he was flying forward, the rope support gone. Alarm registered on his face as he fumbled for balance, his feet and legs tripping over each other. Behind him, Caspasian saw Emma on her knees, Horner's knife in one hand, the severed end of the rope in the other. She looked up and caught his eye. But hurtling forward, Horner was almost on top of him. Rocking back onto the canvas, Caspasian stuck his right foot into Horner's stomach and, pivoting backwards, launched the big man over his head in a perfect *tomoenage* somersault throw, projecting him towards the side of the hull. Horner cried out. His arms flailed for a purchase but there was nothing to hold on to. One moment he was there, and the next he had disappeared, flying over the side of the airship and out into the empty air with the grace of a bird.

'Here, grab hold of this!' Emma shouted, throwing the end of the rope to Caspasian. He caught it and started to pull himself towards her. Hand over hand he closed the distance until he collapsed into her arms.

'What the hell do you think you're doing?' he shouted, his mouth close to her ear.

She drew back and frowned at him. 'Is that your way of saying thank you?'

Caspasian looked up for the *Siegfried* but it had drawn clear and was now shadowing the *Fafner* some hundred yards distant. He knew that in the unpredictable winds of the mountain passes it would be lethal for Harrison to attempt to remain in such close proximity to the sister airship.

'Come on,' he shouted at Emma. Pulling himself along the rope, one hand firmly holding onto Emma's arm, he made his way back to the cupola.

Dropping down inside the airship, he helped Emma in after him and checked that the bundle was still securely fastened to the cupola necklace. If all went according to plan he would be using the contents very soon.

He was about to leave the cupola when he heard a voice blasting down the communication tube. He picked it up and put it to his ear. It was the officer of the watch wanting a report.

'Everything under control,' Caspasian barked back at him, ensuring a good blast of air made its way down the tube to disguise his voice. 'It looked like Quesada was caught in a freak gust of wind, but it's all right now. He has moved astern and is maintaining station there, five hundred yards distant.' Caspasian hoped that the stern lookout would confirm this.

He caught something about Lieutenant Davies and answered that he was on his way back to the control car. With luck, he and Emma would have done what they came to do and would be away by the time the Baron missed both Davies and Horner.

Ducking down inside the cupola so he could be heard, Caspasian drew Emma close to him. 'I want you to stay here,' he said.

She shook her head defiantly. 'Not a chance. Suppose they send someone else? What would I do then?'

'That's a chance we'll have to take.'

'No, that's a chance you'll have to take. Not me. I'm coming with you.'

'Look, we don't have time to argue.'

'Exactly. So let's go.'

One look at her told Caspasian he was not going to be able to change her mind. He gritted his teeth. 'Right, but stick close behind me and do exactly what I say.'

She smiled at him. 'As ever.'

He led the way out onto the gantry and edged along it to the top of the ladder. Gripping the top rung he looked down, leaning out as far as he could to check the coast was clear. His head swam at the drop beneath. 'Are you comfortable with that?' he asked.

Emma nodded unconvincingly. 'Easy as pie. I've done a thousand stunts harder than this.'

Caspasian started down, Emma keeping a couple of rungs above him. They stopped every fifty yards for a break, looping arms and legs through the ladder and shaking their muscles to avoid cramp. After the cold of the outside, the exercise quickly warmed them. Caspasian felt confident. They had managed to get aboard the *Fafner* and, he believed, had not so far alerted the Baron or his crew to their presence. Those who did know were dead now, plastered across the Andean rocks below. Their task was to locate and free the prisoners who, judging by past performance, were likely to be held in the cargo hold.

When they finally reached the axial gangway Caspasian was relieved to find it deserted. All the crew were apparently at their stations. Emma was gasping for breath, her limbs trembling from the long descent. Caspasian briskly rubbed her arm and leg muscles to restore them to life.

'Better?' he asked.

She nodded.

Going quickly past the rows of ballast tanks, Caspasian approached the cargo hold, straining to catch the slightest sound that might signal the presence of the Baron's crew. All he could hear was the muffled sound of the engines suspended in their gondolas outside the hull. The airship was now moving through the pass and the Baron had slowed the motors to a gentle cruising speed of barely thirty miles an hour. Caspasian was confident that von Staaden and all his officers would be in the control car, alert to the slightest breath of wind. With limited room for manoeuvre, their full concentration would be on the mountain walls on either side of them. In the engine gondolas and in the lookout stations, every member of the Baron's crew would be similarly occupied, each man doing his job to the best of his ability. The timing was perfect.

Caspasian took a deep breath to steady himself outside the cargo hold, and then entered briskly, striding in, hands ready. At his right hand side a crewman rose from his stool. Caspasian cut him down before the man had even been able to utter a sound. Backfist *uraken* strike to the nose, open hand blow to the neck, and a drop punch to finish him. One, two, three.

The man's companion scrabbled with his holster. The strap snagged. Caspasian's foot shot out in a *mae geri* front kick to the midriff. The force of it lifted the man off the ground, and before he landed Caspasian was on top of him. Two punches, Left hand, right hand. Silence. He spun. Spun again. Checking his arcs. All clear. Emma stood in the doorway behind him, eyes wide and staring at the two bodies flat and unconscious on the floor. Opposite her, bundled together in swathes of rope, sat the four captives. Brigadier Percival looking annoyed at the delay to his rescue, Lionel Domain, dishevelled and clearly not enjoying it, Private Smudger, staring at the bodies that Caspasian had just dispatched with such ease, and finally Richard Edward, tired but bright-eyed, a smile on his lips.

'What took you so long?' the Brigadier snapped, struggling against his bindings.

Caspasian regarded him, weighing the benefits and disadvantages of laying him out cold like the two guards. 'My apologies, sir. Slight problem of coming aboard.' He ran to his side and knelt to undo the bindings. 'In case you hadn't noticed we're flying at several thousand feet.'

Richard laughed good naturedly. 'Don't mind him, John. He's only joking.'

The Brigadier scoffed and muttered something which Caspasian chose to ignore. When all four had been released, they got shakily to their feet, rubbing wrists and ankles where the ropes had bitten. Emma went to Lionel's side and consoled him. He seemed a shadow of his former self and appeared on the verge of tears. She laid his head against her shoulder and stroked him like a child. The Brigadier was quick to act. He went to the nearest of the guards and took a pistol out of the holster on the man's belt.

'I'd be careful with that if I were you, sir,' Caspasian warned.

'I know, I know. The bloody gas cells.' The Brigadier checked the magazine clip in the butt and snapped a round into the breach, ignoring Caspasian's caution. 'You're beginning to sound like a bit of a gas bag yourself,' he added spitefully.

Richard came and slapped Caspasian on the back. 'Don't listen to him,' he said. 'I don't know how you got here, but thank you.' As if it had only just occurred to him, he seemed to realize that they were aloft in the Baron's airship. 'What now?'

'Now we go topside and get off this crate,' Caspasian said, gathering them together and heading for the door.

'How?' Smudger asked, astounded at the way Caspasian made it sound so simple.

'Two options,' Caspasian said. 'Either Captain Harrison can get close enough to drop a rope ladder. Or in case the winds are too strong, I've brought parachutes. We found some that the Baron must have placed on board the *D200*. We can parachute down to the valley below.'

Everyone froze, the blood draining from their faces. Lionel

Domain was the first to speak. 'That's absolute madness! I can't do it.'

'Do you have a better plan?' Caspasian asked.

Domain mouthed but nothing came out.

'Couldn't we seize the airship?' Smudger asked, desperate to avoid either option just outlined by his rescuer.

Caspasian shook his head. 'There are too many of them. It would be bound to end in a fire.'

Smudger swallowed hard, accepting the fate that awaited him.

Caspasian led the way out onto the axial gangway and back towards the central ladder. Their luck was just too good. He knew it could not last.

'Just a minute,' Brigadier Percival said, stopping in his tracks. 'What happens if we abandon the airship?'

Caspasian stared at him. 'Once we're off we are free to shoot it down. A few rifle shots should be sufficient.'

'Shoot it down?' the Brigadier gasped as if Caspasian was the most obtuse officer he had ever come across. 'Shoot it down? Are you daft, man? Not only is the *D100* worth a considerable amount of money, not to mention national prestige, but according to the guards, before the Baron abandoned his island, he loaded his entire store of diamonds on board. At this very minute they're in the radio room.'

Caspasian began to get the drift. He could feel himself starting to boil, the anger rising from deep within. 'Brigadier, we don't have time for this. Come with me now or else we'll leave you behind. In case you've forgotten, the *Victoria and Albert* is steaming just off the Peruvian coast and the Baron means to intercept her. Possibly to sink her. Balancing the two, I would have thought that even you could see which was the priority.'

The Brigadier went scarlet. 'Don't you dare lecture me, Caspasian. Damn you, who do you think you are? We will both save ourselves, and the *D100* with its treasure.'

'And who's the treasure for, sir?' Caspasian asked sarcastically, his voice betraying his hatred of the man.

In answer, the Brigadier brought up his pistol, the muzzle pointing directly at Caspasian's chest. Caspasian smiled bitterly. 'I see. So that's the whole strength of your argument, is it?'

'Don't push me, Caspasian. I should have shot you when I had the chance four years ago back in India. I should have finished the job then. You're a rotten officer. Rotten to the core.'

Caspasian refused to back down. 'Even you must recognize that a gunfight will end in one thing. The destruction of all of us, airship, diamonds, the lot.'

He could see that his words had struck a distant chord. He rammed the point home. 'At least let the others go. I'll come with you. We can get the diamonds, just you and I, and still make it back for a pick-up by Harrison. The *D100*'s as good as lost already. There's no way we can seize control and Harrison won't let it escape to bomb the Royal Yacht.'

The mental struggle was written across the Brigadier's face. Finally, just as Caspasian was bracing himself to rush him, Percival relented. 'All right, then. The others can go.' He jabbed the barrel of his pistol towards Caspasian. 'But you come with me.' Without Caspasian, the Brigadier knew that he would not have a chance. And Caspasian knew that once the Brigadier had what he wanted, Caspasian's life would not be worth a jot.

He turned to Emma. 'Can you find the way back to the top lookout?' he asked. She nodded. 'Good. Go then. Harrison will try to pick you up when he sees you. The air seems pretty stable and the airship's going as slow as can be expected. He should be able to lower a rope ladder. Quick now,' he said, and pushed her away from him.

With one backward glance, Emma led the others away towards the foot of the ladder and started to climb. Caspasian waited until they were all well on their way, climbing hand over hand, and then turned back to the Brigadier.

'I should have known you'd try something like this,' he said.

Brigadier Percival smiled icily. 'Stop complaining. Why not just obey an order for once? You might find you enjoy the novelty of the experience.'

Caspasian's jaw set. He did not trust himself to answer. The Brigadier was careful to remain out of reach. He knew what Caspasian could do. 'Get going,' he ordered, jerking his gun in the direction of the radio room. 'We've got some diamonds to fetch.'

21

Major Westacott sat at his stool gaping absently at the metal chest before him. Although the lid was fastened with a padlock, he could see the contents glistening and glittering in his mind's eye all too clearly. It was tormenting him. If he had not held the Baron in such fear and trepidation he would have sought some way of taking the treasure for himself. As it was, however, he was obliged to sit meekly by and watch over it like some dullard lackey. It was all too bad.

He sighed deeply, exhaling his disquiet and unease across the chilly confines of the radio room. The radio equipment sat idle, as it had done since their departure from the island. The Baron had been adamant that strict radio silence should be observed as he was concerned that any transmission might risk being intercepted. If this happened, it would not be difficult for their position to be deduced by a process of intersection. The readings from two ground stations would be taken, and where the lines intersected, would be the airship's position. The Baron had rabbitted on about how this had happened to him in the war. Westacott did not give a damn. All he cared about was surviving. Preferably with the diamonds in his sticky grasp.

'Hello, Major.'

Startled out of his reverie, Westacott locked up. His jaw just had time to fall open before Caspasian's foot pumped into his chest, knocking him backwards off his stool. He landed with a crash against the flimsy wall. The whole room shuddered.

'Y . . . you,' he stammered. 'How did . . . ?'

Hands laid hold of his flying suit and hauled him to his feet. Caspasian grinned nastily into his face and then slapped him hard across the cheeks. First from the left with the flat of his open palm and then, with the back of his hand, from the right. The two blows knocked all resistance out of him. Westacott started to blubber. The sobs burst from him in great heaving waves and he was shocked by the depths of his own despair.

'You don't understand,' he tried. 'They threatened me. I had no choice.'

Caspasian's knee jerked up into the soft leather of Westacott's overall leggings. Beneath the generous layers of fleece it found his testicles. Westacott felt as though he was going to be sick. His gorge rose and he gagged.

'Sorry, Major?' Caspasian asked sarcastically. 'I didn't quite catch that.' And he kneed him again, managing to turn the Major's body aside just in time for a rush of half-digested breakfast to erupt down the front of Westacott's leathers. 'Oh dear, now will you look at that?' he said, turning to the Brigadier who was covering both men with his pistol from the doorway. 'Some people are such bad flyers.'

Brigadier Percival scowled. 'All right, Caspasian, that'll do. You've had your fun. Now get the diamonds and let's go.'

'What about him?' Caspasian asked, holding Westacott's limp and miserable form in one hand.

'Leave him for the Baron.'

Caspasian glared at Westacott. 'Think yourself lucky,' he said through gritted teeth. He spun the Major round so his back was to him, released his hold, and rabbit punched him viciously on the side of the neck with his open hand.

'Open it,' the Brigadier commanded, jerking the muzzle of his pistol at the strong box.

'What with?' Caspasian asked lazily.

'Don't be smart with me,' the Brigadier replied dangerously.

'Use your fucking initiative. You're supposed to be so damned clever.'

Caspasian scanned the desk. Nothing. He ripped open a couple of drawers. A sturdy-looking screwdriver lay in the bottom one underneath some papers. He hefted it in his hand then put it to the padlock and levered. The padlock groaned painfully and then burst.

'Back away!' Brigadier Percival ordered. His eyes were consumed with an ugly hunger. Caspasian backed away to the far wall. Any minute now, he told himself. Give the old bugger enough rope and he will hang himself. Drop your guard and then I will have you. What I did to Westacott will be nothing compared to what is coming to you, Percy my old fruit, he thought, deliciously savouring the beating he was going to give the Brigadier.

But Percival was far too wily to fall for that. He waited until Caspasian was as far from him as the room allowed, and then bent down to pull the box towards him, his eyes and gun on Caspasian all the time. He flicked open the lid. One lightning glance told him all he wanted to know. Lying a foot deep, diamonds dazzled him. The Brigadier almost choked. He straightened up and with one foot he pushed the box back towards Caspasian.

'Pick it up.'

Caspasian paused, and the gun jabbed in his direction again. 'You don't expect me to lug this all the way to the top lookout, do you?'

'Here. Use this,' the Brigadier said. He plucked an old rucksack off a hook behind the door. 'Quick, man!'

With the Brigadier's eyes burning into him, Caspasian held open the flap and emptied the contents of the strongbox into the rucksack. As he did so, he could hear the Brigadier's sharp intake of breath at the beauty of the glittering cascade. When the last of them had been decanted, Caspasian set the empty box aside, fastened the flap of the rucksack, and hoisted it onto his shoulders.

'Tell me, Brigadier,' he said as he moved back through the vessel's hull, past the rows of ballast tanks. 'What have these got to do with recovering the airship and saving the Prince of Wales?'

'Don't be stupid, man. Think how grateful His Majesty's government will be to get its hands on a treasure such as this. They'll promote me to General on the spot.'

'You must take me for a complete idiot,' he said. 'Do you really expect me to believe that if we ever get off this crate the diamonds will find their way to the treasury?'

The Brigadier chuckled. 'Most of them. Why not? It won't take many to take care of my humble needs,' he said. 'Just a pocketful. Or two. Those bloody misers at the Treasury won't notice if a few are missing. How will they know?'

'What if I tell them?'

The Brigadier laughed, quickly stifling it in case anyone might overhear. 'Yes, you always were a bit of a joker, weren't you?'

'So if you're going to finish me off, what incentive have I got to carry these one more step for you?' Caspasian stopped and turned to face the Brigadier. Quick as a flash and without hesitation, the Brigadier answered, 'What about Miss Emma Lavelle?'

Caspasian's face darkened. 'What about her?'

'It would be a pity if she were to meet with an accident.' He leered. 'In all this turmoil she could easily take a fall. From this height, I'd hate to think what the rocks below would do to such a pretty little form, don't you? And by the looks of the two of you together, you'd know all about her form, wouldn't you, Caspasian? I bet you've dragged yourself all over it, haven't you?'

Caspasian glared at him. 'Jesus, until now I didn't realize just how poisonous you really are.'

The Brigadier snorted. 'Go fuck yourself. Now move!' He jerked the barrel of his pistol towards the ladder. With the anger raging inside him, Caspasian walked on. When he arrived at the ladder, he adjusted the rucksack's straps, and began to climb. With the extra burden, the climb rapidly became a Herculean task. By the halfway stage he was fighting for breath. From a safe distance below, the Brigadier urged him on, the pistol ever present.

Suddenly, from in the distance, they heard a shout. The Brigadier froze. 'Damn! They've found Westacott,' he said. He stared up at Caspasian. 'Move it! Just think of Emma. If you fail in this, she dies. I promise you!'

Caspasian started to climb again. The voices were getting closer. 'What if you don't make it that far?' he said.

'Oh don't worry about that,' the Brigadier answered, his voice savage. 'I can fix it for her all right. Even if it means I die as well. All I have to do is empty the contents of this magazine into the airship. One of the bullets is bound to hit a gas cell. It would be as easy as hitting a barn door at twenty metres. And you bloody well know it.'

And Caspasian did. The Brigadier had secured his cooperation. For now there was absolutely nothing Caspasian could do about it.

They were almost at the gantry when they heard shouts from directly beneath. They looked down and saw a large group of men pointing up at them. Even from such a distance they could make out the stern figure of the Baron in the centre. Together with his men he started to climb towards the Brigadier and Caspasian. Steadily hand over hand, up towards a final confrontation.

'Quick, damn you!' the Brigadier cursed. 'This is your last chance! Now move!'

Caspasian took a deep breath and set off on the last leg of the climb. Several minutes later he hauled himself over the gantry.

'Move away,' the Brigadier commanded, clearing a space before he himself climbed over. The two of them stood panting. The Brigadier glanced down at their pursuers. He looked around at the gas cells. Caspasian could see the calculations going on in his mind.

'Let's give them something to think about, shall we?' the Brigadier said. And before Caspasian could stop him, he leaned over the side of the gantry and fired off a round, aiming it neatly down the narrow tunnel between the two gas cells on either side of the ladder. There were outraged shouts from down below and their pursuers hesitated.

The Brigadier looked at Caspasian and laughed aloud. 'Well, life's all about gambles, isn't it?'

'I'm not sure who's the madder,' Caspasian said quietly. 'The Baron or you. You should have changed sides like Westacott. You and the Baron are two of a kind.'

'Ha! I don't intend to secrete myself away on some god-forsaken island. I'll get what I want in my own way and in my own time, thank you very much. And I'll do it without having to become an outcast.' He jabbed the pistol at Caspasian, indicating the cupola just behind him. 'Now get out there!'

Caspasian shrugged out of the rucksack's straps in order to duck inside the cupola. He pulled the pack in after him. Once again he felt the blast of the icy air.

'Out!' the Brigadier commanded.

Caspasian hoisted himself up and out of the cupola, lifting the pack behind him. He crouched on the upper surface of the airship. The *Siegfried* was suspended close overhead, the control car some hundred yards in front of the cupola where Caspasian crouched beside the pack loaded with diamonds. A rope ladder dangled the thirty yard drop from the gondola door to the broad canvas-covered back of the *Fafner*. Captain Harrison's anxious face appeared briefly at the door looking down. He waved frantically. Caspasian could see the *Siegfried* drifting all over the place, the rope ladder trailing wildly from side to side. Harrison and Wolter were obviously having trouble maintaining station directly overhead. Mountains rose sheer on either side of the two airships and sudden winds gusted savagely.

The Brigadier climbed out of the cupola. He looked over his shoulder and gauged the distance to the ladder. He reckoned he could make it on his own.

He smiled nicely at Caspasian. 'I'll have that, thank you,' he said, indicating the rucksack.

Caspasian picked it up but held it against his chest, using it as a shield. He backed away. 'You must be joking. Let's go together. I'll be right behind you.' He waved a hand towards the ladder. 'With the diamonds,' he added.

'We don't have time for this, Caspasian,' the Brigadier said. 'The Baron and his men will be joining us at any moment.'

'My thoughts exactly,' Caspasian shouted back. 'Better get a move on then, hadn't we?'

The Brigadier boiled with rage. He studied Caspasian to see if he could be sure of a clean shot. But Harrison might see. He could not risk it. Reluctantly Brigadier Percival began to make his way along the back of the airship towards the ladder. He moved at a crouch as if balancing on the top of a speeding train. To his relief the airship had slowed and was now relatively stable, but he did not like the look of the mountains. They were far too close and the pass appeared to be narrowing the further they progressed along it. He had to get into the *Siegfried* and escape soon, but only with the diamonds. The thought of them consumed him.

At every step he glanced over his shoulder to make sure Caspasian was behind him, but not too close. Somehow he had to get the sack away from Caspasian. He could not allow him into the *Siegfried* as well. Not after all he had said. But then who would believe him? Nevertheless, the Brigadier did not want to take the risk.

He glanced back over his shoulder and glared at Caspasian. At that moment, someone blundered into him. Percival spun round. It was Emma. To his surprise he found that he had already reached the ladder. Emma had clambered down to steady it for him. She clung to the lowest rung, one hand on the rope, one reaching out to Percival.

'Give me your hand,' she said. But then she saw his gun. She looked up and saw who it was pointed at. 'What's going . . . ?'

Before she could react, Percival grabbed her and snatched her off the ladder. She crumpled at his feet. He picked her up and hugged her to him with one arm. The other waved the pistol at Caspasian, beckoning him forward to within earshot.

'The diamonds for the girl, Caspasian. That's the deal.'

Caspasian stared at him, his mind racing.

'But then you abandon us to the Baron,' he said. 'How long do you suppose we'd live?'

The Brigadier grinned. 'That's not my problem.' He jammed the muzzle of his gun under Emma's jaw. 'You've run out of time, Caspasian,' he said. 'Hand them over. Now!'

Caspasian kept hold of the pack. 'First let her go.'

'Damn you!' the Brigadier howled, 'Give me the . . .' He stretched out a hand towards the rucksack in Caspasian's arms.

Caspasian held it towards him, offering it. Bait on the hook. The Brigadier's eyes flickered between the pack and Caspasian's face. 'Put it down,' the Brigadier commanded. Caspasian shook his head, knowing that the moment he relinquished his shield the Brigadier was likely to shoot him.

Suddenly, the ladder drifted into the Brigadier's back. He glanced up. Harrison was leaning out of the gondola door.

'What the hell's going on?' He shouted down, barely audible above the noise of the engines and the wind.

'Caspasian's injured!' Percival shouted back.

Harrison stared uncomprehending, his concern focused on the ever narrowing gap between the two airships. A sudden gust rocked both vessels. 'I can't hold this position any longer. We're going to collide!' he screamed frantically. 'Get up here!'

In a flash, the Brigadier took his arm off Emma, hooked it through the ladder's rungs, and snatched hold of her jacket again. She screamed, almost losing her footing. Percival placed first one foot, and then the other on the ladder.

'The pack, Caspasian. Now! Or the girl gets left behind with you. You know what that means.'

Caspasian looked at Emma. She shook her head. 'Don't do it,' she shouted. 'He'll kill you!'

But he did not have a choice. He could not allow her to be stranded on the *Fafner*. He took a step forward, holding out the pack. At that moment there was a roar from overhead and the *Siegfried*'s engines surged. In front of them a mountain ledge had reared out of nowhere to block their path. The mountain pass had closed and they were flying straight towards a wall of rock. Any second now, the Baron's airship would have to rise in order to clear the rocks. The moment it did so, it would climb straight into the *Siegfried* overhead.

At the elevator wheel in the *Siegfried*, Gustav Wolter was spinning his controls to climb out of the way. The engines were surging to maximum power to add aerodynamic lift. As the nose of the *Siegfried* reared up, the ladder fixed to the control car gondola went with it, and, clutching the bottom rungs, the Brigadier was pulled upwards, away from the *Fafner*, away from his hostage who fell from his grasp into Caspasian's waiting arms, and away from his precious sack full of diamonds. He howled with rage and pointed his gun at the hated Caspasian.

But as his finger tightened on the trigger, he hesitated, angling for the right shot. It was impossible. Any bullet would pass down through the hull's fabric and into the gas cells inside. The explosion would burst directly upwards and the *Siegfried* was still too close. It would be engulfed along with its sister ship.

The Brigadier scuttled up towards the top of the ladder but

remained there, declining the helping hand of Captain Harrison who was trying to pull him into the safety of the gondola. Percival was biding his time. The instant he judged it safe to fire, Caspasian knew he would pump the *Fafner* full of bullets. He would not stop firing until he had seen it explode. Caspasian had only seconds to act.

He darted forward and pulled Emma to her feet. 'This way!' he shouted. He looped the pack over one shoulder and with his other hand holding tight to Emma's hand, struggled back to the cupola. Any moment now the Baron and his men would appear and then he would be caught between the Baron and the Brigadier. It was not a sandwich he particularly wanted to sample.

At the cupola's side, he thrust Emma down onto the canvas. 'Hang on tight,' he said. He knelt beside the bundle he had lowered from the *Siegfried* when he had first come aboard, and struggled with the bindings to free the individual parachutes. Emma saw what he was doing and blanched. 'I can't use one of those.' She shook her head and started to get to her feet, glancing desperately back towards the departing Siegfried, now drawing out of range.

'You don't have a choice,' Caspasian replied. 'You'll be fine. Believe me.'

From inside the hull he heard shouts. The Baron and his men had made it to the gantry. They were approaching the cupola.

The parachutes came free in his hand. He thrust one at Emma, stuffing her arms and legs roughly through the straps, clamping the fastening and yanking them tight.

'I can't do it,' she shouted in terror, tears springing to her eyes.

'You can and you will!' he shouted back. He put her hand on the ripcord handle and closed her fingers around it. 'The moment you jump, pull this. Just open your arms outwards and take the handle with them. The parachute will do the rest.'

'But where will we land?'

Bloody good point, Caspasian thought, glancing at the sheer rock faces around them and the snowscape beneath. To Emma he just smiled confidently. 'Don't worry. It'll be fine.'

There was a shout from below him and he caught a glimpse of a man's head. It was the Baron's cap, the gold braid clearly visible. Then he saw the flash of a gun. There was a second man close behind him. This was it. There was no more time. He would not have a chance to get into his own parachute.

Snatching it in one hand, he grabbed Emma and pulled her after him, the sack of diamonds still around his shoulder. They raced towards the stern of the airship. Slowly the gradient started to angle downwards. In front of them they could see the vast tail and rudder assembly towering into the sky. It was time to jump. Caspasian looked down. Sheer rock, snow and ice. The *Fafner* was passing over the ledge linking the two mountains. The snow was barely a hundred feet below. There was not enough room for the parachutes to be deployed. The canopies would not have time to open. Caspasian and Emma would crash into the rocks and be dashed to pieces. He had to wait. Just a moment or two more.

At the cupola, the Baron's head popped up, scanning around for his enemies. He looked up and saw the *Siegfried* drawing away. He raised his pistol.

'Baron, is this what you want?' Caspasian shouted, holding the pack of diamonds aloft. The Baron's head snapped round. He stared hard at the pack. Caspasian undid the strap and flipped open the top cover. He held it up, pouring ever so gently. A thin stream of glittering diamonds sprinkled out, bouncing off the taut canvas roof of the airship and rolling away, snatched by the wind and whisked out into space like dust. The Baron screamed and swung his pistol onto Caspasian. But the tail and rudder were at Caspasian's back. He could not fire. He aimed again at the *Siegfried.* Caspasian poured more diamonds. He saw the Baron's jaw set hard. He knew he had lost them. This was the end.

Caspasian saw the frail blue puffs of gun smoke and heard the little cracks of rounds as the Baron shot at the *Siegfried.* In response, Harrison and Wolter spun their controls and veered away, safely out of harm's reach. But as they did so, the Brigadier got the one thing he had been waiting for. Caspasian's death warrant. He aimed and fired into the *Fafner.* And whereas the Baron's rounds had been fired at maximum range and into the underside of the *Siegfried* where the accommodation, control car, ballast tanks and other encumbrances acted as a shield for the gas cells, stopping the bullets from the Baron's gun, the Brigadier's shots, fired from above, pumped easily through the fragile canvas fabric of the *Fafner's* topside, through the gas cells fashioned of rubberised cotton, and straight into the heart of the hydrogen, brooding within. *Fafner,* the dragon, was awoken.

The first shots punctured the *Fafner* towards the prow. There was a moment of complete hush as everybody froze, watching. Waiting. Lives balanced on a knife edge. Then, with one mighty lurch, a jet of flame shot skywards as the furthest gas cell exploded.

The Baron threw up his arms, crying out, his words lost in the immensity of the valley and of space. Flames cartwheeled towards him as cell after cell exploded, each one greater and more ferocious than the last. The whole airship rocked, losing all stability. Caspasian felt the shock waves pass up through his legs, almost knocking him off his feet. This was it. He glanced down, his balance starting to go. The main keel had been fractured. It was giving. There was a sickening groan of metal being twisted asunder and a blast of heat and burning fabric struck Caspasian and Emma, prising them from their precarious hold. But beneath the buckling airship, as flames spread like an avalanche, he glimpsed green far below. The ship had cleared the ridge. Beneath them a valley had opened up. They were over the pass.

He grabbed hold of Emma by the shoulders and braced himself to project her out into space. The sack tumbled from his grasp, diamonds scattering across the airship's breaking back. From the distant *Siegfried* he caught an echo of the Brigadier's howl of rage, frustration and hatred. But he was far away now, his rounds expended. He floated beneath the escaping *Siegfried* like a child on a rope swing, his empty gun waving at Caspasian like a toy.

Caspasian glanced at the Baron just at the moment the flames reached him. His arms were still outstretched as if fastened to a cross. He was shouting at the top of his voice. And then the flames engulfed him. The airship was breaking in two, its spine snapped. The nose and tail both began to rise.

'John, your chute!'

Caspasian snatched at his parachute sliding innocently away across the rearing hull. But it was gone, drawn into the fires of hell. As the nearest tongues licked out towards them, Caspasian pushed Emma clear, launching her out into space and leaping after her himself, hanging onto the straps of her chute with both hands.

Down they plummeted. Caspasian counted. One second. Snow struck him in the face as a rock ledge whipped past. Two seconds. The *Fafner* was now one enormous ball of flame. It dropped like a stone, veering off to a flank and crashing into a rock face. Explosion after explosion resounded through the mountain pass, and the sickening groan of twisting metal as it crashed downwards.

Caspasian tugged the ripcord handle. The chute unfurled above them, snatched open by the wind, and Caspasian drove his arms through Emma's straps, gripping tight. The jolt of the opening chute almost tore his arms from their sockets. His grip gave way and suddenly he was hanging by his fingertips. Emma grabbed him by the shoulders, clinging to his jacket. Caspasian looked down. They were at least three thousand feet up. But with his extra weight they were descending too fast. The force of the landing would kill them both.

He could see Emma's lips moving. She was urging him to hold on. His fingers burned, the straps threatening to tear them from his hands. Her grasp on his jacket was weakening but fierce. As determined as the woman herself. The *Siegfried* was out of sight now. It had veered away from the neck of the pass and was heading back on the far side of the mountain range. They would not have seen the chute open. Just the explosion of flames, Caspasian and Emma still on the *Fafner*'s rearing tail.

Caspasian looked up into Emma's eyes. She read his intent and tightened her grip. 'Don't you dare!' she screamed at him. 'I'm not going to let go!'

'Emma,' he said simply, appealing, resigned.

Then, as he prepared to release his hold, she shouted, 'I can't survive down there. Not without you. Look at it! I'll die.'

It was just enough. For one second he faltered. And then he saw it. The ledge. Covered with banks of deep snow. He swung himself like an acrobat. Once. Twice. Each time increasing his arc. On the third giant swing he looked up at Emma, winked, and let go.

He was falling. As he fell he twisted in midair, angling his body towards the ledge like a diver towards the pool. He would have to trust that the snow was deep enough and soft enough to break his fall. If not, if there was rock close beneath the surface, he was dead. One. Two. He struck. Every particle of breath was smashed from his lungs. Sliding. Falling. Snow in his eyes, ears, nose and mouth. Sparks stung his eyes. Stars like diamonds. Then blackness.

Epilogue

＿〜＿

'Gentlemen, we've only got time for a couple more questions.'
Positioned in the centre of the little group, Frederick Giles
dominated the podium. Before him, the audience of journalists
thrust their arms frantically into the air, jockeying for attention
like a classroom of children bursting with the answer.

Giles ruminated over his choice, enjoying the melée. He hated
the gentlemen of the press and liked to torment them whenever
he could. So much so that he broke off in mid-selection to turn
to Brigadier Percival beside him. 'This shouldn't take much
longer. The Governor was keen that you should all be put on
display. Publicizing the thwarted plot against the *Victoria and
Albert* helps wondrously to divert attention from the fact that the
Baron was able to pinch not one, but two of our airships in
the first place.' He allowed himself the most cynical of smiles.

Percival shrugged carelessly, but refrained from answering.
Giles revolted him, as did Georgetown and this whole dastardly
business, most particularly the outcome. Harrison and Wolter
had successfully navigated the *D200* back to Guiana, located the
Demerara and followed it downriver until they had arrived at
the shocked capital which had turned out in its entirety to cele-
brate the airship's return from the dead. Since then, Harrison,
Wolter, Percival and the others had been fêted as heroes, day
and night. Signals had been sent to London informing the Air
Ministry and government of the outcome, and the words of
praise that had been returned were fulsome.

A replacement airship crew was on its way out by steamer

and, on arrival, would come under Captain Harrison's command. The *D200* would then fly back to Cardington where a reception was being arranged that would make the arrival at Georgetown seem desultory by comparison.

' . . . Caspasian?'

The mention of the name fired through the Brigadier's consciousness like a burst from a machine-gun. He looked up to find the eyes of the entire room upon him. There was a sudden silence of bated breath.

'Erm . . . I'm sorry, what was that?' Percival stammered.

'The gentleman over there,' Giles prompted quietly, directing a short but excessively pudgy arm towards the expectant earnestness of the relevant reporter.

'Is it fair to say,' the man repeated, enunciating each syllable as if teaching the English language to a roomful of foreign students, 'that in all probability the *Victoria and Albert* would have been sunk without the singular bravery and self-sacrifice of Captain John Caspasian?'

A shudder passed through the Brigadier's body as if he had just been wired to the mains.

'I, er . . . , that's difficult to say, I mean, one can never attribute . . . what I mean is, we all, as a team effort . . .'

'Yes, it is perfectly fair to say that.'

The Brigadier's head snapped round to find Richard Edward leaning forward to answer the question for him. On either side of Richard, Captain Harrison and Gustav Wolter were nodding their sincere agreement, heads going up and down, spring-mounted. Around the room, pencils scribbled furiously on note pads.

'Indeed, throughout the entire business, I would say that virtually every idea and initiative stemmed from John Caspasian, and it was then his courage and determination that drove each one forward to the final successful conclusion, though at the terrible cost of his own life and, of course, the life of Miss Emma

Lavelle.' Richard slumped back in his chair. The statement appeared to have drained him and only his immediate neighbours were able to see the moisture clouding his eyes.

Around the room there was a muttered chorus of 'Hear, hear.'

The reporter nodded gratefully to Richard but declined to let the Brigadier off the hook. 'Brigadier?'

Brigadier Percival's neck manoeuvred in its collar which had suddenly become very tight. 'Erm, quite so, quite so.' He crossed his legs and tried desperately to appear relaxed. 'Fine man,' he mumbled.

'Presumably you'll be nominating him for some sort of posthumous bravery award?' a voice from the back of the room called out.

There was another chorus of 'Hear, hear!' and several people started to stamp in unison.

The Brigadier smiled, bobbing his head from side to side, debating the issue. An icy silence told him he was starting to offend the gathering. He coughed and quickly added, 'Yes, indeed I shall.' There was a murmur of approval.

Captain Harrison pitched in, prefacing his statement with an icy glare at Percival. 'And I will be supporting the citation when the Brigadier submits it. I think it is the least we can do for the late Captain Caspasian.'

Frederick Giles was delighted with the Brigadier's evident discomfort and scoured the room for the most aggressive reporter he could find. But as he did so, Lionel Domain rose from his chair at the end of the row. An expectant hush descended on the room.

Although groomed and dressed to perfection once again, Lionel Domain seemed to have shrunk as a result of the entire experience. The certainties of his world had been challenged and overturned, more so, in fact, than for any of the other survivors. For his certainties had been the most strongly held, and consequently had proved to be the most wounding when exposed as illusory. Like Icarus, he had been closest to the sun, or so he believed. Being the highest, he had been the one with the furthest to fall.

He spoke now into the silence, filling it with a quiet and restrained passion.

'All of you were asking at the beginning of this session, about Emma Lavelle. Myself and the others have replied to your questions, and all of us have lamented her passing. But as we draw to a close, I feel the need to say something more.' He paused for a moment, searching for words. He held up his hands as if weighing something. Unable to do so, he let them drop noisily against his thighs.

'Emma was a star,' he said at last. 'She was a bright star in a firmament which holds only a few such stars. A star of great brightness and purity . . .'

Anonymous in the crush of reporters, someone sniffed. A nose was blown loudly.

'Valentino described her as his little angel. Well, now, more than ever, she is an angel for us all.' He paused again, raising one hand and pointing heavenwards. 'And her career was only just approaching its prime . . .'

With his public face of sincerity firmly in position, Brigadier Percival leaned towards Giles and spoke out of the corner of his mouth. 'That's a bit rich, isn't it? Her career was more on the rocks than Caspasian's bloody Scotch.'

Giles responded with equal care. 'Well she's certainly on the rocks now. Spread right across them like strawberry jam. Mind you, if she wasn't, she'd be able to demand any part in Hollywood after all this.'

Domain was now into his swing. His voice strengthened as sentence after sentence poured onto the parched soil of the audience. When he finished, a handkerchief flourishing across his dry eyes, the room erupted in a thunderous hand clapping. From their seats at the very front of the audience, Scratch and

Smudger clapped the loudest. The very instant it had become known that both Westacott and Horner had perished, morale in the garrison had rocketed to previously unknown heights. A new commanding officer was due to arrive with Harrison's replacement crew, and the future that beckoned appeared brighter for them than ever before. Yet for now, neither soldier was able to take any pleasure in it. For both of them, as for the whole room, the deaths of Caspasian and Emma Lavelle snatched away all joy.

Domain sank back into his chair and Frederick Giles rose from his with the majesty of a hot air balloon untethered.

'And now, ladies and gentlemen, I really must insist that these brave and heroic individuals be allowed some respite from your questions. I will therefore draw this session to a close. Thank you.'

Ignoring a barrage of shouted pleas, Giles presented the assembly with his barn door of a back, and began to usher Percival, Harrison and the rest from the podium.

Outside the building, strong sunlight dazzled them. Hats were put in place, brims pulled low, and everyone prepared to retire to the hotel. Harrison and Wolter fell easily into step beside one another, Richard Edward joining them a moment later. They slowed the pace to accommodate him.

'I can't believe they're dead,' Richard said as they pushed their way through a gaggle of persistent reporters who were refusing to be dismissed.

'We all saw the *Fafner* explode,' Harrison answered. 'No one could have escaped such a conflagration.'

'Besides,' Wolter added, 'the Peruvians have sent search parties to scour the area and all they've found is wreckage and charred bodies.'

Richard shook his head despondently. 'I just hope he gets the recognition he deserves. Both him and Emma.'

Harrison glanced across to where Domain had readily

succumbed to a further interview on the other side of the street. 'I think Lionel will see to it that Emma's memory is suitably honoured. Even if it is out of self-interest.'

'But Caspasian,' Richard persisted. 'We have to make sure he's honoured as well. Somehow.'

Harrison placed a hand comfortingly on his shoulder. 'Don't worry, old man. We'll certainly do that. Never fear.'

'I would like to have had the chance to get to know him better,' Richard said. 'I think, given time, the two of us might have become friends.'

'I'm sure you would have,' Wolter confirmed. 'I'm not a bad judge of character. From what I saw of the two of you, you could have been brothers.'

Richard smiled with delight, flattered beyond measure. He was wise enough to recognize that dear Gustav was being diplomatic as ever and doing his utmost to console a friend, but all the same, Richard felt there really was a grain of truth in what he had said. He would so enjoy telling his sisters about Caspasian when he got home. How they would love to have met him.

Far away from the slowly dispersing crowd, Brigadier Percival strode like a man possessed. He was like a caged animal. But for him, it was not the remembrance of a lost liberty that antagonized him, but the spectre, branded on his mind's eye, of the most fragile and glittering of cascades tumbling out of a haversack and dissipating into the remoteness and inaccessibility of the Andean mountainscape. Fury burned in him. Anger threatened to consume him, so much so that he half feared spontaneous combustion.

'Damn him!' he murmured to himself. 'Damn him to hell!'

A single consoling image was the Brigadier's bitter salvation. The image of Caspasian in flames, like a heretic lashed to a post, heaped faggots erupting in flames at his feet. Caspasian plunging down into the inferno's heart of the dying *Fafner*. A

Götterdämmerung more justly deserved, Brigadier Percival could not imagine.

He stopped dead in his tracks, hands on hips, and inhaled as deeply as his lungs allowed. 'Goodbye, John bloody Caspasian. And good blasted riddance.'

But as he set off again, his step was lighter for barely ten yards, before the glitter of sunlight on falling diamonds tormented him anew.

Frederick Giles closed the door of his office behind him and walked down the corridor, heading for the back entrance. It was another scorching hot day, not the most pleasant for what he had in mind. Checking that the way was clear and that all the fuss and commotion was confined to the front of the building, he located his car and driver, engineered himself into the back seat, and directed that he be conveyed to the cathedral. The short drive was speedily conducted, fortunately so, for Giles' anticipation was not easily contained on such occasions as this.

As the car drew near to its destination, Giles leaned towards the window and spied what he was after. He tapped the driver on the shoulder and indicated. Several seconds later the car drew up alongside a large, exotically-dressed woman. Giles opened the door and moved aside to make what room was possible for the person about to join him.

'There you are, my dear,' he said. 'Were you missing me?'

The woman squeezed herself in beside him, the car's springs withstanding this ultimate test. She beamed at him, eyelids fluttering coyly. 'Of course,' she purred. 'Admit it, you love your Annabella, no?'

The shepherd's hut in the remote Peruvian valley was invisible from any distance beyond ten yards, and such had been the intention when it had been constructed many years before. Now, after countless seasons, the last few of which had seen it unused, moss and vegetation had so enveloped it that it appeared to be more of a natural outgrowth of the hillside itself rather than an edifice made by man.

A lively brook tumbled past the front door, the crystal-clear water ice cold from the melting snow that flowed into it higher up the mountainside. A shepherd, long gone and forgotten, had once fashioned a single window in one of the cabin's log walls. Wooden shutters had been used instead of glass to cover it, and on this morning of bright sunlight, they stood open once again, thick wedges of freshly torn moss evidence of the struggle it had required to force them apart.

A heavily rusted metal chimney stack leaned precariously on the overgrown roof, and from the top of it, woodsmoke briefly smudged the air until waved away into nothingness by the constant breezes of the high altitude.

A head and shoulders suddenly appeared at the open window, leaning on the sill and gazing contentedly into space. Emma sighed deeply, tasting the chill air and revelling in it.

She smiled hugely, speaking to someone in the room behind her. 'All this time, and you still can't get that fire to work properly.'

Caspasian burst from the hut's door, choking and rubbing his smarting eyes. He bent over, hands on knees. With one enormous cough he cleared his lungs and then stooped to the brook and scooped up a palmful of water to throw in his eyes. Blinking them clear, he sat back on his haunches and surveyed the mountaintops that towered overhead. A moment later Emma joined him. She was carrying an armful of parachute silk which she draped round her shoulders. She sat down beside him and they settled to contemplate a bird that soared so far up, that they were hardly sure whether it was a bird at all.

'Is that a condor?' Emma asked.

Caspasian considered it. 'Not sure.' He turned to her and grinned. 'Don't care, either.'

'I hope you're going to care about finding us some supper,' Emma said. 'And preferably something other than rabbit. I've eaten so much of it over the last few days, I'll probably hop down the mountain when the time comes.'

They laughed, leaning shoulder to shoulder. But unintentionally Emma had broken the spell. Caspasian regarded the mountains again. 'We can't stay here forever, you know.'

Emma looked at him, studying every line of his profile. 'Why not?'

'There are people down there who think we are dead. It's not fair on them.'

'Who?' Emma asked, suddenly angry. 'Tell me who?'

'Lionel?'

She laughed. 'I meant, who can we think of, between the two of us, who isn't motivated by self-interest?'

He turned to look at her. 'Very well then, Harrison, Wolter.' He paused. 'Richard,' he added, picturing for a moment, the strange sincere young man he had discovered to be his half-brother. 'How about them?'

Emma was silent. She found a piece of loose turf at her feet and worried at it with the heel of her boot.

Caspasian put his arm round her and held her close. 'What was it your mother used to say? It's not what we achieve . . .'

'I know, I know,' she said, the anger draining from her. 'It's what we do to others that defines us.' She had worked the turf free and reached to pick it up. It lay soft and cold in her hand. She tossed it into the brook and watched the rivulets of water scurry it rapidly downhill and out of sight.

'Of course, that doesn't mean we have to go right away,' Caspasian said. He shrugged. 'It could be several days' walk to the nearest settlement. We'll need to gather supplies. Dry some meat, catch some fish perhaps.' He grinned at her. 'There are all kinds of preparations to be completed first.'

'It could take a while, eh?' Emma asked.

'Most certainly.'

'How long do you reckon?'

Caspasian thought about it. 'Days, at least. Maybe a week or more.'

Emma lay back with her hands behind her head and gazed up into the clear blue sky. 'I like the "more" part.'

'Me too,' Caspasian said, lying down beside her. 'You know, when you get back, the world's going to go absolutely berserk. You'll be able to . . .'

'I know,' she said quickly, stopping him. 'Why do you think I want to stay up here?'

'Oh. I thought it was because of me. My irresistible charm and magnetism.'

She laughed. 'It is! Of course it is. But . . . don't you see? It's so easy here. The two of us can simply be who we are. There's no pretence. No public face to be maintained.' She heaved an enormous sigh. 'God, I really hate it sometimes.'

'But only sometimes?'

She nodded. 'I suppose so. I only hate it sometimes.' She turned her head towards him. 'I must sound very ungrateful.'

'No,' Caspasian answered. 'You sound just like the rest of us. The good and the bad. Every life has both. Why should your life be any different?'

'And will I still see you? When we've been resurrected from the dead?' she asked.

'What would you want from a pauper?'

Emma grinned. 'Right now I could use some lunch.'

Caspasian kissed her once and then stood up. He held out his hand. 'Come on. Let's go hunting. I envisage jugged hare for supper.'

Emma groaned. She took the parachute silk back into the hut and put it with the rest which Caspasian had fashioned into a vast and luxurious bed.

Coming back outside, she found Caspasian trying on the

parachute's outer case. He was tightening the shoulder straps to fit. 'I thought I'd give this a go,' he said. 'Just like a haversack, isn't it?'

Emma frowned doubtfully. 'Very smart.'

One of the straps had snagged. Caspasian tugged at it irritably.

'Why not take it off and start again?' Emma suggested.

Caspasian did so, kneeling beside the bulky pack and wrestling with it. 'With all these belts and bits it's like a bloody octopus.' His hands were deep inside it, feeling for the source of the problem. 'I sometimes wonder if . . .'

He stopped in mid-sentence as his fingers encountered something.

'What is it?'

'Nothing,' he said, grimacing as he worked at the blockage. 'Just some stones. Probably in the fall, they got snarled up in the pack with . . .' He pulled out his hand.

Side by side, Caspasian and Emma looked down at the sparkling cluster of diamonds in his palm. A further search produced a second handful. And then a third. Until a neat little pile lay innocently on the ground beside the cabin door.

Emma stared, hardly able to believe her eyes. 'What was that you were saying about a pauper?'